"I LIKE WHAT I FEEL."

"Don't," Grace said, but heat welled in her veins. "I should not be here."

"But you are here. Kiss me, Grace."

He nibbled her lips apart. He kissed her deep, and long, and hot until she grasped his shoulders and kissed him back. His hands supported her. His fingers sought places she had never thought to feel touched by another human, least of all a man.

With his lips still on hers, he worked his hands to the small dimples at the base of her spine, and then forward over her hips to her belly.

She tore her mouth away. *"Please!"* she said, struggling.

"You do not have to plead," he whispered, close to her ear. "I have no intention of stopping."

D0441899

If You've Enjoyed This Book,
Be Sure to Read These Other
AVON ROMANTIC TREASURES

FORTUNE'S FLAME *by Judith E. French*
MASTER OF MOONSPELL *by Deborah Camp*
SHADOW DANCE *by Anne Stuart*
THEN CAME YOU *by Lisa Kleypas*
VIRGIN STAR *by Jennifer Horsman*

Coming Soon

ANGEL EYES *by Suzannah Davis*

Avon Books are available at special quantity discounts for bulk purchases for sales promotions, premiums, fund raising or educational use. Special books, or book excerpts, can also be created to fit specific needs.

For details write or telephone the office of the Director of Special Markets, Avon Books, Dept. FP, 1350 Avenue of the Americas, New York, New York 10019, 1-800-238-0658.

STELLA CAMERON

FASCINATION

An Avon Romantic Treasure

AVON BOOKS NEW YORK

If you purchased this book without a cover, you should be aware that this book is stolen property. It was reported as "unsold and destroyed" to the publisher, and neither the author nor the publisher has received any payment for this "stripped book."

FASCINATION is an original publication of Avon Books. This work has never before appeared in book form. This work is a novel. Any similarity to actual persons or events is purely coincidental.

AVON BOOKS
A division of
The Hearst Corporation
1350 Avenue of the Americas
New York, New York 10019

Copyright © 1993 by Stella Cameron
Inside cover author photograph by Brant Photographers
Excerpt from *Breathless* copyright © 1993 by Stella Cameron
Published by arrangement with the author
Library of Congress Catalog Card Number: 93-90344
ISBN: 0-380-77074-1

All rights reserved, which includes the right to reproduce this book or portions thereof in any form whatsoever except as provided by the U.S. Copyright Law. For information address Curtis Brown, Ltd., 10 Astor Place, New York, New York 10003.

First Avon Books Printing: November 1993

AVON TRADEMARK REG. U.S. PAT. OFF. AND IN OTHER COUNTRIES, MARCA REGISTRADA, HECHO EN U.S.A.

Printed in the U.S.A.

RA 10 9 8 7 6 5 4 3 2 1

For Denis Farina,
a Dangerous Man.
And for Adventurous Women everywhere.

Chapter 1

March 1822. Castle Kirkcaldy, Scotland

"Teeth? *Teeth!*" Arran Francis William Rossmara, Marquess of Stonehaven, flung wide his arms and collapsed onto a sofa. "Teeth, Calum? I ask you to describe this female and you tell me she has *good teeth!* In God's name, man, we are not discussing a brood mare."

"Are we not?" Calum Innes's dark eyes shone with innocent surprise.

Arran leveled a finger. "You, my friend, are trifling with a desperate man, a man who may shortly take your miserable throat in his hands and squeeze out your miserable *life*."

"Hm." A broad smile revealed the true, irreverent, and wholly roguish nature of Calum Innes. "As you say, we are definitely *not* discussing a brood mare."

"Well?"

Calum inclined his head, and firelight sought the red in his brown hair. He was a tall man, almost as tall as Arran himself, his lean elegance and economy of movement guaranteed to turn the heads of many men—and every female with an eye for a handsome man.

He arched a brow. "Grace Wren? That's who you're asking me about?"

"Yes, Grace Wren." With a single irritated tug,

1

Arran wrenched off his black neckcloth. "That is the name of this woman I'm supposed to welcome into my home, is it not?"

"It's the name of the woman you sent me to London to find."

"I did not *know* the woman's name when I sent you to London. I did not know the woman. Confound it, I *still* know nothing of her."

"Her name is Grace Wren."

"Calum," Arran said warningly.

"And she has good teeth. At least, from what I could see—"

"*Calum!*" Arran roared. "Enough. I am considered a quiet man. A patient man. But, as you well know, this matter holds no humor for me."

"Nor for me," Calum said with a deep sincerity his twitching mouth belied. "Securing a wife for the Savage of Stonehaven is an exceedingly serious matter, one that carries weighty responsibility."

Arran had known Calum since they were both small boys when, through circumstances neither of them ever mentioned, Calum had come under the protection of Arran's parents. They had grown up together, attended Eton and Oxford together, and bedded their first woman together—a lusty and willing farmer's daughter who had been bright-eyed and still eager for more energetic games when her two young partners wanted only exhausted sleep. Together they had grown to manhood and had already watched the passing of their thirty-third years, yet Calum Innes's merciless baiting could still drive his oldest friend, companion, and trusting employer to near madness.

At this moment Calum was regarding Arran's thunderous face with feigned surprise. "Could it be, my lord, that I have caused you some annoyance?"

"The Wren female is coming—*if* she comes—

strictly on approval," Arran said coldly. "If she suits, there will be a marriage."

"Almost her exact words."

Arran draped his arms along the back of the sofa. "Surely I have misheard you."

Calum cleared his throat and went to examine sheets of hand-drawn music strewn atop one of three pianos in the vast, heavily paneled gallery that was Arran's music room. Calum rested the tip of a long forefinger on a page and began to hum.

"No, no, *no!*" Arran shot to his feet and strode to jerk the music away. "Not like that. You murder every note you attempt, so do not attempt them at all."

"You wound me. Is this a masterpiece intended as an offering at noble George The Fourth's visit to our honored land?"

Arran had to smile. "You are particularly bloody tonight, Calum. We both know that neither Sir Walter Scott's Fat Friend nor any other shall ever know who penned this piece. Not that it is likely to be heard outside these walls."

"No doubt it is terrible," Calum said with an enormous sigh. "A monstrosity, as are so many other works being played around the world for people who applaud yet do not know that yours is the name that deserves the praise."

"Enough of this." He could not face another discussion about the way he chose to live his life. "What did you mean when you said my words were almost the same as Miss Wren's?"

"Merely that Miss Wren absolutely agrees with the terms you laid forth." The mythic garden scene in an Oudry Tapestry Calum must already know thread by thread suddenly became freshly interesting.

Arran eyed him suspiciously. "Good."

"She is rather a small thing."

"How small?"

"Oh, I don't know." Calum frowned and held out a hand. He made airy estimates at varying heights from the glistening, dark wooden floor. "Perhaps this small."

Arran found his palms were unaccountably damp, and folded his arms tightly. "If that is correct, then you have arranged to bring me a child."

Calum raised his hand several inches and leveled it against his body. "There," he said, smiling afresh. "The top of her head definitely approached my shoulder. Yes, that is her height."

"Good God." He hated this, all of it. "One of those wretched, simpering, weeping, frail creatures who need a firm anchor in the mildest of breezes."

"I really don't think Miss—"

"I told you she must be healthy and strong, and you know why."

"She assures me she is very healthy and strong. Lack of height does not always denote frailty."

"What of her body?"

Calum pulled his watch from a waistcoat pocket and consulted its face. "Hector left a message for me. He wants to see me as soon as possible."

Hector MacFie was Arran's faithful estate commissioner, a tireless man who tended to be over-zealous. "Hector can wait. Do not change the subject. Her body, Calum, and do not continue to toy with me."

"Diminutive."

Arran curled his lip. "Scrawny, you mean?"

"Slight might be a better description."

"A pox on you, Calum. You've retained a fragile waif."

"Be calm, my friend. I hardly think *retained* is the appropriate term. And the lady is delicate, nothing more."

"Puny!"

Calum caught Arran's shoulders in strong hands. "Miss Wren is a small woman of extremely compact and appealing proportions. I would never have approached her with our proposal had she not met all the requirements you stressed."

"Do *not* use the word *proposal.*"

"That is what it is."

"It is no such thing. We are merely offering a trial period to see if she will suit."

Calum's hard fingers dug deeper. "She will suit, Arran. She must. You need heirs, man, and you need them now."

Arran closed his eyes. "There is time."

"Not if you want to be certain there is at least one thriving offspring in your nurseries to ensure that Sir Mortimer Cuthbert and his son never get their hands on the Rossmara estates."

"Do not speak my cousin's name in my hearing. Not tonight."

"Two years, Arran. All you have is two years, and if you still have no heirs, Mortimer—your cousin will have the right to be consulted on the—"

"On the administration of *my* estates in consideration of their eventual passage into the hands of his oldest son, *and* he will immediately draw a portion of all revenues," Arran finished, the ice-cold spear of disgust driving at his gut. "You need not remind me. How my father could have allowed such an outrage, I cannot collect."

"He gave you thirty-five years to ensure the continuation of your line. The old marquess knew what he was about. He knew you might need incentive to tie the ball and chain of matrimony around your ankle."

"I tied it once," Arran said through gritted teeth, and instantly regretted the remark. "If Father hadn't died on my wedding day, he'd have written the new will he promised to write." Their eyes met, and the other, the episode he could never forget, was present and horribly alive again. There had been a woman, and a child . . .

"Forget Isabel," Calum said gently.

Never. "Struan could have saved me this," Arran said, referring to his younger brother. "He's the stuff of good husbands and fathers. The will provided for him to produce an heir in my stead—and gave him until my fortieth year to do it."

Calum clapped Arran's shoulders. "Do not torture yourself with these reminders. Let it all go. Struan will never be a husband or a father, and you are taking the steps that must be taken."

Arran turned away and went to draw back heavy red draperies from the casement. Only the blackness of a wild early March night greeted him.

"Her hair is pale," Calum said from behind him.

"Perhaps she is so small and so pale that I shall not notice her at all. Perhaps I shall be able to accomplish what must be accomplished and scarcely notice the event."

The sound Calum made was probably a cough, but it sounded more like a choked laugh. "Come, Arran, do not tell me you've lost interest in that for which you once held a formidable reputation. Surely my tireless lord of the bedchamber—and anywhere else where he could find his way beneath a fetching piece's skirts—surely he has not become indifferent to planting himself between soft, white, and welcoming thighs."

Despite himself, Arran felt the stirring of arousal. "How do you know that Miss Wren's thighs are soft, white, and welcoming?" he asked in low tones.

"I have a talented imagination," Calum responded, equally low. "The lady *is* a fetching piece. She has a tiny waist and hips rounded just so." He drew the appropriate outline in the air. "Her neck is slender, and her breasts . . . small, certainly, but firm and high, and . . . Ah, yes, Miss Wren has breasts that should not be wasted either on spinsterhood or on a man who does not appreciate the very best.''

Stirring became insistent pressure inside Arran's breeches. ''You observed the lady who may become my wife very closely.''

Calum bowed, all hint of amusement lost to his finely drawn features. ''I tried to see her with your eyes. Who better to do so than your best friend and adviser? You charged me to find a woman who would satisfy your requirements, and your instructions were exacting. I could hardly select a suitable candidate without looking at her. When she is your wife, you may depend that my regard will be of a very different nature.''

Calum's reputation as a rogue and a rakehell was legendary in the best of circles. ''It will be different from *this* moment forth,'' Arran said. ''And, yet again, she may never *be* my wife.''

''As you say.'' Calum spread the tails of his dark blue coat and dropped into a leather wing chair close to a white marble chimneypiece that shimmered like an ice sculpture. ''Her hair is pale, a silvery blond. She has dark brows and dark brown eyes—delightful in a startling manner. And I am assured that she will meet all your requirements.''

The hour grew late and Arran was anxious to return to the work he intended to accomplish before dawn. ''She is mature, then?''

''Indeed. Four and twenty and nothing of a foolish paperskull.''

''Modest?''

''Exceedingly modest.''

''Of a docile nature?''

Calum leaned to toss a coal from the hearth back into the fire. ''I found her most agreeable.''

''She would disdain excitement?''

Another coal required attention. "Miss Wren gave not a single report of any exciting event in her life."

Arran put a fist to his mouth. "And the, er, other?"

"I gained the distinct impression that the lady will be more than satisfactory in the capacity that concerned me most during my search."

"So you say." Nothing in his experiences with women encouraged him to trust their word. "You made it plain to her that my habits are . . . unusual."

Calum hoisted a boot atop a long-muscled thigh. "I told Miss Wren that you are confined . . . er, reclusive, I think was the term I used."

"She *fully* understands what that means?"

"Well . . ." Calum's brow furrowed. "Now that I think of it, I should probably have mentioned your habit of using a disguise to masquerade as a peasant. And that you spend your days in the said disguise whilst working among your tenants—who think you are another man entirely from the Marquess of Stonehaven. And—"

"You will never speak a word of that," Arran said.

Undaunted, Calum continued, "And I definitely omitted to speak to Miss Wren of your need for almost no sleep, that you work here all night and require physical labor upon which to vent your pent-up strength during the day. I did not tell her that I suspect you might turn to violence were there no outlet for that strength. Hah! Yes, and in faith, I forgot to inform Miss Wren that you have a friend!"

There were times when Arran itched to pounce upon Calum as he would have when they were children. "Which friend would that be?"

"Why, the fair actress in Edinburgh, of course. Naturally, since you are so set upon complete openness, you will wish your prospective bride to be aware of your mistress."

Arran approached Calum with determined steps.

"Ah, ah." Calum leaped from his seat and moved to put it between them. "I jest, of course. No mention of Mrs. Foster shall ever pass my lips in front of the marchioness."

"There *is* no marchioness. Go and plague Hector. He probably wants to discuss his damnable sheep or some crippling new scheme for Yorkshire. I'll inform you if I decide we should send for Miss Wren." He went to the piano and began picking out notes. Solitude was what he needed.

Calum cleared his throat.

The music began to make patterns in Arran's head. Perhaps the piece would do after all.

"We seem to have misunderstood one another," Calum said loudly.

"Later, later."

"I fear it will not be later."

"What do you mean?" Arran looked up to find Calum crossing toward the door on tiptoe.

"Miss Wren and her mother were to depart London within the fortnight."

"No! I will not be ready for this ordeal within a fortnight. Send word that I will let her know when the time is convenient." Which it might never be.

"That won't be possible."

"Of course—"

"No, Arran. You forget that I did not return to Scotland direct from the drawing rooms of London. I had to deal with the West Indies issue and—"

"Get to the point, man."

Calum opened the door. "It has been well more than two weeks since I last saw Miss Wren. By my calculations she is very likely to arrive . . . tomorrow."

Freedom! Grace Wren all but bounced upon the carriage seat. Freedom, and at last the hope that her

mother would stop wishing her only child had been
a son. No more pinching pennies. No more wistfully
watching other ladies decked out in marvelous finery she could never hope to possess. No more walking when she might prefer to ride. No more trying
not to notice threadbare furnishings in less than sa-
lubrious rented accommodations. *No more deferring
to the wishes of any other human being!*

"Grace, do settle. You quite exhaust me with all
that wiggling and grinning. Really, grinning is
something you should not do at all with that large
mouth of yours."

"Yes, Mama," Grace said.

No more trying to entertain and indulge her
mother when the available means were definitely not
adequate.

"I do wish you had not chosen blue for today."
Mama primped pale pink ribbons that secured a rose
satin bonnet decorated with full white ostrich feath-
ers. "Blue does not at all suit you, Grace Charlotte
Wren. Particularly so dark a blue. It accentuates your
unfeminine lack of flesh. It is positively dull. It
makes you appear far too thoughtful. Gentlemen do
not at all appreciate thoughtful females. If only you
would listen to me in these matters."

"Yes, Mama." Poor Mama, her life with dear Papa
had been so confining. Little wonder she had such
an insatiable appetite for frippery, endless gossip,
and what she termed "her little pleasures" now that
she was a widow. Ichabod Wren, a barrister of mod-
erate success, had provided tolerably well for his little family. The inheritance he left Blanche should
have been more than enough to sustain her and their
daughter in passable comfort for many a year. Really, it was difficult to understand why, only five
years after Papa's death, they were evidently already almost penniless.

"I hope we shall soon become acquainted with the marquess's neighbors."

"Yes, Mama."

"Oh, really, Grace! Can you say nothing other than 'yes, Mama'?"

Grace sighed and smiled. "I'm sorry. We shall be there quite soon, and I confess that I am preoccupied."

"No doubt. I know little of Scottish society, but assuredly the marquess moves in the very best of circles, so we shall be invited absolutely *everywhere*."

"We shall see." There was no point in ruining Mama's happy dreaming so soon by reminding her that the peculiar circumstances under which they were to take up their new positions were unlikely to lead to amiable socializing. Grace looked at the scenery beyond the carriage. "Is it not beautiful? So green and wild."

Mama sniffed. "Uncivilized. I am a Town woman. Give me a crescent of beautiful London houses and the rattle of fine carriage wheels on London streets. Far preferable to this barbaric wilderness."

Silently Grace agreed that the hills they'd passed since traveling north from Edinburgh were indeed barbaric. A thrill climbed her spine and she hunched her shoulders. "Not all of London is fine, Mama." Their own rooms in St. John's Wood, the best they could afford after selling the Chelsea house to pay off debts, had been anything but fine.

"No matter," Blanche Wren said, unmoved. "Mr. Innes told you the marquess has a house in London, did he not?"

"He did."

"Belgravia," Mama said reverently. "With luck we shall be installed there before the end of the season."

Grace very much doubted that they would be installed anywhere but in Kirkcaldy, the marquess's house some miles west of a village called Dunkeld, for many months to come. All of Scotland was a mystery to Grace, but Calum Innes had assured her the marquess's house was agreeable, the staff compliant, and the marquess himself an undemanding man. Yes, she would tolerate Scotland's mystery well enough under such circumstances—particularly while contemplating the pleasant rewards the final result of this liaison promised.

"Do you suppose the other ladies of our station hold regular salons?"

"What is our station?" Grace could not resist asking.

Mama straightened her spine. "You know perfectly well. You are to be a marchioness." At forty-five, Blanche Wren was a pretty, plump woman with rather too many chestnut ringlets and a magpie's fascination with flashy finery.

"There cannot be much farther to go," Grace said. Her high spirits began to waver. "I do hope the marquess is as congenial as Mr. Innes told me."

"Of course he is."

"Of course." And, after all, she must not forget the situation would be temporary. "Mama, please tell me what your friends said of Lord Stonehaven."

"I see cottages," Mama said suddenly, leaning toward the window. "Beside the river."

"Yes. Do not evade me on this yet again. What did the ladies in your sewing group say?"

"They said nothing derogatory. Do look, Grace. This is quite a pretty place. See how it nestles in the valley."

Grace looked where her mother pointed. "That will be Dunkeld and the River Tay." The river was satiny and wide, and the hills the color of dark emeralds. Here and there patches of snow still clung to the higher reaches. "Which of the ladies knew Stonehaven the best?"

"Oh, fie!" Mama fell against the black leather squabs of the luxurious coach the marquess had so generously provided. "How you do persist. All right. Since you insist, I must tell you the truth. I cannot bear any misunderstandings between us."

Apprehension made Grace shiver.

"I did not ask about the marquess at all. There. Now you have it."

Grace laced her gloved fingers tightly together. "Mama, you *promised.*"

"I did no such thing. I *agreed.* But then I changed my mind, and I don't want to hear another word about it."

"I'm afraid you shall have to hear several more words on the subject." Vexation and anxiety thinned Grace's temper. "You assured me that I had nothing to worry about in agreeing to this marriage. You implied that you had been told positive things about the gentleman."

"I told you I had heard nothing derogatory about him. Which I had not."

"Mama, that was deceitful. You said your friends knew the marquess."

"Some of them probably do. And I deliberately said nothing of the matter to them. Nothing at all."

"Nothing?" Grace moved to the edge of her seat. "Where do they think we have gone?"

Mama smiled archly. "They believe we are staying with rich relatives in the North. Soon that will be perfectly true."

"It will *not,*" Grace said, infuriated.

"Certainly it will. Stonehaven lives in the North. He is exceedingly rich, and we are about to be related to him."

The whole thing was impossible. "Why didn't you tell the truth and try to find out more?"

"Because I could not risk our losing this plum opportunity, you peagoose." Red rushed to Mama's already rouged cheeks. "Half of those women have unmarried daughters. Do you think I would risk one of them trying to usurp our position?"

Grace turned a shoulder to her mother and closed her eyes. She refused to enter into these silly imaginings Blanche indulged.

"It's getting darker," Mama said after some time had passed. "Perhaps we should have found an inn in Dunkeld to spend the night."

"We will be there before dark," Grace said, keeping her eyes shut. "The coachman assured us." Was it too late to turn back?

"I only did what I thought was best."

"I'm resting."

"You are not. You are angry with me."

Angry because again her mother put her own gain before her daughter's happiness? *Yes.* "It really doesn't matter." She studied the landscape again. "The entire business cannot last too long." She tried not to worry the question as to why her future husband had sought a wife through such unusual means.

"What an amazing offer this is, Grace," Mama said, as she had said at least once an hour for the past four weeks since they had met Mr. Calum Innes. "A title. A comfortable home on a thriving estate."

"Indeed." Grace's spirits lifted. "The marquess keeps to his house and requires only my loyal attention in trying times."

"Yes." Mama nodded solemnly. "I suppose he will make funds available to you immediately."

"According to Mr. Innes, the marriage will take place almost at once."

"The poor marquess needs you."

He needed her. Grace tapped her toes together and fiddled with a loose thread on her pelisse. *Needed* her. "Mama . . ." Surely now was an appropriate time to ask the questions that had formerly and summarily been dismissed. "Mama, what exactly do you suppose the marquess will require of me?"

"You have already been told." Mama's face took on the cross look that warned of a possible ill temper to come.

There might never be another opportunity to seek guidance in what was clearly a most sensitive area. *What occurred between a man and a woman . . . a married man and woman . . . when they were alone?*

"Mama, if I were not marrying an exceedingly ancient and mortally sick man, what might I need to contemplate when . . . ?" Oh, she knew so little of life. She knew *nothing* of life, and the most terrible part of it all was that she *knew* she knew nothing of life. "What do a man and woman do after they marry?" Grace asked in a rush.

"*Do?*" Mama pulled her brows together over a wrinkled nose. "What can you mean?"

She meant that she had never been allowed the opportunity to make any friends her own age, had never known a single female to whom she could turn for guidance, and there were things she simply *had* to know. "It is all so puzzling. I've heard things your friends have said about marriage. Or *started* to say. Whenever they realized I was there, they whispered behind their fans and uttered long-suffering sighs as if they were withholding something quite terrible." It was a beginning. "And I want to know because even though I shall probably never experience such matters for myself, I wish to be treated as an adult and to be aware of what I am *missing*." There. She had said it all.

Mama's bosom rose and fell once, mightily. "*Well,*" she said, averting her face. "They say there can be hidden depths in deep waters."

New boldness loosened Grace's tongue. "I should

certainly imagine there is. After all, one cannot see everything in water that's deep, can one? Any more than one ever knows absolutely everything about a person from the outside—not if they have a single brain. Of any dimension at all, that is.''

Mama's mouth, which had slowly opened, snapped shut. *"Well!"* Her fingers were wound together into a quivering knot. "I never thought my daughter capable of such . . . You know everything that a gently born young female should know about . . . about the subject you so indelicately raise.

"As you say, you are to marry an old invalid. When you are alone—after you are married—you will read to him from the Bible, keep your voice and eyes lowered at all times, smooth his bed sheets, and smile. *Smile*, my girl, not *grin*.''

Once more Mama presented her profile, and Grace felt the subject close. Frustration made her wriggle afresh. It was abominable to know that there was something one did not know. But she would be patient. After all, she was not so old that—if the marquess did not linger overlong—she might not eventually experience some deeper harmony of the mind. With a man equally interested in *her* mind.

The trap opened behind Grace's head, and the coachman called down: "Yon's Kirkcaldy, lassie. Ye'll see it well fra' here.''

Grace and her mother turned their attention to the view from the hill they now descended. On hills to the north and east lay dense forest. A river running from the southwest forked like a silver divining rod and snaked to circle a broad valley. Small clusters of cottages dotted endless fields on the valley floor, and to the west a village huddled about a church.

And on a flat-topped mound in the center, surrounded by parkland and ringed all about with a wall as thick as any two cottages standing side by side, was a massive gray stone structure fronted by twin drum towers and cornered on all sides with many-turreted angle towers.

There was no house of any size to be seen.

"Where?" Grace said hoarsely. "Where? Angus, where is Kirkcaldy House?" She directed her question through the trap.

"*Castle* Kirkcaldy, lassie. Ye canna miss it. Home of the Rossmaras for many a century."

"Oh, Grace," Blanche Wren whispered when the trap had snapped shut.

"A castle," Grace mouthed. She looked out once more. "*That* castle?"

Mama spread her fingers over her mouth. "Yes. That castle. And it will be ours. *Ours*, Grace."

This time it was nervousness that started Grace bobbing in her seat once more. "Mr. Innes did not mention a castle."

"What is the marquess's will be ours. Mr. Innes said so."

Grace could not stop her teeth from chattering. "This is all too much."

"*Nothing* is too much." Mama's blue eyes sparkled. "We need never worry again. We shall have the very best of everything."

"Oh, dear. Surely he could easily have found a wife from nearer at hand." What could be so awful about the marquess that he'd been forced to seek a distant stranger as a companion? "I am becoming quite fuddled. Mr. Innes did say all that would be required of me would be to give Lord Stonehaven my loyal regard in the trying matter of his remaining earthly demands, did he not?"

"Oh, yes, yes!" Mama also bobbed.

"Mr. Innes said several times that the marquess keeps mostly to his rooms," Grace said. "Marriage to a man too sick to go about will undoubtedly be short."

"And Mr. Innes said there are no children."

Grace nodded.

"So there we are. There is nothing to fear. You will be what the marquess needs, and then we shall be *rich*."

"Mama!"

Blanche Wren pursed her lips. "I am merely stating the obvious."

"I do intend to be most faithful to his lordship's demands, Mama," Grace said disapprovingly.

"Of course you do."

"I would never care to be considered a heartless opportunist."

"Absolutely not."

Grace frowned down upon Castle Kirkcaldy. "Yet that is what I am. Or what I was."

"What do you mean?"

"I do not even know the marquess, so he knows that I cannot have a tendre for him. Just as he cannot have a tendre for me. The proposal Mr. Innes made was by way of being in part a business arrangement. But I am completely set on making my husband glad that I was found for him."

"I'm sure you are." Now Mama's eyes were round and earnest.

Grace drew herself up. "I shall wed him—in his bed if necessary. Then I shall give complete attention to his remaining earthly demands." She concentrated on remembering her mother's instructions. "I shall read to him from the Bible as often as pleases him, and do all the other things necessary."

"I know you will make the gentleman happy."

"If anyone can, I will. I'll marry him and tend him."

Mama shook her head sadly. "And bury him . . . and mourn him."

"Exactly as I should." Grace felt a rush of guilty relief. "Everything will be as the marquess wishes."

And then she would be *free!*

Chapter 2

C alum had deliberately brought about this un-
speakable aggravation. Now the wretch insisted upon standing at a window in the highest
room of the Adam Tower, his eye clamped to Arran's telescope.

"For God's sake, come away from the window."

"Have patience, Arran."

"A stranger. A female I've never set eyes upon.
Hell and damnation, I am like some virgin bride
awaiting her unknown fate."

Calum chuckled. "Hardly. And there are enough
eager misses among your neighbor's households.
May I remind you that you could have any one of
them."

"Never." At least he would have the pleasure of
surprising the dear, malicious surrounding gentry.
"My desolation at . . . They enjoyed my misery
when they thought I was destroyed by . . . We will
not talk of that. I will have none of them."

"So it will be Miss Wren."

Damn Mortimer. And damn the misfortune that
had been Father's scheme to ensure the clipping of
his elder son's wings. "No. No, I will not see her."

"I think I already do."

"Not only a strange female I'm supposed to take
as my bride, but her mother to boot."

"You sent me to London in your stead, Arran. It
was unthinkable that you should take the time to go

yourself. I did my duty as prescribed by you. One could hardly expect a young female to travel to Scotland without a companion.''

Nothing could lessen this awful premonition that his life was about to change forever. "I will not see her, I tell you."

"As I've already said, I think I see her now. A black carriage and . . . Yes, it's yours, right enough."

"Mine? Ah, yes, mine." He vaguely remembered Calum coming to the gallery one night some weeks previous and mentioning sending old Angus Creigh to London with a coach in case it was needed. "You should not have rushed ahead, Calum."

"If I'd waited . . . if I'd come back and told you about the girl and asked what you wanted me to do, you know you'd have cried off the whole thing. You would not do this for yourself, so I've done it for you."

"Then you can *marry* her for me, too, dammit." Arran waved a hand. "Forgive me. It's not your fault. You thought you were acting for the best."

"I was and I am. She'll be here shortly."

Arran was anxious for his night's work. "Greet her kindly. Make sure she rests for as long as necessary—a day, two even. Then return her to London."

"I cannot!"

"You can and you will."

"I *cannot* and I will not." Determination tightened Calum's firm mouth. "You are confronted by potential disaster, yet you will not see any of it."

"There is nothing about my affairs that I cannot spin to my advantage."

"You cannot *spin* the dictates of your father's will into anything but what they are."

"I should never have allowed you to talk me into this madness with the girl."

"Arran—"

"No." He held up a finger. "I have spoken my piece and now I have work to do."

"You cannot shut yourself away with your infernal music and trust that the world will remain as you wish it. This affair *must* be dealt with."

"Soon. I will deal with it very soon."

"The coach will soon reach the courtyard. We should go down."

"*You* should go down. Kindly apologize to Miss Wren and her parent." There must be a way to deal gracefully with them. "I will decide upon a suitable, er, gift to show my gratitude."

"Very well, we might as well deal with all your rage at once."

"I beg your pardon?"

Calum turned up his palms. "I am ready for your wrath. I may even deserve it. What I did not tell you was that I encountered Mortimer in London—at White's. He was tossing blunt at the tables as if he already had the Rossmara fortune at his disposal."

"That is nothing to me." Except a further reminder of his untenable position.

"I fear it is. He was foxed. I heard him speak of his son's inheritance."

"He would not," Arran said. "He would not dare before it is time."

"It was said for my benefit. The drink made him daring and he could not resist baiting me. Any other would assume he spoke of what he himself would leave to Roger."

Arran's jaw clenched. "The fool. He will never get what he wants."

"No, he will not, but nevertheless, he took note of what I mentioned. Said he'd soon be bound for a stay in Edinburgh. Be certain that as soon as he can gather his poisonous wife and whatever other en-

tourage he considers desirable, they will flock to this
castle like vultures.''

For an instant Arran did not understand. ''The man
hasn't been here since Father died. He knows he isn't
welcome, but . . . How did he find out . . . ?'' The
sheepish look in Calum's eyes was answer enough.
''You told Mortimer I was getting married, didn't
you?''

''I am only a man.''

''Yes. And so am I. How long before Mortimer
descends?'' He shut his eyes tightly. ''Do not say
that he is also fast upon my doorstep.''

''He'll be a week—perhaps even two.''

''Good.'' Arran strode across the room.

Calum caught up with him amid standing suits of
armor in the passageway leading to his apartments.
''Wait, Arran. What do you intend to do?''

''No more questions,'' he told Calum. ''Kindly go
down and greet my *fiancée.*''

Grace had watched the scene they passed with
mingled awe and anxiety. Smoke curled from the
chimneys of tidy cottages set amid small but equally
tidy gardens. Those people still abroad appeared
cheerful and well fed—until they saw the marquess's coach.

''Did you see how the people looked when they
saw us?'' Grace asked her mother with a shudder.
''As if they thought we would leap forth and attack
them? Even as they stood respectfully by, they
cringed.''

''You read too many of those dreadful novels,''
Mama said, covertly studying the castle courtyard,
which lay behind the grand fortress. On this, the
north side, it was revealed as L-shaped and but-
tressed on all corners by towers. ''Dwelling on silly
romantical stories will inevitably cause aberrations
of the imagination. Better to spend more time im-

proving indispensable skills. How to adequately
defer to a gentleman. How to compensate in delightful conversation for the girlish charm you lack. Oh,
really, what *can* be keeping that wretched coachman? Tell him to hand us down.''

"He's gone ahead to announce us," Grace said in
a voice that wobbled annoyingly.

"And he's taking entirely too long about it. You
must complain to the marquess."

Graced lacked the composure to respond. Once
inside the great wall that surrounded the base of the
castle's mound, the carriage had bowled upward
amid acres of ancient beechwoods and lush fields
where sleek, fat cattle grazed. Immediately about the
castle were gardens edged by low hedges and endless smooth lawns.

"There he is," Mama said, shifting to the edge of
her seat in readiness.

"Perhaps this is the wrong Kirkcaldy," Grace remarked weakly and not without some hope.

"No," Mama announced, smiling. "There is Mr.
Innes. My, I do admit I'm relieved to see him."

"Oh, dear."

"Collect yourself, Grace. For once in your life will
you do something useful for your poor mother, you
ungrateful girl? Haven't I suffered enough for not
producing a son?"

Grace sighed and gathered her reticule onto her
lap in time for the door to swing open. "Mrs. Wren,
Miss Wren," Mr. Innes said heartily. "Welcome to
Kirkcaldy." He helped her mother down but looked
directly at Grace.

She studied his dark eyes and found nothing of a
reassuring welcome there—nor on his unsmiling
mouth. "Thank you." She took the hand he offered.
"This is a magnificent place. I was almost certain
you referred to it as a house."

Innes's laugh added no cheer to the moment. "It

is a house. What we scots call a great hoose. Do you not like the place?''

''Oh, it's beautiful, I'm sure, but—''

''But a little overwhelming.'' He watched Mama, whose chin pointed skyward as she surveyed the clock tower that crowned a castellated balcony around the roof of a massive, oak-doored vestibule. ''Your mother appears quite pleased with her prospective home.''

· Grace took a calming breath. ''Mama is interested in everything. How is the marquess?''

''Well.''

Tiny cold ripples spread over Grace's skin. ''I'm glad.''

''Let me show you inside Kirkcaldy.''

''Thank you. Exactly how well is the marquess?''

''Very well.''

''I see.''

Angus passed them, hefting one of Grace's smaller trunks.

She marshaled the courage to say, ''I'm glad the marquess is so much improved.''

''Improved?''

''Yes. Over his former indisposed condition.''

''Ah.''

The coachman had reached the top of the entrance steps. He set Grace's trunk down and pushed the door wide open.

''Surely there is someone to help with the luggage,'' Grace said.

''Damn muck wallop,'' Mr. Innes said sharply. ''I never thought to . . .'' He closed his mouth firmly and inclined his head, indicating for Grace to precede him up the steps.

She forbore to ask the nature of a muck wallop.

''Do hurry, Grace.'' Mama hovered, half inside and half outside the vestibule. ''Does the marquess

not have sufficient servants, Mr. Innes? We shall
have to rectify that situation immediately.''

"Mama.''

"There are more than enough people wandering
about with nothing to do. I have no doubt many of
them will be glad of the employment."

"Mama!''

"We have an adequate staff, Mrs. Wren," Mr.
Innes said in a voice that was too pleasant.

He waved them ahead of him . . . inside Castle
Kirkcaldy.

On the threshold Grace drew in a breath and
held it.

"Muck wallop!" Mr. Innes's roar shook her to the
bone. He drew himself up, and she saw muscles jerk
in his lean cheeks. "Please come in. We'll get you
settled shortly."

She could never, ever, be settled amid all this.
Grace shook her head slowly. Dark red Persian rugs
did not soften the stark flagstones. No fire brightened a huge marble fireplace at the opposite end of
the vestibule. Above the fireplace stretched a grim
plaster relief of some battle scene. Dully glowing
suits of armor stood guard around the walls, each
one grasping a vicious-looking weapon in its iron
hands.

"Grand, isn't it?" Mama said, catching Grace's
eye.

She thought it quite terrifying. "Yes. Grand."

"Och, Master Calum, d'ye not see any o' the laddies about?" Angus staggered in with another trunk.
"I'm afraid Shanks may have forgotten to tell them
we're expectin'—"

"What's all this then?" A stocky man burst from
an archway to a dark corridor and marched into the
center of the vestibule.

"Nice of you to come, muck wallop," Mr. Innes

said, silkily menacing. "Do you suppose we could rouse the rest of the appropriate staff?"

"I should *think* so," Mama murmured.

Crowned by a thatch of curly red hair, the man had the ruddy face and brawny body of a vigorous laborer. He jutted his square chin ferociously. "Appropriate staff, sir? Nothin's been said to me about needing any particular staff. Therefore I'll away back to my duties and assume ye've made a mistake."

"Kindly stay where you are." Mr. Innes's smile was not reassuring. "Miss Wren, allow me to introduce you to his lordship's steward, Mr. McWallop."

For a dreadful instant Grace thought she would laugh hysterically. "How do you do?" she said, and giggled—and coughed. "I'm very pleased to meet you, Mr. McWallop."

"Aye." He straightened his claret-colored jacket and smoothed the dashing yellow silk waistcoat he wore beneath. "Aye, well, that's as may be. Here's Shanks. If he weren't deaf, he'd o' been here when ye made all that racket comin' in."

"I'll thank you not to cast aspersions on my hearing, McWallop." The newcomer strutted into sight on spindly legs encased in black breeches. He wore the reassuringly familiar uniform of a butler. When he saw the little assembly, he raised a beaked nose, causing the vestibule's dim light to shimmer on his bald head.

Mr. Innes flexed a hand at his side. "This is Miss Wren, Shanks. And her mother, Mrs. Wren."

Barely taller than Grace, Shanks eyed her with the interest a dog might show a dinner he didn't want. "We are not expecting visitors," he said.

Mama huffed loudly.

"Ring for Mrs. Moggach," Mr. Innes ordered. "*Now.* And send one of the footmen I haven't seen since I got back to help Angus with the luggage."

"Oh!" Grace realized she'd unknowingly rested

her hand on the head of half a polar bear, stuffed and with a gray-green fish clasped in its paws. She crossed her arms.

Mr. Innes advanced upon her, deep concern in his eyes. "Are you unwell, Miss Wren? I expect you are exhausted from your travels. And your dear mother. Please accept my apologies for the delay in showing you to your rooms."

"It's quite all right. Evidently the servants are surprised by . . . our . . . appearance," she finished slowly, warily watching the latest arrival in the vestibule.

Tall, large-boned, and heavily flashed, the woman dwarfed Shanks, who smiled happily at the sight of her.

"There you are, Mrs. Moggach," Shanks said. "Really, it's a shame to disturb you at such an hour, but—"

'Such an hour?" Mr. Innes said through his teeth. "For God's sake. Who is this household run for?"

"Ladies present," Shanks said, disapproving, undaunted, and stately all the way to the tips of his shiny black slippers. "These are visitors, Mrs. Moggach. Seems Mr. Innes expects rooms prepared for them."

Grace's courage deserted her completely. "This is too much trouble," she said, turning up the corners of her mouth and retreating. "Perhaps Angus could take us to the village. I'm sure we'd find a place at the inn for the night."

"Verra sensible, don't ye think, Mr. Shanks?" Mrs. Moggach said.

"Indeed," Shanks agreed.

"My God!" Mr. Innes said.

Very suddenly Mr. McWallop swept up a hand-held gong and sent a resounding bong echoing from stone walls.

Grace's hand went to her heart and she heard her mother gasp.

"I'll attend to this, Mr. Innes," the steward said. His face became even redder. "I'll thank ye to keep your opinions to yoursel', Shanks. Mrs. Moggach, Mrs. Wren will do well enough in the Serpent Bedroom."

"Serpent?" Mama echoed faintly.

"The girl can be put in Delilah."

"But that was—"

"It's the only other room suitable at short notice," Mr. McWallop interrupted Mrs. Moggach. "Make certain everything is made as comfortable as possible for the ladies' stay—including a good breakfast before they leave in the mornin'."

Four untidily liveried men appeared, each one showing signs of having hastily donned his white wig. A few short commands from Mr. McWallop sent them rushing in different directions.

"The ladies will not be leaving in the morning," Mr. Innes said. "Be prepared for a discussion, McWallop; you, too, Shanks. Mrs. Moggach, your presence will also be required. I'll speak to the marquess and let you all know when you'll be called."

"The marquess is not interested in—"

Mr. Innes waved McWallop to silence. "He will be now."

"I dinna see why he—"

"I'll take Mrs. and Miss Wren to the old marquess's drawing room."

"Ye'll do no such thing!" Mrs. Moggach's voice rose. "It's not been used since—"

"It will be used *now*. And it will be used a great deal in the near future. I've no doubt your new mistress will wish to reopen many rooms."

Grace attempted a smile but failed miserably.

The three servants stood quite still. "New mistress?" Shanks said clearly.

Mama bustled forward. "Yes. New mistress. And not a moment too soon from the look of this place." She wrinkled her nose. "Cobwebs. Dust!" One white-clad finger made a trail over the breastplate of the nearest suit of armor.

"Well!" Mrs. Moggach said, rolling in her lips. "And who are you?"

"I'm the mother—"

"Please, Mama. This is all quite outrageous."

"Mrs. Wren is the mother of your new mistress," Mr. Innes said calmly.

The woman looked from Mama to Grace, and her eyes made a disbelieving journey from the top of Grace's "too-thoughtful blue" bonnet to the matching slippers that peeped from the hem of her velvet pelisse. "I don't understand a word o' this."

Grace recognized a petty adversary and rallied. Rudeness was one thing she could not abide. She raised a hand, signaling for silence. "That will do, Mrs. Moggach." Her own sharp voice startled her, but only for an instant. "If you wish to keep your position, you will follow the instructions you've been given. At once! Do I make myself clear?"

"And who is it that gives me orders?"

"I do," Grace said firmly, taking pleasure from the look of surprised glee that transformed Mr. Innes's serious face. "If I hear even the smallest complaint, I shall inform the marquess that you are to be discharged at once."

"He'll not listen, ye wee upstart."

"He most certainly will. As his fiancée and soon to be wife, he will listen to whatever I have to say."

McWallop dropped the gong.

Why purple? Grace wondered. Purple draperies, purple counterpane and canopy, small purple armchairs; even the silk carpet that completely covered the bedroom floor was purple.

No matter. At last she was alone. Mama was taken with the opulence of the extraordinary Serpent Room and had already retired, exhausted, for the night.

Grace decided she would probably never sleep again. She went to hold her cold hands over the fire that had been lighted in the bulbous, black metal fireplace—surrounded by purple and white plaster depicting grape vines.

Mr. Innes had assured her the marquess would not be able to see her tonight. Grace hoped her relief had not been too apparent. Perhaps the marquess was not so well after all. Guilt made her grimace.

A light tap came at the door.

She frowned and called, "Come in."

The door opened a few inches, then a few inches more, and a girl cautiously popped her round face into the room.

Grace smiled. "Hello."

Shoulders appeared. Fine brown hair escaped from a knot to trail around the face. Bright blue eyes regarded Grace with alarm.

"What is it?"

"Mairi, miss. It's Mairi."

"Come in, Mairi."

Alarm visibly approached panic. "Are ye certain ye want me to?"

The day had been too much. The past weeks had been too much. "If you would *like* to come in, then I'm certain."

"Verra well." In she came, plump, with a sweet face and jerky movements. A white apron clearly intended for a much taller woman trailed below the hem of her brown woolen dress. She wound her red-knuckled hands together.

"Come by the fire," Grace said. "You look chilled."

"Och, no. I'm not chilled. Not a bit o' it."

Grace smiled and nodded—and waited.

Mairi made a faint humming sound.

"Did someone ask you to come and tell me something?" Preferably that she was to be returned to London forthwith.

"Dearie me."

"Something's wrong?"

"Nothin's wrong, miss. Except that I'm to be your new maid, and I never was anyone's maid before."

"I see." She didn't.

"They came for me in the village since there was none here at the castle as would do the job."

Grace made a grim note to have words with Mrs. Moggach about that. "You did not have another job, Mairi?"

"I've a job here—in the kitchens. It's not enough to keep me livin' here, so I come in evra mornin'. I come in to cook the servants' puddin' for Grumpy."

"Isn't that the housekeeper's job?"

"Aye, but she's not a good hand at it." Mairi puffed at the hair that flitted near her eyes. "I'm not good either, but Grumpy doesna care to spend her time on anythin' . . . Och, I'm talkin' too much. I always talk too much. It's been the bane o' my poor father's life, and doesna he tell everybody so."

"You can say whatever you please to me," Grace said. She'd welcome a little friendly chatter inside this silent stone edifice. "Who's Grumpy?"

"Och!" Mairi layered her hands over her mouth, and her face turned scarlet. "Will ye listen to me blatherin'? Mrs. Moggach is Grumpy, an' she'll have my skin for the haggis for sayin' so. Please say ye'll not tell hersel'."

For the first time since she'd arrived, real laughter welled in Grace. "I won't tell her if you don't tell her I'm going to call her Grumpy, too. It's a perfect name for her."

"Aye, and it's true enough. Moggach means grumpy in Gaelic, y'see."

Grace saw. "So, Mairi, what are we to do tonight?"

"Ye're to do nothin', miss. I'm to be your maid."

"It's late."

Mairi hunched her shoulders. "I know, but I was told to see to your needs."

They looked at each other.

"So I'll start on that, I suppose."

Grace didn't move. Neither did Mairi.

"Mayhap ye'd tell me what I should do first?"

"Sit down."

Mairi frowned.

"Sit down," Grace repeated, sinking into a purple chair herself. When Mairi had hesitantly followed the instruction, Grace leaned back. "How old are you?"

"Eighteen, miss."

"I'm twenty-four."

"So old?" Mairi nodded sympathetically. "I s'pose that's why."

"Why?"

Mairi went to rise, but Grace signaled her to remain seated.

"Why what, Mairi?"

The girl fidgeted with her apron. "Well, why ye'd agree to come, I s'pose."

Some things were better left unasked for a while. "Perhaps you'd best start being my maid some other time."

"Dearie me," Mairi said, her eyes darkening with worry. "I was afraid o' this."

"Of what?" Already Grace felt herself warming to this girl.

"Ye'll not want someone who's not a real maid. I was afraid to come, but I did, an' now you're not so fearsome." She caught a quick breath and sat on the very edge of her seat. "Not so fearsome at all. Ye might find me quick to learn, miss. Honestly, ye might. I've always learned quickly, everyone says I do. Why, even Grumpy says I sometimes do somethin' right an'—"

"Of course you do," Grace interrupted hastily.

"I so hoped ye'd let me stay, miss. I've not much o' a place o' my own with father. He's a new wife these past years, and she'd be glad o' the space I take up. If I had a place here with ye, it'd be a blessin' for sure."

Grace shook her head—then nodded. "As far as I'm concerned, you're my maid, Mairi. Don't concern yourself for another moment."

"Och, thank ye!" She bobbed up from the chair, made to embrace Grace, but pulled back. "Thank ye. They're to give me a room o' my verra own if I suit ye. So I'll start now. Would unpackin' the trunks be the first thing ye'll be needin'?"

"No!" Grace gripped the arms of her chair. "No, thank you, Mairi. I'd prefer to do that myself."

"Ye would?"

"Yes, I would." At the bottom of those trunks, carefully packed in oiled cloths, lay another part of Grace's plans for the future. No one could be allowed to touch them. "If I tell you a secret, will you promise not to laugh and not to tell anyone else?"

"I promise," Mairi whispered. She bent to bring her honest face close to Grace's.

"All right." Grace whispered, too, and put a finger to her lips. "You've never been a maid, and I've never *had* a maid. What do you think of that?"

Mairi's blank expression slowly changed to amusement. She grinned broadly. "Ye never have?"

"Never."

"Then who's to tell who about it?"

"We'll just have to tell each other," Grace said, and they laughed together. "Do sit down again. I'm so glad you're here. You can start being my maid by telling me all the things I need to know about this place." And about the marquess, she thought, although that subject must be carefully approached.

"We all live well enough," Mairi said seriously. "Though Father tell o' how it used to be before . . . It used to be different here. There was laughter and balls and the gentry comin' for parties."

"That would be before the marquess's, mm, sickness?"

"Aye, ye could call it that."

Poor man. Now he was reduced to seeking the aid and company of a woman he didn't even know. How quickly friends could desert one when grave illness occurred.

"D'ye think there's any reason to be afeared, miss?"

Grace screwed up her eyes. "Why should there be?"

"Well. At night, I mean. With what goes on an' everythin'."

A slow thud, thud, made Grace very aware of her heart. "I'm afraid I don't know what you're talking about."

The girl glanced nervously at the door. "*Him.*"

Grace lowered her head encouragingly.

"Ye know. *Him.* Is it true that ye're to marry him?"

Was it? "It appears so."

"Are ye not afeared?"

Such lack of understanding in the face of illness was very sad. "No, I'm not afraid."

"Och, ye're verra brave. D'ye know all about him, then? And do ye still not fear for yersel'?"

"Why don't you tell me what you think I should be afraid of? Then I'll tell you if I am." Despite her resolve, Grace had to swallow around the tightness in her throat.

Mairi looked over her shoulder again, and into the dark recesses of the room. "He's never seen by day."

Grace nodded. "I'm sure he's not."

"But the lights are on all night."

"Are they?" Of course, a poor, sick man's lights might be needed at night.

"There are terrible stories, ye know."

Grace was afraid she soon would know.

"Have ye heard them?"

"I don't think I have."

"Are ye set on it, then?"

The fire had begun to burn low, and Grace shivered a little. "What are you asking me?"

"If ye're determined to marry *him*."

"It appears that I am."

"Aye." A tremendous sigh raised Mairi's rounded bosom. "I was afraid o' that. A woman as old as four an' twenty and still a spinster is likely to feel desperate, I s'pose."

There seemed no response.

"Surely ye'd be better off a spinster than with *him*? What'll ye do when he goes on one o' his wild tears?"

"I don't know," Grace said. As hard as she tried to remind herself that these local people were ignorant, she could not completely quell her own nervousness.

Mairi began to wind her hands together again. "If ye decide to go ahead with it, I'll be here for ye. Let me know if there's a babby an' I'll do me best to save it."

Grace felt her mouth drop open but was helpless to close it.

"I could rush in and help ye take it away from him." An upsurge of enthusiasm brought a smile to Mairi's pale lips. "If ye wanted me to, I'd help ye hold him down until he subsided."

"What baby?" Grace managed to ask.

"Och, ye poor, wee thing, ye dinna know at all. He's *mad*. No one sees him. Not ever."

"The marquess?"

"Aye, the marquess. And the stories they tell. It's the babbies that twist your heart, though."

"What babies?" Grace almost screamed.

"The ones he steals o' a night." All color left Mairi's face.

"How . . . how does he steal them?" She could hardly breathe.

Mairi's eyes opened wide. "Och, I'm not sure, but they say as he looks for any left lyin' about."

"Whose baby was stolen most recently?" Perhaps there was some monster on the loose, and the poor, sick marquess was being blamed for sins he was incapable of committing.

"I'm not certain, but I'll find out for ye. That's if I can get anyone to talk about it."

"If someone's child has been stolen, they'll talk about it."

"Och, no." Mairi slowly rocked her head from side to side. "Ye don't ken a mother's pain at knowin' her bairn's suffered so. She'd not be likely to talk about it easily."

Grace had to ask: "What exactly does he . . . ? What is supposed to happen to these babies?"

"Och, miss," Mairi moaned. "He *eats* them."

This time Grace did scream.

"Calm y'sel'," Mairi said, taking hold of Grace's hands. "Ye'll need your wits about ye for marriage to the Savage o' Stonehaven."

Chapter 3

Midnight had come and gone. But for her mother, Grace was alone among strangers in a castle hundreds of miles from her London home and faced with the probability that she was about to become the wife of a dying marquess.

The courage to leave her chamber had not been easily summoned, but there was a task to be accomplished, and it must be done quickly lest someone more determined than Mairi took an interest in Grace's trunks.

There was not a moment to be wasted. Especially on foolishness. Eating babies! And she had allowed the lateness of the hour and her formidable surroundings to sweep her into ridiculous and unfounded fear.

Widgeon! Sapskull! Peagoose!

Never again would she succumb to such girlish nonsense.

Grace settled her oiled-cloth-wrapped bundle more firmly beneath her arm, turned the corner of yet another gloomy, deserted corridor, and tried to ignore the suits of armor that stood like silent iron sentries all over this great building—at least, all over as much of it as she had so far observed. The plastered walls supported banks of weapons and shields between portraits of dour-faced, richly dressed men and thoughtless-looking females holding flowers or books.

37

She eyed the paintings with disdain. Lifeless. Useless. Who would want such ill-tempered scowls on all sides?

This was the fourth turn she had taken since creeping from her chamber. She stopped and looked back. One left, two right, and another left. Only she must reverse them all on the way back.

A draft as if from some deep, bone-cold place wafted about her ankles, plucking at the hem of her thin dress. She stepped closer to a wall. If she listened, there seemed to be hushed swishings and breathings and a faint irregular ticking like the last efforts of a dying clock.

And, so very far away, music?

No. Nothing.

There was absolutely nothing unusual about this place, except that it was a huge, confusing, mostly dark, and mostly empty castle in which she was an interloper.

To turn back would be to give up—at least for now—and she wanted to waste as little time as possible finding a place to continue the work she could only do in private.

She eased away from the wall. Another door, heavy and crooked like several others she'd already opened, stood ajar on her left. She pushed it open a little and peered inside. The shapes of draped furniture loomed, and a most unpleasant and strong smell of dust hung over all. This house—*castle*—must be cleaned and it must be cleaned promptly. If she did little else that was useful here, she would ensure that the lazy servants attended to their duties.

A weak moon cast scant light into what was obviously a bedroom, but it was enough to show Grace that the room would not do for her special purpose. The windows were too narrow, and there was not at all a welcoming atmosphere.

She pressed on. The bare stones beneath her feet

struck an icy chill into her flesh. Her slippers made dry, scratching sounds as if hidden fingers tried to crawl a way out.

Music.

A rush of notes like a distant silver waterfall.

No. Mama, and Papa before her, had warned Grace to ignore her otherworldly senses. Yet . . .

She had *not* heard ghostly music, and faint-hearted, she would not be. The days ahead would require a cool head, and Grace would be up to the ordeal.

At intervals, wall sconces puddled their yellow glow over the scene. Lights at night, indeed! Of course there were lights at night.

One more room, and another, showed no more promise than the others until Grace finally reached a staircase. Cautiously she stared up steps worn thin at their centers by the passage of many feet. The weight of stone around her pressed in. She could almost feel the hundreds of years this home of rock had weathered. "And the people," she murmured to herself. "All those people."

She heard it again, and this time almost clearly. The same fluid, descending notes played, over and over, on a piano.

Perhaps Mr. Innes was the pianist. Perhaps his rooms were here, although she'd been led to believe they were in the opposite direction.

The music stopped. In her mind the remembered sound made an image of a cobweb strung with early morning dew. Then, as if a breeze blew the shiny threads and droplets away, the web was gone.

Otherworldly nonsense.

At a square landing, the staircase angled away to the right and upward again. And at the top was a door.

And under the door shone a slice of subdued light.

". . . the lights are on all night."

A watery sensation attacked Grace's limbs. She stood quite still and listened.

There was no sound.

She let out the breath she'd held and climbed again. *Peagoose.* No doubt she'd expected to hear babies crying to the tune of her cobweb music. Or perhaps the crunch of tiny bones . . . "Oh." The small cry could not be contained. Silliness it might all be, but quite horrible to contemplate.

"Courage," she told herself. "You are afraid of nothing. And you must get started on your work again."

The words felt decidedly hollow, but she settled a hand on the doorknob and turned it slowly.

Soundlessly the door swung inward over glossy wooden floors. Grace was faced with an expanse of dark blue silk carpet and towering paneled walls hung with rich tapestries. In the center of the room stood a piano upon which were heaped untidy piles of papers. More papers littered the floor. No welcoming flames lighted the white marble fireplace.

Grace stared at the piano and swallowed painfully. The lid was up, exposing the keys. A bench with a tapestry seat stood at an angle.

No one sat upon that bench.

Inching forward, she peered around. There was *no* ghostly pianist hovering in the vicinity.

She should flee.

She would *not* flee.

This was supposedly to be her home, and she must learn to make it so for as long as she remained . . . Again Grace guiltily recognized that she was contemplating the death of a man she had not met but whom she might well marry.

With hesitant steps she entered an extraordinary room. The arches of a domed Gothic ceiling were ornately plastered with garlands of leaves and musical instruments. Grace was no expert on such things, but a group of armchairs pushed at careless angles around a marquetry table appeared to be upholstered with Aubusson tapestry like some she'd seen in the home of one of Mama's needleworking friends.

The light came from beaten brass wall sconces.

"Hello," she said softly.

No one replied.

"Is anybody here?"

There was in the air a feeling of energy . . . emotion. And there was only silence.

She should leave.

She *would* not.

Quickly, before she could change her mind, Grace hurried determinedly across the room and stood before the fireplace. Holding the bundle against her middle, she looked around.

To the left, in a corner, stood a second piano. A third, this one very large and with the top raised, occupied a space some feet from a curved casement over which were drawn red velvet draperies.

Grace surveyed the entire scene and had an unnervingly poignant insight. This was a place that had been filled with music. The marquess, when he'd been a young, well man, must have loved music. A violoncello rested against a couch, and several violin cases were placed, open, on its seat.

This had once been someone's beloved place. She could feel it. And now it was kept ready as if the musician would one day return. The little part of her she'd been taught to ignore must have heard music from long ago. The arched ceiling above Grace's head, the plaster garlands and fanciful images, had caught and held the beautiful sounds, and she had somehow snatched them away again, if only for a few moments.

"So sad," Grace said. Who could be taking such care of all this? Certainly not the slothful band of

servants she'd so far encountered and of whom,
with the exception of Mairi, she'd seen nothing since
dinner

She closed her eyes to feel the energy that had
managed to remain alive here.

Alive. Yes, it was alive and the energy still
hummed, audible to that magical part of her mind
that she and only she had welcomed since child-
hood.

This was a good room, a perfect room.

Grace opened her eyes and looked around keenly.
That window was wide, and the exposure should be
perfect for her needs. Why not? Surely if she told
the marquess she'd like to care for his music room,
he would be happy to agree. Perhaps in time—if they
found a kindly companionship—she would be able
to tell him about her secret. If he was the type of
man she was beginning to think he might be, he
could only be inclined to encourage her in the passion she'd been forced to hide.

And now she was being truly foolish. No man
would encourage such pursuits in a woman, particularly in a woman who was his wife purely for the
purpose of providing care in his dying days.

Grace walked to the gloomy window alcove and
swept open a drapery. "Oh, yes," she whispered,
and tears sprang into her eyes. The moon hung in a
misty bowl of silver sunk into a sky as soft as draped
black muslin. By day there would be sunshine here
and the crystal blue of high hill heavens. "Yes, yes!
This must be the place."

"Must it indeed?"

Grace all but collapsed. She whirled about to face
a man, a very large man. The lumpy bundle slipped
under her arm, but she caught and clamped it
against her chest.

He was so close, she could see how his narrowed
green eyes caught light and darkened.

"I . . . I am Miss Grace Wren."

"Really?" Tall, extremely tall, and dressed in black except for his white linen, the man must have stood, silent and unmoving, watching her from the shadow of the casement.

With difficulty, Grace lowered her gaze from his face. "I am . . . I am to live at Castle Kirkcaldy," she said, appalled at her wobbly little voice.

"Really?" There was a cool amusement in his deep voice.

Grace raised her chin. "Yes, really. My mother and I arrived only hours since. I could not sleep, so I decided to explore."

"Perhaps you might have considered inquiring as to whether exploring, as you call it, is appropriate under the circumstances. I take it you did not ask?"

"There was no one *to* ask," she told him defensively.

"Then would it not have been prudent to wait until there was someone?"

Grace remembered the music. "You were playing the piano!" Of course. She had not imagined anything after all.

He lowered his gaze as if deep in thought, then he said, "No one was playing the piano."

"But . . ." He *had* been playing. "You were . . ."

"You are mistaken." He held a small brush in his hand, and a cloth.

"Who are you?" Grace said. "Are you . . . are you supposed to be cleaning this room?"

His dark brows rose a fraction. "Perhaps I am." The black hair that curled across his brow was pulled back and tied at his nape in a manner that was unfashionable yet decidedly and rakishly appealing.

"You're taking care of it for the old marquess, aren't you?" She gripped the oiled cloth tighter. He probably wasn't supposed to be using the piano, and that's why he'd denied playing. But, and more important, if this man was close to her supposed future husband, he might be willing to tell her about him.

The man moved, and Grace drew in a sharp breath. This was part of the energy she'd felt in the room. His black coat fitted perfectly; fitted perfectly over a powerful chest and shoulders and moved about solid muscle as he circled to stand between Grace and escape.

"You did not tell me your name," she said, feeling vulnerable and trapped.

"It isn't important. Why is this room the place you were looking for?"

Grace crossed her arms over her untidy burden. "I'm not sure. All I meant was that I like the way it feels. And I like the window. The light must be wonderful here in the daytime."

"You like light?"

"Oh, yes. Light is a marvel. It's full of life and it changes all the time."

"You don't find merit in darkness?"

"Not for . . . Darkness can be beautiful if one feels safe and can reflect upon it without anxiety." She reflected now. "When I looked outside just now, I thought the sky was like black muslin, as if it would be soft to touch."

He turned the corners of his mouth down.

She was in a strange room, in a huge, strange castle . . . with a large and exceedingly strange man. "I expect you think me fanciful."

"I think you interesting. Unusual even."

"What a coincidence. I think you interesting and . . ." Completely unfamiliar occurrences could make one say such unsuitable things.

"Interesting and . . . ?" A smile revealed straight white teeth and showed unexpected dimples beneath high cheekbones. But the smile did not soften or relax his harsh face. "*And*, Miss Grace Wren?"

"I'm sure I cannot remember what I meant to

say." But she did not intend to appear an empty-headed widgeon. Neither did she, for one moment, intend to let him think her afraid of him. Grace smiled at him directly. "Do you know the old marquess?"

His reaction was extraordinary. The smile became a grin, and then he laughed.

"I'm sure I cannot imagine what is so humorous about that question, sir." Perhaps she should try to make her escape and look for another hiding place for her treasure.

He sobered but continued to grin. "No, clearly you cannot, Miss Grace Wren."

What an arresting mouth, wide and clearly defined, the lower lips much fuller than the upper . . . And his nose was so straight, the narrow bridge an elegant blade.

This was one more outrageous event in an unbelievably outrageous day. "I asked if you knew the marquess. Was that an inappropriate question?"

"Not at all. I know him better than anyone."

Her heart bumped. "Do you like him?"

He raised his sharply defined jaw to look down upon her. "A complex question. There are those who would say the marquess is not without virtue." The growth of his beard shadowed his cheeks, and she saw the sweep of thick, dark lashes. The face of a barbarian, a barely tamed barbarian.

If he was tamed at all.

"He is a good man?" She tried to relax but failed.

The wicked smile flashed again. "The best of men. None better."

"Oh. Oh, that is very relieving to hear."

"I'm glad to have pleased you."

"Was this room his?"

"It still is. This castle is his."

Grace blushed. "Forgive me. Since he is so ill and

confined, I . . . He loves beautiful things, doesn't he?''

The man planted his feet apart and considered, and whilst he did, his green eyes never left their close scrutiny of Grace.

She hunched her shoulders a little. Leaving her chamber wearing only a thin blue muslin dress had been a mistake, but it was not only the chill that made her shiver.

''Why do you think the marquess loves beautiful things?'' the man asked suddenly.

''This room.'' She inclined her head. ''And Mr. Innes took us to a drawing room which he said belonged to the old marquess. That, too, is magnificent.''

''Is it?''

''Oh, yes. I'm sure the marquess must find it very difficult to be denied all pleasures of life. The room did not appear to have been used in many years. Not since the old gentleman became ill, I should imagine.''

''How *old* did Mr. Innes say the marquess is?''

Grace thought. ''I don't believe he did say exactly.''

''But he told you . . . he was ill?''

''Oh yes. Already confined to his room, Mr. Innes told me.''

''Did he? *Confined?*''

''Yes. He told me the marquess doesn't go about anymore.''

''He told you that, hm?''

''Yes. Not at all. Isn't that sad for a man who must have been so vital.''

''What makes you so certain he was vital?''

''Why, this room.'' Grace smiled around. ''Look at it. Feel it. Can you *feel* it?''

He frowned. ''I'm not sure. Help me.''

She hesitated a moment before saying, ''If you

close your eyes—'' she did so herself ''—there is something in the air. It's vibrant as if there were colors one cannot see with one's eyes open. When you . . . There's music here.'' And there was, like a shimmery echo of the notes he'd played. ''I can hear music here, can't you?''

Very faintly, as if drawn like a brilliantly hued silken ribbon, notes seemed to carress her mind. ''Can't you?''

A touch, so light it might have been imagined, passed along her jaw.

Grace's eyes flew open. He did not appear to have moved, but the darkness in his eyes had intensified. He looked at her mouth.

She passed her tongue over her lips and saw him draw his own bottom lip between his teeth.

''Can you?'' she repeated, and her voice broke.

''Oh, yes,'' he said. ''Yes, I can hear it. Who are *you*, little night imp? Other than Miss Grace Wren?''

His meaning wasn't clear. ''I . . . I am no one really. Except that I am here to marry the marquess. Since you know him so well, I expect he has spoken of this event.''

''There has been some mention. What is in your parcel?''

Grace held it the tighter. ''Just some things.''

''Just some things you carry around in the middle of the night whilst you search out a hiding place?''

''No—'' How could he know? ''That is . . . they would not be valuable to anyone but me.''

''They?''

''My things,'' she said, desperately trying to think of a way to leave.

''But they are very, very important to you, aren't they?'' he said softly.

''You are like me,'' Grace said, and immediately wished the words away. But they had been said. ''I mean, you feel things others don't always feel.'' And they were both hiding something for which they cared very, very much.

"I doubt if we are at all alike," he said. "No deep intellect is required to see that you hold something dear to you. But that is your affair. If you should require a place to keep possessions in safety, why not use the window seat behind you?"

She glanced back.

He moved without sound, setting aside the brush and cloth and leaning past her to lift a heavy oaken lid. "There. It is yours, and you have my word that neither I nor any other shall touch whatever you choose to leave here. Do you believe that you can trust me?"

"Yes." It was true because they were alike, she and this stranger. How miraculous to chance upon someone so obviously different from oneself in every visible way but whose very heart touched one's own. Relief made her stupidly weak—and grateful. "Thank you! Are you certain . . . You are sure the marquess would not mind?"

"Absolutely."

Carefully Grace bent to set the parcel into the deep space. As she straightened, she found his face close to hers. "Thank you," she said again, and awkwardly played with the thin gold chain at her throat.

"The pleasure is mine." He tilted his head, looking upon her so intently that Grace felt heat rise to her skin. "Oh, yes, the pleasure is definitely mine."

She took a deep breath and could not fail to note that his gaze briefly shifted to her breasts. "I was right, wasn't I? This was the marquess's special room?" This deep, trembling sensation was not something she recalled feeling before.

Putting the lid of the window seat down, he straightened. "Yes, indeed."

"I wish I had known him then."

"Fate brings us surprises," he said.

Grace frowned. "I beg your pardon."

"Mm?" The green of his eyes was so searing, it had the power to burn. "I simply meant that sometimes reality proves quite different from that which our imagination has anticipated. Yes, indeed, reality can present us with some interesting prospects."

"I'm sure I do not understand you, sir."

"No, I'm sure you don't. But you may one day."

She might like that. "You say you are the marquess's companion."

"His closest companion."

"I thought that was Mr. Innes's position."

"He would be the first to tell you I am closer."

This was most puzzling. "You deal with his . . . personal needs, perhaps?"

Once more there was that smile that made her want to smile, too. "His most personal needs."

Now she understood. "So it is *you* who need me." Impulsively she rested a hand on his arm. "And the marquess himself, of course. But you need me to help you look after him."

His manner of taking his bottom lip in his teeth caused the oddest sensation within her. "In a manner of speaking," he said.

She leaned closer. "I really am very capable, you know. My mother is not at all strong—in some ways, that is—and I nursed my father through his final illness. You will not find me one little bit hesitant in dealing with the . . . with whatever needs to be done."

"Whatever?"

"Whatever," she agreed fervently. "And he will find comfort in a woman's gentle touch—the touch of someone bonded to him."

"What a delightful thought."

"I beg your pardon."

His hand, warm and strong, covered hers upon his arm. "You need never beg my pardon."

Truly, men could be so difficult to understand.

"Why did you agree to marry a man you have never met?"

Grace bowed her head.

"Come." He shook her gently. "Answer me this."

"It . . . It was a solution."

"To what?"

Was the decision she'd made wrong? "To the problem of how to care for my mother," she told him in a rush. "And to finding a way to be free to make my own choices."

With his forefinger he eased up her chin. "Now you speak in riddles. What choices could a young female possibly want to make for herself?"

There it was again. Even in this sensitive man. The wretched and annoying male certainty that females were inferior and in need of guidance in all things. "Really, it is *too* infuriating. Why do men think they have the right to tell women what they should do and what they should want? And what they should *think*, for goodness' sake? I wish to marry a man who considers me his equal in all things. I should like to help him with his business and the decisions he makes. And I should like him to consult me when he is troubled and expect me to give him comfort and to offer sensible advice." She paused for breath. "And I want to have to ask no man's permission to do what I consider important."

There seemed a loss of focus in his eyes. "Extraordinary."

"Oh, fie! There is no point to this, and I cannot imagine why I am speaking of such things. This is not something I speak of, and it is amazing that I should have chosen to tell you."

"Amazing? When we are so alike? You already told me as much, you know. But I am confused. How will your marriage to the marquess aid you in achieving your goal?"

Grace blushed once more. "I would not have thought of such a plan if Mr. Innes had not approached Mama and me at Lady Armstrong's. He came to a salon there, and Lady Armstrong introduced us. Afterwards he reacquainted himself with me at several gatherings. He said he had been told about me and wished to approach me on a matter of business."

"But how did you—"

"He asked me many questions and was pleased with my answers," Grace said quickly. "Just as he was pleased with the exceptionally boring . . . um, the quiet life I have lived. At first his suggestion seemed quite appalling."

"Appalling?"

"The thought of marrying a decrepit old man for his money." She clapped her hands over her mouth. "I mean—"

"You mean that marrying a decrepit old man for his money repulsed you before you considered the money in more depth?"

"Yes . . . No! Well, not exactly." How dreadful she sounded.

"I am not clear as to how you intend to use this money to fulfill your requirements whilst your husband still lives. Other than taking care of your mother, that is."

"Oh, I could not! No, no, I have every intention of being the very soul of kindness, a true pillar of strength to my husband whilst he lives.

"But once my duties are discharged, there will be no impediment to my seeking a husband of my choice, d'you see. Then it will be no different than a man of means seeking the wife of his choice . . . As men always have . . . I'll have the means myself . . . d'you see . . . ?

"Men have always done it, haven't they? Wealthy

men?'' Surely any reasonable man would understand. ''Are you married?''

''No.''

''Don't you think that if you were rich, you could easily find a wife who would please you?''

''It appears less and less likely.''

There was an altogether confusing inflection in his voice. And why was he watching her so strangely? ''Anyway, Mr. Innes said I would be very well compensated for my efforts.''

His eyes narrowed even more. ''A bargain. Your young life for an old man's pleasure?''

Grace felt fuddled, and yes, more than a little unnerved. ''Mr. Innes's offer was sincerely made. He made it clear that all that is required of me is to care for the poor old man in his final days and to take care of his remaining earthly desires.''

He coughed and averted his face. ''Mr. Innes explained all this to you?''

''Oh, yes.''

''And he said you would soon be free.''

She frowned. ''That is what I'm sure he implied.''

''You would not have considered coming here to marry a man who was not on his deathbed?''

''Oh, no!'' Why would he ask such a question? ''I'm sure that if he were young, he would not have been at all what I wanted in *that* kind of husband.''

''What, I wonder, would your kind of husband be?'' The comment was evenly enough made, and Grace did not anticipate his next move. He reached out and caught an untidily trailing tendril of her hair between finger and thumb and tugged lightly. ''No doubt you would want a man who told you often that you have the most glorious mass of pale blond hair he has ever seen.''

The careful pull on her hair spun a thread of intimacy between them. ''The matter of a suitable husband will not be at all difficult,'' she said.

He increased the pressure on her scalp, pulling her closer until she stood almost toe to toe with him, looking up. "Perhaps there is already a fortunate man waiting for you somewhere?"

"Absolutely not!" Grace tried to ease her hair from his fingers.

"So adamant." Abandoning the tugging, he concentrated instead on smoothing her cheek with the back of a finger. With his thumb, he stroked her bottom lip. "I have no doubt that you would make a passionate wife for a young and virile man."

Tingling warmth spread in Grace's belly—and lower. "This seems an inappropriate conversation," she told him, and heard the breathlessness in her voice. "I should return to my chamber."

"Which chamber is that?"

"One with a silly name. The *Delilah* room, of all things."

His hand fell to her shoulder like a stone, and his fingers closed on her neck. "Who put you there?" he asked sharply.

"Mr. McWallop," she said, aware of the pressure of long, strong fingers at her throat. "Apparently there was none other anywhere near readiness. It is all purple and rather vulgar, but quite comfortable. This castle needs cleaning," she finished uncertainly.

"You shall have a different room soon enough." A white line formed around his compressed mouth. "*No one* is supposed to enter that chamber. I ordered it locked."

She did not imagine his anger. "I expect they forgot. In the morning I'll mention your concerns to—"

"You will mention my concerns to no one. Not a soul. Do I make myself clear?"

Grace opened her mouth, but no sound came.

"You will not tell a soul that you came here to-night. Or that you saw me. Is that also clear?"

She nodded.

"Now you will leave." He did not remove his hand from her neck. "But you will return tomorrow night at precisely the same time."

"Could . . . could I not come during the day?"

"You are never again to enter this room without my permission."

"Perhaps the marquess would like me to look after it for him."

"He would not."

"But it would ease a burden for you, and—"

"It is unseemly for a female—particularly one in such a peculiar circumstance—to argue on such a matter."

Grace found a little courage. "I think you would do well to remember who you're speaking to. I am shortly to be your master's wife, and as such, you will be *mine* to command." She did not sound particularly courageous.

His touch gentled and slipped to her bare shoulder. He rubbed the sensitive skin there with his palm. "I will be *yours* to command?" A fresh smile made of his face a dark and devilish mask. "Tell me, Miss Wren, how will you know when you meet the man you wish to marry . . . after the marquess's death, of course?"

"That is simple," she said, defiantly shrugging free and slipping past him. "I shall *feel* it, sir, as I feel anything that matters to me."

"And how will this momentous event feel?"

Grace backed away toward the door. "It will feel full of love. I will feel the man's love for me with my heart and soul."

"And you will never doubt that his love is for you rather than for the enormous wealth you plan to command?"

"No doubt at all!" she told him triumphantly. "Because he will not know I have money until *after* he has declared his love. And *I* will love him."

"This love is essential?"

"It is everything."

"A pretty notion." He put his hands on his hips beneath his coat. "But at least we know there is no misunderstanding in what you intend to do at Kirkcaldy. You intend to *use* the marquess, just as he intends to use you. And that is quite fair, do you not agree?"

Every word he spoke felt like a trap, although she could not guess why that should be so. "I agree."

"And what if the marquess *lingers* on somewhat longer than you anticipate?"

She chewed the inside of her cheek. "Then I shall simply have to make the best of it."

"Perhaps you could consider turning to another who is, as you have already suggested, very like you. Time might pass quite pleasantly in the company of one with whom you share so much."

He was offering her companionship. *Friendship!*

Grace brightened. "You really are very perceptive and forward-thinking for a man." Her more favorable impressions of him had been correct. "Of course. That is a perfectly wonderful idea. I accept and I intend to enjoy every moment of our time together. Thank you."

"You seem certain there will be no problem with such an arrangement."

"None at all, thanks to you. You are by way of making me an offer of . . . *friendship,* are you not?"

His brows raised. "It would seem that I am."

"I scarcely comprehend such immediate good fortune, but I feel that you and I will be a great comfort to one another." Reaching the open door, she paused. "Until tomorrow night, then, when I may surprise you with my ingenuity."

"What man would not look forward to such an occasion?"

"Only one with water in his veins and no passion in his soul. Clearly you suffer no such affliction. Tomorrow I will show you that within this simple body of mine lies an innovative imagination. I will show you things you have never experienced before. And I hope you may offer of yourself with equal disregard for what our dull, tiresome society regards as acceptable."

He mumbled something she could not hear.

"What did you say?"

"I said, Godspeed you back to your chamber . . . And Godspeed the hours until tomorrow night."

Chapter 4

*"**A** mighty, monstrous excess."*
Kirkcaldy.

So had Arran's father described the place—and his father before him.

Arran planted his feet, pushed the brim of his shapeless woolen hat up from his eyes, and squinted against the late afternoon wind. The turrets and towers of the fortress that had been his family's home for three centuries scarred a gray sky like dark, mocking fingers.

Mighty, yes. *Marvelous*—yes. Monstrous? Perhaps. And only excessive in its insolent beauty.

He loved Kirkcaldy.

In the early hours of the morning, the hours after his encounter with Miss Grace Wren, Arran had felt, almost as never before, the weight of his responsibility for his home and his people. As he should have known would be the case, a day spent as most of his days were, on the land—with those people— had renewed his determination to remain accountable for both.

The day had also fueled a bone-deep weariness. Even a strong man grew tired of standing alone. Arran smiled bitterly. Did the longing for love— whatever that might be—ever completely die? The answer was of no moment. For the Marquess of Stonehaven, there would be no trusted lover. Experience had taught him not to expect to share his life

57

with a woman who would want him if he were *not* a nobleman with vast wealth.

"Och, there ye are," Robert Mercer said, arriving at Arran's side and clapping him between the shoulder blades. "I didna see ye go. Will ye no take a bannock fresh from the hearth with us, Niall?" Tenant son of tenant forefathers, with a history as long as Arran's on this land, Robert never failed to ask the man he trusted, but did not know, to break bread with his young family.

Arran ducked his head and wiped a heavily gloved hand over his grimy face. "My thanks, Robert, but I'll away home." The manner of speech slipped to his tongue as easily as the rough peasant clothes fitted his big body—as easily as he became "Niall" to pass among the souls who found their living on his estates.

He loved these people. They were simple and warm and generous—and their future was his trust as surely as had they been his children. The lords of Stonehaven had all had their faults, but they had never skirted responsibility for their tenants.

"Things go well with ye?" Robert asked. The invitations to share the Mercers' table were never pressed, although Arran always heard hope in the other man's voice. "Your place weathered the winter?"

Again Arran glanced toward the castle. "Aye. Well enough. It's stout." Robert had no knowledge of where the tall man with long, wild hair spent the hours after he disappeared from the fields and forests of Kirkcaldy, and had long ago ceased to ask. "How are Gael and the little one?" Arran added.

Robert shifted at his side. Yet in his twenties, he was straight-backed and fair with brown eyes that looked at a man direct. "There'll be another bairn afore long," he said, flushing slightly. "I'd have wished my Gael stronger first. God forgive me, it's too soon."

Arran heard fear and self-recrimination in Robert's voice—and deep love for his tiny, red-haired wife. "Ye're but a man," he said, floundering. He looked at his own scuffed but sturdy boots. "Ye've plenty of good food? And your place is sound?"

"Aye, Niall." There was a hollowness. "Mr. Innes never fails to make certain o' that. A miracle, he is. We all say as much. He seems t'know our needs almost as soon as we know them oursel'."

The system worked well, Arran thought with satisfaction. He told Calum what needed to be done, and Calum dispatched what was necessary—to the occasional confusion of the estate's commissioner. Hector MacFie was a good man, but the fewer who knew of Niall's existence, the better. "Take heart, Robert," Arran said. "Take heart."

"A man ought to be more for the woman who gives him her life," Robert murmured. "I'd be naught without my Gael."

"She'll do well enough," Arran said, awkwardly settling a hand on the other's shoulder. "And she'd not do other than carry your bairn within her. Away, home t'her, Robert. Tell her I've a small treat I'm planning to bring soon."

"Ye're so good. Have ye no—?" Robert closed his mouth, but the unasked questions hung between them. Had Arran no one to love, no one to give meaning to his life? Where did he go when he left this place? Why did he come and go like some great, solid apparition?

Arran only fastened his gaze on his castle, his empty castle, which he must find a way to keep from the evil, grasping hands of his cousin—just as he must ensure that Mortimer Cuthbert never controlled the fate of the tenants of Kirkcaldy.

"I'll bid ye good day, then, Niall," Robert said.

''Thank ye, friend. I'd have taken two days t'mend that wagon without ye. I'll tell Gael of your treat. Mayhap it'll make her smile.''

Robert swung away and loped downhill from the knoll where Arran still stood. He watched until the straight, blond hair and flapping coat sank from view.

A poor man who worked the earth with his hands. A man for whom music was an old harp crudely played beside a smoking peat fire while he and his neighbors sang the simple songs they'd learned at their parents' knees. That was Robert Mercer. Yet Robert Mercer had no need to search out a strange female to bear his child, a strange female who would take him to her bed for her own selfish ends . . . as selfish as those of Arran Rossmara, Marquess of Stonehaven. Robert Mercer's fragile little wife would bear his children no matter the cost to herself, and would do so in love.

Grace Wren, *if* she eventually produced an heir to all that Arran saw before him, would not do so willingly.

Anger drove his fists together. Were all so-called *gentle*-women shallow, ambitious adventuresses?

Grace Wren welcomed the *friendship* of a man who was neither father nor brother nor any other kind of relation. They both knew what manner of friendship that was to be.

When she discovered who he really was, she would hate him, and so much the better. Her hatred would make it easier for Arran to feel no remorse over his side of a loveless match.

He turned his back on the way Robert had taken and strode toward the hidden mount that would take him to his castle . . . and he remembered Isabel, and the black night that made him what he was today.

Wedded to his music.

Bonded to his inheritance.

The keeper of his own heart and soul, and invulnerable to the wiles of any woman.

March winds were wild upon the hills this year. By the time Arran reached his horse—sheltered in dense forest—tree limbs whipped and creaked before a growing storm, and his boots stirred the rising scent of wet and rotting leaves.

Quickly he shed the sagging woolen coat and breeches, the shirt of crude cotton, and the heavy boots that were "Niall's" trappings. In moments he was once more dressed as Arran, Marquess of Stonehaven, with his hair secured at the nape by a black ribbon.

Darkness had fallen when he thundered, head bent over black Allegro's neck, past the castle walls to the stables, where he left the horse for the stable-boy who would come as soon as he heard the door close behind Arran.

Sodden, raging within at the intrusion of necessity upon the privacy he craved, he stalked through the walled garden that was his sanctuary alone, to the entrance at the base of Revelation—the tower that housed all of his private rooms except the music gallery.

He gained his bedchamber, tore off his drenched cloak, and sprawled in a chair by the fire that was kept burning at all times.

Fate had trapped him. Father, in a whimsical tantrum, had trapped him . . . and failed to set him free by dying, equally whimsically.

He *had* to marry. He *had* to produce an heir. Damn it all, he *had* to marry this conniving female Calum had found, because there was no time to do otherwise.

What manner of woman would choose to marry a man she'd never met? What manner of woman would marry a man she thought to be "decrepit," near to death?

Arran smiled bitterly. The questions didn't need to be answered—or even asked.

What kind of man would marry a woman who had already shown such delight at the prospect of passing time in a "friendship" with a stranger whilst she awaited the demise of her husband?

A desperate, trapped, ruthless man.

They were well matched—almost.

Miss Grace Wren and Arran Rossmara deserved each other. He drew his bottom lip between his teeth and tasted the rain that was still on his skin. They deserved each other, but Miss Wren would be the one to learn that fact last . . . and to learn most . . . to learn the true price of bottomless greed.

Arran Rossmara would teach her.

"Mama, I really wish you wouldn't."

"Pishposh, I shall do as I please, Grace, and you will show me the respect I deserve." Mama, resplendent in an aqua silk gown and elaborate white ruff which Grace had not previously seen, reclined upon a gold brocade chaise. "As soon as that sensible—and, might I add, charming—Mr. McWallop arrives, we shall begin treading the path upon which I intend us to remain firmly footed."

Grace made up her mind. "We must discuss this, Mama. Whether you wish it or not. I am not at all sure—"

"Well, *I* am sure. For your own good we must make certain that your position in this household is immediately made clear. The condition . . ." Mama picked up a dusty Vincennes vase in dark blue and gold, and wrinkled her nose. "It's an outrage. It is deplorable. A clear case of servants quite out of hand. They have—have—*mutinied!*"

"*Mama.* We are not at sea." Although from the

violent winds that battered the windows, they might as well be. Grace turned her eyes determinedly from the dark menace beyond the glass. "I *have* no position in this household. Which is exactly what I wish to discuss with you."

"I should *think* so."

This was not getting in the slightest bit easier. "I have made an error. A grave, grave error." Wind had frightened her since she was a little girl, and nowhere had it ever sounded so furious as here.

"I'm glad you finally see things my way."

"Coming here was a mistake." There, she had finally said what had to be said.

"An error?" Mama sat more upright on the chaise and let her fan drop open. "What *can* you be saying?"

Grace trailed around the beautiful little drawing room on the floor below her bedchamber. Her mother was right in saying that, although the castle appeared in perfect repair, it was sadly in need of a very good cleaning. Beautiful things met the eye wherever one looked, and despite an oppressive abundance of armor and weapons and rather nasty stuffed animals in spots, Grace thought that for a castle—not that she'd ever been in a castle before— Kirkcaldy was remarkably tasteful.

"Grace, answer me at once."

"I like this drawing room better than the old marquess's, don't you?"

"Yes. Stop avoiding my questions, my girl. And stop suggesting that you should have done other than accept Mr. Innes's marvelous offer." Mama closed the fan and pointed it at Grace. "You are twenty-four years old. *Twenty-four*. Had you been a son, the picture would have been entirely different. As a son you would have cared for me after my dear Ichabod died, and I should never have had a moment's worry. Not a moment! But you are not a son and you are on the verge of becoming an old maid. If I were to allow you to do so, what would become of us then, I ask you? *What?*''

"We should have to learn to live within our means," Grace said quietly.

"Oh!" Mama fell back against the cushions. "Oh, I cannot believe I am hearing this. Our means? Our *means*, you say? What means, you little sapskull?"

"Papa left—"

"Your sainted papa left enough to keep *me* in a modest manner for the rest of my life—should that be very short—and to provide for you until marriage—a very *early* marriage. Need I remind you that *you* have caused my dearest Ichabod's plans to be completely inadequate."

Grace shook her head. Mama was wrong to berate her for not being a son, but it was true that keeping two on what should have supported one for the past few years must have put a great strain on Mama's inheritance.

"I'm glad you see the error of your thinking, Grace Charlotte. Kindly cause me no more frights like that."

"I did not intend to frighten you."

"Well, you did. And it is your duty to make sure that my wishes are met in this great wreck of a place."

"It is not a wreck," Grace mumbled. "And I am not in a position to order the servants about."

"You soon will be," Mama declared. "*Where* is Mr. McWallop? I sent for him ten minutes since. Really, the tea things have not been removed, and it is already well past the dinner hour. I feel quite faint from hunger."

Grace did not say that she thought it possible the maid Mama had sent—with a good tongue whipping—to bring Mr. McWallop had never delivered the message.

"Ring the bell."

"Very well. But—" A fresh and mighty blast of wind slammed the building and whined its way upward between towers and turrets. Grace flinched, and flinched again.

"Oh, do get over that silliness, Grace," Mama said, then tutted. "You think me very harsh, and perhaps I am. But I have suffered a great deal, and I'm not as well as I once was. Ring the bell and come here to me, child."

Grace did as she was told and allowed her mother to pull her down to sit beside her.

"You are my sweet lamb," Mama said, patting Grace's hands. "Kiss me and promise you'll allow yourself to be guided by one much older and wiser."

Again Grace did as she was told and breathed in the rose-scented warmth of a rare embrace. She did love Mama. And she did want to be the one to provide for her and make her proud.

"Ye called, Mrs. Wren?"

At Mr. McWallop's firm, deep voice, Grace sat up.

Mama opened her fan. "Indeed. And you came almost before Grace finished ringing."

"Florence brought me your message a while since. I'd retired to my quarters for the evenin'. It's usual for guests to call on Shanks or Mrs. Moggach. Or it would be if we ever had guests. I answer to his lordship."

Grace held her breath and dared not look at her parent.

"In that case I am deeply appreciative of your making a special effort to give us some time."

There appeared to be no false note in Mama's voice.

"The tone of your request suggested we'd as well take the measure of one another smartly."

"I always admire a man with sound judgment and

foresight. Did I not tell you that Mr. McWallop was just such a man, Grace?''

"Mm." Grace looked at the man's face and decided he was handsome in a ruddy, exceedingly physical sort of way. "Mama said as much."

There was a slight relaxing of Mr. McWallop's rigid, square-shouldered stance. "Verra generous of ye, ma'am." He actually smiled—directly at Mama—crinkling the corners of dark brown eyes in a quite pleasing manner.

"Don't mention it, Mr. McWallop. Grace wanted to speak with you about certain household matters."

Grace turned sharply to Mama.

"Yes. She is—as you will discover—industrious and very, very observant. And she is a stickler where matters of household efficiency and appropriate management are concerned."

Mr. McWallop looked at Grace.

Grace stared hard at her mother.

"Every room in this establishment requires a thorough cleaning," Mama said.

Mr. McWallop's impressive red brows drew together. "Is that a fact?"

"It is indeed. Ask Grace. And meals are served at totally erratic hours, and they are of indifferent quality. Also there needs to be attention to fires—they are frequently allowed to burn low, and the servants in general appear a surly, untidy group badly in need of discipline and a good bath!"

"Mama!"

"Isn't that so, *Grace?*"

Really, Mama could go too far. "You have said that Kirkcaldy rarely has visitors. I have no doubt that our sudden appearance has caused unexpected stress on the staff," Grace temporized.

"Aye." McWallop did not appear mollified.

"Grace—"

"My mother and I are still recovering from our long and arduous journey. Forgive us if we seem less than gracious."

"Grace Charlotte!"

"I should particularly like to commend the choice of Mairi as my maid. She is industrious and intelligent, and I am delighted with her."

"Thank ye, miss."

"Really," Mama said darkly. "You must take the reins at once, Grace."

"That is not possible, Mama."

"As the marquess's wife, it is your duty to do so."

"I am *not* the marquess's wife."

"You will be very soon."

Grace tried to avoid Mr. McWallop's eyes. "This is an inappropriate moment to discuss—"

The door sweeping wide open to reveal Mr. Innes stopped Grace in midsentence. He entered the room and stood before them. Once more his smile failed to reach his dark eyes. "You sent for me, Mrs. Wren? One of the maids found me, and she seemed exceedingly distressed."

Grace's limbs felt unaccountably weak.

"My daughter sent for you," Mama announced, letting Grace know that yet again her parent was manipulating events. "She wishes to know exactly what is the marquess's current condition."

"I see." Mr. Innes clasped his hands behind his back. "I think the best way to describe the marquess at this time would be as, hm, changeable."

There was a moment's silence before Mama narrowed her eyes and said, "You mean he is in varying degrees of . . . debility?"

"Very varying."

"As in he could become dangerously debilitated at any moment?"

The nostrils of Mr. Innes's straight nose drew in.

He tipped his face toward the delicate plasterwork ceiling. "I would say his lordship's condition could most accurately be stated as dangerous, yes."

"In that case, there must be no delay. Not one moment." Mama rose majestically to her feet and settled her skirts. "We wish to see the marquess at once. He has asked Grace to marry him, and she is here to do so."

Grace opened her mouth to speak and promptly closed it. Another man had arrived in the open doorway, this one tall and dark and slender. His curly hair had been disheveled by the storm, and he was in the act of unfastening his cloak whilst Shanks scurried in his wake.

"Good God!" Mr. Innes's exclamation made Grace jump.

"I'm glad you approve of my arrival, Calum," the newcomer said cheerfully. "Always nice to get a warm welcome to Kirkcaldy."

"Your—"

"Good to see you, too, Archie," the man cut Mr. McWallop off. "What's this I hear about a wedding?"

"Not right now, man," Mr. Innes said. "The marquess will want to see you. We'd best go immediately to Revelation."

Revelation? "What is this about the marquess and Revelation?" Grace said. "Is that his lordship's preferred biblical reading?"

"Revelation is a tower," Mr. Innes said curtly. "To be precise, it is the tower that houses his lordship's rooms."

"Did I not hear the lady say that there was to be a marriage?" the newcomer asked, clearly uninterested in any other subject.

"You did indeed, sir," Mama said, settling her elbows at her waist. "The marquess is to marry my daughter." She indicated Grace.

"He is?" The cloak hit the floor, and Grace's hand was enfolded in a crushing grip. "Praise be to God. That's the best news I've heard in years. Haven't I always told you the Lord provides, Calum? I've arrived just in time."

Mr. Innes made a strange sound, like a word inhaled, and said, "You always were an irritating bastard . . . Ahem. Miss Wren, allow me to present your future brother-in-law, Father Struan Rossmara."

Chapter 5

The trouble with women was that they were necessary.

God, were they necessary.

Arran cocked his head at a fresh onslaught of wind and rain against the windows and checked his watch. The hour of his proposed meeting with Miss Wren was long passed and she had not appeared.

Damnation. He ought to be glad. If Calum had not come—with Struan, for God's sake—to inform him that his *fiancée* was impatient for her marriage, he might take her failure to keep their appointment as evidence that she had some sensibilities he'd failed to discern. He might wonder if she had regretted her forwardness of the previous night and decided to give her future husband the loyal consideration he deserved!

Arran smiled darkly. He'd been tempted to reveal their first meeting to Calum, and might have done so had dear brother Struan not been present. *Father* Struan—pious priest—had a way of rousing some spurious shreds of conscience in Arran. Struan made one feel vaguely sinful at all times.

Vaguely? Hah!

Damn the girl. He had better things to do with his precious night hours than await her pleasure.

Pleasure. Ah yes. As soon as the business of the marriage was attended to, he would consider resuming his affair with Mrs. Foster. Mrs. Foster asked no questions, made no demands in excess of his considerable consideration of her—and she knew a great deal about *pleasure*. No, perhaps he didn't have better things to do, but he'd do them anyway. The latest piece—for piano and violin—did not yet please him.

He went to his favorite piano close to the windows and played again the theme that had seemed so engrossing only yesterday but which now bored him.

It would not do.

Absently at first but quickly engrossed, he began to play a waltz he'd composed whilst recalling the longing young faces of partnerless misses at a London ball. Arran bent to the keys. He saw the music as he'd thought the girls saw it. And he felt in the notes an inward swaying.

How different were the real and the perceived natures of the privileged nubile female. All sweet innocence on the outside. All calculated maneuvering behind their simpering smiles.

The music was at odds with the storm that had continued to gather strength since his return home. Arran took pleasure in the dichotomy, playing as if his music laughed at nature's rage.

He raised his face . . . and looked directly into the startled brown eyes of Miss Grace Wren.

Instantly his fingers stilled on the keys. "You are late." Damnably stupid thing to say. She would think him impatient for her.

"I've come," she said, sounding breathless. Gold tipped her smoky lashes and cast a gilded gleam into dark brown. Unusual eyes. Large and unwavering—and deeply intelligent if he trusted his instincts. The thought disconcerted him mildly.

Then she smiled.

My God. She smiled like a magical, merry imp set

free from captivity. She smiled . . . openly . . . *honestly?*

"Caught!" Glee clung to the word. "For a moment I was too engrossed to realize. You *were* playing the piano last night."

He made to rise.

"Oh, no!" She freed one hand from the bulky package she carried and waved him back to the seat. "Please continue. It's so beautiful."

"Is it?" Isabel had pretended fascination with his music. That had beguiled him. Never again. At least he had not made the mistake of telling her the pieces she heard were of his own composition. Only Calum and Struan knew.

"My own skills at the pianoforte are abysmal. Mama tells me I should not let gentlemen know as much." She turned up her palm. "I'm sorry I interrupted you. *Your* skills are very considerable."

Very considerable? "You are too kind."

Her brow puckered. "Do you doubt that you are talented?"

Might he be spared inane conversation with foolish females. "I doubt very little." In fact, he usually felt extremely sure of himself. How peculiar that he did not feel particularly certain now . . .

"Then carry on. Do."

"I think not. I should prefer you to forget that you ever heard me play."

She pressed a finger to her mouth. Such a soft, full mouth. Her smile remained, but it was more whimsical than merry now. "My, my. Mama would say that it was unsuitable to refer to a gentleman as charming, but I find you so."

"I beg your pardon?"

"Do not be cross with me."

The girl was a riddle. "I fear I do not understand you."

Miss Wren giggled, a delightful sound. "You are

shy! I find that charming in a man who is so obviously . . . physically . . . *powerful*. You are too shy to play for me!''

''Shy?'' He stared at her. Impertinent chit. ''Ridiculous nonsense. I choose to play only for myself.''

''Oh.'' He saw her swallow and color rose in her pale face. ''I have misjudged you. I thought that we . . . No matter. I find you very mean. And I really see no need for you to snap at me like that.''

He frowned. Mean? Snap? The little female was decidedly odd. Decidedly and unfashionably direct.

''If I could play beautifully and make people see pictures with my music, I should be delighted to do so as often as possible.''

Arran spread his fingers on his knees. ''Would you indeed, Miss Wren?''

''Most definitely.'' She passed him and carefully lowered another of her mysterious burdens onto the window seat. Without looking at him, she continued, ''I do not believe in keeping special gifts to oneself. Not if there is an opportunity to do otherwise.''

As she bent, the little enameled bluebird she wore on a chain around her neck swung forward, and her breasts seemed perilously close to popping free of her bodice. Yes indeed, he decided, Miss Wren would definitely be generous with her gifts. That gown had been no accident. She wore it intending to encourage him to take what she offered. How simple it would be to help her in that particular task.

''You made me see lovely colors.''

She made *him* see a slender white body opened for him, and silver hair spread wide, and pink lips smiling a welcome, a very worldly welcome.

And she made him disconcertingly, inappropriately, angry. It should not matter to him that she was shallow and grasping.

Damn, but he still, in some crevice of his otherwise cynical mind, wanted a woman who was tender and true. He wanted to *love* again, God help him.

"Such marvelous colors," she murmured.

Arran started. "Excuse me?"

"Your music," she said very softly. "It was like twirling ball gowns. But the feeling was wistful, as if one wanted to be part of the music rather than an observer. It made me want to dance."

Everything within him grew wary. She knew what he'd intended. He looked at the music before him and realized that, of course, he'd been playing from memory. *Fool.* Even had she seen the piece on paper, she could not have known what the notes depicted for him. She'd made a clever guess, that was all.

Arran gathered his composure. "I take it that you and your parent are settling well at Kirkcaldy."

She did not appear to hear him.

"Miss Wren?" Arran said, frowning. "Are you and your mother—"

"Yes." She interrupted him abruptly, but her voice was barely audible. "Well, thank you." She stood as if transfixed, her face averted toward the black, rain-washed windows.

He rose. "Your plans are going ahead satisfactorily?"

She did not respond.

Arran tapped his jaw. Something had distracted her. "Are you satisfied with your progress at Kirkcaldy?"

"No." She shook her head.

She was an enigma. "How so?" he asked, aware of a stillness that emanated from her.

"I fear it will all take too long."

Distaste assaulted him. "You think . . . You are afraid the marquess may take longer than is convenient to die?" His lip curled. "For your purposes, that is? Surely the matter of a *decrepit* old husband *confined* to his bed need not stand in the way of whatever pastime you choose to pursue?"

"Probably not. However, I should prefer to be a free woman."

"Freedom is very important to you?"

"Freedom and power," she said, her voice, with its suggestion of forgotten laughter, rising a little with each word. "I do think power is intoxicating, don't you?"

"Very. Would you care to share with me the nature of the power you crave?"

"Power over my own destiny. Power that makes me any man's equal."

Any man's equal indeed! Never had a small, lithe female form been so deceptive. Her back was very straight inside the dark blue crepe edged at its low, square neck with pleated satin as creamy as the soft skin it touched. With her head erect, the mass of pale ringlets cascaded from her crown past a vulnerable neck so slim that Arran knew he could surround it with one hand. The hips were, as Calum had pointed out, just so—as were the fragile white shoulders. From where he stood, Arran could see the curve of her cheek, the flicker of thick lashes.

Deceptive indeed. The next time his overburdened brain whispered thoughts of love in connection with Miss Wren, he must remind it that the woman within her appealing exterior was pure steel.

And he wanted to touch her, curse it. He wanted to touch and taste and possess *all* of her—*now*.

The wind's voice became a scream.

Those white shoulders drew up sharply. The girl chafed her crossed arms.

"Perhaps we should discuss how best to pursue the matter of filling the empty hours that lie ahead of you." His mouth was unaccountably dry.

"Not now."

Arran locked his thighs and willed away his body's unwelcome yet mounting response. "When then?"

"Soon . . . perhaps, soon."

He searched for a means to distract himself and found none. "How soon?" Innocent her wide-eyed, soft-mouthed face might appear, but he saw beyond the angelic mask.

And still he had to make tight fists to stop himself from sweeping her into his arms and stripping her naked. Even as she protested and blushed, and tried to cover herself, her chin would be defiantly high and she would become softly, urgently, pliant. Soft white thighs . . . Arran drew in a long, slow breath that did not fill his lungs. He would need to be careful with one so small, and he would be careful—with each thrust into her body, he would be careful not to crush her.

Her teeth would clench between parted lips.

Her eyes would glitter with the fevered light of passion.

Her breasts would tighten and swell in his hands.

Her nipples would bud against his tongue and she would cry out.

Her hips would arch to receive him and her legs would wrap and hold him.

And her slick, moist center would clench . . .

Arran had to open his mouth to take in a complete breath. The pulse in his groin became a driving throb.

He was obsessing on a stranger; a stranger who would become his wife only to use him.

Arran allowed himself a scornful smile. Miss Grace Wren would learn all about using from a man who had learned the art from the best. He would enjoy instructing her.

Lightning cleaved the darkness outside. For seconds the girl's hair was turned to shimmering white gold. Then thunder burst, at first like a mighty stroke on a huge drum, then as reverberating crackles that split the air in slowly fading ripples.

"A wild night," Arran remarked.

She did not speak or move.

"Should you like to put your bundle inside the window seat?"

Not a word.

Arran narrowed his eyes. "Miss Wren?"

If she heard him, she gave no sign.

Lightning shot earthward once more, and thunder followed immediately in its wake. The girl jumped violently and he saw a fine tremor pass through her.

She was afraid of the storm and she did not respond to him because she had ceased to hear anything but the howling night.

Arran stepped closer. The set of her body was so rigid, he feared the slightest contact would fracture it.

Cautiously he touched the fingertips of his right hand to the side of her waist and felt a jarring start.

"Hush," he told her, settling his hand where his fingers and thumb could measure the tiny proportions of her ribs. "You are safe here with me. The storm cannot penetrate these walls."

Thunder rolled once more and she shuddered.

Slowly, so slowly, Arran drew his hand behind her. With the back of one finger, he stroked her rigid spine all the way to her neck and back to her waist. "Let me comfort you," he murmured.

She drew in a shallow breath and her head fell forward.

Smiling, Arran traced her spine again—and again. The tension was not gone, but this sensual little woman reacted to his touch despite her fear.

A voluptuary indeed, he thought, with deep satisfaction. All else aside, this marriage he had not wanted began to promise intriguing possibilities.

"I . . . I'm sorry," she said at last. "You said something?"

"You are afraid of the storm."

"Of course not." But her breaking voice betrayed the lie.

"There should be no shame in a small weakness. There is no man—or woman—who fears nothing."

Arran splayed both of his hands on her back and smoothed upward, over her cool, bare shoulders. She tilted her head backward and he slipped his thumbs up the sides of her neck and made small circles in the tender hollows beneath her ears.

Grace Wren sighed. "What do *you* fear?"

He opened his mouth to assure her he feared nothing, but smiled instead. "I fear . . . mm . . . cold soup when it is meant to be hot and hot soup when it is meant to be cold."

"That's silly." She wriggled a little, and Arran realized he'd stopped exploring her delectable skin. *Such* an appetite for fleshly pleasures. Pure carnal desire speared him. Rather than bracing his legs and pulling her soft hips against the swollen ridge she'd created, he schooled himself to wait . . . not a long wait, but at least until he could gain the satisfaction of seeing her squirm and beg. And she *would* squirm when she learned the true identity of her *decrepit* old marquess. And she *would* beg when she learned that any pleasure they shared would be upon *his* demand and only to achieve *his* ends.

"I do not believe any woman has ever called me silly," he told her, stroking her arms, then settling his hands at her waist.

"Mama has called me silly ever so often. Mama says I am childish—especially in the matter of storms."

In Calum's words, the Wren parent was a shrew. Arran disliked cruelty, particularly cruelty by those who should be gently strong . . . the way a mother

should be gently strong toward a child . . . Some
women were incapable of natural instincts. "I think
you are delightful—in all ways." It seemed only kind
to say as much, even to a scheming female. "And I
offer my services to ease you through any storm."
The nature of the services he had in mind would
ease them both.

"What is your name?"

Arran stopped chafing her midriff. "As I told you
last night. My name is unimportant."

"It is . . . If we are to be friends, I should like to
know how to call you, please."

She did not as much as pretend that she did not
want him. "You do remember my request that you
not mention our meetings to any other?"

"I could not."

The answer puzzled Arran. "*Could* not?"

She made to move away. Arran clasped her cool,
bare shoulders and held her in place before him.
"What do you mean, you could not mention our
meetings?"

"To do so would jeopardize my reputation."

"Ah, of course." He must be losing touch with
reality. So preoccupied was he that he'd completely
forgotten propriety. "A young, unmarried lady
keeping late night appointments with a man. You
are right. The slightest rumor of such an indiscretion
could indeed be ruinous to your character."

"There will be no such rumor."

"Why so certain?"

"No one will ever know. How would they?"

Arran pressed his lips together. She intended to
make him her *friend* and assumed such an act would
bind them together in silence. Why would a servant,
the marquess's trusted companion, reveal that he
was secretly rutting with the man's soon-to-be wife?

"How indeed?" he asked evenly. Particularly

since she would be at great pains to help protect her fornication.

"My name is Grace."

"I know."

"I should like to know yours, sir."

Arran considered. "Niall." She would never encounter those who knew him by that name.

"Niall?" She turned to face him. "A strong name. How is your family known?"

Such a curious miss. Curious and—much as he might prefer to ignore the fact—captivating, although he couldn't for the life of him decide exactly why. She was certainly not pretty, or beautiful—not in the manner acceptable to society. Not that the dictates of society had ever influenced Arran.

"Niall is enough. And it is used only by those with whom I choose to be familiar." He smiled, telling her with that smile that he intended to become very familiar with Grace Wren.

A faint blush bloomed in her cheeks. "My name is unfortunate."

He inclined his head. "Grace? How so?"

"Mama says that had she known . . . I am really rather clumsy."

Arran ensured that his face revealed no changing emotion. "Grace seems a perfect name for you." Her parent would be taught to mind her sharp tongue. "I hope I may call you Grace?"

She nodded, and he noted that she avoided his eyes. "You play the piano very beautifully," she said.

"Thank you." He would not remind her that she had already said as much—effusively.

"Do you also play the violin and the violoncello?" Grace indicated other instruments in the room.

"Sometimes."

"But you prefer not to speak of it."

"That is so."

She gestured thoughtfully. "I understand. You have been forced to keep these things secret because you expected to be misunderstood—chastised, even?"

Arran watched her. She puzzled him. *Chastised?* She sounded sincere about whatever her mysterious mind was concocting. Could there be a deeper level to the girl, or was he mistaking her designing nature for something he'd find so much more appealing? Such as simple concern for another.

"No matter," she said airily. "You are not yet comfortable enough with me to share too deeply. I must respect your privacy. How long have you known the marquess?"

If he were not cautious, he might be diverted into a careless response. "I've known him all my life." The deception fell naturally enough from his lips.

"I met his brother earlier this evening. Do you know him?"

Damn that brother's ill-timed arrival. "Oh, yes. Obviously Struan is considerably younger. I have known him all of *his* life, too."

"Do you suppose Father Struan has come because he's been told the marquess is close to death? Very close, perhaps?"

She wanted to spend as little of her life as possible on the fortune she coveted. "I do not think we know Father Struan's true reason for being here now." A fact that troubled Arran greatly. "His brother's health has nothing to do with the visit. Of that I'm certain."

"Perhaps . . . Oh, dear." Grace crossed her arms tightly beneath her breasts—with delightful results. "Of course. That is what he meant when he said his arrival here was fortuitous."

Arran waited.

"You do see, don't you?"

He didn't see at all. "No."

Grace rocked up onto the toes of her slippers and bounced. "Father Struan intends to marry the marquess and me."

Her nipples, just concealed by pleated white satin, pushed visibly against fine crepe. Arran imagined those twin berries pressing into his palms, the firm smoothness of pert breasts filling his hands. She would reach for him, find him, fondle him . . . Yet again his manhood grew heated and heavy. When he took a nipple into his mouth and sucked, she would shriek, imploring him to release her from exquisite torture. He would make her wait, and wait . . .

"Do you think that is what he intends?"

"Most definitely . . . I beg your pardon?"

"Do you think Father Struan is here to marry the marquess and myself?"

Curses. Why hadn't he thought of that? Struan had appeared totally surprised at the prospect of Arran's marriage. But Father Struan was no less wily as a priest than he'd been as the Viscount Hunsingore of his boyhood; he could have heard rumors about the marriage and decided to offer his services at the ceremony. "Father Struan is Catholic." Damn him. He'd taken the faith of their ancestors out of some malicious desire to annoy; Arran had always been sure of that.

"The marquess is not Catholic?"

"No."

"How strange that one brother . . . Very strange."

"Immaterial, actually." How he wished he truly did not care that Struan had announced his conversion and the decision to become a priest at the precise moment when Arran had needed him most—the moment when he'd hoped Struan might agree to marry and produce the needed Rossmara heir.

"I should return to my chamber."

"Why?"

"I . . . I might be missed."

"By whom?"

Her eyes slid away.

"Quite. You are shamefully neglected here, night imp. Your mama is in another wing. You have no companion nearby, no maid close enough to answer your call—should you call in the dark, silent hours." He let the comment hang a moment. "And you have not been moved from the Delilah room."

The smooth skin between her brows pleated. "How do you know all this?"

Much as he detested the thought of her being in what had once been his dear wife's room, it had been his decision to leave Grace there. Her isolation from the rest of the household suited him perfectly.

"Niall?"

Her use of the name startled him. "I know because I am closer to the marquess than any man, and I know what he knows. *He* knows everything. Are you comfortable in that purple monstrosity?"

"Comfortable enough."

"And you are not disquieted that should you perceive yourself to be in some danger, there might be no one to aid you?"

She hesitated an instant before saying, "No." Outside, the wind changed direction, and rain beat a staccato rhythm at the windows. Grace glanced sideways and back again. "Why should I be in danger? Why?" Her voice cracked.

Arran shrugged. "I cannot imagine. But I suppose there is always a chance. After all, one cannot be certain that no villain is afoot in such a large establishment. But you are right. Of course there is no danger."

Raindrops clattered like handfuls of ice chips flung against the glass. "I wish it would stop," Grace murmured.

"It will—eventually. What is it that you carry so stealthily through the night? In your bundles."

Wariness sprang to glittery life in her eyes. "You do not wish to share your own secrets. I shall not share mine. I carry nothing that would interest you. And I am not stealthy."

He laughed aloud. "Not stealthy? If I didn't know better, I would suppose you were stashing stolen treasure."

Grace drew herself up very straight. The top of her head truly did not reach his shoulder. "What I brought is treasure to me, sir. Of no value whatsoever to any other, but *priceless* to me—as it may be to others one day."

Intrigued, he looked at the bundle on the window seat. "Do tell, Grace. I swear I shall think of nothing else until you do."

"You fun me, sir." She turned and moved her "treasure" beneath the lid of the window seat. "As I have already intimated, just as you do not care to share your music with any other, I do not care to share my . . . I do not care to share what is precious to me with you. Kindly do not press me further."

He gave her a mocking bow. "As you say, Grace. But how do you know I will not wait until you leave and simply take a look?"

There was a rustle of petticoats and she planted her small, slippered feet apart. "Because I know I am not entirely wrong in my first assessment of you. You are like me . . . in a way, like me." She moistened her lips. "And because you are a gentleman. Gentlemen do not break their word."

He would disregard her fanciful comparisons between them. "Did I give you my word?"

Her chin came up. "You will, won't you?"

Arran considered. "Let me see. If I do give my word, I think I should receive some bonus for exemplary behavior."

"Will you give me your word?" She stepped closer, and he looked down into her earnest face. Innocence shone in her eyes.

The lady was an accomplished actress.

"Will you give me a bonus, Grace?"

My God, her skin was translucent. From his vantage point over her, he saw her white, pointed breasts, the shadow between almost as if she were naked. Rising and falling with her rapid breaths, the rims of pink areola were no longer hidden from him.

Unable to restrain himself further, Arran tilted up her chin with a crooked finger. "Answer me. What shall be the price of my silence?"

Once more she passed her tongue over her lips—with predictable results. His body tightened to unbearable readiness.

Very slowly Arran slid his fingers down the side of her neck until they rested, spread wide, over the swell of her breasts above her bodice.

"Oh!" Her eyes widened and she made to jump away.

Arran was quicker. "I cannot possibly allow you to leave me now," he said, slipping a hand around her waist. "You have yet to tell me about my prize."

"I do not understand you," she whispered. "A gentleman requires no payment for his honor."

Arran chuckled—deep in his throat. "My honor is not at stake here." The baggage had decided to spice the game with a display of virginal skittishness. She intended to entice him the more, and she was succeeding, by damn. "*My reward, Grace?*" he urged.

She shook her head. With each breath she took, her warm breasts pressed against his hand. He almost grimaced at the force of his arousal.

"What are you asking of me?"

Arran inclined his head. "Very little, my clever imp. A mere nothing between a man and a woman destined to share so much." Careful not to move too quickly, he bent to pass his lips over her brow. At her temple he placed a light, lingering kiss. "Very, very little from one with so much to give."

She trembled, and Arran smiled secretly. Never had he been presented with so desirable a package that was so ripe for the taking.

"Perhaps I should allow you to suggest suitable, shall we say, payment?" he said.

"I cannot imagine what that would be." Her body was stiff.

He was happy to play her game. "Ah, but I think you can."

"I do not think you should . . . That is to say, I think you should not touch me . . . A single female should not be alone like this with a man. But I think there is a special need for me to be here with you."

"How very true."

"Yes, well . . . However, I do not believe I should allow you to *touch* me."

Very, very clever. Very artful. "Perhaps not. At least not in the ordinary way of things. But you and I are not ordinary people to be governed by ordinary rules, are we? You and I are destined to discover wonderful things together. Closeness, physical closeness, is bound to be part of such things, don't you agree?"

Grace looked up into his eyes, and her own seemed to glimmer with unshed tears. "I believe we are meant to be very close." She caught her lower lip between her teeth. "I wish . . . I hope that . . . Niall, I do have a feeling about you. No doubt I am reckless to say as much, but even last night I thought there was something intimate in you that reached out to me."

Perfect. "Indeed, imp. And there was something intimate in you that reached out to me."

"I knew it!" Lightning struck afresh, snapping and crackling and thrusting a path of blinding white light. Grace flinched and covered his hand where it still lay upon her breast. "You are strong and warm and . . . and there is an energy within you that searches out the same energy within me. Could it be that we are like souls?"

Ah, yes, she was very, very good. "Quite possibly. Are you perhaps ready to discuss the future of our *friendship* now?"

"I don't know. The storm . . . you. Everything is so confusing."

All an act. All a delightfully concocted drama intended to bring him falling before her knees. "You excite me," he murmured, bowing to kiss her temple once more, and then her cheek, her jaw, the arched line of her throat. "I know what you want from me, Grace. You may be sure that our interests are mutual." He would gladly fall before her knees—and bury his face in her belly, between her legs—and pull her down until her breasts hovered like tender fruit above his mouth.

Her hands caught at his shoulders. He wore no coat, and she plucked at the fine linen of his shirt as if seeking a way inside. "This is . . . I have never felt quite like this before."

Arran drew his lips back from his teeth. She might never have felt quite like this perhaps, but close enough to know that her sexual appetites would need to be met again and again. He would not think of the other men upon whom she must have bestowed her favors. She was what he needed, what he must learn to find satisfying—a woman who could match his passion without demanding love. Whatever that was.

He licked the hollow above her collarbone, and below. Grace began to pant and make small, mewling sounds. "Dear me," she said breathlessly. "Are you certain this is what should be part of our closeness? I don't think you should . . . That is, I don't think *we* should do this.''

Pretty, so pretty. "Sometimes it is appropriate not to think at all. Simply feel. You deserve what I can offer you. You are a woman meant for intimacy with a man—the right man.''

"You are right.'' Her tone had changed, become certain. "Yes. You have made up my mind. I shall share my secret self with you at once.''

Arran almost laughed aloud. "I am honored,'' he said against her skin. He raised his head and regarded her steadily. "But we should definitely not hurry, my dear. Oh, no, these things are far better when enjoyed in a leisurely manner.''

She frowned, a perfect parody of perplexity.

Glancing down, Arran bracketed her breasts with his hands and pushed them together.

Grace let out a sharp cry and clutched his arms.

"There is no hurry, sweet. Trust me in this.'' Trust him and he would lead her to joy that was agony . . . and frustration that was endless torment. This avaricious, deceitful, predatory, carnal little woman would learn the agony of knowing ecstasy, knowing its source, knowing that it was physically within her reach, but knowing also that it would never be hers to command.

"Niall?'' Her hands sought his. "What . . . Do you want me to share what is most intimately mine with you now?'' Her gaze darted to the window seat.

Her nipples were all but freed. She would share *what* he wanted her to share, *when* he wanted her to share it. Arran jerked satin and crepe down and rubbed work-roughened thumbs in circles that skirted contact with distended areola.

"Niall!''

"Cry out my name,'' he told her, narrowing his eyes. "Cry, my sweet. This is a most gratifying be-

ginning to our friendship.'' He concentrated, tracing
the paths again and again, slowly, very slowly, coming a little closer to that which she sought from him,
and a little closer, but not touching.

"I want . . . I want . . .'' She writhed and plucked
ineffectually at his fingers.

"What do you want? Tell me.''

Grace only moaned and pressed her eyes shut.
She let her head fall back, and Arran bared her
breasts completely—and gasped at their small,
thrusting perfection. He must control himself. He
must. If his plan was to be brought to the satisfying
conclusion he demanded, then he had to curb his
impulses.

Half-lifting her from the floor, he bent to kiss the
underside of one breast.

Grace cried out.

With his tongue, he followed the circles he'd first
made with his thumbs.

She filled her hands with his hair, and he felt it
pulled from the ribbon at his nape. "Oh, please,''
she said on a deep sigh.

Please, indeed, Arran told himself. Please myself.
Suck you so deeply into my mouth, you cry out your
pleasure. Tear off this damnable gown and plunge
into your body until you scream, not knowing if you
plead for more or beg to be spared.

The tip of his tongue dragged across one swelling
mound, into the vale between the onward across
petal-softness to the very edge of the other rosy
circle.

Grace tugged his hair. She clamped his head between her hands and attempted to force his mouth
to that aching spot she yearned for him to claim.

And he wanted it.

With his eyes squeezed shut and his teeth
clenched, Arran held Grace close and rested his

cheek where she would have his mouth take possession.

Another second of this and his legs would give out.

"Niall," she said, pleading. *"Please."*

Please, please, please. His manhood pulsed, drove against his trousers until he longed to be naked.

Her struggling shifted her nipple back and forth against his cheek. The smallest shift . . . just a tiny turn of his head and he could claim it.

Stop. Now.

"Thank you, Grace," he said, certain that she would not notice how his voice rasped. Standing straight, he shook back his hair and straightened his shirt. "You have proved to us both that we will be a great comfort to one another in the days to come."

"But . . ." Her face was flushed. Rather than cover herself, she held her bodice where Arran had drawn it—to frame her breasts.

"It is very late, Grace," he told her, taking hold of her elbows and backing her around the piano and across the room. "You must go to your bed now."

"But I don't want to. I want you with me."

So brazen. "Soon enough, sweeting." Soon, just as soon as he could adequately set the scene.

"I am afraid," she told him, and tears filled her eyes. "You are my only friend, the only one I can turn to. Please do not make me go away without you."

He brought her to the door. "What are you afraid of?"

"Of being alone. Of—of what is supposed to happen to me."

"That you are to marry the marquess, you mean?"

"Yes!"

"I'm certain you will cope most satisfactorily with that event. For everyone's sake." He reached behind her and opened the door. "Go to bed, Grace."

"No."

"Yes." Slowly he brought his face closer to hers, and her chin rose. He parted his lips, and so did Grace. He wetted his lips with his tongue—and so did Grace. She was a passionate man's fantasy. "Oh, *yes*."

Arran kissed her, kissed her lips for the first time. Her mouth did not respond, but she tasted sweet. He knew he risked falling into the seething abyss he had sworn to avoid as yet, but he had to drink of her.

Just one last, long sip to last the night. Slowly her lips softened and he felt her sigh.

With gentle desperation, he lifted a breast into his hand and his manhood leaped.

He reached his tongue deep into her mouth. She became very still. Arran stroked farther inside, and finally her tongue met his. His groan was echoed in her hushed moan, and Arran pushed his thigh between her legs.

Grace threaded her arms beneath his and wrapped him tightly, pressed her center to him with all her might.

Stop!

Arran broke away.

"Niall!" She groped for his shirt and tugged until he heard buttons tear loose. "Don't stop holding me."

"Go to your room," he told her, avoiding her eyes, locking his legs, willing the burning need to die. "Go now."

Instantly her hands fell away from him.

"Go."

"Yes," she muttered. "Yes, I must go at once. Quickly."

He could finish this as soon as he chose. There was no need to delay.

"You've decided you do not want to share yourself with me?'' she said. ''My friendship no longer interests you?''

Then he did look at her. ''Oh, yes. Oh, yes, it interests me very much.'' Steeling himself to resist the urges of his flesh, he pulled her bodice back into place. Why be in too much of a hurry? Restraint could only make the ultimate capitulation more tumultuous. He would not allow his mind to make those pictures now. ''Come to me again tomorrow night.''

''I do not think that is wise.''

Arran regarded her sharply. ''It is absolutely wise.''

''No. I should not come here again.''

Surely she wasn't feeling guilty. He surveyed her tumbled curls, her kiss-swollen lips, her disheveled dress, and smiled. No, any protest was simply another ploy to bind him more tightly in her sensual snare. ''Tomorrow night, Grace.''

Taking a step backward, she shook her head. ''I do not know what has possessed me here, but I know it has been wrong. I must not return.''

Inclining his head, he smiled slowly, hooked a finger into her bodice between her breasts, and drew her close. ''We both know what we must do, don't we?''

She shook her head again but less vehemently.

''Of course we do. We have only begun what will become a great comfort to both of us.''

''Niall—''

''A very great comfort, and I thank you for it.'' He thanked her deeply. ''The same time tomorrow?''

She stared at him as though mesmerized, but formed a silent ''no'' with her enticing lips.

''Yes,'' he murmured. ''Yes, because there is so much more for us to accomplish together.''

With that, he found a nipple and squeezed very gently with a finger and thumb.

Grace's lips parted and her eyelids drooped. She sought his arm and held on.

He replaced his fingers with his palm and made tight little strokes back and forth.

Her knees began to sag.

Arran's hands went to her waist and he shook her lightly. "So much more, Grace. Don't you agree?"

Her eyes flew open. Her cheeks were wildly flushed.

"Of course you agree." He straightened her bodice again. "Run along now, there's a good girl. We'll meet here tomorrow at the same time."

Once he'd urged her out, Arran shut the door and all but threw himself against it. He had not spilled his own seed since he'd taken his first female. Tonight he was perilously close to breaking that record.

Somehow he returned to the windows and forced one open against the straining wind. Leaning out, he turned his face upward and closed his mind to everything but the cold rain that took too long to douse his ardor.

Chapter 6

Grace said a prayer that the dark circles beneath her eyes would not be noticed, and knocked on the door to which Mrs. Moggach had gruffly directed her.

"Mr. Innes wants to see ye," the woman had said the moment Grace entered the dining room that morning. Mrs. Moggach's mouth had turned down in surly disdain. "Ye're to go to him now."

Grace had set off at once and without breakfast. Not that breakfast appealed in the slightest, so disturbed was she by the previous night's events.

No voice commanded Grace to enter, and she knocked again. These rooms—on the ground floor of the castle's most easterly wing—were far-flung from her own quarters. Really, this place was ridiculously large. What a waste it was for one old man and a gaggle of mostly nasty servants to occupy so little of so much.

Impatient, Grace turned the door handle and slowly entered a small study beyond.

Empty.

She walked to a rosewood desk strewn with papers, and looked around. Books were scattered everywhere. Bending, she studied titles. *A Romany History. Kings Without Countries. People of the Moors. The Heather Crown.* Grace sniffed and straightened. She had no idea what might be contained in such volumes. Mr. Innes was a silent, apparently thoughtful man who made her slightly uncomfortable. Nevertheless he was very handsome, and women undoubtedly found him attractive.

But he was not Niall. Scalding heat dashed up her neck and into her face. Places in her body for which she knew no names began to throb as they had throbbed last night.

A suspicion had been swelling within her ever since she'd left Niall and rushed back to her chamber. Her first reaction to his touching her must have been correct. Regardless of what he said and regardless of how much she wanted to believe him, it was not appropriate for a man to see, let alone put his fingers where . . . She was freshly afire over every inch of her skin.

Liberties. The ladies who were Mama's friends had—on many more than one occasion—spoken darkly of *liberties.* These were apparently the inappropriate actions of gentlemen toward females to whom they were not related. She had not quite understood what was meant, but heads had been wagged in her direction and Mama had been reminded of her heavy responsibility as the sole parent of an unmarried woman.

The females who had supposedly been prey to these liberties had been referred to as wicked and weak and as *strumpets.* The inference was that they had caused the understandably susceptible gentlemen involved to lose their heads and do things that were absolutely wrong and which they would not have done unless tempted beyond endurance.

Grace clutched handfuls of her skirts. Niall had been taking liberties, she just *knew* it.

She was *wicked.*

She was a *strumpet.*

She was so *weak.*

She must *not* go to him tonight.

Her hands stole up to cover her breasts and she closed her eyes.

"Niall," she whispered. "I want you to touch me again." She was wrong, but she wanted to forget the marquess and think only of the man who filled her thoughts in every waking moment.

They did share something deep, something that drove her to want to be with him. And that same deep something made Niall mistakenly feel that he needed to touch her to *share* himself with her in that way.

That was exactly what caused last night's happenings.

And—wicked as she might be—she wanted them to happen again.

Rattling startled her. She dropped her arms and spun around.

Mr. Innes, with Father Struan at his heels, opened French doors and stepped in from a stone-balustraded terrace, bringing with him a gust of fresh, rain-washed air. At the sight of her, his dark brown brows shot up. "Miss Wren. What are you doing here?"

She hoped she was no longer red-faced. "You sent for me."

"I did?"

"Good morning to you, Miss Wren," Father Struan said, stepping around Mr. Innes and smiling as if the very sight of her made him enormously happy. "You are looking particularly fetching today, my dear. My brother is a very lucky man."

Grace tried to smile back, not a particularly good attempt. "Thank you." She did not feel at all fetching. "Good morning, Father." In her experience, no man of God had ever looked remotely like Father Struan. Even in his threadbare black garb, his impressive bearing and physique were impossible to ignore. And his face . . . Father Struan was exceedingly handsome.

Mr. Innes tugged a watch from his waistcoat pocket and frowned at its face. "It's later than I thought," he said, sounding irritable.

Grace decided that Mr. Innes was a trifle formidable. "Mrs. Moggach said she'd sent Florence to you with a message and that you would want to talk to me."

He closed the door behind him. "No doubt that's what this is about." Patting of pockets produced crackling, and he pulled out a crumpled sheet of paper. "Here we are. Does Florence ever speak coherently?"

"I'm sure I don't know." She forbore to point out that she had been at Kirkcaldy but a short time and hardly knew the servants—or anyone else here—at all.

"Four Meissen-style porcelain flowers," he read aloud. "Gilded leaves. A gold brooch in the shape of a bow and set with sapphires. One small bleu celeste cup and saucer—Vincennes. Pearl earrings with diamond drops. An enameled chicken—Russian—with five topaz eggs. Gold fork with single large ruby set in handle. Mm. Hmm. And so it goes."

Grace worried the muslin ruffle at the wrist of one yellow sleeve. "What is this about, Mr. Innes?"

"Theft," he said simply, tossing the paper on the desk. "A series of thefts, to be precise. Mrs. Moggach reports that there are small treasures missing all over the castle."

Grace's mind became blank. She stared from Mr. Innes to Father Struan. The latter winked at her and showed no particular concern with the discussion.

"Evidently our trusty housekeeper expects me to inform the marquess that we are under siege from

what she terms wicked villains,'' Mr. Innes said.
''What do you think of that, Miss Wren?''

She approached until she stood across the desk
from him. ''What should I think? Why would Mrs.
Moggach . . .'' A dreadful notion formed. ''Is Mrs.
Moggach suggesting that *I* know something about
these thefts?''

''Not a possibility,'' Father Struan said lightly.
''Don't give it another thought.''

Mr. Innes looked at her, and she noted how very
dark his eyes were. They appeared to be quite black.
''Of course that is not what she's suggesting.'' When
his lips settled **together**, Grace noted how the corners turned up in repose and how distinct were the
curves of his lips. She decided she would like to see
him laugh.

''Since you are to become mistress here, I presume that Mrs. Moggach thinks you should be informed of what she considers to be a serious
matter.''

''Then why didn't she simply tell me herself?''

''The workings of the female mind have never
been clear to me.'' He did smile then, and Grace felt
her own mouth twitch in response. Mr. Innes was
indeed a *very* well-favored man. He might be unfamiliar with the workings of the female mind, but
Grace was not. There were more than a few feminine thoughts revolving around this tall, lithe, darkly
compelling man on this morning—of that she had
no doubt.

''Well, Mr. Innes. You have told me about this
unfortunate situation, and I thank you. I fear I cannot help you decide how to proceed.''

''The marquess will decide—if there is any decision to be made.''

Father Struan made a slight humphing sound.
''He's very good at that sort of thing—decisions, that

is. Tossing them about. Tossing them out entirely, I shouldn't wonder.''

Grace frowned at them both. "What do you mean?"

"I mean," Mr. Innes said, "that I cannot imagine it being possible for anyone to be certain as to what is where—or where it is not at Kirkcaldy. Do you agree with me, Struan?"

"Bit like thinking one sees a fat fish among the rocks in a river, I should imagine," Father Struan remarked. "Blink, and you'll probably discover your fish was one more rock. Do *you* agree with that, Miss Wren?"

Grace suppressed a chuckle. "I do agree."

"Would you think it impertinent of me to suggest that you call me Calum?" Mr. Innes said, somewhat gruffly.

To her surprise, she felt a warming toward him. "I should like that. And you must call me Grace. You also, if it pleases you, Father. Are you certain the marquess is well enough to be bothered with petty household matters?"

Calum hesitated before saying, "Do not concern yourself further with this. I'll speak to Mrs. Moggach myself."

"Perhaps I should go to the marquess now." Grace became utterly still as she awaited his response. She wasn't certain why she had made the suggestion unless it was that she'd become desperate to end her suspense. "Would it not be a good idea for me to speak to him about this issue?"

Calum had rested his broad, long-fingered hands on the desk and braced his weight. He was reading the note again and absently said, "His lordship doesn't care for daylight."

"Not at all," Father Struan echoed.

"What does that mean?" Perhaps she'd misheard them. "Did you say he doesn't—"

"Doesn't like daylight," Calum repeated. "Yes, that's what I said. He sleeps in the early morning and prefers not to see anyone before nightfall—not then if it can be avoided."

Grace puffed up her cheeks and let the air slowly escape. "How peculiar." Then she remembered what Mairi had said. "He is only seen . . . He is truly a night person? He never goes about in the daytime?"

Calum's face came up. "No—yes. That is, he finds the night soothing."

"Very soothing." Father Struan sighed and nodded.

"Oh, I see. His illness, I suppose. For some reason he feels more pain in daylight. Perhaps his eyes are affected?"

"Perhaps." Calum's expressionless stare had returned. "It is simply his preference. I think he would prefer that you not question his habits. His lordship is a very private man."

"So private that he chooses not to see the woman he is supposedly to marry," Grace retorted. "When you approached me in London you said the marquess wished for someone to ease him in trying times. Surely these are trying times and I should be with him."

Father Struan, very serious now, said, "We must not hurry these things."

Calum said nothing. He folded Mrs. Moggach's note and returned it to his pocket.

"Well," Grace said, irritated at his high-handed silence. "Evidently my suggestion does not meet with your approval. But I'm grateful to have been included in this domestic detail. Now perhaps I can eat my breakfast."

"Absolutely. We cannot have you fading away before the nuptials."

Predictably, Father Struan added, "Absolutely

not," before seating himself in a chair beside the desk and pulling a small book from his pocket. He began to read.

"Let me start you on your way to breakfast," Calum said.

She cast him a sideways glance as he ushered her from the study. "One begins to wonder when those nuptials will be. Of *if* they will be."

"They will *be*, as you put it. And soon, I think. Very soon."

Grace's stomach turned most unpleasantly.

"I'm glad you are so anxious to be joined with the marquess."

The term "joined" had never been something she understood in this context, but she nodded at Calum. "My mother assures me that we will all be happier after the wedding has taken place." Grace did not agree, but she was tired of uncertainty.

In the great hall, Calum took his leave of Grace and strode away toward stairs that led down to the kitchens. She hovered beside an intricately carved stone screen. Above her head was the minstrel's gallery, draped all about with heraldic and military colors. Even her breathing seemed to echo upward into the painted ceiling domes.

She did not belong here.

Another's breath made rapid gasping sounds and Mairi arrived, panting, at Grace's side. "Och, there ye are. Ye fair worried me, miss."

"Why?" Grace patted a plump shoulder and tucked wisps of fine hair behind the girl's ear. "Calm yourself, Mairi. I can't imagine why you were worried about me."

"Grumpy—" She ducked her head and glanced quickly all around. "Mrs. Moggach said she hadna seen ye this mornin'. I was afeared somethin' had happened to ye."

There was no point in stirring up trouble among

the staff by telling Mairi that Mrs. Moggach certainly had seen Grace. "Well, as you see, nothing has happened. I'm in fine health."

"Ye didna wait for me to dress ye. Ye're supposed to let me do that. Florence told me so, and I'm sorry I didna know as much yesterday."

Grace doubted she would ever care to be dressed by someone else. "You need not trouble yourself to come to me in the morning." Particularly since she could not be certain of exactly when she would be back in her room . . . The now familiar heat washed her body and she looked away.

"Och, I must or I'll lose my place here. Florence says I should ask for a room close by yours, too."

"No! No, that's not necessary."

"Florence says I wouldna know if aught happened to ye in the night unless I could hear ye."

Grace almost moaned with frustration. "You told me you like the room you were given." A great deal had been happening in the night, and—might she be forgiven—she wasn't certain that a great deal more might not happen on future nights.

"I do like the room. It's the coziest place I ever had, but—"

"There is to be no *but.* I insist that you stay in the room you've already been given. I take it you have been told about the thefts that have taken place in the castle?"

"Everyone's all aflutter about it," Mairi said. "Grumpy says heads'll roll. She got that funny look on her face—like an evil gnome from the moors— and said she'd a good idea who the villain was."

"There are no evil gnomes," Grace said severely, whilst wondering who Mrs. Moggach's suspicions were trained upon.

"Och, and there are, too," Mairi said with unexpected fierceness. "Scotland is fair full o' gnomes and beasties and fairies—and kelpies in the lochs.

You'd do well not to make any o' them angry with your disbelief, and . . .'' She caught Grace's eye and her voice trailed away.

"Did Mrs. Moggach make any suggestions about the identity of this *villain?*''

"Only that it was a person or persons who'd not been long in these parts. But I dinna know who she can be speakin' of.''

"No,'' Grace said, setting her mouth in a grim line. She had a very good idea who the old *gnome* referred to. "Come along.''

Grace marched away in the direction of the dining room. Mairi followed and insisted upon serving her heavy oatcakes and cold porridge laden with butter and salt. "Ye're a waif of a thing,'' she said, chuckling. "There's no flesh on your bones. Ye'll need your strength for the trials that lie ahead.''

Grace's spoon clattered into her bowl. "Why do you say that, Mairi?''

The girl blushed and busied herself with removing unused covers from the long, gleaming mahogany table.

"Mairi?''

"Och, take no notice o' me, miss. I'm blatherin' again. My father's always tellin' me to mind my tongue. Will Mrs. Wren be having breakfast soon?''

"Mama never arises before noon. Close the door, please.'' Grace was not about to miss an opportunity to pry more information from Mairi.

When they were safely shut inside the oppressively paneled room that seemed to Grace to be large enough to hold a ball, she pulled a chair beside hers and motioned her maid to sit down.

Mairi came slowly, reluctance weighting every step.

"Sit,'' Grace ordered. And when Mairi did so, Grace added, "Why do you say I'll need my strength for the trials ahead? What trials?''

"Och, ye're not to pay me any mind." She rocked her head. "It was just a manner o' speakin'. Ye're too thin."

Grace ignored the last comment. "I don't believe you."

That resulted in a truly furious flush. "I'm sorry," Mairi muttered. "I never was good at untruths. I only meant ye'd do well to make sure o' your health afore ye're married."

"Why?"!

"Och, miss," Mairi moaned.

"Why?" Grace persisted.

"I've already told ye about the babbies."

"Foolishness," Grace snapped. "You're not to listen to such nonsense and you're not to repeat it, either."

"But—"

"You are not to do so. Do you understand me?" Mairi nodded miserably.

"There's far too much gossip and mean-spirited whispering in this castle."

"Aye, miss. But ye shouldna be alone in that room."

They were back to that. "I am perfectly fine." She knew she should have a companion, just as she knew she should not be running around in the middle of the night, seeking the company of a man . . .

He *fascinated* her, drew her, made her someone she did not know but whom she was unwilling to abandon.

She had to concentrate on her reason for being at Kirkcaldy. "Mairi, tell me about the marquess."

"I already told ye about him."

When light touched Niall's face, it carved shadows into the planes beneath his cheekbones. And it pointed out the cleft in his chin—and when he smiled, there were those grooves in his cheeks. And light made his eyes as green as . . . as pale, clear, flawless emeralds . . .

"Are ye feelin' poorly, miss?"

Grace jerked her face up. "Not at all. Tell me more about the marquess."

"Och, I dinna know. I'm sure I dinna." When she spied Grace's steady gaze, Mairi swallowed noisily. "Well, he's always been quiet—accordin' to Father, that is."

"Your father's seen him?" Grace shifted forward in her chair.

"No, no. He's heard about him is all. There's not a soul hereabouts as hasna heard about him."

"What does he look like?"

Mairi's pale, round eyes grew more round. Her brow furrowed.

Grace cleared her throat. "Is he . . . is he very ugly? Deformed?" She chewed her bottom lip. "Does he have any teeth?"

"Teeth?"

Grace flapped a hand. "Silly me. Of course he has teeth. He eats babies."

"Och, miss!"

"I was joking." She managed a little smile. "Tell me what he looks like."

"Och, miss."

Grace pursed her lips. *"Don't* say that again."

"But I dinna know what he looks like. I doubt anybody does."

"That's . . . Of course someone knows what he looks like."

"No. No one except Mr. Innes, o'course."

"And—" Grace snapped her teeth together. She'd almost said, *and Niall.* Calum and Father Struan had told her the marquess didn't like daylight. Perhaps that was why no one knew what he looked like. "Oh, fiddlesticks, Mairi. Don't expect me to believe no one has any idea about the man's appearance."

"He did used to go about a bit. So my father says."

"He did?" She was instantly alert. "Where did he go?"

"I don't exactly know that, either. Except that it was in London. And in Edinburgh, I think."

"Well then, someone will be able to tell me more."

"No one here, miss. If they know, they'll not speak o' it."

"That is the most outrageous thing I've ever heard. What can they be afraid of?"

"Ye've not been told at all, have ye?" Mairi's mouth jerked down. "Ye're a poor, innocent lamb about to become a sacrifice."

Despite her resolve to be strong, Grace's stomach plunged. "Kindly stop this nonsense and tell me what you're talking about. In simple terms."

"I'll be close by. I promise ye that."

Cold crawled over Grace's skin. "I don't understand you."

Mairi leaned close. "After ye're married. I'll be close enough to hear if ye cry out. Please say ye'll call me if . . . if he . . . if ye need me."

"I thank you for being concerned, but there is absolutely no need for you to worry about me. And I cannot imagine why you should be worrying about something you have no true reason to expect."

Mairi sighed—a very long sigh. "D'ye not know the marquess was married once already?"

Grace screwed up her eyes. "No." Her heart beat faster.

"Well, he was. And she was verra beautiful and verra young."

"How long ago was this?"

Mairi sprang to her feet. "I've got to away back to me work, miss. I'll need to go now."

"Nonsense." Grace caught the girl's wrist and drew her close. "I expect it was a very long time ago that the marquess was married."

"Not so verra long," Mairi muttered.

"How long?"

"I'm not sure. Six years, mayhap. We're not to speak o' it."

"*Six* years," Grace said. "Only *six?* What happened? How did she die?"

"Och, miss!"

Grace bit back a reproach. "It's obvious that the marquess's first wife died. I'm simply asking you to tell me how."

Mairi pressed her lips together.

"Was she ill? A fever?"

Mairi shook her head.

"Did she have an accident? Riding, perhaps? A fall?"

"Someone's got to tell ye. It might as well be me."

"Indeed," Grace said while her skin continued to draw tight over her bones.

"D'ye know about Revelation?"

It was Grace's turn to shake her head. "No—" She held up a finger. "Yes. When Father Struan arrived, Mr. Innes—Calum—said they should go to Revelation at once. It's where the marquess lives."

"Aye. It is."

"Where is it exactly?"

"Over there." Mary pointed west. "It faces the hills behind Kirkcaldy—on the side where there's nothing but forests and sky t'see. They say he doesna care to look upon people at all, or the places where they live."

"He sounds most unpleasant," Grace said before she could stop herself. "That is, he sounds . . . private," she finished for want of a more acceptable description.

"They say there's a secret chamber under Revelation." The folds of her plain woolen skirts became of great interest to Mairi. "They say there could be a way out from below—but there's no one who can tell ye where it is."

Grace digested that. "What does a secret chamber have to do with the marquess's wife?"

"Ye will scream if—"

"*Mairi.* Tell me what you're trying *not* to tell me, please."

Distress clouded light blue eyes. "She was there at night. In the morning there was no sign of her."

"The marchioness left?" Grace asked. "At night?"

"Not by carriage. Or on horseback. And it was deep winter, so she couldna have walked."

"Oh." With her heart thudding as if it intended to escape her chest, Grace pushed to the back of her chair and gripped the seat. "You think . . . ? They think . . . ?"

"Aye," Mairi whispered. "That's what they think. And her bairn with her."

Grace raised sickened eyes to her maid's face. "Her bairn?"

"Her ladyship was increasin'. That night the marquess's voice was heard, and it was a horrible thing, so they say. A howl that shook even Kirkcaldy. Like an animal with an arrow in its heart, so me father told me."

The thudding of her own heart beat along Grace's veins and into her ears.

"That night a beautiful woman who was to bear the marquess's bairn went to her bed in her own chamber. Later the marquess was heard shouting in Revelation. The next morning the marchioness was gone, and his lordship never spoke her name again."

Thoroughly shaken, Grace moistened dry lips. "I am certain this is all foolish speculation."

"He used to go down under Revelation. They say he kept a special store o' spirits there. He doesna go anymore. He hasna since that night. Sealed it up. And then he ordered her room locked. Something awful would befall anyone found in it—that's what his lordship warned.''

''Oh, dear,'' Grace said, mostly to herself. ''Oh, my. Poor woman. There has to be another explanation.''

''If ye think o' it, it'd make me feel less afeared.'' Mairi wound her apron about her hands. ''I'll be away now.''

''Mairi!'' Grace rose as the girl reached the door. ''Is there anything else I should know? *Anything?*''

Mairi hesitated, her hand on the door handle. ''No. No, nothin' . . . except that the last person to see her ladyship alive—apart from the marquess, that is—was her maid when she took hot chocolate to the marchioness's room.''

''I see.''

''In the morning the marquess called in the maid.''

''Yes?''

''She was never seen again, either.''

A small shriek escaped Grace's throat.

''Aye, ye'd do well to be concerned. It'll make ye more careful. And there's one other thing ye ought to know.''

Grace could only stare.

''Ye're sleepin' in the marchioness's room.''

Chapter 7

There were times, like now, when Grace wished Mama were someone with whom she could share confidences. But here, as had always been the case, they saw each other rarely, and only when Mama chose to do so.

Should she go to Niall tonight?

Naturally, Mama would say no. After all, Niall could not offer what the marquess could offer.

Not that Niall was particularly likely to offer anything at all—except companionship while she was here.

But they did seem so admirably suited . . .

Wasn't what she felt with him *exactly* what she'd hoped to eventually feel with a man, a man she would wish to marry?

He was some sort of servant.

Grace did not care.

She hesitated by the door of her room.

The pelisse robe had been the perfect answer to Grace's dilemma. Of amber-colored velvet, the garment covered her from throat to ankle and was closed along the length of its front with sturdy hooks and eyes concealed by flat, knotted silk bows in a shade like russet autumn leaves. A narrow ruff of cream lace rested about her neck.

A guard to keep her own errant responses trapped.

And a shield to turn back any misguided notion

110

Niall might have about repeating last night's definitely questionable performance.

She raised her chin, set her shoulders squarely, and slipped from the room she wished she need never enter again. It seemed full of silent screams. And draped about with shifting shadows.

Paperskull. Whatever might or might not have happened in that chamber could not have left anything behind, and it certainly had nothing to do with her.

Last night Grace had taken a wrong turn on her way to the music room and arrived late. Tonight she knew exactly where she was going.

Her skirts brushed a suit of armor.

Metal joints rattled.

Tiny hairs rose along Grace's spine.

She drew back against the wall and looked up into the painting of a man's narrow, sardonic face. "Very well," she said, wrinkling her nose. "Sneer at me. I am not afraid. I am *not*. And I think you were a greedy, self-indulgent creature. Those wet, red lips tell me so."

Talking to portraits? This place was fuddling her mind.

Carrying the one small package she had still to place with her other bundles, she took several more steps and stopped again.

Panic swelled up and she clasped her throat.

"What should I do? *What should I do?* Oh, please tell me what I should do."

No wise voice answered.

If she doubted that what she might share with Niall was pure, she needed no wiser voice than her own.

But she didn't trust herself in this.

"Tell me to return to my room. *Please.* Make me go back there and close the door and never see him again. *Please.*"

All she heard were the creakings and hushings

and whisperings that had accompanied her on her previous trips through these corridors.

But no music.

Last night there had been music, just as on her first venture. Again it had enveloped her and lured her on. She strained to catch the sound now, but not a note reached her. The absence increased her uncertainty. It was Niall's music that had so helped convince her that they were alike. They both loved beauty and were not free to pursue it as they should.

Earlier in the day she'd been determined not to go to Niall, but her fortitude had failed.

Go to him. Explain that you were not yourself last night. Tell him you understand that you may somehow have been responsible for those marvelous . . . those undoubtedly inappropriate touches. Say you do not blame him at all and beg him not to think ill of you now that you have come to your senses and are firmly resolved never to allow further moral lapses. Ask him about the stories you've heard—about the marquess and the marchioness and the room.

Brushing away formless things that seemed to wind about her face and neck and pluck at her hands, Grace scurried on, faster and faster, until she could scarcely breathe. Niall could tell her what she needed to know. She would ask her questions, go to her bed, and never seek out his company again.

Or she could decide not to marry the marquess and ask Niall to take her instead.

Out of the question! This would be their last meeting.

There. That was decided.

The final flight of stairs was gained and she ran upward.

"Good evening, Grace."

She had not heard the door to the gallery open. Off balance, she stumbled on the top step and would have fallen into the room—had Niall not caught her.

Grace's face collided with his solid chest. The next moment she found herself swept up by an exceedingly strong pair of hands at her waist, swung around, and deposited on the blue silk carpet.

"So eager," he said, a smile making the dimpled grooves she'd imagined so many times whilst waiting to see him again. "I'm flattered that you ran all the way to me."

"I did not run all the way," she told him, gasping. "I merely tripped." Fortunately she'd managed to keep a grip on her package.

Before she guessed his intent, Niall pulled her into an embrace that threatened to suffocate her. His mouth covered hers, opened hers, and his tongue slipped past her teeth in that strange, mystical way it had done so last night.

Grace forced her eyes to remain open. She would not succumb to these abandoned desires. With a great effort, she tore her face from his and pushed at him.

Raising one dark, slashing brow, he released her at once. "What is this, imp? A return of maidenly modesty?"

"I have never lost my maidenly modesty," Grace informed him.

"Really?" Niall paced around her, studying every inch from the top of her tightly coiled chignon with its few restrained curls that fell forward at the ear, all the way to amber satin slippers that barely peeped from the hem of the matching pelisse robe. "Intriguing. Truly intriguing."

Grace walked past him and set her package down by the window. "There are a few things I wish to tell you. And one or two questions I should like to ask. Would that be acceptable?"

When he didn't reply, she swept the full back of her skirts around and turned to look at him. "Niall? May I proceed?"

He made an expansive gesture with one arm. "Please do."

"First there is the matter of a rumor that has been spreading today. Are you aware of it?"

"Something about missing trinkets? A handful of small gems? Yes. It is of no importance."

"But Calum did tell the marquess." Grace picked up her parcel again. "He would not have done so if he hadn't thought it important."

"Mr. Innes has become Calum? I had not thought the two of you were on such intimate terms."

"The use of a first name is hardly intimate."

"It is more intimate than the form accepted between strangers."

"We are *not* strangers."

Niall came closer and stood, looking down at her. "You find it remarkably easy to become closely acquainted with men, don't you?"

His meaning was obscure, but Grace doubted she would like it made more clear. "Calum has been kind to me. For that I'm grateful. It has been mentioned to me that certain suggestions have been made about the identity of the supposed thieves."

"No such suggestion was made to me . . . by the marquess."

"I'm told that a member of the staff thinks the crimes are being committed by someone recently arrived here." She stared at him hard. "How many people can you think of who are recently arrived at Kirkcaldy?"

He strolled away, and for an instant she thought he might sit at the piano. Instead, he picked up a violin and peered at its bridge.

"You can think of no one but my mother and myself, can you?" Without waiting for his reply, Grace tugged open the oilcloth that wrapped her package and spread the contents upon the window seat. "It occurs to me that someone may have observed me bringing my supplies here and decided that I am hiding things I have stolen."

"Are you suggesting *I* may have made that connection?"

"I don't know. Come here, please. You will see that any such suspicion is false."

"You really are an intriguing little baggage." He did as she asked and silently regarded the jumble she'd set out for him. "Paintbrushes? Paints?"

Grace drew herself up. "I am a painter." She raised the lid of the window seat enough to drag out another bundle and wrestled a canvas into the light. "I do not expect you to understand my form. It is not necessary that you do."

Niall took the canvas from her and propped it against the drapes. "Oils?" he asked, predictably enough.

"Indeed. *Oils.* I have no interest in the dull watercolors ladies are supposed to take such delight in daubing." Why was she showing him, telling him? Was it truly because she feared he might make a connection between her hidden possessions and the things that had been stolen? Or was it because she needed, so very desperately, to share what she had never been able to share, and to do so with another human being in whom she felt a kindred passion for beautiful things?

He had crossed his arms. "Your parents approved of this?"

"No."

His expressive brows rose once more. "Then how have you been able to pursue such an . . . unusual pastime?"

"It is not a pastime. It is a vocation. And I have pursued it in secret because what I am doing is important. One day it may be of the utmost importance to other artists who follow in my footsteps."

"I see."

Grace regarded him with narrowed eyes. "No, you don't. I thought you would. But you think what I do is trivial. If I were a man, you would take something so innovative seriously, but a daring female artist must be regarded as foolish—and with deep suspicion."

"Painting . . . this type of painting—" he appeared bemused "—cannot be . . . *suitable* for a woman."

"Why?" She began to seethe. "Because I should not tax my poor little brain with anything more than insipid flowers? And of course, there is needlework. No doubt that would meet with your approval."

"There are, my dear girl, your duties to your husband."

"I do not have a husband."

"But you will. Very soon. I cannot imagine the marquess approving of a wife who, er—" puffing up his cheeks, he made a vague, all-encompassing motion with his hands "—who applies such, mm, *dramatic* and unconventional swaths of color into compositions that are difficult to . . . *interpret?*"

Speech deserted Grace. He did not understand at all.

Niall glanced at her. "No, no, my dear. Your husband will have quite different demands to make of you. Although, of course, creativity is always to be commended."

His superior smile did something odd to her spine.

"What exactly *is* this supposed to be?" he asked, indicating her painting.

"I—" Grace planted her fists on her hips and turned her head away. "Your arrogance appalls me. Total, impossible, male arrogance. High-handed, cabbageheaded, completely insensitive . . . I—I—"

"Please do not strain for superlatives on my behalf." He was still smiling that infuriatingly tolerant smile.

"In generations to come," Grace said when she could finally speak, "there may well be a school of painting for which my work is the pattern. One day they may speak of the Grace Wren school."

He looked at her, simply *looked* at her, then at the painting, and said nothing at all. The silly smile remained on his lips.

"You do not think my work has any value at all, do you? You find what pleases me ridiculous and unworthy of fair comment."

Niall drew his bottom lip between his teeth, then slowly released it. "Not at all. I am merely speechless before something so unusual."

She did not believe him.

"Hmm." Clearing his throat, he pointed to the canvas. "Enlighten me. What exactly do you call this *school* of yours?"

She was tempted not to tell him. But he deserved to learn that she had given all this much thought. "Suggestive."

Grace was gifted with an unblinking and brilliant green stare. Slowly Niall's sensual mouth spread into a frank grin. "What?" He coughed and then she was almost certain he was trying not to laugh. "*Suggestive?* Suggestive of *what*, pray?"

"You are laughing at me!" Forgetting herself, Grace poked a finger into his chest. "*Laughing*, sir. That is despicable. Unconscionable." A jab punctuated each word.

"Hah! What an admirable vocabulary you do have." He convulsed, apparently at his own brilliance, and bent over.

"Ooh!" Grace poked him again and again. "I shall never forgive you. I thought you would understand."

"You assault me unfairly," he sputtered, making futile grabs for her finger. "Suggestive, eh? Black and red and white. A gaping hole, I think. Suggestive of a large mouth, perhaps? Yes. You see, sweet imp, I do not have the least difficulty understanding what you think you painted."

To her horror, Grace felt the prickle of tears sting her eyes. "All you do is play music other people create." She sniffed. "I create my own beauty. I expect that is what makes you so mean and jealous. There is nothing original in you."

He became still.

"You were right about the mouth," she told him, holding her anger about her like a thorny skin. "It is—appropriately—a man's mouth. Wide open, yes. Shouting, yes. What else does a man's mouth ever do?"

"Men do not always shout."

She did not care to listen to him. "That is not the point here." Indicating the painting, she explained. "This is the essence of a man, his soul reaching through the flesh to find meaning in the wretched life with which he is shackled."

Niall scrubbed at his face.

And Grace jabbed him again. "Pay attention! You may learn something of interest. *You* may be complacent in your lot, sir. It is not so with all men. Or all women. *This* man is made of fire and passion. *This* man cries out his love and his desire to be free to bestow that love upon the object of his desire."

"All of that?" Niall said quietly.

"Yes. All of that."

"You have an incredible imagination."

"I do, indeed. And I find I burn with the need to resume my work."

"Mm. Tell me more about this man."

He no longer appeared amused. Grace smoothed back loosened wisps of hair. "He is naked."

Niall's gaze shifted slowly from Grace's face to the painting. He bent low to look closely. "Naked?"

"Naked. I never paint clothes."

"I see—or perhaps I should say that of course I see there are no clothes. May I ask upon whose form you base a painting such as this?"

Grace waved a hand airily. "Upon previous impressions."

"Indeed? Do tell me more."

"I think not." She did not trust his sober countenance. "You were kind enough to allow me to keep my supplies here. You deserved an explanation, and now you have one. Nothing more need be said on the subject."

"I am beginning to find the subject fascinating."

"Please do not mock me further."

"I find *you* even more fascinating."

At last everything was safely stowed away again. "And now there is the other matter I wished to speak to you about."

"And there is another matter I wish to speak to *you* about," he said. "At great length and in great depth."

Niall was rubbing his chest. Grace noted the shadow of dark hair through fine linen. The shirt was unbuttoned at the neck, and the same hair curled in plain view. "I have never known a gentleman to come into a lady's company without his coat before. Or his waistcoat and neckcloth," she remarked, and instantly regretted the comments. "Not that it concerns me, of course."

"Of course. A woman of the world who paints naked men could not possibly be affected by such a sight."

Grace shook her head. "Not possibly."

"You have very pointed fingers, imp. I do believe you have wounded me beyond repair."

She frowned. "A bruise or two. Nothing more. I could not have injured you badly." But she did feel some remorse. "I'm sorry if I hurt you, but you made me very angry."

"I did not intend to make you angry. But do not give it another thought. You have shown me another level of yourself, and I like what I see. A little temper can be titillating in a woman, particularly during certain, shall we say, *encounters?*"

He muddled her. "I should return to my room quickly. I had made up my mind not to come here tonight."

He planted his feet apart. Doeskin breeches fitted his powerful thighs without a wrinkle. "Sweeting," he said, his voice deep and warm. "You could not possibly have made up your mind to such a foolish thing."

With an effort, Grace raised her eyes. "Why? Because it is unthinkable that I should be able to resist you?"

"Exactly. I understand you better than you understand yourself. You wanted to come as much as I wanted you to—if not more so."

"Oh, that is . . ." Grace sputtered, "It is insupportable. I shall leave at once."

"I think not."

She made to go around him. He stepped into her path. Grace dodged in the opposite direction, only to be foiled again.

He took hold of her wrists and, ignoring her attempt at resistance, drew her toward the fire. "You are overset. Come and sit with me."

"I am *not* overset," she told him, but she had no choice but to go with him, to allow him to press her down into one of the Aubusson chairs.

"If you are not overset, why are you scarcely able to take a breath? And why are your cheeks so charmingly pink?" He rested a big hand on each chair arm and leaned over Grace. "And why are you behaving as if you think I might *ravage* you?"

Her hand flew toward her mouth. She dropped it and straightened her back. "I may know very little, sir, but I know you are suggesting something quite beyond the pale. You are entirely too familiar. The time has come for you to understand your position—what your position will become."

"Sir? I was not *sir* last night." He sounded . . . *dangerous*. "Surely you have not forgotten how *familiar* we were last night."

He enjoyed humiliating her. "Matters have changed. I have considered my behavior and decided the less said about it, the better. I was simply caught off balance by unusual circumstances. You would do well to look to the future and forget the past yourself."

"Look to the future and my position?" The soft linen of his shirt draped hard, flexed muscle. "I can hardly wait for you to explain that to me. What exactly will my position be?"

There was a threat in his voice, in the attitude of his extremely tall, extremely strong body. *Poised to pounce*, Grace thought, pressing herself into the chair.

"Um, I think we should discuss this at another time," she suggested.

"And I think we should discuss it now."

So tall. So forceful. And *so* angry. Green fire flashed in his eyes. His lips were drawn slightly back from his teeth, very white teeth.

"My position, Grace?"

Her only escape would require that she duck beneath him and scramble away, with a complete disregard for decorum. "I wish you would not loom over me like that, Niall."

He smiled. Definitely dangerous. "Do I make you uncomfortable?" Firelight rippled across his tanned skin. "Do I, Grace?"

"No."

"Do you want me to kiss you again?"

Her own skin blazed. To kiss and be kissed by

Niall? Delightfully tempting. And it was also wrong. With or without the whisperings of Mama's friends, Grace knew that men and women did not kiss—as they had kissed—in a casual manner. Did married men and women kiss in such a way frequently? she wondered. Really, this preoccupation with such matters was out of hand.

"I asked you a question, Grace."

She was to marry another man, and she had already betrayed him in her heart. She shook her head fiercely.

"I think you do want to be kissed." His eyes flickered lazily over her.

Might she be forgiven, but he was right! His nearness alone made her dizzy with longing.

"Last night we barely began to explore what we can enjoy together."

"There can be nothing more." But if only there could.

"Let us consider my position. At the moment I am above you. Over you."

"I did not refer to—to—*that* type of position."

"Well, we can deal with whatever other position you have in mind later. For now we shall experiment with some I have in mind."

He made no sense. "I shall speak to the marquess. I'm sure that if I explain that you are, er, supportive of me, he will understand."

"Supportive?" he repeated thoughtfully. "Mm. Yes, I think that will do well for a start."

"And—with his lordship's approval—we will be able to continue our friendship. If it pleases us both."

She thought the smile on his lips fixed. The narrowing of his extraordinary eyes was impossible to mistake. "Naturally, if you do not wish to—"

"What makes you think the marquess could possibly approve of his wife's *friendship* with another man?''

Grace shifted awkwardly. ''His lordship is unlikely to know exactly what it is that we share, Niall. Therefore he is unlikely to be jealous of—''

''We must see how things progress,'' Niall said, interrupting Grace again. ''Your gown becomes you.''

Her heart and soul were torn by confusion. ''Thank you.''

''The color. Not the cut. It is too severe. Take off the ruff.''

Grace did not immediately understand.

Niall's next move shocked her. Smoothly he parted her thighs and sank to kneel between them. ''Every position is made up of many parts,'' he said, his gaze centered on her mouth. ''This is but the beginning. Kindly remove your ruff.''

She found that the next breath she took went no farther than her throat.

''Do it, Grace. *Now*.''

Slowly she raised her arms and found the fastening behind her neck.

''No,'' he said sharply. ''Don't. I've changed my mind. Undo these.'' He touched the silk corded bows that hid the fastenings on her gown.

Grace made no attempt to do as he asked. Very slowly she lowered her arms. Very slowly Niall slipped his hands beneath the hem of her gown and smoothed the backs of her legs through lace stockings. He smoothed all the way to her knees.

''Stop!''

''Ah, Grace, your protests excite me. Just as you intend they should.''

''I'm sure this is wickedness. You must not continue!''

''If it is wickedness, it is wonderful wickedness,'' he argued, his nostrils flaring. ''I must continue and

I will. You and I both need this. You know it and so do I. Your skin is soft. Is every part of you so soft?''

"No!" She should have listened to her head and remained in her rooms.

"No? Tell me which parts are not soft so that I may avoid them."

"I did not mean . . ."

"I thought not." At the sensitive spots behind her knees, he stopped and feathered little strokes back and forth.

Grace's legs jerked and Niall smiled—a purely wicked smile. "A soft part? A tender part?"

She tried to wriggle away.

Niall's smile broadened. "Mm. Move like that again, sweet imp. You can have no idea what you are doing to me."

Grace attempted to lift her legs from his hands.

"Thank you." He slid his hand up the backs of her thighs. "I'm so glad we both want the same things."

"Niall!"

Her skirts rose to reveal smooth, pale skin and the tops of her stockings, where delicate lavender daisies decorated satin garters.

"Pretty," Niall said. He no longer smiled. "These things a woman keeps hidden tell so much about who she really is. Teasing little flowers. They tell the truth, don't they? And the austere gown is a lie."

His fingers kneaded higher—and higher.

"Don't," Grace said, but heat welled in her veins. "I should not be here."

"But you are here."

"Only extraordinary circumstances make it so." She swallowed. "Unchaperoned . . ."

"Unchaperoned, indeed, thank God. How tedious a hovering chaperon would make moments such as this. Kiss me, Grace."

"I have never before been left alone . . . I mean, I have never before been in such a situation."

"No?"

"Oh!" Shock traveled the length of Grace's spine. "What are you doing?"

He was, she already knew, cupping her bottom in his broad hands.

"Kiss me, Grace," he said, bringing his parted lips closer. "I like what I feel. You are round and firm and warm—and so smooth. I can easily imagine how every other part of you is as smooth, and warm—and inviting."

Grace shook her head. Each twitch of her muscles served to tighten his grip on her. His fingers found a most sensitive crease. Leaning toward her, lifting as he did so, Niall pressed himself firmly between her legs and dragged his tongue along the outlines of her mouth. "Open for me." His fingers found an even softer spot, and a small, sharp, raw sensation penetrated Grace. She felt . . . *wet*. "Open," he murmured, and nibbled her lips apart. He kissed her deep, and long, and hot, until she grasped his shoulders and kissed him back.

His hands supported her. His fingers sought places she had never thought to feel touched by another human, least of all a man.

With his lips still on hers, Niall worked his clever hands to the small dimples at the base of her spine, and then forward over her hips to her belly.

She tore her mouth away. "*Please.*" Struggling, she attempted to work her gown down. Impossible.

"You do not have to plead. I have no intention of stopping."

Grace turned her face away. He seared her, stripped her nerves open, made her want to close out the denials and give herself up to these wonderful sensations.

"Not even a shift beneath your gown?" he said,

close to her ear. "Such a very passionate woman. You wished to be ready for me as quickly as possible."

"I . . . I was not coming," she told him weakly. "I changed my mind and there was not time for . . . Oh, I have never felt like this."

"Good. I want you to tell me that again and again. And I want you to make me feel the same—again and again. And you are to do exactly as I instruct you, do you understand?"

Dazed, disoriented, she returned her gaze to his face. Glittering eyes. Lean features. That sensual mouth promised more of what she'd already come to need. Once, not so many years ago, when he'd been very young, his looks must have hovered on the brink of beauty. In potent maturity, he was the dark embodiment of angel become fully man. In Niall's mesmerizing features, Grace saw how sin had somehow touched beauty and made it a study in the image of impure desire's fascination.

"Do you understand, imp?"

She nodded, not remembering what he'd asked of her.

"Good. Undo your gown."

"*No.*" Shaking her head vehemently, she plucked at her skirts again.

Niall laughed, a low, possessive laugh. "But I think you will." And his thumbs delved into her most secret folds.

Panic brought Grace's hips writhing up from the chair.

"That's right," he said, rubbing back and forth over velvet skin turned mortifyingly slick. "You are wonderful. The most accomplished performer I have ever encountered."

His words only grew more confusing.

"Undress. *Undress*, Grace."

She started to speak.

"Do as I tell you." A flush crept over his cheekbones. Perspiration shone at his temples. "I could
not have expected such fortune."

"Fortune?"

"As you are, sweeting. As you are. The gown?"

With fingers that felt stiff, Grace touched the silk
bow at her neck. "The ruff?"

"No. I think not. I've decided the ruff will do well
where it is."

Undoing the hook and eye took both of her hands.

"And the next one," Niall said as it parted.

She did as he asked.

"Go on."

The gown was open to her breasts. Grace slipped
out another hook.

Niall's iron hands left her body and he gripped
her wrists. "Velvet was meant to entice men," he
told her. "Feel how your breasts respond to me
through their soft covering?"

He rubbed her with flattened palms, hooking his
fingers inside her bodice to graze the fullness he
found there.

Grace caught at his arms. He ignored her and
pushed his flattened hands inside the gown and over
her shoulders whilst he kissed her again, fully, pos-
sessively.

He left her gasping.

"Carry on."

It took seconds for her mind to focus once more,
and when it did, it was to the vision of Niall unbut-
toning his shirt and pulling it off. His muscles flexed
in the firelight.

"You should not." Grace looked into her lap,
gasped at her near nakedness, and quickly turned
away. "It isn't appropriate."

"Appropriate!" he shouted. "My dear little miracle. You enthrall me. I want to see you without the
dress."

"You cannot."

"Yes, I can. Undo it, or I will undo it for you, and if I do, I might tear something. That would be hard to explain."

Hesitantly, her eyes still averted, Grace released another fastening, and another—and another. Slowly the gown fell apart until she knew her nude body was his to stare upon.

"Look at me," he commanded.

She wanted to. Turning up her face, she studied every line of his and found nothing there that did not pump fresh heat into her blood.

"Look at yourself."

Grace shook her head.

"Yes. *Yes*, Grace. Look at what it is that makes my manhood swell with its need for you."

She glanced down and her face throbbed with rushing blood. Between the tumbled folds of amber velvet, her body was white. The dark gold curls between her legs glistened, and whilst she watched, he touched her there, slipped a finger within and worked back and forth. "What *is* that?" she cried, her hips bobbing up from the chair. Such a feeling had never before been hers.

"It is good, sweet. And you are good. I do believe I am having difficulty containing myself. But I shall try. Do not look away."

Swiftly he bent and drew a nipple into his mouth, suckling so insistently that Grace gasped—with sweetly painful pleasure. Her hands found the curling hair on his chest and held on. Niall made a growling sound in his throat and turned to running his tongue around the nipple while he squeezed the other between his fingers. Then he shifted, drawing his beard-rough jaw across tender skin until he could nuzzle and nibble on her other breast.

Grace clamped his head to her and forgot everything but the waves of fire that shot from her breasts, deep into her belly. That place between her thighs throbbed.

"I need," she panted. "Niall, I *need.*"

"What do you need?" he asked, pulling away from her once more. "Look now. See now."

As soon as she saw her rosy, wet nipples, swollen from the attention of his mouth, she tried to cover herself.

"A virtuous maiden," Niall said in that odd tone she did not understand. "Take the gown all the way off, my virtuous maiden."

"It is . . . it is almost off."

"I want you absolutely naked before me. Do as I order, Grace."

His expression was implacable, and her heart tripped in her chest.

When she did not move, he began undoing his breeches.

Grace's hand flew to her mouth.

"I'm glad you are excited," he said, stripping the doeskin down to his knees.

Amazed, Grace gripped the arms of her chair and stared at him.

"Yes, indeed, your enthusiasm is gratifying."

"It is . . . *huge.*"

"It is very ready."

"Y-Yes." How strange that men were so differently made. "Angry-looking, too."

"Its rage is to possess you, sweet one. To enter your warm, wet, ready body and possess it. But that's what we both want, isn't it?"

She nodded slowly. "I expect so." His condition did not appear comfortable. Had she caused such an extraordinary effect?

"The gown, Grace."

Unable to look away from this new vision, she struggled awkwardly to work the bodice from her shoulders and down her arms. Tight sleeves, together with her position in the chair, made the task difficult, and by the time the fabric strained at her elbows, Grace was desperate to be free of restraint.

"Allow me," Niall said. He lifted her, but instead of pulling away her sleeves, he tugged the gown tight behind her, trapping her arms at her sides. "A delectable picture."

Her slight weight made it simple for him to settle her astride his thighs.

"Oh, no." Grace struggled helplessly. "Oh, Niall. This is . . . this is . . ." But she didn't know what this was, except heat and searing need, exquisite pain that must never end, and encroaching blackness that seemed bent on claiming her mind.

The smooth, swollen mystery he'd bared pressed against her sensitive woman's place. He pushed her backward over the seat of the chair and lavished her nakedness with kisses. Tender, whispering kisses. Biting, demanding kisses. Sucking kisses that drew small screams from her throat. Her mouth, her shoulders, her breasts, her belly, he missed no fraction.

She heard his rasping breath and felt the powerful rocking of his hips against her.

"There is more?" she panted.

"Oh, yes. We both know there is more."

Niall rose abruptly to his feet, leaving Grace kneeling, her back bent over the chair. Standing above her, he stepped out of his breeches and braced his legs apart.

"You are . . ." Her mouth grew dry. "I never knew there could be such power."

"And you want my power." His smile was cruel but served only to excite her more.

Very deliberately, he drew her up against his length and stripped away the robe. "Can you tell me exactly what it is that you want now?"

She could tell him nothing.

Niall stepped back and surveyed her. Grace's hand went to her neck and she fiddled with the ruff. She made to undo it.

"No," he commanded. "Leave it. Prim spinster chignon. Governess ruff. And the rest is perfect, naked wanton—all the way to those, those . . ." He waved at her legs in the lace stockings and satin garters that made her feel even more revealed. "You are the stuff of a virile man's fantasies. You inflame me, imp. Wicked, wonderful imp. But you already know that. Your body is small, yet voluptuous, and it weeps as no cold woman's body ever weeps."

He took her by the shoulders and turned her around. "I want to say things you are to carry with you always." He pulled her to lean back against him.

Grace closed her eyes. This should not be happening, but it was, and she was glad. Could it be that she truly had, in the strangest of manners, met the man with whom she would eventually share all of her life? Could it be that she should tell him now that he owned her heart?

"And I want to give you feelings to remember always—to want always," he said, his voice deep and rough.

He slipped his hands beneath her arms and covered her aching breasts. He covered and teased and aroused them before pressing downward to her belly and beyond. With his rough jaw resting on her shoulder, he drove a finger against her feminine flesh and began an inexorable stroking that sent Grace sagging into the support of his arms.

"Remember this feeling, Grace."

"Yes," she whispered.

He dipped and that frighteningly engorged part of him drove forward between her thighs. It drove and drove again. And his fingers brought once more the singing black bliss.

"Niall! Please. I want to lie down. *Lie* with me."

The stroking, delving drive, stopped. Grace turned in his arms and pressed her breasts to his chest. "We will bring great comfort to each other." She reached up to run her hands into his long, tangled black curls. "I could not have hoped for such good fortune."

His hands settled over hers. "Good fortune, indeed. Infinitely better than could be expected."

She would tell him what she hoped could exist for them—together. "There is even more than this for us, Niall."

"No doubt." He pulled her arms from his neck. "But there are things that can only be improved by restraint."

"What things are those?" She did not understand him.

With fluid grace, he stepped back into his breeches and caught up his shirt. "They are things that are the essence of control, Grace. Things that allow one human being power over another. No doubt you get my meaning."

"I don't."

"Oh, I think you do. Does your body still ache, my dear?"

Blushing, she nodded.

"Good. That is one of the feelings I wish you never to forget. And I want you to remember how you look with your prim hair and governess ruff— and your stockings and garters and nakedness. Then there are your breasts, sweeting. Your lovely, begging breasts with nipples still glistening from my mouth. Think of them often."

"Niall!" She covered her mouth.

"Should it be your face that you cover? What of the pulsing place that yearns to feel my fingers again—and my *rod* that excites you so? Fear not, you shall feel it."

Her eyes widened. He mocked her, and she was powerless to hide her shame.

"And these are the words I want you to remember me speaking: I can do again to you what I've done tonight. I can do it whenever I please, wherever I please. And, as I did tonight, I can stop when I please and leave you still wanting."

"You cannot!" The words broke from her lips and she backed away.

"Charming. Such an intoxicating vision. If I had more time, I would indeed lie with you here and now and finish what we have started."

"You frighten me. Don't say these things."

"Oh, but I will. I say to you that whenever you see me, you will know that I am imagining you naked before me, seeing you exactly as you are now. You may be sipping tea with your mother, or chattering stupidly with my . . . with Father Struan, or *Calum*, and when you look into my eyes, you will see your reflection and wonder if they can all see you as I do."

"Stop it!"

"Never. The nature of your kind of woman demands a man's dominance, and you shall have it. You shall have *mine*. Does that please you, Grace?"

She wanted her gown.

Niall approached the door. "I have other matters to attend." He bowed low. "Thank you for a most wonderful interlude. Stimulating, my dear."

Grace snatched up her robe. "Why are you tormenting me? You have changed. I thought we might become friends."

"We will. The best kind of friends. Friends who learn how best to use one another. In the meantime, there are two more thoughts with which I leave you. I meant it when I said I can have you whenever and wherever I please. That is absolutely true. You will never know when or where I may decide that I want you just as you are now. No place will afford you safety from me. Not that you would desire safety from me, would you, my pet?''

Bemused, she shook her head.

''I thought not. I have met women like you before, although never with *quite* your magnificent appetite.'' With the door open, he pulled on his shirt. ''And last of all for tonight; *I* will be the one to decide the nature and frequency of our entertainments. I leave you craving satisfaction. That satisfaction shall not be yours until and unless *I* decide to give it to you.''

Grace could only stare at him.

''Be here tomorrow night.''

He was mad.

''Sleep well.''

Chapter 8

*S*he had not come to him last night!

She had *not* come.

"Hold hard, Arran!" Calum's voice came to him on the cool dawn air, and Arran reined Allegro in beside the river.

He did not turn in his saddle.

"What in God's name ails you?" Calum galloped to his side, his big gray snorting into the mist that still hung in gauzy ribbons above the moorland. "Neither Struan nor I saw you all day yesterday. Neither did McWallop. You've banished us all from approaching you in the gallery. Now we receive this bloody rude summons." He flapped the note Arran had sent via Shanks, who had trembled visibly at being called to Arran's chamber—something that had never before happened to the butler.

"Arran? Is something wrong?"

"In God's name, Calum, let me think in peace."

"Gladly. It was *you* who sent for *me* hours before I might have left my bed. I'll happily doze here while you make up your mind what it is you want from me."

"Do that."

Arran had spent all day yesterday burning from the memory of the previous night's near ecstasy with Grace. Last night he'd gone to the music room anticipating another delightful interlude. And he'd waited for her until almost dawn—in vain. Then he'd

sent word for Calum to meet him at what had been
their favorite boyhood fishing spot.

She had not come to him. Unbelievable.

He'd played his game so well. The girl was his to
do with as he wished, he'd been certain of it.

Arran was still certain. The little witch had decided to spice the chase even more. She would discover that Arran, Marquess of Stonehaven, had been
used once and would never be so again—not by any
manipulating female.

"Good morning, brother."

Arran glared around and saw Struan, elegant despite his hated cleric's garb and comfortable as always astride a chestnut he'd favored since
adolescence. "You've not forgotten how to ride,
then, Father?"

"I've forgotten very little, particularly in the area
of your foul temper."

"Do not waste your priestly condemnations on
me." Arran wheeled Allegro and let the big beast
drink from the river. "I told Calum to meet me here,
not you."

"Ah." Struan's dark eyes held innocent surprise.
"How could I have misunderstood?"

"Why did you tell him to come?" Arran asked
Calum.

"He didn't," Struan said. "Shanks made such a
racket delivering your note to Calum, he woke me.
I went to see what all the fuss was about. Poor fellow's knees were knocking. Really, Arran, I do think
you could try coming into the world with the rest
of us."

"I thought you were angling for me not to be of
this world at all. I thought you were hoping to groom
my poor, black soul for heaven."

Struan settled his flat-brimmed black hat at a rak-
ish angle over his brow and fixed Arran with one of
the "I shall always forgive you" looks he'd per-

fected. "I am a man of faith. As such, I trust the Lord to show you the way home when it is time."

Arran looked skyward through the vaporous, gray light. "May your Lord restrain me from knocking you off that horse and leaping upon your holy neck."

"It's cold, Arran," Calum said. "Your note says you've matters of desperate importance to discuss."

"Does it?" He hadn't planned on Struan's presence. There were things he didn't care to speak of in front of his brother.

"Why did it have to be here?" Calum said, winding his cloak more closely about him. He wore no hat, and the damp early morning had scattered glistening moisture in his dark brown hair.

"Because it pleases me to be abroad when others are not."

"You sound petulant," Struan remarked. "It does not become you. And we already know your penchant for mystery. When do you plan to stop skulking abroad in the night and hiding in the day?"

"God grant me patience!" Arran pulled on Allegro's reins and circled him about. "It is day now and I am not hiding." He set off at a trot, with the two other men in his wake. Only Calum knew how Arran really preferred to spend his days.

"It's barely dawn," Struan called. "And I've no doubt you'll soon dash for home and dive into whatever cupboard is your sanctuary. Father should have put a stop to your peculiar ways, brother. You should never have been allowed to develop such unacceptable habits."

Arran had no patience for this prattle. The work he should have accomplished last night had not been touched. The three hours sleep he required in the early hours of each day had been ignored. He would be in no humor to move among his tenants this day.

"I am an angry man," he ground out, spurring Allegro into a gallop. "A very angry man!"

"An amazing announcement," Struan said, lengthening his own mount's stride. "Don't you find it amazing to learn that Arran is angry today, Calum?"

"Damn you, Arran," Calum shouted. "Your capricious ill humor is no laughing matter. I'm a tired man with a great deal to think about. Let's get to business and I'll away home to my bed, where I belong."

"*I* am not laughing," Arran roared. He gained the brow of a hill and hesitated. Below lay a clutter of tenant cottages, among them the home of Robert and Gael Mercer. He had a visit to pay there, and soon. "What can be making you so tired and thoughtful, Calum?" Allegro pawed at the ground, and Arran swayed in his saddle.

Calum arrived at the top of the hill and said, "You, my lord, are an unpleasant and ungrateful devil. You know full well what occupies my mind presently."

"Arranging for the attachment of my new ball and chain, no doubt."

"You cannot possibly be referring to your marriage to that delightful Miss Wren," Struan said, catching up with his companions. "To be joined to one so lovely will doubtless be a joy indeed—to a man with fleshly desires."

"*Shut* up," Arran commanded.

"I, of course, know nothing of such things, but I can imagine that lying with such a desirable female would give a creature such as you great pleasure."

"*Struan* Nicholas Rossmara, I warn you."

Struan's black eyes, so like Arran's in their expressiveness, gazed dreamily over the land. "Yes, very great pleasure indeed. When did you say the nuptials were to take place?"

"I did not. Calum, in the name of goodness—and for his own safety—take him back to Kirkcaldy."

"We have hardly spoken since I arrived." Struan sounded wounded. "I had hoped we could have many brotherly discussions."

"*That is enough.* That is the very last inane comment I will bear from you."

"Arran—"

"You may also be silent, Calum. I am a man beset by his responsibilities." And his burgeoning desire. "I cannot tell you how I long for garters . . . I mean peace."

Silence fell.

"There. I knew it. You have not considered my feelings in this matter for one moment. Marry, you say. Marry now or Mortimer Cuthbert and his simpering wife will be telling you what you should and shouldn't do with your own estates." Damn the girl. He would find a way to bring her to heel soon enough. "I shall have my way with her . . . I mean, I shall have my way in this . . . I shall have my way. Do you hear me?"

"I do indeed," Calum said, smiling in that infuriatingly knowing way of his.

"Indeed," Struan echoed, not smiling at all. "Do you not agree that Miss Wren is delightful?"

"He has not seen her," Calum said quietly.

Struan opened his mouth. And snapped it shut again.

"Arran sent me to London to find him a suitable wife. Then he changed his mind and said he didn't want one after all—after she was already on her way here." Calum cast Arran a narrow-eyed glare. "He will not see her. He *knows* he must produce an heir, but continues to behave like a blushing girl over the issue."

"Have we forgotten that in the area of marriage I

have already had one notable, shall we say, *disaster?*'' Arran made sure his voice conveyed menace.

"How could we forget?" Struan said, frowning. "A sad, sad event. But this is a new start for you, Arran."

Arran leaned over Allegro's neck. "If you had not decided to become a priest and take *unnatural* vows, I could have taken as long as I pleased to find another wife—if I ever found one at all."

"I should have denied my own heart to relieve you of your duty?" Struan straightened broad shoulders inside a black cape. His hands held the reins casually. "Each of us must follow the path that becomes us."

"How true. I remain here, doing my duty. And you, Struan, *Viscount Hunsingore*, should have taken your place at my side. I have needed you."

There was an uncomfortable silence. Calum looked away. Struan met Arran's eyes, unflinching. "We have need of each other," he said gently. "We always will and I am here for you, Arran. Believe that I shall never fail you. But it is you who should produce the Rossmara heir, not I."

Arran felt his anger waver. The cold air made his eyes sting and he blinked. "I envy the church her ownership of you," he said gruffly. "My bark is sharp, but it is the bark of a dog denied the company of the man he trusts most. And loves most."

"Dear brother." Struan brought his horse beside Arran's. "You and I have shared much. No man will ever be closer to my heart than you. If you ever should need me, send word and I will come." He rested a hand on Arran's shoulder and, as quickly, removed it.

Smoke rose in thin coils from the cottage chimneys below the hill. "Our people are stirring," Arran said, moved by Struan's words.

"Aye," Calum agreed. He had an unspoken kinship with the common folk of these parts. "I hear Gael Mercer is well advanced in her . . ." He caught Arran's warning glance and stopped.

"Who is Gael Mercer?" Struan asked.

"Just the wife of a tenant," Calum said offhandedly. "She's with child and a delicate thing. Well loved, too. I've heard talk about concern over her health among the other tenants."

He would go down to the Mercers' tomorrow, Arran decided. There was the matter of a treat for Gael. He'd have to think about that.

They settled, the three of them side by side upon their mounts, relaxed in the saddle, looking out over the blue-green countryside.

Noisy scuffling broke from nearby bushes and a pair of gray-rumped fieldfares flew up, *chack-chack-chack*ing as they fought for possession of a plump worm.

"What does that remind you of?" Arran chuckled. "We three did our share of fighting over this and that, didn't we?"

"I sometimes wish we could return to those days," Struan said.

Arran stirred. "We can never go back." And he was not abroad at this unkind hour on this dismal morning to mourn the past like a foolish woman. "What I have to say might as well be heard by you, Struan. You may have withdrawn from the world of mere mortals, but I doubt if you would welcome the frequent tramping of our Cuthbert relations' demanding feet upon Kirkcaldy land."

"I would not," Struan agreed.

Calum flipped the reins back and forth across his horse's neck. "The solution to the problem is within your reach, my lord."

"I have come to dislike the sound of respectful address upon your lips, Calum. You think what lies ahead is simple. I tell you it is anything but simple—

for me. And I am most uncertain that you have made as good a choice as you should have."

"Well!" Calum cast back one side of his cloak and splayed a hand on his thigh. "Forgive me for doing as good a job as any man could do. And—since you haven't as much as set eyes on Grace—how can you presume to judge her suitability to be your wife?"

"Oh, I've set more than my eyes upon . . ." Damn his tongue.

"I beg your pardon," Calum said slowly, shifting to face Arran. "What are you saying?"

"I owe you no explanations. I wanted to talk to you because I'm deeply suspicious of my cousin's failure to appear on our doorstep. He—"

"Arran," Struan said, interrupting. "What did you mean just now? About setting more than your eyes upon Miss Wren?"

"I meant nothing. There is something afoot with Mortimer, I tell you."

"No, no," Calum said, pursing his mobile mouth. "Don't try to divert us. *Have* you seen her?"

Arran shrugged elaborately, turning up his palms and assuming a blank expression.

"You have," Calum murmured, jutting his chin and beginning to smile. "Damn you for the slimy slyboots you are. When? Where?"

Damn him for the loose mouth he was. "When is Mortimer coming here?"

"What I'm hearing concerns me," Struan said. "Am I to understand that you have kept secret company with Miss Wren?"

"Nothing a man does in his own house is secret . . . not from himself . . . and it is himself who is the law in that house." Arran knew he blustered. "Answer me. When is Mortimer Cuthbert arriving?"

"Just yesterday afternoon Mrs. Wren approached me again on the matter of your refusal to meet with

Grace. And Struan can confirm that Grace asked the same question herself the previous morning. He was there."

Arran frowned. "Hold your tongue, Calum! And do me the great favor of not calling my . . . She is *Miss Wren* to you."

Calum's grin was smug. "Your . . . ? Your what, my lord? Oh, I will gladly call your . . . ? Certainly she shall be Miss Wren if it makes you jealous for me to address her otherwise."

"It does *not* make me jealous."

"There is something most unorthodox afoot here." Struan shook his head slowly. "I'll thank you to explain at once."

"And I'll thank you to keep your sanctified nose out of my affairs. Calum, Mortimer appears when, man? I have to know and I have to know now."

"Because you wish to be married before he arrives?" Struan asked, not without a note of hope in his voice. "I'm sure that can be arranged. I know certain people. In fact, I could probably—"

"You could do *nothing*. For the last time, I wish to know exactly when my cousin is likely to bring his loathsomeness into my presence."

"I don't know," Calum said.

"You must." And Arran must know. Know exactly, so that he could decide on the best course to take with Grace. "Think, man. Work it out."

"I told you I thought it likely he'd decide to come. I am not certain."

"He'll come. Calculate, Calum. *Calculate.*"

"Well, whenever he's had time to gather his odious family and make the journey, I suppose."

"And how long would that take?"

"For God's . . . Excuse me, Struan. You are unreasonable, Arran. I told you I had rashly allowed Mortimer to know that you would be married and that I assumed he would come here to witness the event."

"To try to halt the event, you mean," Struan remarked.

Arran stared at him. So did Calum.

Struan continued, "We all know Mortimer would do anything that might put this fair estate, and the estate in Yorkshire, into his hands."

"What could he do?" Calum asked. "If Arran chooses to marry and have a child, he chooses to marry and have a child."

"Choice has no part of this," Arran muttered.

Struan sighed. "For two worldly men, you are pathetically innocent. I think you would do well to watch our cousin, Arran. Marry in great haste. And bed your wife in great haste." He coughed. "Please forgive my indelicacy."

"The devil take your indelicacy," Arran snapped. "I want to know Mortimer's plans. *Immediately*."

"What difference does it make?" The gray danced and Calum smoothed its neck.

"*Immediately!*"

"*Marry* the girl, damn you." Calum caught at Allegro's bridle. "And the devil take Mortimer."

"Stay," Struan said. "Both of you. There's something Arran isn't telling us. You've had some exchange with the girl. Doesn't she please you?"

"That is of no consequence."

"What kind of exchange did you have?" Calum asked.

He would not give them the information they wanted.

"Your silence leads me to believe the worst," Struan said, pretending to study his nails. "You have already bedded her, haven't you, my dear rakehell brother? I take it she is not to your liking between the sheets."

"You take entirely too much," Arran retorted.

"But I am correct?"

Arran made fists. "You are *not* correct."

"Then what can possibly be holding you back from the obvious?" Struan said. "Hurry, man. She may already be with child."

Calum sputtered. "Grace Wren has been here only a week. Less. Arran may be a potent bastard. He is not a wizard."

"Wizardry is not required in the matter of impregnating a woman," Struan said, moving to an examination of the back of one hand. "A fertile and receptive female—"

"In God's name—"

"God's name is frequently forgotten in these affairs, Arran. A fertile, receptive female and a man with a healthy, functioning rod and adequate seed is all that is required. Am I to take it that one or the other is missing in the case under examination?"

"Bloody hell!" Turning away, Arran covered his mouth with a gloved hand.

"Forgive me if I am too plain," Struan said in silken tones. "But in the interest of expediting matters, it will help if we know which exact element is unsatisfactory."

"What do you mean, *Father?*"

"Is it the female's lack of receptiveness or fertility? Or your malfunctioning rod and lack of seed?"

"Get him away from me, Calum," Arran ordered through his teeth.

"I think you should answer the question."

"You conspire against me! You seek to make me a madman. All right. You want truth and you shall have it. I have *not* bedded Grace Wren. I have indeed spent time with her on three consecutive nights, but I have not bedded her."

"Three *nights?*" Struan and Calum chorused.

"How did you . . . ? How?" Amazement colored Calum's voice.

''It is far too complicated to explain. Suffice to say that the young woman and I encountered one another and had three separate, er, discussions.''

''Discussions?'' Calum said, blatantly disbelieving.

''Discussions,'' Arran insisted.

''On the subject of your marriage, no doubt?'' Struan asked.

Damn them for the prodding fellows they were. ''No. We spoke of . . . art.''

Calum made a thoughtfully hissing sound and said, ''Art?'' as if it were a new word.

''Art, yes.''

''I see,'' Calum said, but Arran knew full well that his friend and adviser was completely bemused. ''So you had pleasant encounters and discovered that you have common grounds upon which to build an enduring relationship.''

''We did not.''

Calum released Allegro's bridle. He threw up his hands. ''I do not care whether or not you and Grace had a meaningful exchange on the artists upon whom you *cannot agree*. Time is running out. The important thing is that you are now acquainted with one another—we will not continue to explore how well—and so the wedding can take place.''

''We are not acquainted.''

''You—''

''Calum, Calum,'' Struan said consolingly. ''Do not excite yourself further over this *dolt!* For the last time, Arran, *explain* yourself.''

There was no point in continuing the farce. ''Grace is a fetching piece.'' It was a start. ''She pleases me well enough—physically.''

''Yes?'' Struan said encouragingly.

''We have—er—enjoyed certain small exchanges? Of the—er—fleshly variety.''

Calum laughed. ''You slick devil. You haven't lost

your touch after all." He chortled. "Five days and you have her eating out of your . . . hand?"

Arran scowled.

"Or perhaps she is eating from whatever other part of you pleases her."

"For God's sake, Calum! Remember Struan."

"You need not waste remembrance on me," Struan said grimly. "God remains your primary concern. There appears to be nothing further to discuss here. We shall return at once to the castle and make the necessary preparations."

"But she is an opinionated little *shrew*," Arran argued, growing irate. "And she has independent ideas quite unsuited to any wife of mine."

"Nonsense. A strong woman is exactly what you need."

"I need to know how long I have before Mortimer arrives," Arran insisted.

Struan gestured impatiently. "It makes no difference now."

"It makes every difference, I tell you," Arran said. "I *need* time."

Calum turned away and made to start back downhill. "Why?"

"Because there is still work to be done—on my situation with the girl."

"Might I suggest that any further work of that nature be done *after* the marriage?" Struan said, and frowned. "I'll allow it's odd that Grace hasn't mentioned you."

"I told her not to."

Struan smiled approvingly. "Loyal to her future husband already. A most encouraging sign."

Encouraging sign, be damned! Grace thought Arran was Niall, her *friend*, and it was to him she'd come, not to the man she expected to marry.

"I have to know how much time I have before Mortimer arrives," Arran said desperately. "He'll

have installed himself in the Charlotte Square house.
Go to Edinburgh, Calum. If he is indeed there, de-
tain him.''

"Will you explain yourself, man? Will you tell me
why you want me to do this?"

"Because I've decided I *will* marry her. There. You
have what you want. And if I'm to do so, it had
better be before Mortimer appears and interferes."

"He could not," Struan said.

"He might. Unless I misjudge her, Grace will be
in a formidable rage before she agrees to the wedding. If Mortimer arrives before I have dealt with
that rage, he will have an advantage I would never
choose to give him."

"Enough of this twaddle." Struan reached for Arran's arm. "Speak plainly. What is afoot here?"

"Will no man allow me the honor of keeping at
least part of my own counsel?" When neither Struan
nor Calum answered, Arran's blood began to pound
in his ears. "I've placed myself in a pretty fix, dammit. The woman who is to become my wife thinks
that I am another man."

Two pairs of eyes stared blankly.

"She has spent hours with me alone. Without a
chaperon. Allowed me certain—*liberties.*"

"Yes?"

"Good God!" Arran shouted to the skies. "You
should sing together in the chapel choir. Miss Grace
Wren has been keeping company with a man she
thinks of as one of the marquess's servants. She has
suggested to that man that they become friends and
remain *close* friends after her marriage to the marquess."

Both men's mouths dropped slightly open.

"She asked him to become her consolation whilst
she suffers the decrepit old recluse she is to marry."

"Are you ill?" Struan asked.

"*Listen* to me, you fuddle-head. *I* tricked her. *I* led

her to believe I was not the marquess, but his closest companion. She does not know that when she is finally called to meet with her future husband, she will be confronted with *me!* And when that confrontation takes place, she will know that I have deceived her. She will know that I have listened to her plans to use me and take the money I am expected to leave her just as soon as she can encourage me to draw my last breath.''

''Mon Dieu,'' Struan murmured.

Arran scowled. ''Observe, Calum. Even in French, he prays.''

''We've got to get to Mortimer,'' Calum said. ''Hurry. I can't go. I'd make him suspicious. So would Struan. More so. We'll send Hector MacFie. Mortimer is always impressed by Hector. He can take some missive from you relating to estate business. It will be a sop to Mortimer's ego, and Hector can use it to delay him.''

''How quickly the wind changes,'' Arran said, his stomach clenching. ''A moment ago there was no need to divert Mortimer. Now we must rush to head him off.''

Calum and Struan spurred their horses in a wild downhill scramble. ''A moment ago,'' Calum called, ''we did not know that you'll need all the time we can gain you to subdue a shamed woman.''

''How much time, do you think?'' At his master's urging, Allegro's hoofs flew, spewing pebbles. ''How much?''

Calum's shout carried clearly. ''Perhaps Hector should suggest that Mortimer visit the Indies plantations—for a year or so.''

Chapter 9

T hirty-eight, blond, blue-eyed, and forceful in every move he made, Hector MacFie carried with him an air of absolute confidence. Estate commissioner to Arran for five years, since his father's death, when old Amos Cameron had decided that he wasn't interested in serving a new master, Hector was his own man, and a tough, hardheaded one. He was also the best estate commissioner in the land. Arran knew that many an envious landowner had tried to woo Hector away. A more than handsome wage and enough freedom in the matter of deciding policy for Arran's holdings kept Hector on Rossmara lands.

Having been summoned to Arran's study in Revelation at ten o'clock in the morning, Hector was regarding Arran with curiosity. "McWallop came for me," he said. "A rare tear, he said you were in."

Arran did not acknowledge that he knew what Hector was thinking. Their meetings took place in the early evening—always. The very fact of their being here now indicated some emergency.

"I find myself in a difficult position. I need your help."

Hector bowed briefly. "Whatever I can do, I will do. You know that."

"Yes. And I thank you." Hector's loyalty had been tested before and shown worthy of trust. "I want you to go to Edinburgh, to my Charlotte

Square house. Mortimer and Theodora are probably in residence there. And Theodora's sister, the delectable, short-heeled Melony Pincham. There is information I want you to gather there.''

Half an hour later, seething, Arran strode into his bedchamber, tore off his coat, and threw it aside. ''Damn the girl.'' There had been no question of not telling Hector the truth. He'd opened and closed his mouth like a handsome blond fish cast upon a beach, before marching purposefully forth to find Mortimer.

''You shall pay for the trouble you have caused me, dear Grace,'' Arran said aloud.

He could simply have told her the truth the moment they met.

Why should he have? Calculating baggage. She had been quick enough to lay out her selfish plans. And she'd been more than quick to explore a *friendship* with him.

No, he'd been right to tell her nothing.

But now he wished he had been honest.

Damnation—he could *love* her. Why was he driven to feel deeply for women capable of wounding him?

It wasn't too late to go to the Mercers. But he was too unsettled, too angry. Gael and Robert needed no ill humor in their time of trouble. Tomorrow would be soon enough.

Fair Grace. How sweetly, painfully erotic she'd looked. Naked but for the foolish ruff, the paltry bird on a chain she always wore, and lace stockings as provocative as any an opera dancer might have chosen. All slender, pale woman's flesh. Swollen, rosy nipples and a small thatch of golden curls to hide what he had yet to take completely.

He would not beg forgiveness for his deception.

She would be the one to beg. He'd make sure of that.

Please God he'd have enough time.

His music was what he needed. Music and the oasis of quiet satisfaction it brought him. He could think there. Plan. Decide carefully how to deal with his dilemma.

Arran could not remember the last time he'd gone to the gallery in daylight. It was possible he could not work now, but he would try. The mood was everything and . . . he would try, dammit.

The only mishap on the way to the gallery was a near collision with a plump, pleasant-faced maid who apologized and showed no sign of recognition. Arran smiled and started up the final flight of stairs. He really had accomplished an admirable degree of anonymity in his own home.

He pushed open the gallery door and entered. By the end of the month he intended to send his latest arrangement for piano and violin to the very talented musician who had made certain that Arran's work was regularly, and anonymously, performed for admiring audiences.

The enthusiasm abroad for "Contemporary Anonymous" was gratifying and conveyed in unsigned missives from a certain Julius VonDerman.

Calum frequently pushed Arran to claim his work. Struan, too. Arran was less than interested in fame of the kind they thought he ought to seek.

The gallery wasn't empty.

Arran halted, his fists on his hips.

The impertinent, bothersome, *fascinating* chit stood with her back to him—painting.

Rising to his toes, Arran advanced on the small figure dressed in a voluminous *thing* that resembled a bed sheet gathered at the neck. She bowed over, keeping her nose close to the canvas. In her left hand was a wooden pallet, and in her right, a brush held aloft.

He had denied her permission to come here during the day.

"What do you think you are doing?"

"Oh!" She spun around and staggered back, almost knocking her precious painting from the easel she'd formed by stacking one of his priceless Aubusson chairs upon another!

"Oh, indeed," he growled, ducking his head and prowling forward until he towered over her. "Did I or did I not tell you that you are *not*, *ever*, to enter this room in the daytime?"

Grace stood up straight, hitched the frightful, graying, paint-splotched garment above her toes by the device of dragging fabric upward with an elbow, and glared at him. "I am not afraid of you, Niall whoever-you-may-be."

She soon would be. "The time has come for us to have a few honest words together," he told her.

Arran advanced.

Grace retreated.

"I have decided to tell you certain things." He reached for her wrist.

"Don't you dare touch me!" She dodged behind her painting. "I have given considerable thought to . . . to . . . Well, I've given it thought, that's all."

"Please don't avoid fully speaking your mind on my account." He felt—*murderous*. But on the other hand, he felt—*amorous* also. "Tell me, Grace. What is it exactly that you've given thought to?" Removing the foolish smock would take little effort.

"We shall not speak of it again."

"As you wish. But we shall know just the same. Am I correct?"

She blushed in that charming, rosy manner—the same blush that tinted her breasts, and belly, and thighs, when he kissed and stroked her.

"Dear little Grace. Dearest little imp. I told you what I would think every time I looked at you."

"Stop!"

"I cannot. I'm sorry, sweeting, but I am helpless

not to see right through that . . . *that*—'' he indicated the smock ''—and see your nipples, wet from my lips.''

''Go away.''

''I just arrived. I'm going to play.''

She raised her pointed chin. ''Play? But I thought you didn't care to do so in front of others.''

''You are exceedingly aggravating,'' he said. ''And exceedingly reckless. I advise you to be silent.''

''Gladly. Go ahead and play. Be my guest. I promise never to tell your employer that you secretly appropriate his instruments.''

Darting an arm around her waist, Arran drew her hard between his parted legs and brought his mouth to hers.

''No!'' She struggled and dealt him a blow with the fist that clutched the end of her brush. ''Stop it at once,'' she sputtered when he leaped away, rubbing his head.

''You invited me to play,'' he reminded her, delighting in her discomfort despite the sore lump on his head. ''Now you've changed your mind.''

''I thought you wanted to play the piano.''

''When I can play with you?'' This wasn't the time to torment her. ''Forgive me. Let us sit together.''

''No!''

''Why not?''

''I remember a former invitation to Sit With You, sir.''

Arran grinned. ''Ah, yes. Don't tell me you've decided you didn't enjoy that episode? I will not believe you if you do.''

''You, sir, are arrogant beyond words.''

''I am *sir* again? After all we have shared?''

''If you are going to play *the piano*, I shall leave. If you are not, I'll thank you to leave and allow me to paint.'' She indicated the canvas, this one different from the one she'd already shown him.

Dubiously Arran eyed a concoction of bold black and brown strokes alleviated only by a single gold slash. "Man with a sword?" he suggested.

Grace looked at the painting and shook her head.

"Man impaled on the sword of another?"

"No." Her marvelous blush deepened.

"It *is* a man?"

"Yes."

"A naked man?"

"Yes."

"Of course. You don't paint clothes." He schooled himself to concentrate. She cared excessively for this so-called art of hers, and it could do little harm to indulge her feelings. He indicated the spear of gold. "Explain this to me. I only want to learn."

"Certainly. Painters are always direct when dealing with their work. He is a man who has invited a lady to Sit With Him."

Understanding dawned slowly. Arran laughed. He clutched his sides and laughed as he hadn't laughed in far too long. And when he sputtered into choking silence, he found Grace glowering at him.

"I have been painted before," he told her. "But never in quite so—*intimate* a pose."

"Kindly leave me."

"I apologize." He was instantly serious. "It's just that you . . . that your paintings are so astonishingly *unexpected*."

"You find them humorous. I would prefer you to go away."

She would *prefer*? "I don't care for your tone, Grace."

"What you care for is of no interest. The other evening before I . . . before I . . ."

"Sat with me?" he finished for her.

"Quite." Her golden eyes flashed. "I intended to ask you some questions. I choose to do so now."

Her fire could become a most entertaining tool on

dark nights in the tumult of their marriage bed. "Grace, I have teased you enough. Now it's time for me to speak seriously with you."

"Do you know that they call the marquess the Savage of Stonehaven?"

He grew still. "I believe I've heard that title. Where did you hear it?"

"It is commonly used."

If he were honest, he'd admit that he'd heard it himself among the tenants. "Old wives' nonsense. Ignore it, please."

"They say he is mad. That he shouts and raves in the night. And they say that he is never seen by day. Is this all true?"

"No ! No, it is not all true." He did not shout and rave. "Grace—"

"He continues to refuse to see me."

"I want to talk to you about—"

"As soon as I see Calum again, I intend to ask him why he's failed to tell me all I need to know about the marquess."

Arran sighed. "I'm sure he's told you everything that could possibly—"

"The man was married!"

Arran dropped his hands to his sides. "Who told you that?" he asked softly.

"I cannot reveal my sources. There is altogether too much mystery here, and until it is all made open to me, I cannot be certain that I'll stay here. Not that the marquess shows any sign of wanting me to."

"Oh, he wants you to. You may be assured of that."

She spun away from him and paced. "How do you know?"

"Because I . . ." Now, he would tell her now. "Because I am . . . very close to him." Damn his cowardice.

"Don't think I have forgotten that fact," she said

sharply, stopping before him. "You should have explained all this to me. Including the fact that his wife disappeared one night—*after* he was heard shouting at her like a madman."

"He did *not* shout at her . . . No, he was angry, certainly, but not in the slightest mad."

"She slept in the room that is mine."

"Yes." He should have had her moved after all.

"And on that night she went to Revelation—where the marquess lives."

"Yes . . . I mean, I assume so."

"And she was never seen again!"

He was horribly afraid that he could guess the direction of this conversation.

"Did you know the marchioness was . . . increasing?"

Muscles in Arran's cheeks jerked. "I knew."

"But both the marchioness and her baby disappeared and were never seen again. And there is a secret room beneath the tower where the marquess lives."

"Yes, there is." He did not want to think about this, to remember this.

"It is believed that the marquess murdered his wife and unborn child and sealed them in that secret room. What do you have to say about that?"

Weakness assaulted his limbs. Arran closed his eyes and saw hazy specks of color dance behind his lids.

"You are a good man, Niall." Grace's fingers threaded between Arran's, and she brought his hands to her breast. "You did not know. My poor, dear friend. I have shocked you deeply, and for this I am so very sorry."

With a great effort, he looked at her again, looked down into her upturned face, into serious eyes the color of the latest amber earbobs reported missing from his long-dead mother's dressing table.

"Listen to me, Grace," he said, and cleared his throat. "We must speak honestly and quickly. There is no time to waste."

"No time, indeed." She clutched his hands tighter. "But I have worked everything out. First, I forgive you for thinking my paintings . . . unusual. After all, new ideas are sometimes difficult to assimilate. Second, forget what passed between us the other evening. We can be the best of friends and never think of that episode again. It was simply the result of our separate concerns becoming one in the most extraordinary, unusual manner."

Arran nodded slowly.

She expelled a long breath and continued, "The very first time I saw you, I knew there were certain things that drew us together. I couldn't have explained them clearly then, except to say that we were two people with a passion for an art. And that we were both forced to indulge that art in secret.

"Niall, you and I need to be *free*. Your anger and wildness—particularly toward me when I am your only friend—proves it. We *must* help one another."

Unbelievable. She had actually managed to completely romanticize the truth. "This is most illuminating," he said slowly.

"You agree with me. Good. Now, listen. It is possible the marquess will not send for me at all. That will mean that I must leave, but I cannot dream of doing so without offering to take you with me."

He was speechless.

"Say nothing. Let me talk. First things must be attended to first. We will give the situation a few more days. If his lordship continues to ignore my presence, I shall arrange to take Mama back to London, and if you wish, you shall come with me. I promise to make a place for you wherever we go. It is the least I can do for a like soul. Is that clear?"

"Clear?"

"Perfect. However, if I am summoned to the marquess, I shall go. Never let it be said that I am not brave, and in truth, I do desperately need the money a marriage to him would bring." She wrinkled her tip-tilted nose. "If a marriage takes place, I shall ask Father Struan to forgive me for hoping it is short-lived."

"A good notion."

"I'm glad you think so. I wish I could forget that I have become so calculating a woman." She lowered her lashes. "However, and this is of the utmost importance since my very life may depend on it, *you* must protect me against any bodily danger the marquess may represent."

"How—"

"By being ready, of course. I have it entirely worked out. If and when the marquess calls me to discuss our marriage—should a marriage be about to take place—*you* will position yourself where you can come to my aid. If he pounces upon me, that is."

"Pounces?"

"Yes, yes, I admit it's unlikely that a dying man confined to bed would be particularly adept at pouncing, but one never knows. It will be simple for you to be near him. So you are to crouch somewhere so that he cannot see you, and be present all the while I am with him. Of course, if the marriage takes place, we shall have to work out elaborate plans for my ongoing safety. You won't mind that, will you?"

"Why should I?"

"Naturally you won't. After all, we are to become the most faithful of companions." The smooth skin between her brows puckered. "And we will be able to make the best of what happened between us the other night? We won't let it stand between us?"

"I'm sure we won't."

"Wonderful. Then we have settled everything. I'll

be certain to send word to you if the marquess summons me.''

Those three hours of missed sleep were making themselves felt—or was he merely losing his mind? Marshaling a neutral tone, he asked, ''What exactly will you have me do if the summons comes?''

Grace regarded her painting once more. She closed one eye and reached to lengthen a stroke—the single gold stroke. ''You will conceal yourself behind the Savage's bed curtains.''

Chapter 10

Her talents, Melony Pincham decided, had definitely been ignored for far too long. Through the ajar door leading from Mortimer's dressing room into his wife's chamber, Melony listened to her sister and brother-in-law argue.

Poor Theodora. So obviously past her prime. So obviously and pathetically clinging to the faded shreds of her youth.

True, Hector McFie's news must have been a considerable shock to dear Mortimer and Theodora—but there was certainly no cause for panic.

Melony knew what needed to be done.

Melony's talents were about to become fully utilized.

"You were so certain there was no hurry," Theodora said. She turned this way and that before her dressing table glass in the tastefully blue and gold room she could never have furnished herself, and finally decided to spear a third diamond-encrusted comb into her too fussily dressed brown hair.

Mortimer's voice was lost to Melony, but whatever he said brought Theodora swinging around to face him, her thin cheeks flushing. "I certainly *do* blame you, Mortie. Roger's inheritance is at stake here. That—that *man's* holdings are our dear boy's one chance at the future he deserves."

"Arran's fortune is me own one chance at the life *I* deserve, don't y'know." This time Melony heard

161

him clearly. "And yours, of course, m'dear. Naturally I want Roger to have the best, and so he shall—after *we* have had the best. There's more than enough."

Melony smiled and wound one of Mortimer's white silk evening scarves about her neck. How like Mortimer and Theodora to make no mention of the fortune Mortimer's father left him and which had already been squandered. *She*, Melony, would be the one to have the very best out of all this. First she must play her hand with Mortimer and Theodora, and play it exactly right. *Then* she would be ready to play the other part she had in mind.

"What exactly are you primpin' for, m'dear?" Mortimer said. "I'd have thought your time better used preparing for tomorrow's journey."

Theodora ignored him. Bending before the glass to assess the flow of her large breasts from the too tight green dress she wore, she dabbed cologne into her cleavage and turned sideways to achieve another angle.

"We leave at dawn," Mortimer said in his familiar tetchy tone. "I hardly think your best and admirable feature will be particularly noted at Kirkcaldy."

In his youth, Mortimer had been a man to turn any female's head. Back then he'd given full rein to his penchant for untried girls. Many had run from that. Not Melony. She raised her chin. She and Mortimer had shared *entertaining* moments before her marriage to Pincham . . . whilst Mortimer had been courting Theodora. Melony used an end of the silk scarf to smother a laugh. She had always outshone silly Theodora.

Mortimer remained handsome, in a slightly blurred way. The drink had done its worst, Melony supposed. Dark blond hair was still thick upon his head, curling in a charming manner across his brow and at his nape, and his eyes were still a disconcertingly silver shade of gray. True, at forty his cheeks were not so lean and his full mouth had developed an even sulkier droop, but he was carnal to the core, and Melony was woman enough to appreciate his potential. Yes, Mortimer hadn't lost his power to excite.

If Theodora's breasts had not been overlarge, her figure would be regarded as relentlessly scrawny. Melony sniffed and ran her hands up over her hips and belly. She had a body no man would ignore. From *any* angle. And her hair was not *brown* but auburn, thick and heavy and shimmering with light. And her eyes were not *brown* but violet, exactly like the velvety flower, as so many gentlemen had told her. Marrying old Ediah Pincham had been a pity and a waste, but how was she to know he hadn't a fraction of the blunt he'd claimed to have when he offered for her? Well, that was over. Ediah was poisoning the roots of daisies in a Devonshire churchyard, and she was on her way to becoming a rich woman at last.

She put her eye to the crack for a better view and drew her mouth into a tight line. For all he disdained his boring wife, Mortimer was smiling at her now—leering more like—and plunging a hand into her bodice.

"Not *now!*" Theodora said, squealing. "I am quite distracted with all this fuss. You should not have been so leisurely in your dealing with the business of your cousin's possible marriage." But she only flapped ineffectually at Mortimer's hand, and when he lifted one obscenely huge breast into full view, Theodora leaned toward him, smiling with lustful anticipation.

Disgusting.

Word had it that foolish King George IV's latest mistress, Lady Conyngham's, most notable feature was what Polite Society delightedly called an "enormous balcony.'' No doubt if Theodora were present in the company of the king and his ''prime bit of stuff'' at any time during the royal visit to Edinburgh later in the year, there might be quite a competition for Outstanding Dairy Specimen.

''I was to have received word if there was any truth to Calum Innes's burblings at White's,'' Mortimer said. He now had Theodora's bodice pushed down over her stays, allowing him to play with the only thing that could possibly interest him about the woman. ''My source failed me. But since this supposed fiancée has been at Kirkcaldy more than a week and no wedding has been announced, I think we may assume that Arran has retired into his customary tiresome seclusion.''

''Such a handsome man,'' Theodora said to the top of Mortimer's head. Her lips parted and her eyes closed. ''Hurry, Mortie. I really do have such a lot to accomplish this evening.''

''Hurry?'' Mortimer asked indistinctly, backing her against the foot of the damask-draped bed. ''Why should we not take our time?''

''You know we cannot,'' Theodora said, giggling.

Melony heard loud suckling sounds and wrinkled her nose. Why did Mortimer not simply send Theodora away? There was serious business to discuss.

''How do you intend for us to proceed?'' Theodora said, panting. Mortimer pulled her skirts up about her waist.

''We shall arrive unannounced. It was brilliant of you to persuade Hector to spend the night and attend the Parsonbury estate auction tomorrow.'' He undid his trousers and let them fall about his ankles. ''We'll be at Kirkcaldy before Arran can be warned that we are coming. Spread your legs.''

''Really, Mortie,'' Theodora whined in her own special little-girl voice. ''You can be so crude.''

His response was to bend her over the foot of the

bed and plunge into her. "As crude as you want me to be, lovie. As crude as you are yourself. We know what we like."

Melony ground a hand between her legs. A burning ache leaped into her belly. She could see how Mortimer's slick rod withdrew, and thudded home again. Theodora cried out, hoisting herself until her body's weight lay on the bed, and she wrapped her legs around Mortimer's muscular hips.

Insupportable. Melony stifled her own gasp. She could not look away.

Mortimer's satisfied grunt mingled with another of Theodora's shrieks, and the whole sordid little performance was over. They parted and quickly replaced their clothing.

"Where are you going, m'dear?" Mortimer asked, tugging his waistcoat straight.

"I already accepted an invitation to a little gathering at Lady McGrath's. If I don't put in an appearance, tongues will wag. Better to let everything appear as usual, don't you think?"

"Much better." Mortimer helped Theodora arrange her breasts in her bodice once more and bent to kiss a nipple before tucking it away and murmuring, "Always a pleasure, lovie. Always has been."

"And always will be," Theodora said, smiling coyly. "Whilst I'm at the McGraths, I'll mention an unexpected visit to your Rossmara relative. That should silence any gossip."

"It should indeed."

They parted pleasantly, Theodora sweeping from the room with the satisfied pink face of a woman well serviced.

Melony heard Mortimer hum. He turned toward the dressing room, and she sank back behind hanging clothes.

The door opened, casting a slice of light from the bedroom across the dark, narrow space. Mortimer closed the door behind him and continued to hum as he passed through on his way to his own chamber.

"Come and find me," Melony crooned. "If you can."

"What the . . . !"

There was silence then. Silence and darkness.

"Guess who's here, Mortimer."

He made no sound, no movement, and Melony grinned. "We need to talk, my love."

"Then we must indeed do so," Mortimer said, and she heard how desire already thickened his voice. "Come out now."

"Find me."

"I fear it might take longer than I can wait—for our conversation."

"Try."

Clothes began to swing and Melony pushed herself into a corner, giggling. She dragged the square neck of her chemise lower. The chemise was all she wore over daring red silk drawers an admirer had brought from France.

"Where are you, you teasing little baggage?" Mortimer demanded. "Enough of this. Come out to me, now."

"Are you too tired for more chase?" she asked sweetly, and grinned at his curse. "Now, now. If you will disport yourself in full view with that cow you're married to, who can you blame but yourself if you're observed?"

"We were not in full view," Mortimer said, and he found Melony's shoulder. Yanking, he pulled her out and held her firmly whilst opening the door to his chamber.

"You always thrill me when you're violent," she told him, wetting her lips and laughing up into his flushed face. "I forgive you for wasting yourself on *her.* We will call it a small exercise to ready yourself for more taxing things."

A slow smile spread his full mouth. "What in God's name are you doing in my dressing room? *While* I'm with my wife? And *wearing* almost nothing?"

She tossed her head and reached up to remove pins from her hair.

Mortimer took advantage of the opportunity to cover her breasts and push them up inside their scanty lawn covering.

"Naughty," Melony said, letting her hair cascade down, but keeping her hands where they were. "Naughty but so nice." She rocked slowly from side to side, rubbing her nipples against his palms.

Mortimer's nostrils flared and, in a single motion, he ripped the chemise down to the waist.

"So naughty," Melony said, covering his hands on her swelling flesh. "And in far too much of a hurry. Silly Theodora had to leave. *I* want to stay and stay."

"I can't wait for you."

"Yes you can. I want you to. Waiting makes you better. We both know that. I like you strong, Mortimer, strong and *slow*. I know what we're going to do about your cousin."

His eyes shifted instantly from her breasts to her face. "That's no affair of yours."

"It certainly is. I have a plan that cannot fail."

For an instant he regarded her lips. Then he kissed her, bit her mouth until she moaned while he began undoing his trousers again.

Melony dragged her mouth away. "Listen." Her appetite could match Mortimer's and a dozen other men in any day. And she was growing bored with too few readily available candidates to draw upon. "Stonehaven is a recluse, am I correct?"

"Correct. I want to do what we did last time."

"Oh, we will." Her skin tingled and she shud-

dered at the thought. "Obviously this insipid thing
Calum Innes secured doesn't have the fire to draw
your cousin into bed. But, given time and necessity,
he'll get to it."

"I'll make sure he doesn't."

"*We'll* make sure he doesn't."

"I want you now."

"Patience. You'll last longer, and you'll like that."

"*You'll* like that."

She chuckled. "Oh, yes. You are going to compromise Lord Stonehaven's little virgin. And we
may be certain she is a virgin."

Melony felt Mortimer's fingers dig into her flesh
and she drew back her lips from her teeth. She'd
known that would secure his attention.

"Deflowering an innocent is a chore, I know, but
what better man to do it than one with your experience?"

"Go on," he said with a deep intensity that sent
Melony's blood thundering through her veins.
"How exactly am I to accomplish this?"

"With my help. We'll be at Kirkcaldy by late tomorrow afternoon. You will immediately show
yourself sympathetic toward this creature and offer
your help in all things. She has no father, I hear, no
male relative. Offer your services. *All* of your services."

Absently Mortimer massaged Melony's breasts
until she clutched at his shirt, dragging it undone,
pulling at his waistcoat until his chest with its gray-
flecked dark hair was bared.

"I think my cousin may rouse himself if he hears
that I am using my charm on his fiancée. And I've
no doubt that he'll hear. I've seen how that castle
moves about him like a smoothly oiled pistol. They
all listen for his whispered commands as if he were
some hidden, all-powerful god."

"The solution is obvious," she told him. "You

distract the female and make certain your cousin no longer considers her a suitable wife.''

Mortimer stared at her.

''He will not want a bride who has made a gift of her maidenhead to you.''

He smiled and ran his tongue over his lips. ''What if the girl doesn't cooperate? She could be determined to accomplish the match. After all, the rewards will be considerable.''

As if she were not considering those rewards above all else. ''I've thought of these things. I shall help you, Mortimer, my love. *I* shall befriend her. She will not question a short, *pleasant* outing to a place upon which we settle. You will be there. I am a very strong woman, remember. Between us we shall carry our task to its conclusion.'' She shuddered again. ''The thought is not without appeal. In fact, a most exciting interlude should be ours, don't you think?''

''Yes, I *do* think so.''

Melony rose to her toes and wrapped her arms around his neck. Gazing adoringly into his steel gray eyes, she contemplated her personal plan—to provide the dear, cuckolded marquess with solace. His fury at his betrayal should make him a willing recipient for the solace Melony understood best. Then she would have to see, but with good fortune she might find herself the new Marchioness of Stonehaven.

That was her goal.

She reached up and drew Mortimer's bottom lip between her teeth—and filled a hand with his heavy manhood.

Mortimer groaned, and broke free like a crazed animal. As always, his strength frightened and thrilled Melony. It thrilled her more.

''Long enough,'' he ground out. ''Over there.''

He hurried her to a divan strewn with satin pillows, turned her from him, and threw her over the seat. She heard his rasping breath and tried to push herself up.

A hard hand between her shoulder blades sent her facedown again.

"This is what you want, lovie. What I want."

She hated him calling her what he called Theodora. "Yes," she said. "What I want." He would pay for that mistake soon enough.

Fabric scraped over male skin.

"Scream, Melony. I like it when you scream."

He pulled up the chemise, ripped apart the fragile red silk drawers, and hammered his shaft into her.

Melony screamed.

Chapter 11

"Kitchens is no place for those who dinna belong here," Mrs. Moggach said. Ferociously wielding cutters, she labored over a large sugar cone atop a great, scrubbed wood table.

Making the staff puddings at which she "wasna a good hand," as Mairi put it, Grace decided. The housekeeper hadn't as much as greeted Grace when she'd emerged from what felt like miles of confusing, dark stone passages that led from the castle's upper reaches.

"Far too much comin' and goin' if ye ask me," Mrs. Moggach said, pushing away a wisp of gray hair with the back of a hand. "I'm all topsy-turvy. Nowheres near enough staff for all this extra work."

Grace would not mention that a household of this dimension should scarcely notice the arrival of two women, and a priest who evidently used to live here all the time. She would also hold her tongue rather than point out that a great deal more labor seemed to be expended on *staff* puddings than anything put before Grace or her mother. Father Struan had never eaten with them, and she assumed he preferred to take his meals with his ailing old brother.

"I've not enough staff for all this, I can tell ye." Mrs. Moggach's voice had a droning quality. "If ye're wantin' to do somethin' useful, ye can see to gettin' more bodies for me. Not that I suppose there's aught ye can do about anythin'."

171

"Good afternoon, Mrs. Moggach," Grace said firmly, and thought, *Grumpy*, with a good deal of satisfaction.

Grumpy grunted. "Too much t'do an' not enough hands."

A woman sitting before a roaring fire in the range had to be the cook. She drank tea noisily and rocked and appeared oblivious to Mrs. Moggach's monologue. Florence, the upstairs maid, sat opposite cook, chopping carrots into a bowl between her feet. Grace counted eight additional maids of various ages. Two applied jiggers to pastry rolled out with a glass pin by a third, cutting piecrusts and laying them in earthenware dishes. Three more maids grated, ground, and squeezed nutmeg, apples, and lemons, respectively.

"I came down to discuss the business of your instructions to Mairi—regarding those areas of the castle into which my mother and I are not supposed to go. Mairi seems unclear about your message." Grace stiffened her spine. The annoyance she felt must not show if she was to preserve what little authority she might have here.

"I've enough t'do without the added bother."

To Grace there appeared to be far more servants than could possibly be kept busy by the disgracefully lax standards at Kirkcaldy. The seventh and eighth maids, very young girls, carried dirty dishes and utensils into the scullery. In the doorway to another passageway lounged a footman swathed in a canvas apron. He polished a silver dish cover upon his braced knee and spoke through the doorway to someone Grace couldn't see. Through a window into the butler's pantry there was a clear view of Mr. Shanks poring over his books whilst another footman dusted crystal decanters and passed them to yet another to replace on shelves.

"Mrs. Moggach, I should appreciate your full attention." Inwardly Grace quaked. Her mother had insisted that she confront Mrs. Moggach, a task for which Grace felt completely unprepared. "Why would you send such messages to us?"

"For your own good," Mrs. Moggach muttered. "Wee upstart."

This woman felt quite secure in her position, which meant she knew something Grace did not know—maybe a great many things. "I'll pretend I didn't hear you say that. I should like an answer to my question, please."

"All o' her ladyship's things are to be left exactly where they are."

Grace dropped her hands to her sides.

"Not a thing's t'be touched."

"Her ladyship?" Grace screwed up her eyes.

"Aye. His lordship gave orders after she died. Shut her rooms, he said. Dinna move a thing—not ever. That's what he said."

"But—" *She* was *living* in those rooms.

"Amber necklace gone," Mrs. Moggach muttered. "And earbobs. And now there's her little ruby ring."

Grace realized her mouth was dry, and swallowed. "I have absolutely no idea what you're talking about." There wasn't and never had been any jewelry in the Delilah room.

Mrs. Moggach sniffed and raised pale gray eyes to Grace's. She wiped her large hands on a cloth and slapped it down in a wad. "I was an upstairs maid when she died," she said, and nodded toward one of the younger maids. "I started in the scullery. I've grown up in this great hoose. Her ladyship was verra fair. Tall and dark with black eyes and a laugh you could hear through many a room. Those days were different, I can tell ye. Back then this was a live place, not a dead one."

Grace swallowed again. "Times change. I'm sure the marquess mourned—"

"She was a great deal younger than him. She dinna deserve t'die so young. It's my job to make sure her things are kept the way she left them—the old marquess charged me wi' the job. And now there's her little treasures disappearin', and me mournin' for the lootin' o' her grave."

Grace could only stare.

"Someone's goin' into the Eve Tower and gettin' into her rooms. She chose them because she could see for miles. The whole of the road leading to Kirkcaldy. She liked to watch for visitors. Before a party or a ball, she'd dress early and stand up there like a wee girl on her birthday."

"Taking things from a room could hardly be termed 'looting a grave,' Mrs. Moggach." The *Eve* Tower? The road leading to Kirkcaldy? The Delilah room was in the west wing, with the Adam Tower separating it from Eve. And a grove of old spruce trees obscured any view of the approach to the castle.

Mrs. Moggach heaved a sigh that raised her impressive bosom inside the gray woolen dress she favored. "A tender heart, she had. When the old king died, she cried for days."

"But . . . but that was only two years ago!" The words were out before Grace could contain them, then she didn't care. "King George died in twenty."

"King George?" The name rang out as if the housekeeper sought to rid it from her lips forever. "I was speakin' o' the king over the water, o'course. Bonnie Charlie."

"But . . . but . . ." Grace looked around and found several pairs of eyes watching her with interest. "But Prince Charles died . . . He died in . . ."

"Eighty-eight," Mrs. Moggach said dolefully.

"In 1788," Grace echoed. "Your late mistress could not have died *that* long ago."

A few titters were hastily smothered.

"I was speakin' o' the present marquess's mother," Mrs. Moggach said haughtily. "Someone's makin' off with her precious things, and it's t'stop."

All hands stilled.

"Goin' through locked doors. Whoever heard the like o' it?"

Grace's heart thudded. "You cannot be suggesting that *we* are responsible for breaking into locked quarters?"

"They're not broken into. There's some as has a way o' gettin' in, though. And gettin' out wi'out anyone knowin' until it's too late."

"If nothing's to be touched, how do you know things are missing?"

Mrs. Moggach raised her chin and narrowed her eyes. "*I'm* to keep her ladyship's rooms dusted, that's how. It was a trust left me by her husband."

They were speaking about her so-called fiancé's parents. They were speaking of people who died long before Grace was born. She knew the answer to her next question. "Has the marquess—the current marquess been informed of the thefts?"

"He has indeed. Ye might o' charmed Mr. Innes, but he'd not risk keepin' anythin' from his lordship."

"And did his lordship give you leave to issue orders to my mother and myself?"

Mrs. Moggach smiled. Not a pretty sight. "Aye, in a way. Ye'd not have to ask that question if the marquess had welcomed ye. But he hasna. Young Calum Innes has overstepped himself, just as he did so many times when he was an upstarty laddie. What can ye expect from a man with his beginnings? He's tryin' to push the marquess into doin' what he doesna want. The marquess doesna want *ye,* lassie. And ye know as much, don't ye?"

"This is none of your—"

"He doesna. And ye and that mother o' yours—uppity madam—ye've decided ye'll not go away empty-handed. Aye, we know what ye're about."

"How dare you!"

"Och, I do dare." The woman threw down the sugar cutters and gathered up a toasting fork. "I've but one more thing t'say to ye. There was another who came to Kirkcaldy and found a way into those rooms. Don't ye forget it."

"Forget what?"

"We'll not speak more o' that."

"Tell me," Grace said, her anger overcoming dread.

Mrs. Moggach pointed the long, evilly pointed toasting fork at Grace. "Gladly. Isabel Dean got herself married to the marquess and then she crossed him."

"And?"

The fork came an inch closer. "No divorce has ever sullied the name of Rossmara. And *ye're* here, aren't ye?"

"Y-Yes."

"Well, then, we both know what happened, don't we?"

Niall was the only person she could talk to.

And he was the one person she absolutely must *not* talk to.

Grace ventured forth through the daunting vestibule and left the castle. Despite her efforts to be stealthy, the doors clanged shut with a bong that resembled a mighty, long-unused church bell.

Catching her breath in the cool air, she hesitated in the shadow of the castellated porch, then fled swiftly toward the back of the west wing. Keeping

close to the building, she didn't stop running until
she'd turned the corner and dashed past tall hedges
to a lawn that stretched to the edges of a lake.

What was she to do?

How could she have been so foolish as to agree to
Calum's proposition?

What was she to do?

Mama wasn't strong. Grace didn't dare to as much
as mention Mrs. Moggach's accusations—or her
threats. They had been threats, hadn't they?

The reed-fringed lake was large and glossy green
in the overcast late afternoon light. Willows, their
leaves still tightly budded, drooped silently into the
water, and on the far shore stood a white marble
pavilion flanked by white marble statues of
nymphs—kelpies, as Mairi had told Grace they were
called in Scotland.

There was simply too much to be confused about
here. Grace trailed to the water's edge and looked
down at her own reflection, wavering on the almost
still surface.

The truth was that there was one thing bothering
her more than any other—although there were certainly others that should be confronted first.

Niall.

Her reaction to him.

What had passed between them.

The fact that she . . . Grace plucked a reed and
swished it in the water. She had never been in love,
so how could she know that what she felt now, for
this man, was love?

Love.

Grace walked toward the willows. She felt something she had never felt before. She felt it for Niall.
It was a sweetly painful sensation. A tightness in her
throat. A lightness in her head. A tingling thrill that
climbed her spine . . . and curled in those nameless
places.

Love, or whatever caused her present condition, held such potential for ecstacy—and despair.

She hardly knew him. Grace picked up her pace. Then she began to march, pushing aside willow branches as she went. The problem was that she knew absolutely nothing about what was correct between a man and a woman. She'd been warned against the evils of spending time, alone, with a man to whom she was not married.

So that, then, was all of it—the underpinning of her dilemma. She, Grace Wren, a single woman, had *Spent Time* with a man to whom she was not married. And she had *Sat With Him!* Pausing, she closed her eyes, hunched her shoulders, and gave herself up to the delicious and obviously wicked shiver that darted over her skin.

Grace opened her eyes. What she had done, and allowed Niall to do, was wrong, and it was all her fault. Although she knew nothing of the particulars, she had been warned that it was a woman's task, a woman's responsibility, to ensure that no occasion for sin occurred. After all, it was a female who was the potential Vessel for Sin, the temptation for the male. Grace shuddered afresh. On the nights when she'd been with Niall, she had certainly proven a temptation for him.

There was too much she did not know. In particular, had she experienced *all* that could occur when a woman spent time alone with a man? Or was there more?

"Grace!" A male voice carried clearly in the stillness. "Grace! Wait!"

Hatless, Calum Innes caught up. His thick, dark hair fell over his forehead. He was handsome, but, and definitely not for the first time, Grace compared him to Niall and knew her preference was for the dashing tail at the nape and green eyes—and a smile that was at once charming and wicked.

"Are you well?" Calum asked.

She started. "Perfectly." It seemed that at Kirk-caldy she was frequently mistaken for an invalid.

"Florence came to me. She said Mrs. Moggach was less than helpful to you when you visited the kitchens."

Grace considered how to answer. "She said that?"

"Exactly."

"That and nothing more?"

"What else should she have said? Tell me, please. Florence is a good girl, but understandably, she would be cautious not to make her position difficult with the housekeeper."

"Mrs. Moggach was inhospitable, nothing more." She must not be seen as a complaining miss.

Calum leaned against the trunk of a willow. A striking figure indeed. "Would you tell me if there had been something more serious than inhospitality?"

Would she? "I . . ." Grace made up her mind. "Yes. Calum, I have a serious problem, and I scarcely know what to do about it. In fact, I have not the slightest idea about it at all," she told him in a rush.

Calum regarded her intently. "I shall be delighted to offer whatever advice I can. You appear disconcerted, Grace. Shall we walk whilst we talk? It might relax you." Bowing, he offered his arm, and when Grace took it, he strolled with her, leading her carefully around tree roots.

"You are very kind, Calum."

"Not at all."

"Oh, yes. Very kind."

"No more than I should be."

She should not have said she had a problem. "I am beginning to think Scotland the most beautiful place." True, but not at all what she had intended to say.

''Then we are agreed upon something very important.'' He grinned, and his face became young and animated. ''Now, share your dilemma.''

Grace lowered her lashes. ''You are not married?''

''No.''

''But you are experienced as a, er, man of the world?''

He stopped walking. ''What a very odd question for a girl to ask.''

''I am not a girl.''

''Excuse me. A *young lady*.''

''There are occasions when there is a female of mature years who is quite without sources of wisdom in some of the more . . . delicate areas. Apart from my mother, I have never had any female relatives—or friends—to turn to. And my mother's sensibilities are exceedingly delicate. Have you ever . . .'' She simply *had* to have answers. ''You are clearly a man of the world. Therefore you must have Sat with a woman. At least once.''

Calum raised one dark red brow.

''Oh, fie!'' Grace pulled her hand from his arm and turned her back. ''I am in need of advice, sir. Of information.''

''Do not distress yourself,'' he said gently. ''I know that you have had some . . . stressful experiences?''

''Most stressful. But you cannot possibly know about them. I mean—'' A pox on her silly careless tongue. ''I mean that I need guidance. I need information of a technical nature on what exactly passes between a man and a woman.''

''A man and a woman?''

''In . . . moments of *intimacy*.'' Her voice rose to a strangled squeak. ''I need to speak frankly with someone of experience who will tell me what I need to know.''

Calum didn't answer.

"It is so annoying to wonder about such things." She faced him again. "What exactly *does* a woman do when she's being a Vessel for Sin? And when she does it, what does she cause a man to do? In the most extreme instances? That is, when the situation is carried to its fullest extent?"

Grace didn't remember seeing a man blanch. Or grow red. Calum did both in turns. Then he clasped his hands behind his back and raised his face to the sky.

"You see," Grace said, touching his sleeve. "If I knew what one does, and if I've already done it, then I might be able to avoid doing it again . . . *if* I've ever done it before, that is." This was dangerous. "Which I probably haven't, of course. Only I should like to be certain because, unlike so many people, I believe it's good for a person, including a female person, to be as informed as possible on all things."

He coughed.

"Then there is the matter of love. Love is truly confusing, and I was wondering if you—"

"Are you religious?"

"I beg your pardon?"

"Religious," Calum repeated.

"God?"

He nodded and echoed, "God," sonorously.

"Absolutely! My father was a very pious man, and that did not always . . . Well, I do think one should practice one's faith with those closest, don't you? Rather than . . . Father was a good man, but not always an easy one." He was staring at her. "Yes, Calum. I am religious, and I find that fact a great comfort."

"Good. I have the perfect solution to this problem of yours."

"You do?"

"Definitely. A man of God is what you need. One practiced in listening to many of life's troubles—from the troubled. Come, we have a task for Father Struan."

Struan forbore to remind Calum that Arran was unlikely to be pleased if he discovered his private walled garden was being used as a confessional!

"There she is," Calum said, indicating a stone bench amid Arran's beloved rhododendron crescent.

"This is the very devil," Struan muttered.

"I fear she thinks she may be."

Struan stopped. "She thinks what?"

"That she may be the devil," Calum remarked without a trace of a smile. "Hence I steered her in your direction. You being the expert on such conditions."

Struan shook his head. He'd known Calum as long as he could remember—and liked him—but he'd always been an obscure fellow. "She's a charming-looking little thing. Quite unlike anyone I've ever known Arran's attention to be caught by."

"If one is to believe his allusions—and hers—they are quite caught by one another."

"Except that she doesn't know Arran is Arran," Struan pointed out.

"Niall is Arran, you mean."

Struan cast his eyes heavenward. "May the saints preserve us."

"I'll take help from anyone," Calum said.

"Have a care," Struan warned. "The saints can be quite contrary on occasion."

"So I'm told."

"Arran always preferred *dramatic*-looking women," Struan mused. "Miss Wren is, um, *ethereal*, wouldn't you say? Not that I've any experience in such matters."

"In this case I couldn't agree more. Ethereal. And engaging. That's why I chose her. I think she is *exactly* what Arran needs and what will bring him out of his damnable hiding."

"The golden brown eyes and pale hair are unusual." Struan kept his voice down, but Miss Wren appeared to be transported to another place, apparently one that caused her deep concern. "Arran's previous females have all been more, um, buxom?"

"Voluptuous."

Struan blew out a breath. "Whatever. This creature is small but perfect, wouldn't you say?"

"I would. When I first saw her, I wasn't sure. Subsequently I decided she'd have the kind of body that might drive Arran wonderfully mad. Appeal to his sense of beauty. Lithe. Slender. Her skin is so pale. And her breasts are . . . *pert.*"

Struan threaded his fingers together.

Calum gave every impression of being oblivious to his companion. "A man of Arran's strength and sensibilities would undoubtedly be driven quite *marvelously* mad in conquering her. She'd be a supple wand. One could easily imagine that naked she'd be . . ." Calum caught Struan's eye and ducked his head. "Ah. I forget myself, Father. Looking for a wife for your brother was a heavy task, one I took with great seriousness. I tried to see her through his eyes, and that is why I have analyzed her so thoroughly. Please be assured that I have no personal interest in the lady."

"I need no assurances of that nature from you. I know you too well. It is time you found your own wife, Calum."

"We both know that is unlikely to occur." The downward jerk of Calum's mouth told of bitterness. "We will not speak of it."

Not now, Struan thought. *But one day.* "As you

say. So I am to hear Miss Wren's little troubles."
Please God let him be equal to the task.

"Be patient," Calum whispered. "I believe I shall
leave you now. She'll be more comfortable with you
alone."

Before Struan could protest, Calum walked swiftly
away.

The little figure on the bench didn't stir until
Struan approached and stood directly before her.
Then she raised her face with its large, intelligent
eyes, its charmingly tilted nose and full mouth—and
she blushed. And leaped to her feet.

"Sit down," he told her, and she sank back, but
her spine remained board-straight. "You wanted to
see me? To talk to me?"

"Yes. I mean, no. I mean, probably not, but
Calum said you were exactly the man I should speak
to, so I agreed." Between parted lips, her teeth were
small and even and very white. "Calum said that
since I find religion—God—such a comfort, I should
most likely find talking to you about my dilemma
quite comforting, too. Because you are a man of
God."

Calum would hear more about this. "If I can help
you in any way, I will." Arran's manipulating best
friend had certainly chosen a lovely creature. The
girl's face held an innocence that twisted Struan's
heart. "Please don't look so troubled. There is very
little in this world that is worthy of deep regard.
Except honor and kindness—and loyalty and honesty and a simplicity of spirit. I'm certain you have
all these qualities in great measure."

An expression of purest misery filled her eyes.
Tears welled along her lower lids. "Those qualities
have always meant a great deal to me." She spoke
softly. "But I fear I have . . . compromised . . . all
of them in my desire to accomplish certain earthly
requirements."

Damn Arran for his thoughtlessness. "No, no, no." Struan hoped he sounded reassuring. "You could not possibly be guilty of any such thing." He also hoped for an early opportunity to give Calum and Arran his opinion of their behavior with this fragile creature.

"There are certain things I wish to ascertain in order to decide exactly what I have done—or not done. And then I must find a way to deal with *feelings* I have for someone. I have no knowledge of the intimate side of relationships between men and women."

Calum should *roast* for this. "There is no need for you to know such things."

"Oh, but I think there is. How can I decide if I have . . . I do not agree with the old-fashioned notions that a woman should be foolishly ignorant of matters concerning her bodily reactions."

He drew in a breath.

"To men."

He puffed up his cheeks.

"When they . . . *Sit Together.*"

Struan exhaled noisily. "*Sit* together?"

"I know you are shocked that I should speak of such matters, but who can I speak to if not to a priest? I am not a Catholic, but I appreciate that your vows cause you to be exposed to many confidences." She shook her head. "I should not at all care for that. Anyway, since you are a priest and the marquess's brother, Calum thought you would agree to enlighten me."

There were trials no man should suffer.

"I have experienced . . . *unsettling* sensations. Completely new sensations."

Struan regarded his boots.

"They are difficult to describe. Sort of—"

"No need at all to be precise," he said hastily.

"Of course not. I expect a man such as you has heard these things in detail many times."

Pistols at dawn would be too good for Calum.

"Are these sensations the usual sort of thing one should expect when with . . . ? Well, in truth, I've been having them all by myself. I expect that's unnatural?"

He used to be as good a shot as Calum. "Not at all unnatural. Not at all."

"Oh, what a relief." Her eyes brightened, only to cloud again. "However, that does not enlighten me in the other matter."

Men of the cloth did not duel.

"You are so patient with me." She smiled a little. "Could you please tell me exactly what happens?"

"What happens? In what regard?" As soon as he'd spoken, he guessed his sickening mistake.

"The entire thing. All of its . . . parts? You see, I think what I'm really wanting to find out is how I will know when I have experienced everything there *is* to experience."

God was merciful. Even a man of the cloth could commit a grave sin and be forgiven. For murder.

"Would it make it simpler if we considered the question in relation to a wedding night?" Grace asked. "It would seem so to me. That does appear to be the event that everyone considers . . . *eventful?*"

Through gathering gloom, Struan settled his gaze on the garden wall behind her head, on the espaliered cotoneaster, on the stones behind the shiny dark green leaves. Please let him find inspiration.

"Miss Wren—Grace, you are about to be married. Trust that your husband will make these things clear to you at the, ah, appropriate moment." *Trust a cad. Trust a heartless monster who deserved to be horsewhipped, and his best friend with him.*

Footsteps on the path behind made him look over

his shoulder. At the sight of Calum Innes, he pulled back his shoulders and glared.

Calum approached, passed Struan without a glance, and stood before Grace. He offered a hand and she took it, allowed him to help her to her feet.

"What is it?" She frowned, and Struan saw what she had seen, the stiff tension on Calum's face.

"Calum?"

Calum waved Struan to silence. "Everything is perfectly fine. We understand your Cuthbert relatives are presently arriving at Kirkcaldy." He aimed a level stare at Struan. "Perhaps you should entertain them awhile. The marquess wishes to meet Grace. *Now.*"

Chapter 12

"You're absolutely certain the marquess has asked to see me?''

''He was adamant.''

Adamant had never been a word Grace particularly cared for. It had an angry, authoritative sound. She walked reluctantly at Calum's side through the confusing twists and turns, the ups and downs and arounds, of Kirkcaldy.

''I thought his lordship lived in Revelation.''

''He does.''

''Then why didn't we go directly in through the door from the walled garden rather than take such a circuitous route?''

''That's the marquess's entrance.''

''He doesn't like anyone else to use it?''

''The marquess is an unusually private man.''

So private, he scarcely wanted to meet the woman he was supposedly to marry. ''Perhaps he intends to send me packing.''

''He doesn't intend any such thing.''

Where was Niall?

She hadn't seen him for two days. Would he be with the marquess? Oh, *please* let him be there.

Calum held her elbow as they descended a short flight of steps, crossed a small hall with plastered walls that rose several stories to a ceiling spanned with arches, and started up a gray stone wheel-stair.

Grace halted. ''Why should the marquess care

who uses his precious door when he never goes out?"

"He . . . That is a question you should ask the man himself."

Grace fervently wished she'd never, ever come here.

She allowed herself to be led, very slowly, onward. "Wh-What am I to call him?"

This time it was Calum who halted. His brow furrowed. "He is Arran Francis William Rossmara, Marquess of Stonehaven." He appeared uncertain. "Stonehaven would be the expected thing. He'll instruct you according to his preference."

The wheel-stair curled elegantly to a polished oak door at the top. A very solid oak door flanked by two portraits. When Calum saw Grace staring at them, he said, "Mary Queen of Scots," of the painting to the left, and "Prince James Stuart," of the other.

Grace said, "They look ill."

"They probably were."

"Living in castles can't be particularly healthy."

Calum checked his watch.

"Damp," Grace said. "Not good for the lungs."

"The marquess is waiting for you." Calum climbed the last two stairs and offered Grace his hand.

Grace crossed her arms.

"My papa always warned me against the evils of damp buildings. He said I wasn't strong. I needed warm, dry accommodations, that's what he said."

Calum crooked his fingers.

"I should have changed my gown," she said, indicating her spring green muslin over which she wore a dark green velvet spencer. "This is not at all suitable for evening wear."

"I doubt the marquess will notice."

Grace felt light-headed. "Is he also blind?"

"Also?"

"In addition to his other infirmities?" Her hands were cold, the palms clammy.

"He is not blind. He is also not patient."

Grace barely stopped herself from moaning. "He has . . . Surely someone is readily to hand at all times in case he needs something?" Her voice was suitably nonchalant, wasn't it?

"What his lordship wants, his lordship gets, I assure you."

She must sound offhand, innocent. "I expect he has a close *companion* to attend him?"

The expression in Calum's eyes changed, became even more unreadable. "His lordship wants *you* as his close companion, Grace. And he wants you at once."

Niall was the marquess's nearest and most trusted confidant. Naturally Niall knew Grace had been summoned. He would be in position exactly as she had instructed.

He had not seemed entirely delighted at her announcement that if she left Kirkcaldy, she hoped he would choose to go with her. In fact, he had not seemed delighted at all. He had said absolutely nothing definite on the subject.

Perhaps his sense of duty had required that he confess to meeting with Grace.

Perhaps the marquess was in a towering rage.

Perhaps Niall had been sent away!

Surely Father Struan's brother could not be a complete monster.

"Is the marquess at all like his brother?"

Calum was turning the heavy brass door handle.

"Father Struan is so nice. Very gentle and understanding. And helpful."

The door creaked open over dark wood floors worn to a satiny patina. The room beyond was large, the lighting low, and Grace had a fleeting impression of masculine opulence.

"The marquess is nothing like his brother," Calum said. "The bedchamber is beyond the far door."

Overwhelmed by dread, Grace stepped tentatively over the threshold and glanced at Calum. "I confess," she whispered, "that I am frightened."

He bowed his head. "I know. It's natural under the circumstances."

"What should I do?" She caught his hand and held on tightly. "I am in the most terrible pickle. Do you suppose—No, of course there is absolutely no truth to the silly stories about him eating people."

Calum laughed and patted her fingers. "He isn't easily roused to anger—or so he says, although I frequently take issue with him—but I should say that his bark is almost always worse than his bite."

"Oh!" Grace's hand flew to her mouth.

"Take heart, little one," Calum said, smiling at her. "Occasionally I am gifted with intuition. Call it second sight, perhaps. This evening I feel a premonition that his lordship will take one look at you and decide you are *exactly* suited to his taste."

"His *taste*?" Grace's throat constricted.

"Indeed. In fact, I think he will consider you positively *toothsome*."

Chuckling, he shut himself out—and Grace in. She covered her face with both hands. Her own gift for seeing what others apparently didn't see was particularly active tonight. She saw darkness and rage and a fearsome creature reaching for her with gnarled and bony fingers.

A level head could divert many a disaster. *Calm*, Grace told herself, *be calm*.

A fire crackled and spat in the white marble fireplace. The room felt different from other areas of the castle. It felt, Grace realized when she managed to make herself turn around, sumptuous and cared for.

A large carpet covered much of the floor. Its colors, dark red and green and gold, held the soft sheen of silk. A huge writing table with papers, ink, and pens scattered on its leather surface stood at an angle, and an Aubusson-tapestry-upholstered *fauteuil* was pushed back as if its owner had only recently sat in it to work.

Grace drew in a shaky breath. In the room beyond lay an ailing man, yet here everything was kept as if he might emerge at any time to resume the activities of his vigorous youth. The lords of Stonehaven had certain things in common with the ancient Egyptians. They liked to store worldly goods, untouched, in the tombs of their dead.

Blood drained so quickly to her feet that Grace swayed.

Widgeon.

Cork-brain.

Just because Grumpy ranted about grave-looting, there was no reason for Grace to become even more fanciful than usual.

Good grief, the marquess wasn't even dead.

Yet.

She must either run away into passages and stairways and dark rooms from which she would probably never find escape, or go to meet the marquess.

A tapestry covering most of one wall was in what Grace recognized as the *Chinoiserie* style. If life in China was at all like the chaotic, capering madness depicted by the Frenchman who had most likely designed the hanging, then Grace was grateful never to have been there.

Whenever she was alone in the passageways of Kirkcaldy—particularly at night—there was a shrill singing in the sounds that wound through chill air.

Such sounds might come from the open mouths of the pigtailed dervishes in the tapestry.

What could possibly be so terrible about a poor, bedridden old man?

Stiffening her spine, holding her head erect, Grace crossed the room and knocked on the door Calum had indicated.

It swung open beneath her hand.

Only firelight relieved the darkness beyond. The red-gold gleam rose and fell over the dim shapes of furnishings and glistened indistinctly on the heavy folds of drapes drawn about a massive four-post bed.

She could still flee.

Grace swallowed the purest terror she had ever felt and took several steps into the bedchamber.

Ninnies fled.

Immature misses fresh off the leading rein fled.

Women approaching advanced stages of spinsterhood held their ground and did what must be done.

"Good evening, your lordship. It's Grace Wren." Her knees wobbled under the weight of spent courage.

She heard a rustle from the bed.

"I do hope I'm not disturbing the rest you must so sorely need, but I understand you wish to speak with me."

Another rustle.

For the first time Grace felt a twinge of pity. The poor man must be too weak to make himself heard.

"Mr. Innes came to London and told me you have need of a . . ." How bizarre it all sounded spoken aloud. She had been selected as one might select a horse—according to the duties it was to fulfill. "I agreed to be what you need at this time." Now that she thought of it, she wasn't entirely certain what it was that the marquess was supposed to need.

Grace went to the bed and cleared her throat. "I

am going to open the curtains. If you prefer me not
to do so, please give me a sign.''

She was met with absolute silence.

Grace parted the draperies.

''Your lordship?'' She leaned over.

The bed was empty. Counterpane and sheets were
folded back, smooth pillows were stacked, and there
was no sign of the Marquess of Stonehaven.

Relief brought a giggle bubbling into her throat.
But where was he? Where could someone incapable
of walking possibly have gone?

''I did as you asked, Grace,'' a man's deep voice
said, very softly, and she clutched handfuls of the
bed drapes. ''Your hair is falling out of its prim chignon, my dear.''

Niall's voice.

She touched her hair, looking around. ''Where are
you?''

The drapes opposite parted. ''Here, of course, exactly as you instructed. Didn't you tell me to hide
behind the marquess's bed curtains?''

Any joy she might have felt at the sight of him
was extinguished by the cold glitter in his eyes.

''You did tell me to be here? To hide in case the
marquess fell upon you and did you violence?''

Grace nodded.

''All the frightful stories you heard—and believed—about him must have made it very difficult
for you to come here tonight.''

''I had no choice.'' Her voice cracked.

''Of course not. No choice if you wanted to reap
the bounty you're prepared to sell your body and
soul to gain.''

He did not sound himself at all. And she did not
understand what . . . Yes, she *did* understand what
he implied, but not why he was so angry. She had
been honest with him from their first meeting.

''His lordship wishes to speak to me.''

"Yes, he does."

"I expect he's decided the time has come to arrange the wedding." Why, oh why didn't Niall smile, or offer her some shred of comfort?

"And then you will get your price, lovely imp." He averted his face, and in the firelight, his profile was harsh, arrogantly masculine. "How I wish this were otherwise."

He regretted that she was promised to another. Grace's heart lifted. "I, too. But this is a matter of necessity. And convenience—and we must make the best of it. My feelings for you will not change."

"And what exactly are your feelings for me?"

Never, ever, must a lady allow a gentleman to know the full extent of his effect upon her, not if she wished to retain his esteem. Mama had told her that much. "I find that I anticipate each of our meetings with the deepest pleasure."

"I thought so. Yet you failed to keep our last appointment."

"You . . . *annoyed* me. You were arrogant and you ordered me to appear. And you left me . . . Well, I was not at all comfortable when you left."

He laughed shortly. "Not at all comfortable? What a quaint turn of phrase you do have. I left you unfulfilled, and women such as you demand fulfillment."

"You misunderstand. I do not care to be told what to do—not by someone who has no authority over me."

"And you decided to punish me? How predictable."

"No. Not at all. I was simply . . . It seemed advisable not to come until I fully understood certain things."

"Tell me about them."

She felt herself blush and blessed the gloom that would hide her pink cheeks. "I prefer not to. It would seem from your cross countenance this evening that you are angry with me. That saddens me, but I have learned in my life to accept disappointment.''

''How so?''

''How is of no importance, but I had noted your lack of enthusiasm at my suggestion that we appeared compatible enough to forge a long-standing friendship.''

''*Friendship!*'' He laughed aloud. ''How I love your little codes. The other evening you wanted to ensure that you could count on satisfactory service whenever you required it. That is the *friendship* you sought.''

''Kindly make yourself plain.'' Her lips trembled and she set them firmly together.

''Very well,'' he said, throwing the bed hangings wide apart. ''Since you insist on basic language. You anticipated that I would be delighted to offer up my body on demand—your demand.''

His words were like none she had heard before. ''You sound so strange.''

''Do I.'' He crammed the back of a hand against his mouth, and Grace noticed what she'd been too shocked to notice before: He wore a black silk robe open all the way to the sash that held it together at the waist. Black hair curled over his broad, muscular chest.

Grace looked quickly away.

''In truth, my dear, I shall be more than grateful to offer up that particular part of my body that most interests you. Even as we speak it is letting me know how ready it is to satisfy you this very instant. But I must teach it that in this, as in all things that concern you and me, it must always be my will, not yours, that is served. Do you understand what I am telling you?''

"You are not dressed," she said, not caring that her voice rose to a squeak.

"Of course not. A decrepit, ailing man rarely dresses for dinner, madam."

Her heart beat so loudly, she could scarcely hear her own thoughts. "I was summoned by the marquess. Where is he?"

"Ah, yes. Forgive me. In the heat of the moment I quite forgot myself. Everything and everyone should be exactly as expected."

Grace dared another peek at him. "You confuse me." Her hands stole to her lips. "What *are* you doing?"

Holding her gaze, he stripped off the robe and stood, legs braced apart, hands on hips.

He was naked.

She turned away. "Please cover yourself!"

"Certainly. But only if you look at me."

"I cannot possibly."

"You looked at me before."

Embarrassment made her dizzy. "That was . . . It was different."

"Not so calculated, you mean? Ah, me. Your act was very titillating and really almost convincing, but, my dear, your every move was *calculated*."

"I shall go now. Kindly tell the marquess I came as he requested. I'll speak with him when he's certain he's ready to do so."

"He's certain."

"Yes. Tell him that." She couldn't seem to make her feet move.

"The marquess is certain now. Let us begin our conversation, *fiancée*."

Grace squeezed her eyes shut, then opened them again. Cautiously she looked over her shoulder. He lay on the bed, on his side, his head propped on a palm.

"What are you talking about?" she asked him.

The white sheet was pulled up to his lean hips, but he hadn't bothered to entirely cover a solid flank—or that *other* part of him.

Grace's face blazed yet again. This time she could not look away. The stark white linen showed his gleaming, bronzed skin to advantage. The base of that *other* part of him sprang from a thicket as dark as all of his hair. The rest, that which the sheet concealed, *moved*.

"Oh, my," Grace murmured.

"Obviously what you see pleases you."

Her gaze shot to his face.

"I'm surprised you insisted on the nicety of modesty," he said.

The curl of his sensual lips, the narrowing of eyes turned glowing green by the fire, the sharp gleam of cheekbone and jaw, held her speechless.

"You suggested I might look forward to accompanying you to London—if things did not work out here. No doubt the prospect of grinding away in a conveniently bucking coach all the way to London brought you near to ecstatic madness. Come, let us consider how it would be."

He was confusing and frightening her.

"Enough of this, sir."

"*Sir* again. How very odd. You always call me sir when we are closest to falling upon one another."

"Kindly give the marquess my regards. I doubt if we shall meet now."

"We already have."

Grace stared into his eyes until they became blurred.

"Don't you understand *yet*? Are you too befuddled by the aching tips of your pretty breasts to *think*? Does the moist, demanding throb at your center completely addle your brain?"

"You—" She could not swallow. Her tongue was too dry to moisten the roof of her mouth. "No. You jest with me. And I don't understand everything you say, but I know you speak in a most ungentlemanly fashion.''

''A gentleman is a gentleman in the company of a lady, my sweet. You and I are on equal footing here—at least in the area of what is required to satisfy our animal lusts.''

Grace went to back away. Niall's free hand darted to grab her wrist and pull until she half-kneeled, half-sprawled across the bed.

''I am Arran Francis William Rossmara, sixth Marquess of Stonehaven.''

This could not be true. She shook her head. The things she had said to this man in the music gallery flooded back.

''Yes, it is true. And you, Grace Charlotte Wren, are my fiancée. You will become my wife on a day appointed by me.''

''No!'' He had made her a fool, or at least allowed her to make a fool of herself.

''No? Of course you will. You will have everything you want. Money, position, and a man who excites you to distraction. Come. Let us start what we intend to enjoy frequently.'' He began to draw her slowly over the mattress. ''The games are finished. The sooner the rutting begins, the sooner we can dispense with the main reason for which you were brought here.''

Grace struggled against him, and he held her where she was with her face only inches from his belly.

''You cannot be the marquess. He is old. He asked me to come and take care of his remaining earthly needs. Then I am to be free.''

''No one ever told you the marquess was old. You merely assumed as much because that was what you wanted to assume. But be glad, my dear one, you are to be saved so much bother. You need not skulk around dark passageways to find your pleasure, because I shall frequently be in your bed. And I shall quickly enlighten you on the subject of my remaining earthly needs." His laugh was bitter. "You shall tend them for as long as you amuse me."

"You told me you were Niall! You told me you were the marquess's closest companion."

"I have been called Niall—by some very dear friends. And I told you I knew the marquess better than any other. Perhaps I was not entirely straightforward, but can you blame me under the circumstances?"

"Yes, I can blame you. How dare you treat me so, sir!"

"I've decided you shall learn to call me Stonehaven. It denotes a certain familiarity, but not intimacy—not intimacy of spirit."

A lump formed in her throat. "You are cruel. You caused us to become . . . It was because of you that I thought we were friends, and now I discover you deceived me."

"No. You believed what you wanted to believe. Now, let us dispense with our business. I find I have developed a very pressing need. I doubt I shall have the will to ignore it again as I did the last time we were together."

"You speak nonsense."

He pulled her another inch over the bed. "You are not what I would have chosen in a wife had I had the time and the patience to make my own search."

"Let me go." She twisted, but he shifted his grip to hold her wrists against the bed.

"Calum could not have known what you intended to accomplish here. You and your parent thought you had planned well. Heartless, both of you. Heartless and greedy. Your pretty speech about wanting a husband who would consider you an

equal had a certain sweetness to it. Outrageous as
the suggestion was, I almost believed you."

"I *do* want that!" She struggled fiercely, and in
vain. "I *did* want it. I even thought that perhaps . . .
No. Now I have decided I want no husband at all.
Not ever. Men are beasts and unworthy of love."

"Love! Hah! Let us not speak of what does not
exist. Enough of this foolishness—although I do find
that the fire in you excites me." He moved rapidly,
scooping her up and depositing her on her back beside him. Evading her flailing hands, he went to
work unfastening the spencer. "You must be roast-
ing in this wretched, tight thing. Off with it at once."

"No! No!"

But he unhooked and rolled and slid and pulled
until the little jacket could be tossed aside. "Better,"
he said, assessing the brief, square-cut bodice of her
muslin gown with its long, tight sleeves and filmy
skirt. He pulled her hands above her head and anchored them to the mattress. "I think I should wait
a little after all. You want what I want, but I certainly don't intend you to get it an instant before I
decide you should."

He'd discarded the sheet and now he swung a
powerful leg over her hips and rose to sit over her,
his weight upon his heels. "You wear that cheap
little trinket all the time," he said of the long gold
chain with its enameled bluebird pendant. "But no
doubt you'll soon forget it in favor of the jewels you
expect to receive from me."

Staring straight up at the canopy above her head,
Grace tried not to think about the solid thing that
pressed against her most private parts. "The necklace was given to me by my grandmother when I
was a child. It is my most valued possession and I
shall wear it always."

"Touching." Trapping both of her hands in one
of his, he lifted the little bluebird. For an instant she

feared he might break the chain and throw it away
in disgust. Instead, he used the bird to trace her lips.

Grace jerked her head away.

"Mm. We shall probably share many interesting
hours in this bed, my sweet. And elsewhere—all
sorts of elsewheres. I expect you've already made
love in a coach, but—"

"I have *not*, sir!"

"Good. Then we must remedy that at my earliest
convenience." The bird was drawn in a fleeting line
along her jaw to her ear. Grace jumped, and Niall—
or Stonehaven or whoever he was—laughed.

"I want to get up."

"*I* don't want you to get up—yet. I'll tell you when
I do. In fact, that brings a quite interesting prospect
to mind. But I'm not ready."

The sharp edge of a tiny wing descended her neck
and toyed in the hollows above her collarbones.

Grace began to tingle. She screwed up her eyes
and willed her body not to react.

"Every bit of you is so delectably sensitive. I shall
do this to you in the coach." With that, the bird
slipped over the swell of her left breast and into her
décolletage. "As soon as we are on the road, I'll
draw down the shades and strip you. Then I shall
instruct John Coachman to drive very fast. And *you*,
my dear, shall sit where I sit now—astride *my* hips.
And the rest . . . ?" His smile was undisguised
evil.

She began to panic. *"Please!"*

"Patience. There is little that is not enhanced by
careful, slow execution. This bodice is a convenient
thing." To prove his point, he contrived to dip the
side of his hand inside and reveal her right breast.
"Perfect. Let us see how it likes this."

Grace squirmed, felt his hardness probe her
through flimsy fabric, and lay still. He used the gold
bird in a way she had never thought of it being used

before. Cool metal drew the full, pink circle around
her nipple.

"Oh!" Breath caught in her throat. She shuddered. "Oh, *please*."

"Yes, yes." The next circle was smaller, and the
next, until, finally, he rubbed the very tip of her nipple. "Yes, Grace. I like watching you. I like it very
much. Your body doesn't lie, and honesty is something I like very much. Such an eager bud. A ripe
berry. I also like ripe berries."

"My arms hurt." And her breasts ached in a way
that frightened her. She mustn't want him to continue, but she did, more than anything else.

Stonehaven let out a long sigh. "Then I must finish what I intend to do."

The next thing Grace felt was his teeth closing on
her puckered nipple. He nipped and suckled—gently
but insistently—then pulled harder with his lips
while his tongue swirled.

She would not let this happen. Grace bucked
against him. "Stop it! Stop it now. Let me up."

He released her arms so abruptly, she forgot to
move.

"You're angry," he said, still sitting astride her
hips. "And embarrassed. Just as you should be.
Your duplicity shames you. Listen and listen well."

When she tried to avert her face, he turned her
chin and held her where she could only look back
at him.

"Within days we shall be married."

"Never."

"Pretty. Very pretty. Your maidenly objection is
noted and given the consideration it deserves. As
soon as we are married, we will set about the primary business for which you were brought here. In
fact, the *only* business for which you were brought
here."

"I will do nothing for you. You do not need a nurse, sir."

He showed his strong teeth in what was more snarl than smile and reached above her head into a pocket in the bed hangings. "Things are not entirely as you had planned. Unfortunate, but there it is. Sometimes we must adjust and make the best of what we *can* accomplish. I do not need a nurse, but I will pay you as handsomely as you anticipated being paid for that service. Here." Onto her breasts, he dropped a cascade of rubies—rubies and diamonds set in intricate patterns of gold and forming a girdle. "This should make a fine down payment for the services you will render me."

Grace began to pant. "Take it! I don't want it. Please take it away."

Stonehaven's face hardened. "Fate appears to have dealt me another blow." His eyes lost focus. "I knew someone else with your flair for drama. How ironic."

"I'm going to scream."

"Scream. No one will come. No one can hear you."

Her heart seemed to stop. Was the secret room immediately beneath this one? As she lay here, did the bones of another lay below?

"I find I have no appetite for what we had in mind," he said, moving off her and standing beside the bed. "Get up."

Shifting limbs grown cold and numb, Grace did as he commanded, sliding awkwardly around him to set her feet on the floor.

"Take the girdle with you," he said quietly, pressing the fabulous thing into her hands and holding them together. "It will look well about a small waist such as yours, although you will have to wait awhile to be able to wear it. First you will earn the right—as many times as it takes to satisfy me of my freedom from a certain untenable situation."

"I shall never marry you," she said in hardly more than a whisper. "You have played with me. And you have shamed me more deeply than any woman would countenance."

"You will recover. I know your heart and soul, Grace Wren—soon to be Marchioness of Stonehaven. You will not turn aside from all that I can provide you."

"Kindly give me my jacket."

"My pleasure. First, let us be clear about my expectations of you. Once they are discharged, then naturally you are free to pursue your *friendships* where you may. I ask only that you are discreet. I should not wish you to make our children aware of your other lovers until they are old enough to accept such things."

Grace felt her mouth drop open and was incapable of closing it.

"Why so surprised? Surely you did not suppose that all I wanted from you was what I can find with my mistress in Edinburgh. I assure you that she is more than capable of filling my needs—all except the one for which I require you. You will provide me with legitimate heirs."

"Heirs? Children? You dare to suggest that you and I should become *parents* together?"

"I not only suggest, I *order* it." He released her hands and swept up the green spencer. "And I have no doubt we shall take our pleasure in the process."

"I find no pleasure in you."

"Liar," he said, and pulled her bodice over her breasts. "Take your bounty. You will earn it easily enough—*pleasantly* enough. I will not pretend that I do not intend to make you want me as you have never wanted. In time you will beg me not to leave you. I will become the only drug your body craves. And then I shall watch you hunger for me in vain. You will pay for every penny of your prize.''

Grace hurled the priceless girdle at him and fled.

Chapter 13

Allegro's sure hoofs found the way as certainly in the near darkness as they did by day. Arran lifted his face to the soft evening sky and willed the peace of the land to calm him.

He'd passed beyond the castle walls and through the tiny village of Kirkcaldy. With the reins loosely held in one hand, he all but slumped in the saddle and allowed his mount's rhythm to sway him.

Peace.

Simplicity.

He had to find a way to purge himself of the anger and disgust he felt—not only for the girl, but for himself. More for himself. She'd been offered a fabulous match and accepted. What right did he have to expect her to hold fine feelings for a man she'd never met? Unless she continued to refuse to marry him, Grace could bring him pleasure and provide the heir he must have. What more did he want? *Nothing.* He must curb his rage at her duplicity. Rage made him vulnerable, and he would never be vulnerable again. How complicated a life could be made by wealth—the more wealth, the more complicated.

In his pockets were small offerings wrapped in pretty paper. The Mercers would be amazed to see him. He'd never come to them other than in daylight. And he'd never approached them for anything but practical reasons—as a neighbor.

On the hill above the Mercers' cottage, Arran

pulled Allegro up and sat, looking down upon the simple dwellings below. The moon, a fragile wafer edged with silver, iced thatched roofs with a pale sheen. Dusky threads of smoke streaked from chimneys.

He should not use these people to fill his own emptiness.

If the Mercers had visitors, he would not intrude.

He touched his heels to Allegro's sides and moved slowly downhill until he could circle the Mercers' place. No sound of laughter or music came from inside.

Arran swung silently to the ground and left the horse some yards distant.

A yipping set up and two dogs tore past. Then all was silent again.

He would give the paltry gifts and leave. Nothing more.

At the cottage door he paused to ruffle his loosened hair. The rough garb of Niall felt as comfortable as the fine clothes the Marquess of Stonehaven wore.

Arran knocked and immediately called out, ''Robert! It's Niall and there's nothin' amiss.''

Instantly the stout wooden door was thrown open and Robert Mercer looked anxiously up into Arran's face. ''What's wrong, man? Are ye ailin'?''

''No, no.'' Arran clapped the other man on the shoulder. ''I've been busy and I'd promised a certain small treat, if ye remember.''

A slow smile spread over Robert's spare features. He pushed back his own fair hair and beckoned Arran inside the cottage.

Arran swept off his shapeless hat. ''Are ye sure I'm not intrudin'?''

''Och, no. My Gael'll be so glad t'see ye. She's not been out in—'' he grimaced before continuing

"—in far too long. It's not goin' too well with her, Niall," he finished in low tones.

Awkwardly Arran entered. He'd had no experience with the intimate domestic details his tenant husbands and wives shared with natural ease.

"She's not sleepin'," Robert said softly. "Just restin' with the little one."

Gael Mercer's long, loosely braided hair was the color of marigolds in the sun. With her back to Arran, she sat before the fire in a rocking chair fashioned from sturdy willow switches. Her head was bowed, and barely visible above her thin shoulder was the child's mass of soft, flaxen curls. Gael rocked and sang, rocked and sang, and Arran had to stop himself from singing, too.

He walked soundlessly across the brushed earth floor and stood on the edge of a mat woven from river reeds.

Firelight made a shimmering nimbus about the heads of mother and child. Arran recalled that the little girl's name was Kirsty and that her eyes were as dark a brown as her father's.

Gael Mercer was engrossed in her song. "Lassie wi' the yellow coatie, Will ye wed a moorland jockie?" She rocked. "I have mill and milk and plenty . . . And I give it all t'thee."

Arran had to go nearer.

"Lassie wi' the yellow coatie . . ." Her voice was high and sweet, like a Scottish harp. "But I want a wife like ye . . ." Arran's mother had sung the old song in much the same way.

He sang softly, "Haste ye lassie to my bosom," and met Gael Mercer's surprised blue eyes. She smiled and joined her clear soprano with his gentle baritone. "While the roses are in blossom, Time is precious, dinna lose them. Flowers will fade and so will ye."

Kirsty squirmed around, a thumb firmly in her

mouth, and promptly slid to the floor. She held tightly to a fistful of her mother's shawl, but watched Arran with no sign of fear on her innocent face.

"It's Niall," Robert said. "He's come t'see us awhile."

"And ye're more than welcome," Gael said, shyly bobbing her head. "I'll brew ye some tea."

"No," Arran said hastily. "I'll not stay but a moment. How are ye, Gael?"

"Well. Verra well, thank ye." Pink rose in her pale cheeks. Her swollen belly seemed a cruel burden for one so frail. "Robert takes good care o' me." Her smile was only for her husband, and what Arran saw in her eyes made his chest tighten. *Love.* Yes, despite his own failure to find it, there was love, and it was in this crude room.

"I've a little somethin' stronger than tea," Robert said eagerly. "Will ye take a dram?"

Arran shook his head. "No, but thank ye kindly. Do ye have all ye need, Gael?" He'd long ago learned not to say too much.

"More than enough." Again there was the trusting smile. Gael fluffed Kirsty's long, fine curls. "Robert sees to everythin'."

"I'd remembered these." He pulled the packages from his pockets and instantly realized his mistake. Thinking rapidly, he said, "The silly flowery paper was in the Christmas basket from the great hoose. Couldn't think what t'do with it till today."

"It's pretty," Gael said. "See the pretty paper, Kirsty."

Arran went to one knee and offered a parcel to the child. She looked up and waited for her mother's nod before taking and holding it in her hands.

Seconds passed and she only stared at Arran. "Open it," he instructed gently.

Kirsty studied him, then the gift.

She'd never been given a wrapped present before. Smiling, Arran nestled her two small hands in one of his palms and parted rose-sprigged paper. "It's soft," he said. He'd not known what to bring. The small, jointed bear had been in the nurseries, although he had no recollection of seeing it before. "Feel how soft it is against your face."

Slowly Kirsty turned her cheek and lowered it to the bear's wooly brown coat. "Soft," she said, and hunched her shoulders with delight.

"Och, Niall," Gael breathed. "God love ye. I dinna know where ye'd come by such a wondrous thing, but Kirsty'll care for it well."

Still on his knee and feeling like a clumsy youth, he pressed the other two gifts he carried into Gael's hands. "I've nothin' for ye, Robert," he said, laughing too loudly and getting to his feet. "It's only ladies I bring presents to."

"Aye, so I see," Robert said with mock gruffness. "Well, since it's *my* ladies ye're good to, I'll recover from my disappointment."

Gael sat in her chair again and parted delicate paper as if it would break. "Och, it canna be." Her voice faded to nothing. "Such fine lace as I never saw. Will ye look, Robert? Niall's brought me a collar of lace!" She promptly pulled it about the neck of her shapeless brown wool dress. "Did ye ever see anythin' so bonny?"

"It's verra fine," Robert said, drawing close. "But it'd not be near so fine if it weren't about your throat, Gael."

She sat still, and Arran saw tears glisten in her eyes. She swallowed and flapped a hand. "Away with ye, Robert Mercer, for the silver-tongued one ye are."

Arran would not let himself look away. He would carry this picture with him and remember it in the months ahead. If only Grace had been . . . He *could* have loved her. God, the moments of longing left their mark. A movement brought his attention back to the child. She cradled the bear like a baby and crooned meaningless words.

Gael caught his eye and put a finger to her lips before opening the last present. Her hands stilled atop its contents, and the bright color in her cheeks drained away.

He'd chosen unwisely. This gift had made her suspicious. Arran held his breath and prayed for another excuse, another explanation.

"Was it your mother's?" Gael asked, so low, Arran had to strain to hear.

Relief made him grin. "Yes," he said, and it was true. "And it was her mother's, too. It's very old."

"I always dreamed of owning a gold cross." She threaded the worn old chain through her fingers and lifted it until firelight glittered on the thin filigree cross. "I canna let ye give it t'me, Niall. I thank ye with all my heart, but ye must keep it for your own wife."

"I've another cross," he said, also telling the truth. "My mother would have wanted ye to have this one. She always said it brought her peace to touch it. You wear it, Gael. Touch it when ye're not feelin too brave. Tell her it's right, Robert."

Arran saw hesitation in Robert's eyes, and smiled reassuringly. "It's *right*, man," he repeated.

Robert took the chain and stood behind his wife to fasten it about her neck. "Aye, it's right," he said, placing a light kiss on the top of her head. "Niall wouldna have brought ye this if he didn't think he should. And we thank him, don't we?"

"Aye," Gael said, and wrapped an arm over her belly. She laughed. "The babbie's tellin' ye so, too. Will ve feel it, Niall?" she asked shyly.

"It's a good thing, Niall," Robert said. "The feeling o' a new life."

Before he could give in to his impulse to decline,

Arran spread a hand on Gael's stomach. He had to shut out the other memories, the memories of a woman who shrieked and cursed—cursed him for giving her the promise of a moment such as this.

"D'you feel it?" Gael peered up at him.

He became quite still. "Yes," he whispered, and brought his other hand to rest where, as sure as if he could see it, an infant turned and kicked in its mother's womb.

"That's my babbie," Robert said, his voice filled with possessive pride. "It's time ye'd a wife and some bairns o' your own, Niall. They'd be a comfort t'ye."

Reluctantly Arran stepped away. "Ye already married the prettiest and best lassie in the land," he told Robert. "There'd be no point in takin' second best."

Laughter, a few more innocent words, many more thank-yous, a promise to return, and Arran was once more alone in the night. He rode slowly toward Kirkcaldy, watching its shadowy bulk grow larger as he drew closer.

He was Arran Francis William Rossmara, Sixth Marquess of Stonehaven, lord of everything he could see and much that he could not.

He envied Robert Mercer.

Several hours later, as midnight drew near, Arran sat at his favorite piano in the music room.

Damn them.

Damn Mortimer Cuthbert and his bloodsucking clan. They had made him what he was—a desperate man driven to measures that sickened his soul.

The crashing notes he played brought his teeth grating together.

No. That was a piece he'd composed in anger and played in anger many times. He did not need more anger.

A woman's hair, smooth, glinting by candlelight. He stroked the keys, picked up the tempo, stroked them again.

Play out of joy, Arran. You haven't really forgotten how.

Hair the color of marigolds in the sun.

His left hand ran down the board.

Hair of silver, like clear springwater slipping over the many small falls in the river.

Rapidly the fingers of his right hand chased the left.

A waltz. A waltz to make silver hair fly like spun silk spraying wide on a summer's breeze.

Sunshine through gold-edged clouds.

Faster. Faster. Satin-slippered feet flying over deep green grass. Muslin skirts swinging, twisting about slender legs, then puffing up and falling to cover elegant ankles once more.

Softer. Softer. The incline of a pale neck. The gentle curve of sweet, full lips, the lowering of smoky lashes over amber eyes.

Around. Around. Hands outstretched . . . to him.

"Dance with me, Arran. Come, dance with me, Arran."

When his hands stilled, he felt his own smile, his own peaceful breathing. And the smile warmed the coldness inside.

He stood and pulled fresh sheets of paper before him atop the piano. As quickly as his hand would move—and it was not quick enough to keep up with the notes in his mind—he dashed the music down. He wrote, played more, and wrote again. Later, he forgot when he'd come into the gallery, and it no longer mattered.

At last—and amazingly in so short a time—it was done.

Bracing his hands, he wondered what to call the piece.

A vague ache had begun behind his eyes. He would sleep soon.

The door, crashing shut, jarred him to his toes. The fault of a draft, no doubt. He must make sure it was shut next time. For a moment he stared across the room. Then it came to him.

He massaged his temple, and at the top of his new music, he wrote, *Grace*.

Chapter 14

Grace ran as fast as she could toward her mother's rooms. There could be no question of remaining at Kirkcaldy a moment longer.

He thought her conniving.

He thought her wicked.

Her heart ached from the pain of knowing how he despised her. She'd tried to sleep for hours until she could no longer bear to stay there in the darkness. Every word he'd hurled at her played over and over in her head.

He'd thought she wanted to be bought, that she wanted beautiful jewels.

Niall, or *Stonehaven*, believed she would become his wife and bear his children after he'd hurt her more deeply than she could ever have imagined possible.

Mama's room was on the floor below Grace's and in the distant east wing. Tonight Grace's mind was too busy to allow her to hear the castle's strange singing noises.

She did hear the music Stonehaven had played. She'd gone to the gallery to retrieve her precious painting supplies, only to find that the reason for her misery sat between her and the window seat. When she'd released the handle and the door had slammed, she'd feared he would discover her, but he had not followed.

How could a man so cruel and deceitful play such beautiful music?

He was unfair! True, what she'd planned had not been entirely beyond reproach, but necessity had driven her, and she'd been honest with him from their first meeting.

His lordship felt affronted! His pride was bruised because, even while he'd encouraged her to care for him as Niall, she did *not* care for who he really was! Oh, *really*, it was all very confusing and horribly infuriating.

And he'd gone too far. She might not have learned the exact nature of everything that was supposed to happen between a man and a woman, but she knew well enough that Stonehaven's actions toward her in his chamber had been reprehensible.

She'd told him she would have none of him. Now she must find a way to escape this wretched place as quickly as possible.

In the corridor leading to Mama's Serpent Room, Grace slowed her pace and breathed deeply until she reached the door. Florence, whom Mama had somehow persuaded to become her maid, slept close by and should not be awakened. And it would not do at all to allow Mama to see how upset Grace was.

Saying a prayer that Mama would be reasonable, Grace tapped lightly and let herself in to the amazing reptilian creation her parent found delightful.

''Mama,'' Grace whispered urgently, slipping across the room to light a candle beside the bed. ''Mama, please wake up. It's me, Grace.''

In sleep, her mother's face was as smooth as a girl's. Her frilled nightcap and lace-trimmed white nightrail added to an air of innocence that seemed absurd for a woman slumbering in a bed encrusted with many-headed gilt lizards.

Grace touched a soft shoulder. ''Mama! You have to wake up now.''

"Mm?" Blanche Wren's eyes opened a fraction. "What are you shouting about, Grace? Do go to sleep, there's a good girl."

Bracing for a tirade, Grace grasped the bedcovers and yanked them down.

"Oh!"

Grace pressed a hand over her mother's mouth and whispered urgently, "Be quiet, Mama. Be quiet and listen to me carefully."

Mama mumbled and shoved Grace's hand away, but she kept her voice down. "It's the middle of the night, you ungrateful girl. You know how I suffer if I don't sleep long enough."

"You will not be sleeping until noon today," Grace said.

"I most certainly shall. Really, what would your dear papa say if he could see how you treat me? Nothing can be so important that it cannot wait until a civilized hour of the day."

"Please get up and dress."

"I shall do no such thing." With that Blanche struggled to pull her covers back in place.

Grace held them where they were. "You are to do as I tell you—please, Mama."

"Ooh, this is too much. I thought by now you'd be a marchioness and we'd be settled and confident of our position. Instead you behave like the feather-brained creature you are and cannot even manage to *see* your husband-to-be."

Sleepiness invariably made Mama difficult.

"I know you are unhappy, Grace," Mama said. "And I know you think you should be comforted. But *my* need for comfort is greater. I was left alone to raise a *daughter*. Something that should not happen to any delicate woman. A son would have been such a joy and a comfort, but—"

"We are leaving Kirkcaldy."

"Do not interrupt me."

"I am not marrying the marquess. We are packing immediately and leaving Kirkcaldy at the first sign of morning—which will be very soon."

Mama slowly hoisted herself to sit up. Her blue eyes opened wide and she leaned toward Grace. "I think I've been having a nightmare. I'm definitely not thinking quite properly. I thought you said we were leaving the castle."

"We are."

"I thought . . . No, we're not. What can you be thinking of?" She swung her feet over the edge of the bed. "And where exactly were you last evening when you should have been meeting your new relatives?"

"I have no new relatives."

"You most definitely do. They are Sir Mortimer Cuthbert and his wife, Lady Cuthbert. Her given name is Theodora and she is most impressive."

"These people are of no interest to me."

"Yes, they are," Blanche said, her voice rising. "They are the marquess's relatives. Sir Mortimer is his *only* cousin. And then there is a rather flashy creature called Mrs. Melony Pincham. She's a widow. I don't suppose she's really related to the marquess except that her sister is married to his cousin. She wears too many jewels and talks too much. And she expects everyone to listen to her but never to have to listen to anyone else herself. Most annoying."

Grace had the fleeting thought that this Mrs. Pincham had things in common with Mama.

"And there's Roger Cuthbert, a quiet boy of ten years. Nondescript really. He's the Cuthberts' son. And they are *all* of importance to us. You should have met them. They expected it."

Grace folded her wrapper tightly around her chilled body. "Did you send someone for me, Mama?"

"I . . . Well, I did not want to draw undue attention to your lack of social graces."

"I do not lack social graces."

"It was mentioned that your absence suggested as much."

"And what did you say, Mama?" Grace asked quietly.

"I . . . Nothing. I thought you were probably feeling a little indisposed and said as much."

"But a moment ago you told me these people were expecting me to appear."

"Did I?" Mama fiddled with the lace at her neck. "Well, perhaps they were, or perhaps they weren't. I really cannot be expected to remember everything under such circumstances."

"If you thought I was indisposed, why didn't you come to see for yourself?"

Mama straightened her back and looked haughtily upward at nothing in particular. "I found the Cuthberts most entertaining. Sir Mortimer is exceedingly charming and was at great pains to ensure that I knew he found *me* charming also."

"In other words, you were too busy and having too good a time to come to me." She held up a hand to halt Mama's denials. "Please, I understand. It is of no importance now. Come, I'll help you pack."

"We will *not* pack."

"We *will* pack."

"Grace Charlotte Wren! Kindly stop this nonsense."

"I have met the marquess."

"I promised the Cuthberts that they would meet you . . . Grace! You met him?"

How long would it take her to forget the occasion? "I did. Get dressed."

"*Tell* me about him. What did he say? When will the wedding take place? Did he *give* you anything? A token to seal the betrothal? Jewels? He should

have spoken with me, really, but I will forgive him.
Oh, Grace, do—''

''*Be quiet!* He is a man approximately in his thir-
ties. Some . . . Most would consider him exceedingly well favored. The man is wickedly handsome,
in fact. He said I was to do as he wished in all things,
and at all times. He said the wedding would take
place on a day he appointed. He gave me a ruby
and diamond girdle that would circle my waist and
hang to the hem of my gowns. There, is that what
you wished to know?''

Blanche clapped like a child. ''Oh, I *knew* everything would be perfect. The day, Grace. Tell me the
day. And where are the *jewels*, child?''

''I declined the offer of marriage and gave back
the jewels.''

''You . . .'' Mama's mouth hung slackly. ''How
can you tease me so when I have suffered so much?''

She could not bring herself to explain what had
brought her to this debacle. At least if she left without a word to anyone, she could assume the marquess would not ruin her by revealing what had
passed between them.

''Grace—''

''I do not care for him, Mama.''

''What does that matter? A girl doesn't make up
her own mind whom she shall marry and why. *I*
told Mr. Innes we accepted the marquess's offer. The
decision has been made.''

''You cannot force me to the altar. Believe me
when I say you must accept my decision.''

''Never!''

She took her mother's cold hands in hers. ''Mama,
you aren't listening to me. I have told his lordship
that I will not marry him.''

''Oh,'' Mama moaned. ''Oh, Ichabod, how have
I failed in raising your daughter? Grace, you did
keep the jewels, though?''

''No. I gave them back, just as I've told you.''
Admitting to throwing them wouldn't be the thing,
but Grace had relished that brief moment of tri-
umph.

Mama pulled her hands away. ''She gave them
back,'' she said, closing her eyes and squeezing two
tears down her cheeks. ''Never mind that we absolutely *have* to have money and we have to have it
now!'' Her eyes flew open, and the blazing light
there shocked Grace.

''We can return to London and—''

''We can *never* return to London, you little sapskull.''

While Grace looked on, Mama got to her feet and
began to pace. ''You know nothing. *Nothing.* All
those afternoons I spent with the ladies, and you
never, ever knew.''

''I knew you went to sew with your friends. And
play cards.''

''*Did* I? I did no such thing. I met with a certain
group of ladies, but we did not play cards, and if
you had ever noticed, *I* can scarcely sew a stitch! I
hate sewing. It *bores* me and it always did.''

''But—''

''We have to have money. A great deal of money.
It is only the promise of your brilliant match that has
kept disaster from our doors in the past few weeks.''

''Mama!''

''The man is wickedly handsome, you say. He wants
you to marry on his demand, you say. He gave you a
gift worth hundreds of thousands of pounds, you say.
And you declined. *And now you will go to him and beg
him to allow you to accept.*''

''I cannot.'' Grace's heart seemed determined to
jump from her chest. ''What is it? What is wrong?''

''Has the marquess accepted your refusal?''

''Yes . . . No. I mean, he is too arrogant to believe
that I will not have him.''

"Praise God!" Mama clasped her hands together and raised her eyes heavenward. "You will do as I say. First thing in the morning, greet the Cuthberts as I have promised them you will. Smile and do or say nothing to suggest there is anything amiss between you and the marquess."

"I cannot," Grace moaned.

"You have no choice." Mama stopped pacing and held Grace's shoulders. "As soon as he will agree to receive you, go to your *fiancé* and tell him you were bemused—overcome by his generosity and by the wonderful fortune that has come your way. Tell him he has only to appoint the day of the marriage and you will be forever grateful to prepare for the greatest event of your life."

Grace began to shake. "You don't understand. I *hate* him."

"Foolish, headstrong girl. You are not listening to me. Whether or not you hate him is of no importance. If you do not marry him, we are *finished*."

"That cannot be so."

"*Listen.* That man's money has to be ours. On the days when I *wasn't* sewing fine seams, I was engaged in another occupation, one which I will one day master. *I was gambling.*"

"Mama!"

"Do you know what pugilism is?"

"Mama!"

"Fighting. A most exciting sport, so I'm told, although I have never actually seen it. There is a fortune to be made betting on the matches, only, naturally, a lady cannot go where bets are taken. No matter, my friends and I made the acquaintance of a gentleman who was more than happy to place bets in our name—for a fee."

Grace felt sick.

"Unfortunately, I lost rather more bets than I won."

''I s-suppose that can happen. I don't see why it—''

''I spent almost every penny I had and then placed bets with money I did not have.''

''How could you do that?''

''You are such a ninny, Grace. Vowels, my child. Notes against money owed. Gentlemen issue them all the time. Why shouldn't a lady?''

''What does all this mean?''

''It means that there is a man in London, a very ruthless man, to whom I owe a vast amount of money. I was already deep in debt, but when I knew you were to make this marriage, I placed one last, outrageous wager and hoped to win enough to be free. I lost yet again. The promise of payment with handsome interest is the only reason everything we have wasn't taken from us.''

Grace pulled her hands from her mother's and sat on a little stool with dragon-footed legs.

''You will marry the marquess, Grace. If you do not, and if that man finds us—which he most certainly will—we shall end our days in a debtors' prison.''

Chapter 15

Their "understandable fatigue" had saved Grace the difficult task of facing the Cuthbert party that morning—and at luncheon. Now dinner was about to be served—in fact, it should have been served some time since—and her reprieve was over.

"Mortie! Really, you can be such a naughty boy." Lady Cuthbert delivered her husband a sound thwack to the shoulder with her closed fan. "What *can* you think of us, Miss Wren? Not concerned about punctuality? Hah!"

Sir Mortimer must once have been very dashing. He was still dashing—in a rather *dissolute* way, Grace thought. At this moment he was smiling lazily at his overwhelmingly cheerful wife.

"Look at him," Lady Cuthbert said to Grace whilst smoothing the skirts of her purple gros de Naples gown over skinny hips. An impressive diamond collar sparkled at her throat. "One wouldn't think a naughty thought ever formed behind that innocent-boy face, would one?" Lady Cuthbert's bosom was enormous, and a great deal of it showed above the scalloped neckline of her gown.

The corners of Grace's mouth twitched.

"Of course one wouldn't," Lady Cuthbert warbled. "But they do, Miss Wren, take it from me, they do. Mortie, you are to tell Miss Wren at once that punctuality in all things, particularly the serv-

ing of meals, is of the essence in the Cuthbert household. Our dinners are *never* late."

"Come, come," Sir Mortimer said. He winked at
Grace with the eye his wife could not see. "We cannot pretend that our little abode is as complicated to
run as Kirkcaldy, can we, Theodora? And, after all,
the castle staff wasn't expectin' to put on somethin'
grand tonight."

"You're much too generous, Sir Mortimer,"
Mama said. Dressed in bronze jaconet muslin, with
a bronze ostrich feather draped from crown to ear
through a cascade of fussy ringlets, she had been
twinkling and giggling, blushing and hanging on Sir
Mortimer's every word, from the moment she had
finally persuaded Grace to leave the seclusion of her
room and come down for dinner.

"Isn't he, Grace?" Mama poked Grace's ribs.
"Too generous? Haven't we been saying the servants need a good shaking? Haven't we been saying
it from the instant we arrived? At least this salon
appears to have been cleaned. An improvement, I
can tell you, Lady Cuthbert. Let us hope the dining
room has fared as well. *If* dinner is ever served. Not
at all a certainty. Tell them so, Grace."

Grace inclined her head and met the marvelous
violet eyes of Mrs. Melony Pincham, who instantly
offered a sweetly sympathetic smile. "You must be
a little overwhelmed, Miss Wren," she said. Her
voice was unexpectedly high. "Do not allow anyone
to intimidate you. Not ever. Remember, he who
takes the biggest chair may find himself on—"

"I think you mean, he who sits at the head of the
table may find himself at the foot, or some such
thing," Lady Cuthbert interrupted her sister. "Although what that has to do with anything, I fail to
see. Roger, please come and be introduced to Miss
Wren. It's time for you to go to the nursery."

The boy, tall for ten, fair-skinned, blond, and gray-

eyed like his father, came forward and executed a
creditably grown-up bow. "How do you do," he
said. Then he smiled, lighting those intelligent eyes,
and Grace decided he was not at all the nondescript
child Mama had described.

"How do you do, Roger. Are you not to eat with us?"

"I have already eaten, thank you," he said po-
litely.

"He came to meet you. And now it's time for
bed," his mama said.

The Cuthberts and Mrs. Pincham wished the boy
good night while Grace wandered about the red and
gold salon. She'd never seen the beautiful room. According to Mama, "that wonderful Mr. McWallop"
had instructed that this evening was to be festive
and selected this room and an adjoining dining room
for the occasion.

Grace did not feel festive.

She studied a portrait above a lavishly carved
marble chimney piece. A beautiful, dark-haired
young woman had been painted wearing a red ball
gown.

"Marvelous-looking gel, wasn't she?"

A masculine voice rumbling close to her ear made
Grace jump. She glanced up into Sir Mortimer's
face. "I was just thinking as much," she told him,
uncertain she liked his standing quite so close. "Do
you suppose this room was decorated to comple-
ment her dress?"

He breathed in noisily through his nose. "That's
dashed clever of you. Course it was. Can't think why
I never thought of it before meself. She was Arran's
mother. Damn handsome woman, too."

Arran.

"Stonehaven . . . not an intimacy of the spirit."

Grace swallowed and felt, as she'd felt so many
times since her mother's shocking revelation last

night, a turning about her heart that brought her near to tears. How could Mama have placed them in such an impossible pickle? Gambling, no less!

"They say Arran's like her," Sir Mortimer remarked. "Can't see it meself. What d'you say, Miss Wren?"

"Call me Grace," she said absently. She knew what she had to do. *Do it.* "There is certainly something similar about the eyes. And the hair." She must give no hint that all was not perfect between the Marquess of Stonehaven and his blushing bride-to-be.

Sir Mortimer guffawed. "The hair! Long and pretty, hey? Dash me if you don't have a subtle wit, Grace. Can't imagine why a fella doesn't keep up with the times meself. Pigtails went out with tricorns, don't you know. Someone ought to inform the marquess."

"I like . . ." She stopped. She did like Arran's hair. She liked it very much—too much—just as she liked everything else about him too much—except his cruel temper, his suspicion, his unreasonable pigheadedness, and his ability to make her think of nothing but him even as she wished she need never set eyes on him again. "The marquess is rather singular," she said faintly.

"Hah!" Sir Mortimer threw up his chin and laughed hugely. "Will you listen to the gel, Theodora? She's a gem. A jewel. What a perfect turn of phrase. Arran is *singular*, she says. Not dashed peculiar. Not a blackhearted recluse. Not—"

"Mortie," Lady Cuthbert said severely, and dropped open her fan.

"Oh, you know I think the world of that cousin of mine." Sir Mortimer gave Grace another wink. "No fun if a fella can't joke about his oldest and dearest friend and relative, eh, Grace?"

"No," she murmured, secretly thinking that he had barely begun to list Stonehaven's faults.

"Don't mind Mortimer," Mrs. Pincham said, slipping her arm through Grace's. "He's a *terrible* tease. We should be doing what we came to do, and I intend to make certain we start at once."

"And what was that?" Mama asked rudely.

"I think Mortimer should be the one to explain," Mrs. Pincham said. Her white gauze dress was striped with violet the exact shade of her eyes. Little bunches of violets confined white satin bows in the full auburn curls at each ear. Grace admired the charming picture the woman made.

"Where's Father Struan?" Mama asked suddenly. "Mr. McWallop said he'd be dining with us."

Lady Cuthbert cast up her eyes. "Who can possibly rely on such an impossible man? He's been throwing the family into fits since he was a difficult little boy."

"You didn't know Struan when he was a little boy, lovie," Sir Mortimer said.

Mrs. Pincham made an odd sound and said, "I expect Theodora means that he's seemed unconventional for as long as she's known him."

"Don't you presume to explain what I mean, Melly!" Lady Cuthbert's narrow face turned an unpleasant shade of red.

"Now, now, lovie." With yet another wink in Grace's direction, Sir Mortimer slid an arm around his wife's waist and hauled her against him. "Tired, aren't we? Overwrought, aren't we?"

"Addlepated, aren't we?" Mrs. Pincham murmured for Grace's ears only.

Grace tried not to grin. She failed.

"May I call you Grace? I should very much like you to call me Melony."

"Please," Grace said, warming to the other

woman, who did not appear much older than herself.

"I thought Mr. Innes was to dine with us," Mama said. Pouting, she sat alone at one end of a red damask couch. "And Mr. MacFie, so I was told."

"Calum Innes won't be here," Sir Mortimer said shortly. "He keeps out of my way. Just as well."

"Don't mind Mortimer," Melony said. "Calum rubs him the wrong way and—"

"Calum Innes is an upstart. They should have left him—"

"*Mortimer*," Lady Cuthbert said. "You do not care for Calum. We need not bore Grace with the details of old family quarrels."

"He's *not* a member of this family, although he'd—"

"*Yes*," Lady Cuthbert said, glaring. "We know. For goodness' sake, *where* is dinner?"

"Should have thought MacFie would have put in an appearance by now," Sir Mortimer said. "Useful chap, that. Best estate commissioner in the land, so they say."

"I saw him earlier," Lady Cuthbert said. "He sent his apologies. Problems at the dairy or some such thing. Said he wouldn't be able to be present."

"Shouldn't have thought he could do much about dairy problems at this time of night . . ."

How could she be standing here in this sumptuous room, making polite conversation with strangers, listening to their empty prattle, when her entire life was in ruins?

Grace had a wild notion to shout, *I don't care about any of you*, and rush away.

But she couldn't do that. She would probably never be able to do anything but stay in this castle she hated . . . with a man she hated . . . or wished she hated more.

Praise be that Stonehaven had made no attempt

to see her today. She'd made no attempt to see him—despite Mama's pleadings. And there was no danger of having to deal with him tonight. According to every source, the man never left his private quarters, so he wouldn't be at dinner.

"Speakin' for meself," Sir Mortimer said, approaching Grace on the balls of his feet, "I'm remarkably glad to have this time alone with you . . . and your charming mama."

Mama gave a fluttery giggle, which Grace determinedly ignored.

"Indeed," Lady Cuthbert said. "This is a very special time, my dear."

"A *family* time," added Sir Mortimer. "We're here to offer you our support. We want you . . . and your dear mama . . . to think of us as your nearest and dearest. I understand you have no relatives . . . ?" He let the question hang.

"Only distant ones with whom we have no connections," Grace said.

Sir Mortimer bent from the waist. "Quite. But now you *do* have relatives."

Melony squeezed Grace's arm and dropped a soft kiss on her cheek. "I am so happy, dear Grace. We always had one another, of course, but Theodora and I were still very much alone as children. We *know* how it is to be lonely and to long for a confidante. We are warmed to our hearts to know that we now count you a dear friend—and that you share our feelings."

Sir Mortimer extended a hand to Grace. "Come, my dear, I want to have a few private words with you—if your mama agrees."

"By all means," Mama said from the couch.

Grace allowed Cuthbert to fold her fingers into his palm and draw her a short way distant from the others.

"Permit me to say a few words that are to be be-

tween the two of us alone,'' he said in low, intimate
tones. ''Arran is an excessively uncomfortable . . .
He's not *warm*; I'm sure you agree?''

Be careful. ''He is private,'' Grace said. ''I'm sure
we can agree on that?''

''Indeed.'' He led her to a window alcove where,
to her slight alarm, Grace found the two of them to
be shielded from the rest of the company. ''It pleases
me deeply to discover that you are already so loyal
to my cousin. However, I don't think it would be
less than loyal for us to agree that he is not a happy
man?''

She lowered her lashes.

''Yes, well, I'll take that as an affirmative. Arran
is a quiet, withdrawn man. I sincerely hope that,
with you to help him, he will learn to embrace the
world of the living again.''

The living. Grace dug her fan sticks into her hand.
Would this man tell her about the dead marchioness?

''I do not know exactly how you came to meet
Arran.''

Grace said nothing.

''Not that it is my concern—or that it matters.
However, I cannot help wondering if you know him
well enough to embark on this marriage.''

She looked up into his gray eyes. Yes, he was still
a good-looking man, if a little the worse for too much
good food and drink.

''Grace . . . oh, my dear, you are such a gentle
soul. I feel that.''

To her amazement, he caught her chin between
finger and thumb and placed a slow kiss on her
brow.

Before she could pull away, he released her and
held her arms. ''That was a mark of affection, dear
little girl. And a mark of my concern for you. Please,

if there is anything I can do to help you in the days ahead, *come* to me. Promise me you will.''

She couldn't think of an answer.

"How overwhelming this must be for you. All this. Tell me you will count me your nearest and dearest friend in times of great stress . . . possibly great *danger*.''

Grace felt her face pale. Danger here. Danger in London. There was nowhere to turn, yet she could not leave this place, where there was at least a chance for financial security.

Dimly she heard the rustle of fine fabrics in the room—and noticed the women had stopped talking. They must be straining to hear what she and Sir Mortimer were saying.

"We should return to the others," she said. Her voice sounded shaky.

Sir Mortimer rubbed her bare arms. "And we will. Listen, Grace. Listen well. This is a desperate step, but I implore you not to enter this marriage in haste. Give yourself more time to be certain it's what you want. Put off the wedding, dear one.''

"Why—?" Grace stopped. A movement had caught her eye.

Another, taller figure loomed behind Sir Mortimer. "What a pretty little domestic scene. Come, my dear, allow me to escort you in to dinner.''

Stonehaven, magnificent in austerely cut black evening dress, brushed his cousin aside and took Grace's arm. He swept her into the middle of the room and on to the dining room without a sideways glance at any of his guests.

Grace glanced. The gathered company stood and sat in utter unmoving silence.

"You decided to put off your departure?" Stonehaven said, very low. "Your renouncement of me was quite convincing. What can have made you change your mind?''

"We have nothing to discuss."

"We have a great deal to discuss. I shall look forward to dealing with much of it later—when we are alone."

"We shall not be alone until I decide it is appropriate."

"When we're married, you mean? How very provincial of you."

"You are unkind, sir. You enjoy tormenting me."

"Nonsense," he said. "That gown is charming. Gray is unusual for one so young, but it becomes you."

"Thank you, my lord." The others were coming, but for the moment she remained alone with him.

"A ruby and diamond girdle would be a dazzling addition, don't you think? To the gray gown?"

She would not let him goad her further.

"Should I have a servant bring it to you?"

"I want *nothing* from you," she said under her breath.

Stonehaven laughed softly. *"Au contraire.* You want *everything* from me." His narrowed green eyes sent a thrill down her spine. "And you shall soon get exactly that."

Chapter 16

The girl had spirit.

Arran watched her covertly, this complicated creature who would become his wife. The gown was demure, and the more enticing because a pelerine of palest lavender silk covered Grace all the way from her charming neck to the neckline of her bodice.

Not beautiful, but the most unforgettable, the most distracting, woman he'd ever met. Tonight her hair was pulled smoothly back from her finely boned face and wound into a simple, braided chignon. A deceptively demure facade. *Fascinating.*

Grace spoke intimately with Mortimer, who sat on her other side and appeared captivated by her every word—none of which were audible to Arran.

Mortimer had been captivated by her throughout dinner, although he had managed to devour duck pâté with lemon jelly, salmon with lobster sauce, pigeon *en croûte*, chicken fricassee and sweetbreads, Florentine rabbits, and was now about to demolish a last mouthful of venison and black olives. The man had scarcely paused to allow servants to remove or place a dish throughout the meal.

Blanche Wren, who had met her introduction to Arran with avid delight, was clearly impressed by Theodora's pompous largess. Theodora pronounced such gems as "One must be ever vigilant in the management of servants," whilst Blanche's brow

235

puckered in concentration as if she were committing a timeless teaching to memory.

McWallop, in the company of Shanks, stood by, observing the conduct of the understeward, under-butler, and the minions who bore up admirably under the weight of great platters covered with gleaming silver.

He had not, Arran thought idly, missed such events as this piece of nonsense. Five years had passed since he'd last presided over his own table to entertain guests. The next few months would probably necessitate similar annoyances, but he would tolerate them whilst he must and set them aside as soon as possible.

"The venison is heavenly, my lord."

Unwillingly he turned his attention to Melony Pincham, who sat at his left. "I'm glad you approve."

"Is it from your own estates?"

"One hopes so." Where else would it come from?

She leaned forward and pressed his arm. "Silly me. Of course it does." She dropped her voice. "You must think me a hopeless widgeon, but I am always looking for ways to improve myself. Should you feel inclined to instruct me in matters of importance to you, I assure you I take instruction well."

A coy, downward flutter of her lashes, the discreet slipping of her fingers behind his wrist to his palm, alerted him. The comely widow was engaged in the first step of the most ancient game of all: prelude to seduction.

"I shall remember that." Mrs. Pincham was the embodiment of all he detested most in women, but she could prove diverting if the need for diversion arose. And she might have other minor uses also. A moment might arise when he'd be glad of a means to reinforce the fact that his heart had no part in his arrangement with Grace.

The double doors at the end of the dining room were thrown open, and Struan, dressed in his abominably shabby cleric's garb, strode in. "Evening, all." He favored the entire company with his damnable benevolent smile and nodded at Arran. "Forgive me, dear brother. Sorry to be late, but there was a small professional matter I needed to attend to."

"Do tell," Mrs. Pincham caroled. "Something frightfully wicked? I'm sure you have to listen to some quite dreadful things, Father. When people want to be forgiven, I mean."

"A man thought he was dying," Struan said simply. "One of the villagers. Heard I was here and wanted reassurance. Tends to be the good who feel they've something to confess. The wicked are too busy convincing themselves they're just. Actually, he wasn't dying, just in his cups and wishing he were already dead."

Blanche Wren giggled—stupid bitch. Theodora's sharp nose rose and turned disdainfully away from Struan. The rest of the company appeared uncomfortable—with the exception of Mortimer, damn his grasping hide. Mortimer was still assessing Grace as one might a piece of fruit ripened to perfection.

The evil bastard was almost drooling.

Time enough to deal with Mortimer. As far as the marriage was concerned, everything would be done with perfect decorum. No unseemly rush. Arran had overheard Mortimer's plea that Grace should delay the wedding. For an instant there'd been an impulse to rush her off to the nearest minister who could be *persuaded* to perform a ceremony without the usual waiting period.

Mortimer would be looking for any means to question the validity of the match and its issue.

There would be no such means.

Before Shanks could close the doors behind

Struan, Calum arrived, looking calm and unruffled—and elegant. "Evening, all. In time for the festivities, am I?"

"Upstart," Mortimer said, just loud enough for his closest neighbors to hear.

Arran fixed his cousin with an icy stare that didn't waver until the other man looked at his plate. "Sit down, Struan, and you, Calum. Eat something. We have business to accomplish here, and I don't have all night." He ignored his brother's reproachful frown, and Calum's knowing little smile. "This is an important occasion. But I'm sure everyone present knows that."

He was rewarded with the complete attention of all assembled—including Mortimer, whose high color took on a purplish tinge.

"Shanks, serve the champagne. I'm anxious to say what I came to say. Thank you all for coming, by the way."

A mumbled chorus rose and instantly faded.

Vultures.

Arran snapped his fingers, and McWallop came instantly to his side. "Here you are, your lordship." A shabby black velvet bag was placed at his right hand.

He waited until champagne glasses were filled before raising his own. "Shall we toast the future of the lords of Stonehaven?"

The slightest of pauses followed before Mortimer swept up his glass, said, "Here, here," and downed most of its contents. The rest offered a smattering of "Stonehaven," and "The future," and drank.

Arran spared a level look for Grace. She stared back, unblinking, her pretty mouth set. Spirited she might be, but he saw through her. She remained at Kirkcaldy because she expected to get everything she wanted from him, *everything*. Behind that intelligent, engaging face she was already scheming, plot-

ting how she would turn him into her slave. He
would not forget what she'd come to Kirkcaldy to
gain: a title, vast wealth, and widow's weeds . . .
and then the passionate enslavement of a man who
could satisfy her considerable sensual requirements.

Grace now knew widow's weeds were unlikely to
come readily to hand. But he was no fool; the girl
found pleasure with him, and he had no doubt that
she'd decided he could be brought to heel—her heel.

In their high-backed Jacobean chairs on either side
of him at the highly polished table, Arran's guests
waited expectantly.

Let them wait.

Switching his attention to flickering candles in
lofty golden candelabra, he drank of his own champagne.

"Now." He set down his glass and reached into
the velvet bag to withdraw a green silk pouch. From
inside he took a brooch. "I thought you might enjoy
this, Mrs. Wren. I understand you have quite an affection for such things."

He gave the gold dragon with one eye of sapphire
and one of ruby to McWallop, who carried it in two
hands to Blanche Wren and placed it beside her
plate.

Arran tried to shut out the squeals and shrieks
and exclamations that followed. He smiled benevo-
lently, all the while aware that Grace watched, not
her mother, but him. Eventually, while the company
still exclaimed over Blanche's treasure, he met
Grace's eyes.

Puzzled?

Accusing?

Perhaps . . . *fearful?*

Arran bowed discreetly and made certain his smile
held mockery. If only these tiresome games were
not necessary.

"You are too kind, my lord," Blanche cried.

"Think nothing of it." This eternal, bloody smile would shortly crack his face. "Only appropriate."

The neat fingernails of Grace's left hand drummed the table.

Arran rested his own right hand beside his plate.

"Isn't that Great-Aunt Maud's brooch?" Mortimer said, peering down the table.

"It *was* Great-Aunt Maud's." Arran's mother and Mortimer's had been sisters. An aunt, Maud Fenwick, had raised the two girls.

"Mother always admired that dragon. She'd hoped Auntie Maud would leave it to her."

Arran shifted his fingers closer to Grace's. "How disappointing for your mother."

Mortimer pursed his lips. "When your mother died, she felt she had reason to hope again."

Grace had stopped drumming.

"Life can be fraught with little disappointments."

"After all, your mother didn't have a daughter."

Another small shift and Arran's small finger came very close to Grace's. "Neither did yours, as I remember. Seems to me you were an only chick. My mother had two sons. She chose to leave the dragon to me. And now I choose to give it to my future mother-in-law," he said, growing bored and disgusted with his cousin's avarice.

"My mama's disappointment at not receivin' that dragon has known no bounds."

"Your dear mama's been dead for years."

His finger and Grace's touched. Arran waited, but she did not pull away.

"Not the point," Mortimer said, all petulant annoyance. "Some things should remain in a family. Theodora would have enjoyed that brooch, wouldn't you, my love?"

"For *God's* sake, Mortie!" Theodora's plummy voice rang out. "I don't give a damn about the wretched dragon. Do stop being a perfect ass, there's a good boy.''

By pure strength of will, Arran managed not to howl at the outrage and shock on Mortimer's face. Others were not as successful in hiding their mirth. Not for the first time, Theodora had shown herself to have some spirit and common sense.

''Dash it,'' Mortimer muttered. ''Worth a pretty penny, I can tell you.''

Arran's fingers stole over Grace's. He turned up her palm and held her hand. ''Let's dispense with the details.'' He reached into the black velvet bag once more and produced a handful of jewelry that caught the candlelight and sent flashing prisms in every direction. ''Second installment on our agreement,'' he said, dumping a ruby and diamond collar, bracelet, earbobs, and tiara into Grace's lap.

A collective ''oh'' went up.

Grace tried to withdraw her hand.

Arran held her tightly and extricated another fabulous bauble, this one from his pocket. ''My future bride is fond of pretty things,'' he said. ''This should seal our bargain.'' With that, he slid a ring onto her finger.

The light in Grace's eyes was like heated ice. When Arran released her, she wiped her palm on a napkin, never glancing at the twelve-carat cinnamon-colored diamond that glowed warmly from her hand.

''A diamond that matches your eyes, my dear.'' *And it is as hard as your heart.* ''You are now officially my fiancée.''

''Was that Great-Auntie—?''

''No,'' Arran told Mortimer shortly. ''The ring was *not* Great-Aunt Maud's. It is the Brown Beauty and it's been in the Rossmara family for generations. An ancestor of mine took it in trade for sparing a life.''

"Whose life?" Mortimer demanded. "Probably paid too much for it."

Arran favored his cousin with a disgusted glance. "It was taken in trade, I said."

"I meant the poor bastard who owned it. His life probably wasn't worth what that gem is. Thing's as big as a duck's egg. Must be worth—"

"It isn't," Arran said, beginning to lose his temper.

"Oh, yes," Mortimer said, undaunted. "Worth at least—"

"It isn't as big as a *duck's* egg," Arran said. "Try a hummingbird. Grace and I will be married on Saturday four weeks from tomorrow. The wedding will take place in the castle chapel."

Blanche Wren scrambled from her chair like an excited girl and rushed to Grace's side. "Oh, my darling child, such exquisite things." She scooped rubies and diamonds from her daughter's lap and held them aloft. "My little Grace. I always knew she was a gem worthy of gems." The idiotic creature tittered at her own small joke.

"You cannot be serious, Arran!" Theodora's voice pealed through the room. "You cannot *possibly* intend to marry in *four* weeks."

"I can and I do," Arran said.

"The guest lists must be drawn up," Theodora persisted. "And the trousseau bought. And the wedding journey must be arranged."

"No need for guests."

"*Well.*" Theodora thrust her chin forward. "The idea. No guests. I can imagine the sort of rumors *that* will generate."

"Good. I sincerely hope those rumors will be justified in short order. It is my aim to produce several heirs in record time."

"We shall take poor Grace to Edinburgh," Theodora announced. When Arran started to speak, she spoke louder. "I will not take no for an answer. We will not, will we, Blanche dear?"

Blanche dear, an earbob held to the light between finger and thumb, shook her head vaguely.

"Blanche, I implore you," Theodora continued. "Men are such thoughtless creatures. If we do not insist, Arran will—"

"I'll send to Edinburgh for a modiste—a whole army of modistes. Everything shall be brought here, and Grace shall have whatever she wants." He tried to make her look at him, but her eyes were downcast in a fiery face.

"A girl deserves to enjoy this time." Theodora's voice took on a relentless tone. "She should be feted, Arran. Theater. Musicales. Salons. Balls—not that there are any *real* balls in Edinburgh at this time of year. But you must show her to Society or tongues will wag."

"Wagging tongues have never concerned me."

"Be that as it may," Theodora said icily. "*We* have family reputation to consider. Where do you intend to go for your wedding journey?"

"There will be no wedding journey."

"Arran." Struan, speaking suddenly from his place much farther down the table, silenced the rest. "Is this what Grace wants, too? Does she want a four-week imprisonment during which she is outfitted for . . . for what, one wonders? And then a marriage followed by . . . by what, one wonders?"

An awful tension followed. "Thank you, Struan," Arran said at last. Time enough later for words with his brother. For now he must keep matters smooth with his *family*. "Thank you for pointing out how thoughtless I can be. I am a selfish man when it comes to things I . . . things that are mine. If Grace would enjoy a short visit to Edinburgh, so be it."

When Grace said nothing, Mortimer slapped the table, causing glass and china to jiggle. "There you have it, then. Capital, Arran, capital. Know you can't stand the city. We'll take Grace under our wings, won't we, Theodora?''

"It will be our pleasure. The house in Charlotte Square will be perfect."

His house in Charlotte Square.

"We'll make certain Grace sees and is seen and—"

"You will take Grace to Charlotte Square," Arran said, cutting off Theodora's babbling. "She may purchase whatever she pleases. As much as she pleases. You may arrange whatever entertainment can be accomplished in one week. Then I shall expect her back at Kirkcaldy."

"He's in such a hurry," Blanche said, her smile beatific. "Is there anything so wonderful as true love?"

Arran stared at Grace's bowed head, at her smooth hair and the clear-cut bones of her face. Something odd stirred within him, a tightening of the gut, a long drawing in of breath he couldn't seem to release. His jaw clenched—and his fists where they lay on the table.

He felt . . . *possessive.*

The next sound he heard was a chair scraping. "I think we should call it a night." Calum's voice was different, harsh.

Arran ignored him. "Do you want to go to Edinburgh, Grace?"

Her lips trembled, then tightened into a line. She whispered something he couldn't make out.

Possessive? My God, he would not allow himself to crumble before another woman with Thespian skills.

"Grace," he said clearly. "Kindly answer me. Do you wish to go to Edinburgh?"

"Of course she does," Theodora announced.

"Naturally," Mortimer agreed.

"My little lamb always did enjoy entertainments," Blanche said. "And we'll all take great care of her for you."

Grace bent farther over the table until her face was obscured.

Arran was disquieted to feel his heart thud. Her hands were in her lap, and he covered them there. "Grace?"

She shook her head.

"You'll *love* it," Melony said. "We'll go *everywhere* and do *every*—"

"For the love of *God*," Calum shouted. "Are you all mad? Can't you see this is too much for her?"

Arran's head snapped up. He scanned the circle of faces. Blanche, greedily clutching jewels, Struan frowning, Calum glowering, the servants turned to see-nothing, hear-nothing stone—and the Cuthberts' avid concentration.

"Get out," Arran said, low, menacing. Then he roared, *"Get out, I tell you."*

Calum and Struan left at once, striding from the room side by side.

Tears, one, and two, fell on the back of Arran's hand in Grace's lap. Her shoulders began to shake.

"You may go to Edinburgh if you wish," Arran said. His heart turned completely and unpleasantly in a way he had never felt before. "Will that please you?"

"I don't know," she whispered.

"Out!" He swung his attention to the servants, and they smoothly departed.

Blanche placed the earbob on the table and poked Grace's arm. "You silly girl. Such a fuss. How could you shame me so?"

"Get out, I say." Arran directed the full force of his rage at Blanche Wren, then at the rest of them. *"All of you."*

Amid the swirling rustle of silk and satin skirts, the room cleared in moments.

"Thank you," Grace said softly.

Her neck was white and childishly vulnerable above the silken lavender pelerine. A single wisp of hair escaped into a curl at her nape. Arran had an overwhelming longing to touch it.

He must not. "Please don't cry. I'm sorry if I was unduly harsh." Females were given to fits of the vapors, particularly females skilled in manipulation of the male. "Please don't upset yourself further."

"No. You are kind. I knew you were."

This was not as he had planned for the evening to end. He had intended to make his announcements, then leave the company with no doubt that he was a man in control of himself and his destiny. "Would you like to go to Edinburgh? For the shopping and so on?"

Her shoulders rose. "I . . . I think I might."

"And then you will be satisfied to live quietly here?"

She looked up. Her lovely amber eyes glistened with tears. "As long as . . . Niall—*Arran,* as long as we can . . . I would not have married the marquess," she said in a rush. "I intended to tell you as much, but . . ."

He withdrew his hand, and where they'd touched hers, his fingers burned. "I *am* the marquess." What trick was this?

"I mean that when I thought the marquess was someone else . . . when I thought you were *Niall,* then I intended to tell you that I wanted you, not the marquess."

"Then why didn't you?"

"You were so angry. You are *always* so angry. Please listen to me. Please believe me. We did not meet under the best of circumstances, but I quickly learned that we *do* have an intimacy of spirit. The yearnings of my heart are the yearnings of yours. As soon as I allowed myself to think clearly, I knew it. That's when I decided that I could not marry some old marquess for the security he could give my mother and me, because I would never be happy with anyone but you.''

She lied. She lied to try to get what she wanted, everything she wanted—Kirkcaldy, a title, perpetual wealth and comfort . . . and the adoring attention of the man she desperately wanted to control with her body.

Isabel had seduced him into marriage with her charm, with her body.

Isabel had nearly destroyed his soul and ended his life—with her body.

''I wonder when you intended to reveal your enlightenment to me.'' He rose from the table.

''I told you. On the night when I almost changed my mind about coming, but did so anyway.''

''Ah, yes, the night of the ruff and the pretty stockings.''

''Please, my lord. Do not speak of—''

''The night when you wore nothing beneath your robe.''

''I told you I almost did not come, but—''

''You changed your mind? Yes, I remember. But I do not remember your attempting to declare your undying devotion to me.''

''I was confused!''

''Confused? Conveniently confused. I also cannot recall any announcement of your decision to refuse the decrepit old man you had agreed to marry—sight unseen.''

''You muddled me.''

''And the following evening, when you could have come to me again and revealed your true feelings, you stayed away.''

''You—''

''And when I sent word for you to come to me—

as the Marquess of Stonehaven—you did come. What have you to say about that?''

Slowly Grace stood up. She raised her chin and stared straight into his eyes. ''Why am I trying to convince you of something you don't wish to believe? You are exactly what they say you are: a *Savage!* You are without human feelings and wish to remain so. Very well, I give up. You are right. All I want from you is comfort and security.''

Arran crossed his arms. He did not like the tightening of muscles in his gut.

Picking up the black velvet bag, Grace scooped her newfound treasures inside and drew the string tight. She cradled the bounty in the crook of her arm and swept from the room.

Minutes passed and the stillness became unbearable. Arran caught up a decanter of brandy and a glass and trailed back into the salon to sit in a chair near the fire.

The spirits burned his throat—at first. Soon he felt nothing but the dulling warmth seeping through his veins. He studied his mother's portrait. His father had said of his wife that she was the best judge of character he'd ever met. If Elizabeth said a man or woman was true, well, then they were true. If she said otherwise, best steer for clearer waters.

Arran could use his mother's insight right now.

He filled his glass again, drank, and stared morosely into the fire.

It wasn't possible . . .

The girl had lied about her feelings for him. Hadn't she?

Chapter 17

*A*t *last.*
    At last she could go to him.

Too long had passed since they'd been together. An hour was too long; a day—any day when she could not hope to feel his wonderful, strong hands upon her—was too long.

Waiting drove her mad, and made her desperate for him—a condition that could only heighten their pleasure.

Praise God the staff at Kirkcaldy had grown increasingly fat and lazy. They watched nothing with interest except their own comfort. Leaving via the door beyond the meat and fish pantries—the route that brought her closest to her destination—without being seen, and slipping out into the kitchen garden, was accomplished with ease.

He would be so pleased to see her—to enjoy what she had planned for him, for *them.* She patted a pocket in her dark cloak where certain titillating trifles were stowed. First she would show him how they were best to be used, and then he would return the favor . . .

His legs were massively muscled and hard. Oh, yes, he was a *hard* man.

She raised her face and laughed.

Buttocks like iron that did not yield beneath her fingers. Thick hair upon his chest hiding flat nipples that leapt when she licked them. Shoulders so broad

that when he rocked over her, he shut out the light—
when there *was* light.

The night was black and warm—seething. Her
breasts tingled, and her belly—the place between her
thighs, and higher inside where he would reach with
his huge shaft.

She reached the brown gelding she'd managed to
take from the stables earlier and hide behind tall
boxwoods beyond the kitchen garden.

Her destination wouldn't take long to reach. The
gelding trotted amiably downhill toward a cluster of
buildings that lay to the west of the castle but still
inside its great wall.

The evening had been entertaining enough. And
satisfactory enough. Yes, he would be pleased to
hear that their plans were once more going as they
must.

Lights showed in the horse barn she sought, and
the sound of raised voices reached her. She frowned.
He'd said that if she could come, he'd be alone by
now. Dismounting, tossing the reins over the horse's
neck, she hurried to an open doorway and flattened
herself to the wall outside.

"Not there, man." The voice she heard was un-
mistakable. A voice filled with authority. The voice
of a man who always knew what he wanted and got
it . . . almost always. When what he wanted didn't
please her, he *didn't* get it. She smiled. Tonight they
both wanted the same thing.

"William! Distract the mare, damn you."

He was above her, in the loft where they'd met
several times before—but he was speaking to someone below, she could tell that.

Risking a peek into the building, she saw not one
man, but two wrestling with a small mare while a
third stood aside with a gray snorting stallion. The
business at hand took all of the men's attention. She

slipped inside the stone barn, moved swiftly to the staircase leading to the loft, and climbed silently up.

With his hands braced on a low wooden wall running the length of the building, he stared down, completely absorbed. "Damn it!" he shouted. "She'll do him mischief, kicking like that. Get a feed bag on her. Use your heads."

"Mayhap we should wait till the morrow," a voice called from below. "She'll not take anythin' as well bein' this skittish."

"She'll take him well enough." The laugh was strong, deep, and so sweetly familiar. "No different from a woman, laddies. Sometimes they need to be persuaded, but in the end they can hardly wait for more of the same."

A woman. He made the words sound impersonal, as if there were many women for him, and they all as one. Bravado. The strutting call of men to men. He would pay for that by some means she would devise.

"Psst." She stood at the top of the stairs, hidden from the floor of the barn, but not from the man who liked to give orders and watch them fulfilled. "Psst!"

His face turned sharply toward her. He narrowed his eyes and shook his head in dismissal.

He was dismissing *her?*

She almost laughed aloud.

"Go it again, laddies. He's ready for her."

A squirming dart of desire tugged deep inside, and she pressed the heel of a hand down her belly to her mound. The stallion was ready to mount the mare. Lucky little mare. *Poke your head into the feed bag and see what gets poked into you.* She'd seen it often enough, the rearing of sweating, muscled power.

Swallowing a moan, she slid to her knees. Never mind his damn rutting horses, *she* was ready.

"Come here," she whispered loudly.

A hand dropped to his side and he gestured sharply.

Leave? After waiting for this moment until her very skin hurt with need?

"Psst!"

The hand flicked again, and with the subtlest of motions he indicated the men below.

Did he think she was a green girl? A fool? Did he think she hadn't noticed that three men were trying to drag a stallion to mount a mare whilst he looked on?

On hands and knees, she crawled swiftly through loose straw until she was behind him and then sat, her cloak and skirts bundled about her.

With one finger, she tickled the inside of his right calf.

His breath drew in with a gasp.

"Send them away," she whispered.

He made fists at his sides. "William! Again, damn it. Tomorrow could be too late. If we miss her time, there'll be hell to pay."

"Help me take off my clothes."

"Calm her, Rory." He gave no sign of hearing her speak.

"I'll just have to undress myself." She undid her cloak and let it fall. Next she loosened the tapes that secured her bodice and eased it swiftly down, pulling her arms free and wriggling until she was naked to the waist. "Look. I promise you'll like what you see."

"Did ye say somethin', sir?" one of the men called.

His back flexed and he locked his knees. "I said, be careful."

"Oh, dear," she told him. "I'll speak more softly. Things went well tonight. Stonehaven's agreed to send that insipid little waif of his to Edinburgh. By the time we've finished with her, he won't be interested anymore."

He shifted closer to the wall and muttered, *"Not* now."

"Sir?"

"I said, *now!*"

She heard the stallion bellow and the mare's shriek.

"Damn it! Hold that mare, I say."

"Slipped away from the big, bad stallion again, did she?" Clasping his knees, she pulled herself forward between his parted legs. "I won't slip away from you, will I? I know what's good for me."

"For *God's* sake," he ground out, making to step away, but halting abruptly. *"Don't* do that."

"You like it," she hissed, keeping her hands where they were, supporting the weight that bulged and grew inside his tight breeches. "Don't pay me any mind, my love. Instruct your men and *I'll* instruct you."

Wriggling, she turned to sit with her back against the wall and her hips firmly wedged between his feet. "Mmm. Let me see what I can find."

"If he . . . if he starts to lose interest, use your . . . use your hands on him."

She could hear his harsh breathing. "Use my hands on him?" she murmured, and began undoing his breeches.

He swiped downward, searching for her wrists, but missed.

"I am an obedient creature. I'm going to use my hands." A few deft, practiced movements and she tugged until he stood, legs parted, manhood springing free—all but naked from waist to knee.

And she did use her hands.

"I think we'll get her this time," a voice shouted from below. "Mayhap if ye'd come down and lend a hand, sir?"

"Run down and lend a hand," she taunted him. "I'll come with you and help."

"The three of you can manage. Make haste. Finish it, now."

"I will," she whispered. "Give me . . . Oh, it isn't going to take very long at all." Running her palms along his groins, she weighted his ballocks and smiled when his thighs jerked.

"He's got her!" His voice broke.

"And I have you." Opening her mouth wide, she drew him in.

Darkness rushed over her, darkness tinged with red behind her closed lids. She felt his body shudder and heard the wild sounds of the mating animals . . . Using her lips, she sealed him close. Then he spent himself and all but sank on top of her.

For several minutes she rested her head against rough wood and stroked upward over his belly. The man was never less than almost ready, even now.

"Good enough," he said, his voice a hoarse croak. "Lock them in and go. I'll stay awhile."

"Are ye sure, sir?"

"Yes, damn it. *Go.*"

Languid warmth softened her body and ran in her veins. She sighed, looking up, waiting.

At last the barn door slammed shut.

With his hands on the railing, he leaned away until he could see her. The slightest arch of her back made certain he saw enough to make his juices run hot.

"Damn you," he said in tones she didn't like one bit. "I told you to stay away from me."

"You said you'd be here tonight."

"And that I'd be busy."

"You knew I would come to you. I always come to you when I can."

He clenched his teeth. "I have told you this should not continue."

"And I've told you *I'm* the one who decides about that."

"What the hell d'you think you're doing now?"

"Getting you ready to do a masterful plowing job," she said innocently. "It's been too long and I'm a very ready girl tonight."

"Girl? Hah!"

When he tried to wrench away, she grabbed his shaft in the squeezing fingers of one hand and held him tightly.

"Hell's teeth!"

"You may have *my* teeth, if you like. But first let us remember a few things. You and I are lovers. We've been lovers for a long and very satisfactory time."

"It wasn't my idea."

"No, it was mine. But you weren't hard to seduce, my love. I seem to remember that you followed me into that little cupboard at Kirkcaldy quite willingly."

"I thought you needed something."

"I did." With the end of her thumb, she flipped back and forth against the head of his manhood. "I needed you, and you very quickly obliged."

He panted and covered her hand. "You stripped naked. Right in front of me."

"And you spread my legs in an instant."

"That was then."

"And this is now. Spread my legs again. I want you to remind me of what it is I so admire about you."

With a rough moan, he took her shoulders and threw her to her back on the straw. Instantly he was upon her, pawing her breasts, sucking her rigid nipples into his mouth.

"That's right." She hissed through her teeth. Her skirts were already bunched about her hips. "Put it in me now. *Now!*"

In a single, mighty thrust he buried himself in her, and she wrapped her legs about his waist. Their coupling was savage. "I'm just like that woman you mentioned to your men," she panted against his ear. "I can hardly wait to get some more—and some more. The only difference is that I don't need to be persuaded."

Spent, he fell on her, breathing heavily, and rolled onto his back. "I don't want to do this anymore."

Rage swelled instantly. Her eyes stung, and her throat, but with fury, not tears. "You took a married woman, another man's wife. *Me*. I don't have to tell you what will happen if he learns you've cuckolded him."

"If we stay away from one another, he won't."

"If you stay away from me, *he will*. I'll tell him and I'll say you raped me."

For an instant he was silent, then he reared over her, eyes blazing like a crazed animal. "I never raped you."

"No," she said very softly. "*I* raped you—virtually. But he won't believe that. No, Hector McFie, you will do as I tell you, and keep on doing it, or I'll make sure you lose everything you've worked for."

He stared down at her for a long time before scooping her left breast into his big hand and slowly lowering his mouth. "As you say, Theodora. We are bound together, aren't we? Bound by what we both want most: power over others." He bit her nipple until she cried out in exquisite pain.

Chapter 18

"**M**ay I join you?"
"Oh!" Startled, Grace jumped and spun to see Mrs. Pincham climbing the last few steps to an alcove in the Eve Tower where a small window gave a view over the moonlit approach to the castle. "How did you find me?"

"Your maid," Mrs. Pincham said, joining Grace. "I've been looking for you ever since dinner."

"Mairi? She doesn't know where I am."

"Evidently the girl's very devoted to you. She was in the corridor below." In the subdued light from a sconce, the woman's eyes were turned blue-black. "Been following you for hours, so she says. Lucky I saw her. I told her I'd look after you and sent her to her bed."

"That was nice of you." Grace touched her cheek and felt moisture. "Really, Mrs. Pincham, I don't need company."

"I'm wounded. You must not like me at all."

"Of course I do."

"Then call me Melony. Only strangers call me Mrs. Pincham, and I'd hoped we were to be friends."

A friend would be wonderful, especially now when Grace felt so hopeless. "Melony. Yes. I'm sorry, I was preoccupied."

"Then we are friends?"

257

"That would please me." If anything could ever please her again.

"Tell me what's wrong," Melony said, her lovely face full of concern. "Why did you cry at dinner?"

"It was nothing." It was *everything*.

"Friends confide in one another."

Grace turned back to the window.

"Please." Melony put an arm around her. "Let me help you. I feel a great need in you, and I know that if you'll trust me, I can dispel whatever is making you unhappy."

Grace closed her eyes, and fresh tears coursed her cheeks. "Thank you, but I shall have to . . . In time I'll learn to deal with the things I cannot change."

"Oh, my dear." Melony folded Grace against her bosom and rocked her. "You have not spoken of your troubles to your mama?"

Grace jerked away. "No! She is too delicate."

"Hush. Hush." Melony pulled her gently back into an embrace. "You are such a sweet thing. Of course you want to shield your Mama. Do not be angry with me, but may I guess that Stonehaven is the cause of your distress?"

Grace said nothing.

"I thought so," Melony murmured. "Men. They are so necessary and so *difficult*. Is he cruel to—"

"I cannot speak of this." Her throat felt raw from holding back sobs.

"Then let me speak. Has he . . . Has he tried to . . ."

"Oh." Grace buried her face in Melony's sweetly scented shoulder and wept. "I . . . I'm sorry. It's just that I know *nothing*. Almost nothing. About how things are supposed to be between men and women. And I have no one to *ask*."

"Ask me," Melony said soothingly.

How could she ask? How could she explain all

that had transpired and try to describe the tumult of feelings she had for Stonehaven?

"*Ask* me, Grace," Melony urged.

"I *hate* him," Grace said, and began to tremble. "But, on the other hand, it's entirely possible that I *love* him."

"Just so."

"How can I possibly decide which when I don't understand what has already . . ." A great rush of emotion left Grace weak. She had to turn to someone. "A great deal has happened, and I don't understand any of it—*most* of it. Stonehaven and I . . . Well, we . . . Oh, dear."

"My darling friend. Will you let me be your best friend?"

Grace looked into Melony's sympathetic face. "Oh, yes, I would be very glad to."

Melony smoothed Grace's hair. "You have made me incredibly happy. We women only have each other to truly trust, and I need you as much as you need me."

"You do?"

"You'll never know how much. Come, let's go to your room, where we can be completely private. You shall tell me *everything*. Then I'll make certain things work out for the best."

Arran folded the music atop his writing table. He slid the sheets into a large envelope he'd already addressed, turned it over, melted some wax, and applied his seal. This piece was very short, a simple air for piano alone. After leaving the red salon, he'd gone to the gallery and worked into the night until the thing seemed complete. He'd returned to Revelation feeling an urgency to be rid of it. Let the chosen beneficiary of his efforts decide if the little offering was ready for performance.

Gallatin Plethero, Esquire.

Young, extraordinarily talented, extraordinarily ambitious. Arran had heard Plethero play for Prinny—before he became George IV—at Brighton Pavilion. The brilliant performance had been the only worthwhile moment in an otherwise grotesquely excessive night of revelry. Since that evening, more than ten years ago, Arran had sent his compositions to Plethero with the firm instruction that no one should ever know who wrote them. They were to be performed—if they pleased the musician—with a brief introduction explaining that the composer was unknown.

The brandy had dulled his anger—and his confusion—for far too short a time. Then the music had rushed in to distract him once more.

Now the music, like the brandy, was a memory, and there was nothing to divert his pondering.

Grace.

"Grace," he said aloud. "What are you? Who are you? Are you exactly what you appear or are you what I . . . ?" Could she be what he'd vaguely felt her to be when he'd watched her still face, those downcast eyes at the dining table?

Could she be a gentle girl with an artist's soul inside a body led astray by unruly passion?

He touched the back of his hand where her tears had fallen.

Arran got up from the writing table in his sitting room. The fire had been made up whilst he worked in the gallery. McWallop doubled as his valet and saw to all personal comforts. An unusual arrangement, but one that suited Arran's need for complete privacy. The fewer intruders into his world, the better. Anyway, McWallop had been with the family for years and he'd learned to anticipate his master's wishes almost before Arran thought of them himself.

Playing host to the Cuthberts and silly Blanche

Wren had exasperated him. If there hadn't been a need for some public record of his intention to marry Grace, he would never have suffered such nonsense. God, the servants had eyed him as if he were a phantom materialized at his own table by a devil's spell. Some of them really had never seen him before and must have believed the piffle about his having two heads, or whatever.

A kettle stood ready to be boiled on the hob for the green tea he'd learned to relish on the continent in '15. He'd been working behind the scenes, honing his skills as a diplomat for England as she formed an alliance with Austria, Prussia, and Russia. An Austrian princess with a liking for things from the East had introduced him to Japanese tea, drunk very late at night—between athletically strenuous sessions on her embroidered Chinese pillows. The tea, she had huskily informed him, was *most* restorative. And so it was. The princess had also liked rare eastern oils, sultry, aromatic oils that made her ample white body as slippery as a lithe, snowy seal—but much warmer.

Arran sat the kettle on the hob to boil and took the lid off the dark blue Sevres pot that was his favorite.

Princess Annalisse had been very athletic indeed. He recalled her intriguing ability to sit impaled upon him, her knees spread like a nicely plump frog, whilst she excited his belly with her oiled breasts and reached back to squeeze his ballocks at the same time.

The princess had been his last female adventure before Isabel, who, although not at all athletic, had made up in imagination for what she lacked in muscle.

But that had not been his reason for marrying her.

Straightening, Arran stared down into the leaping flames. He'd thought himself in love with Isabel, and her gift to him in return had been to teach him that love did not exist.

Little Miss Grace Wren was something entirely different again. She was an odd mixture of bone-deep sensuality and . . . and achingly naive simplicity.

She had the power to move him.

Steam began to rise from the kettle spout. Arran poured water over tea leaves but stopped with the pot only half-filled.

If she had the power to move him, and if he thought for an instant that her innocence was real, then how could he be so certain that she was nothing other than a conniving opportunist?

In the distant and ugly Delilah room she would be lying awake.

How did he know?

He *knew.*

Should he go to her—simply to talk? He could test her. Only in simple ways, such as to ascertain her fondness for children. And in so doing it might be possible to make a smoother path into this sham of a marriage.

Arran wanted to see her.

No. No, he would never allow himself to again become vulnerable to a woman.

What could it hurt to go to her?

He finished making the tea and paced across the room, waiting for the leaves to steep.

There could be more to marriage than passion. His mother had died young, but his father had frequently spoken of her as that which had made his spirit whole.

Had he made it too difficult for Grace to tell him she'd decided to abandon entering into a bogus marriage? Could it be that she did feel something for him?

The answers weren't really relevant, although if

she should carry any kindness toward him, the months ahead would be made the more pleasant.

Pleasant. Hell's teeth, he didn't want *pleasant*. He wanted heirs and he wanted a warm—no, a hot, willing partner in the making of those heirs.

"Damn it to *hell!*" Grabbing up the evening coat he'd tossed on a couch, he left the room.

Cursing under his breath, Arran made his way from Revelation through the warren of corridors and stairways that eventually took him to the wing he sought. Even if he were seen here, there could not be too much idle chatter since he was merely visiting his fiancée.

"Repeat what you said." He spoke aloud. "You *do* remember what you said? About having intended to tell me—when you thought I was Niall—that you would not marry the marquess after all?" Then he would ask the most important question of all: "Why had you decided to tell me that?"

And therein lay the solution to his dilemma. Should he try to trust her, or should he continue to take the safe route and merely use her?

At the corner that would take him to the Delilah room, he paused. He hadn't been here since the night . . . not since then. Isabel had insisted she wanted that particular room, even though it was so far distant from his. The arrangement had been devilish difficult, particularly since she had declared that she detested Revelation and could not possibly spend nights there. He'd made more journeys across the castle to this wing than he would ever be able to remember.

He did not wish to remember any of them, especially the last one.

Arran turned the corner and collided with a hurrying figure in violet-striped white muslin.

"Oh!" Melony Pincham pressed a hand over her

heart and clutched at him for support. "Oh, my lord! You have quite undone me."

An interesting prospect, Arran decided whilst considering why the tempting jade was abroad at this time of night and in this particular wing, where he knew she could not possibly be housed.

"Pray, forgive me, Mrs. Pincham. I did not hear you coming."

"Please call me Melony." Her auburn hair had slipped free of its pins to hang in luxurious abandon about her pale shoulders. "Mrs. Pincham sounds so very formal, and I don't think we are likely to remain so, do you?"

He raised his chin and looked down at her. "Possibly not."

"I know we shall not. My lord, I am glad we have made this unexpected encounter. I was just with Grace, and I left wondering how I should approach you."

"You were with Grace?"

"Yes indeed. I could not sleep and decided to walk about. My feet brought me here and I saw light beneath her door. I have frequently been told that I have an extraordinary ability to *know* when I am needed. That must be what led me to Grace tonight. But we should not speak here. If she were to hear us and know you were here, the awful stress of it might make her positively ill."

Arran made to go around her. "Grace is feeling ill? How so?"

"Stay," she told him, grabbing his hand. "She is not ill in that way, not ill in body. Please, come with me and we shall find somewhere private to talk."

"I shall go to her."

"That would be most unwise."

"Thank you for your concern. Now, if you will excuse me."

"If you go to Grace now, we shall all rue your decision."

Arran looked directly into the woman's large, glistening violet eyes. "What . . . Don't toy with me, madam. Make yourself plain."

Releasing his hand, she slipped back in the direction from which he'd come. Reluctantly Arran followed and saw her trip rapidly along until she turned another corner. By the time he'd followed that far, she was running up a staircase toward the Adam Tower.

"Mrs. Pincham," Arran whispered loudly. "Let us not continue this mystery."

He gained her side, but she did not halt until she reached a suite of rooms he remembered from the long-ago days of house parties at Kirkcaldy.

She looked in each direction before opening a door and beckoning for him to follow her inside. "Hush," she told him. "And call me Melony or I shall not speak to you at all." Her smile was pure coquette.

Straightening his cuffs, Arran advanced.

"There." She shut them inside a room decorated in shades of yellow in which the fire had burned low and where the light from guttering candles wavered over the walls. "We shall be completely private here." With a triumphant smile, she turned the key in the lock.

"What is all this about Grace?" He remained not far from the door.

"In good time. Kindly be at ease by the fire. Do you care for chocolate?"

"I detest chocolate."

"How unfortunate. There is something so comforting about hot chocolate when one is troubled. It always puts me in mind of nursery days when I was—"

"*Grace.* She is the only reason I am here, Mrs. Pincham."

"Melony. I insist, or we shall simply end this conversation."

"Melony."

"There! Perfect! I have never particularly cared for my name, but when you say it, I find it has a most pleasing sound. Most pleasing. Sit down."

"I prefer to stand."

Melony turned and looked up at him over her shoulder. "But I like to sit." She dropped to a low stool close to the fire and arranged her skirts—skirts that he realized for the first time were all but transparent. "If you insist upon standing over me like an elegant giant, I shall probably snap my neck. But at least come closer where I can see you properly."

Arran strolled to stand beside her. "Can you see me now?"

"A little better."

She tilted her head and openly studied that part of him most likely to betray any response to her femininity.

"The hour draws late, madam."

"Melony."

"Melony," he said. How shallow and foolish women such as this could be. She did not guess how perilously close he was to losing his temper.

"Are you . . ." Slowly her eyes traveled up to meet his. "Are you as tired as I, my lord?"

"Possibly."

"Then why not allow me to help you rest?"

"Good night to you, Melony." He made to turn away. "Perhaps we shall meet again before you leave Kirkcaldy—which will be soon, I presume?"

Her hand snaked out and she grasped a handful of his shirt where his waistcoat hung open. "You don't want me to leave. You are a lonely man, and I would like to help you become less lonely."

"I was on my way to visit my *fiancée*. If you'll excuse me?"

"She doesn't want to see you." Melony dropped her hand and turned from him.

"Explain yourself." Not that whatever she said mattered. The woman's motives for approaching him were perfectly clear.

"I would rather not. Please accept what I've told you."

"Accept and then help make the rest of the night more interesting for you?" he asked. "Is that what you had in mind?"

Her bare shoulders rose. From his vantage point over her, he had an almost unimpeded view of her breasts. More than ample, round and tipped with dark pink nipples that were already budded.

Arran stirred, took a deep breath, but did not look away. "Answer me, Melony. Did I arrive before you in time to present a possible entertainment on a night when you didn't wish to sleep alone?"

"I prefer not to lie. Yes, my lord, you did."

He raised his brows. "I cannot fault your honesty."

"Lying to you would be pointless. A man such as you is not seduced by flattery and falsehood."

"A pretty speech. Explain what you meant about Grace."

She crossed her arms and plucked aimlessly at gauzy little sleeves. "I . . . No, I cannot. Please leave me."

Arran narrowed his eyes. "What manner of game is this?"

"One I should not have begun. I should simply have told you Grace was exhausted and had fallen asleep, then allowed her to find a way to tell you herself."

"Tell me *what*?"

Melony slowly lifted her face. Her small mouth trembled and turned down. "Very well, but you will be angry, and I fear I shall be the one to bear that anger."

"You have nothing to fear from me," he told her shortly.

She toyed with the sleeves, and they slipped farther down her arms. "Very well. I tried to persuade her that she should attempt to make the best of your arrangement. She told me something about having made up a story to convince you that she cares for you after all."

Arran tugged his loose cravat from his neck. "Go on."

"She said you did not believe her. Grace is angry because you are a hard man who does not, mm, play the game."

"What game would that be?" he asked evenly.

"I've said too much. She is resigned to the marriage and to bearing your children. Then she intends to continue in the manner to which you both agreed at the beginning. She will find a suitable . . ." Melony contrived to draw her bodice almost down to her elbows. "She will find a way to amuse herself. I think we both know that she is a woman of considerable . . . shall we say, considerable energy?"

"Shall we?" His gaze slipped downward. Grace had told this woman everything that had passed between them; of that, he was now certain.

"She described your meetings." Her breasts were completely revealed, a fact they both knew. "You were not pleased to discover that Grace intended to marry for position and wealth, and afterward to find her pleasure elsewhere."

"What man would be pleased with such a discovery?"

Her pointed tongue slid over her lips. "Perhaps you should have accepted her story about having decided she wanted you—you, the man she thought you were at the first meetings. Her descriptions of your encounters sounded . . . *satisfying.* People of a certain station in life are accustomed to *compromise,* are they not, my lord?''

''As you say.''

''Then surely you should not be averse to more of what you have already enjoyed with Grace—for as long as it pleases you—before the two of you turn to other diversions?''

''She told you that was what she proposed?''

''I hope I have not made things more complicated for you and Grace.''

When he did not respond, she stood, gathering her dress to her bosom and pretending to be flustered. ''I have managed this badly. Grace asked me to be her friend, and I agreed. Now I have made things more difficult for her—for both of you.''

''I'll take my leave of you.'' Grace had actually confided *everything* in this creature.

''Please don't go until I am assured you are not angry with Grace.''

''My feelings toward my future wife are no concern of yours.''

''But they are!'' Her fingers abandoned the slipping bodice to descend upon his arms. ''I shall not rest again until you listen to me. You must have noted that Mrs. Wren is . . . She is not a sympathetic parent.''

''Agreed,'' he said vehemently.

''Yes, well, Grace is alone. And she does not entirely understand her, um, *urges.* Some women are bemused by the strength of their carnal desires, and Grace may be one of those. That is why one man will never be enough—'' She paused, her mouth forming a horrified ''oh.'' ''I mean she is very, very energetic.''

Arran looked at her breasts.

''Oh, dear. I am doing this so abominably. I'm

certain that given time, Grace may come to appreciate you as she should.''

''As she should?'' His gaze didn't waver. ''You mean that if I wait for her approval, I may, in time, gain something close to constancy from my wife.''

Melony tossed her head. ''Do not muddle me, my lord. I mean that eventually it is inevitable that Grace should come to appreciate you as much as I already do.'' She pressed her hands to her cheeks. ''You have befuddled me. I am speaking as I had no intention of doing. But since I have, I shall finish. I consider it a crime for a man with such obvious . . . *talents* to be less than adored by any woman he chooses to honor with his attentions.''

''Do you indeed?''

''Yes, my lord.'' With one fingertip, she made a line down his chest all the way to the waist of his breeches. ''Let me show you how your needs should be ministered to. I assure you I am very sensitive to your needs.''

''You do not know me at all.'' Yet he knew her— in the way men of the world knew all such women.

She flattened her palms over his shirtfront, spread her fingers, stroked him. ''Should we go to my bed?''

''I think not.''

''Quite so.'' Her breasts rose and fell, large, white-skinned, and traversed with the palest of blue veins, the nipples distended. ''Here before the fire will be better. I can make you forget Grace. That, I promise you.''

Slowly Arran threaded his silk cravat around her neck.

For an instant there was a flicker of anxiety in her eyes. It faded when he smiled. Winding the ends of the cloth about his fingers, he shortened it, drawing her closer.

Melony giggled and slipped her fingers inside his

breeches. "Oh, yes, I will make you forget." Her head fell back and her moist lips parted. "You need a woman who understands the requirements of a man such as you. A woman who can perform for you in Society . . . and elsewhere."

Arran transferred both ends of the cravat to his left hand and smoothed his right down over her shoulder.

"Yes," she whispered urgently, arching her back. "Oh, yes."

Deftly he pulled the flimsy sleeves, first one, then the other, up her arms and tweaked her bodice into place.

"What—?"

A sharp little yank on the cravat silenced her before Arran retrieved the length of silk and stepped away.

"Why . . . ? You can't *do* this."

"Can't I? Watch me, Mrs. Pincham."

"I will not *stand* for it, I tell you!"

He unlocked and opened the door. "I don't believe I ever heard how Mr. Pincham died. Can disgust kill, do we know? Good night, madam."

Chapter 19

❝I do believe he's in love with me.'' Grace regarded Mairi with serious intensity. "I have finally identified the reason for my own distress. There are feelings that can make one very disturbed.''

"Aye?" Mairi waited expectantly.

"As a female I have felt so happy, I thought I might pop. And so sad, I thought I might die. In the end all I could do was cry."

Mairi watched Grace closely. "Aye, miss?"

"Men do not cry," Grace said. "They get angry. Which explains everything. The marquess is completely, painfully, and hopelessly in love with me.''

"Och, I'm sure I dinna understand the ways o' the gentry," Mairi said, her round blue eyes brilliant with anxiety. "How could ye decide his lordship loves ye when he's not seen ye, or spoken a word t'ye, for days? And ye'd only set eyes on him the two times anyway."

Grace inspected the white lace falling collar Mairi held. "I've just explained all that. It's as plain as your nose, Mairi. This will do very well.''

Mairi draped the collar about Grace's neck and shoulders on top of an already high-cut dress in emerald green faille piped with white. "Like one o' them governesses," Mairi said, frowning and swiping at the ever loose wisps of fine brown hair about her face. "Not a bit o' your pretty skin t'be seen."

272

"No," Grace agreed lightly. "Skin is a very dangerous thing, Mairi. You would do well to ensure that your own is well covered. I have given all this much thought, and I cannot think why it took me so long to see the truth."

Mairi blushed a bright pink. "I'm sure I dinna know what ye could be talkin' about. There's none t'look at me, Miss Grace. But ye're different."

"You'll find a wonderful husband in due course. He'll be perfectly charming and very good to you. Meanwhile, I intend to ensure that there is nothing about me that may cause the marquess to feel compromised."

Mairi stared. "What's that, miss?"

"Compromised?" Grace laughed. "It means *endangered*. At risk."

"An' how would a great, bad-tempered man be en—en—put in danger by a wee slip o' a lassie like ye?"

Grace gave Mairi an arch look. "By causing him to have thoughts that might lead to his wishing to . . . Mairi, I would not speak so plainly if I did not think this was for your own good. I have noted that there are events—situations—certain *touches*, that lead a man to want to *Sit With a Woman*." She watched Mairi's wholesome face and waited.

"I see," Mairi said at length. "Sittin' wi' ye?"

"Hush." Grace dropped her voice. "In a man as principled as the marquess, such *urges* may cause grave disquiet."

"I've no idea what t'say t'ye, miss. I thought ye were actin' strange. Ye said ye'd seen the marquess himself? On your own?"

"Of course," Grace said irritably. "I told you he summoned me and we have discussed the wedding." If being told when the event would take place could be counted as a discussion. "And although I would not wish you to mention this to anyone else,

I had met with the marquess on several previous occasions."

"Ye had?"

"I had."

"They'll not speak any good o' him belowstairs. They say he was at dinner! Himself at dinner!"

"Certainly," Grace said, pretending that there should be no cause for surprise over the event.

"But he's not been seen around the castle in many a year, so I'm told. Are ye afeared o' him?"

"Not at all," Grace said with more conviction than she felt. "He is a charming man." A slight exaggeration. He was a pigheaded ogre, but she was—with the help of Melony's insights into masculine behavior—in the process of working out a cure for that condition.

"Is he . . . What does he look like, then? Is he all twisted up wi' great long arms and a mouth like a gash made wi' a dirk?"

Grace tutted and went to sit before the glass to ensure that her hair was suitably restrained. "He is the most handsome man I have ever seen."

"Ah. What a ninny I am. That explains that, then."

At Mairi's distant-sounding comment, Grace turned on her stool. "What does it explain?"

"I'm not supposed to tell ye." Mairi smoothed her apron and plunked her hands on her hips. She began to pace, muttering under her breath as she went.

"But you will tell me," Grace said in a wheedling tone.

"Aye, I will on account o' ye bein' a gentle, carin' soul. Ye've been bewitched by a fair face and form. The devil himself in pretty garments. Och, miss, ye shouldna put yoursel' in the way of such danger as marryin' with the Savage. There, I've said it."

"Oh, come, now. Because of all the silly old sto-

ries about him *eating babies?* Mairi, surely you see
how foolish that is.''

''They're talkin' about him belowstairs. He was
fair ragin' at dinner, they said. An' he sent them all
packin'.''

Grace had no wish to remember the event in detail. ''His lordship had good reason to become agi-
tated. There was a great deal of—er—discussion.
Everybody wanted to tell him what he should and
should not do.''

''About ye goin' to Edinburgh.'' Mairi blushed
brilliantly. ''I'm sorry, miss, but people do talk.''

''Let them. All that nonsense about the marquess's first wife is purely malicious, too. I've no
idea what really happened to her, but I'm sure it
wasn't anything like the wicked stories that have
been invented.''

''He's a foul temper, has he not?'' Mairi said,
making a great deal out of tidying the scarves,
fichus, pelerines, spencers, and other items of clothing Grace had assembled to wear at the necks of her
gowns to render them as modest as possible. ''And
there's none who can tell ye otherwise than that he's
capable of . . . Well, ye know what he's capable of.''

''I do not know that he's capable of the wicked
things you're suggesting.''

Mairi straightened and folded her arms over her
plump bosom. ''I wasna' goin' t'mention this, but I
think I may have to.''

Grace's hair, drawn back to a heavy braid at her
nape, shone smoothly. Not a hint of a wisp escaped
to form a tempting curl. She ran a hand over the top
and inspected her face. Scrubbed clean and with no
hint of blacking on her lashes or color on her lips or
cheeks, she looked satisfactorily plain.

''I probably will tell ye.''

Of course, her lashes were dark anyway, except
for the tips, which, for some odd reason, were gold.

And her mouth managed to appear pink all on its own.

"Mayhap I should just out wi' it and—"

"Mairi! Say what you intend to say anyway!"

"Himself was in that Mrs. Pincham's rooms in the wee hours o' the mornin'! On the very night when he'd announced your weddin' at dinner. There, I've told ye."

Grace sat very still with her hands in her lap.

"A *coorteesan* is what they say that woman is. A *coorteesan* is a woman who—"

"I know that a courtesan is a kind of woman we should not discuss, Mairi." How could it be true? Why, Melony had been with Grace until very late that evening. "I've heard my Mama and her friends speak of courtesans as the destroyers of good husbands."

"Indeed," Mairi agreed.

Melony had been a pillar of strength and comfort in the days since that evening.

"So," Mairi said when Grace didn't continue. "He canna verra well be in love wi' ye, can he? He's a bad man, miss. If ye'll excuse me for sayin' as much about your intended."

A bad man? "I thought poor Melony appeared distracted on the following morning," she said vaguely. "I think I begin to understand why."

"Och, ye're such a sweet-minded lassie. My father would have had an easier life if I'd been half as gentle a soul as ye are."

"Piffle! You are the sweetest, kindest creature on earth, and I'm so glad you came to me. Now. You have helped make things entirely clear to me."

"Deary me, I've turned your poor mind wi' my news."

"Don't you see, Mairi? It's all a theatrical nonsense to hide his true feelings."

Mairi wound a primrose yellow shawl of China

crepe into a creased rope. "I'm sure I dinna know what ye're sayin'."

"The marquess, silly. We're agreed that he's a pigheaded, overbearing man—a cruel man, even."

"Aye." The shawl became a crumpled ball. "I shouldna wonder."

"Only he's not really cruel. He has true *beauty* buried in his soul, Mairi. True beauty." Thinking of how he hid that beauty brought tears to her eyes. "You should hear him play the piano. Sounds of angels, he makes."

"Sounds o' angels?"

"Oh, yes. And this visit to Melony is a direct result of his fears."

"Aye . . . *No*. No, I dinna understand ye, miss. Mayhap ye should go to your bed awhile. Ye dinna sound well."

Grace swung around from the glass. "But I *am* well," she said stoutly. "I have not been better in a very long time. I was right all along. Stonehaven loves me, and that frightens his wits to shreds. He went to Melony in an attempt to prove to himself that he could, er, experience similar feelings with her to those he felt with me. He wanted to prove that they were not at all unusual. And he has not appeared since because it did not work, and now he is forced to confront the true situation."

"And what would that be?"

"He is lost. Lost to me, of course." She snapped her skirts across her legs. "He is a man who abhors weakness, and like most of his foolish sex, he considers falling in love a weakness."

Mairi recollected the shawl and hurriedly tried to smooth it. "If ye say so. But I know what they're sayin' belowstairs, and it isn't anythin' like what you think."

"They are small-minded and mean. And they are gossips. Poor Melony. What a trial for her to have to deal with Stonehaven. You see, Melony is a most loyal friend, and she must have felt deeply troubled by the marquess's behavior—because of that loyalty. But it shall never again be mentioned, and I shall learn from it."

Mairi frowned dubiously.

"Don't look at me like that. I know what I'm saying. And I *do* know what I'm doing. And what I'm *going* to do. I'm going to force him to give up his foolishness. I'm going to do all manner of kind and loving things for him until he cannot help but pack away his silly doubts. He will open like a flower, Mairi. Like a rose to the sunshine. Yes, indeed. I am going to be Stonehaven's sunshine."

Mairi started to respond, but a rap on the door was followed by Melony's entrance. She hurried in, ignoring Mairi and going directly to Grace. "How are you, dear one? Forgive me for taking so long to come. Theodora has been completely tiresome this morning. She insists she's misplaced her wretched diamonds. Can you imagine? Anyway, I couldn't get away sooner."

"I've decided on a course of action with Stonehaven," Grace announced.

Melony cleared her throat and indicated Mairi. "Perhaps we should have a private little chat, dearest?"

"Mairi's perfectly trustworthy," Grace said.

"Of course." Melony looked somewhat cross. "But there are things I would prefer to talk about between the two of us. I'm sure you understand."

Before Grace could respond, Mairi pulled the load of accessories from the bed into her arms and made for the door. "I'll away and see t'these," she said, never looking at Melony. "It'll take a while. Send word if ye need me for anythin'."

As soon as the maid had left, Melony caught Grace's hands in hers and peered anxiously into her face. "You appear pale."

"I know."

"Are you ill?"

"No."

"Has anything been said about our departure for Edinburgh?"

"Mama said that Sir Mortimer said we'll leave by the end of the week."

"Ooh!" Melony squealed. "Isn't that the veriest excitement?"

"The veriest," Grace agreed, but her mind was elsewhere—on a tall, strong man with long black hair tied at his nape and eyes the color of deep-sea waters. "We are to buy my trousseau." She wrinkled her nose, although the idea did bring flutters of anticipation to her stomach.

"You do not appear . . . I see it now!" Melony exclaimed. "You are not yourself. The falling collar. The artless hair. The sorry expression. *Why* do you appear so . . . so *dull* and old-fashioned?"

Grace smiled brightly. "Thank you, Melony. You have made me happy."

"I have?"

"Indeed you have. Dull and old-fashioned—or at least exceedingly modest—is exactly as I wish to appear." Whatever she said, she must not embarrass Melony by letting her know she had learned of Stonehaven's behavior the other evening. "These past days have not been wasted. They have given me a much needed opportunity to analyze what it is that troubles Stonehaven and what I must do to help him."

Melony dropped Grace's hands. "*Help* him." She pursed her lips. "He is absolutely beyond the pale, and . . . Oh, my, what am I saying? He is your fiancé, and I have no right to say anything unpleasant about him. Forgive me. I'm certain the two of you will manage well enough."

Grace smiled at her friend. "You are not to worry further." Melony must be afraid that Stonehaven's

strange humor would continue. "Please believe me
when I say that the marquess is about to become a
changed man. There will be no more exhibitions of
ill humor. At least, there will be no more once he
learns that happiness is within his grasp."

"I surely cannot understand what you mean."
Melony walked smoothly to stand before the fire
and jiggled her fingers before the warmth. Her rose
satin was, Grace thought, a trifle overdone for
early afternoon. Nevertheless, its richness became
Melony's white skin and auburn hair.

"He loves me," Grace told her simply.

Melony swung around. "*Loves* you?" She pressed
a hand to her throat and laughed. "What can you be
thinking of? Men such as Stonehaven do not *love*."

"You are altogether too jaded. No doubt the result of your early bereavement. The sooner you find
someone to love yourself, the better. I cannot bear
to see your sweet, generous nature wasted on a
lonely existence."

"I am *not* lonely."

"No, no, of course not." Great patience and care
must be exercised here. "And I assure you, my dear
one, that no gentleman could look at you and not
entertain thoughts of finding a way to make you his
own. I believe you have been too distracted by grief,
but you will soon be ready to entertain affectionate
advances. *Sincere* affectionate advances," she added
with a meaningful glance lest Melony had any notion at all that Grace had learned of Stonehaven's
presumptuous visit.

"There is no need to concern yourself with me.
You and your wedding are what matter. And I want
you to allow me to help you with every aspect of the
arrangements." Melony smiled sadly. "After all, I
have had the joy of going through the arrangements
for my own, sadly short marriage."

"Indeed." Grace popped up and went to kiss

Melony's cheek. "And you are so generous to put aside the difficult memories to be a support to me."

"What did you mean about Stonehaven?"

"It's simple," Grace said, swaying a little. "The first step was to change my style of dress—although I had not entirely formulated all of the reasons and results when I first made the decision.

"Stonehaven loves me. I told you of our early meetings and how we were carried away on an inrushing tide of incredible *Passion*."

"Yes." The spots of color on Melony's cheeks could only be caused by discomfort at Grace's frank announcement.

"Forgive me for being so forthright on this subject. But we are women of the world, and I know you want to learn every detail.

"Those moments of extraordinary abandonment frightened him."

Melony tilted her head. *"Frightened?"*

"Indeed. Frightened. He is afraid such powerful love will make him weak and that he will not be strong enough to resist such episodes *all the time*."

A strangled noise escaped Melony.

"Shocking, I know, but true. There is such a . . . a *thing* between us that I think it entirely possible we shall be unable to do anything at all but *Sit Together* if we do not find a means to control our impulses."

"Sit together?"

"Oh, you know what I mean. I've come to understand so many things. Like the reason for chaperons. It is important for a man to maintain the notion that the object of his affections is pure. But when a man is alone with a woman and he can see and touch enough of her to cause certain *sensations*, then it is inevitable that he will soon be lost and have a desperate desire to *Sit With Her*."

"Ah."

Grace screwed up her eyes. There was something

a trifle strange about Melony's expression. Probably the result of too much stress of late.

"This in turn leads to the man feeling compromised—because the effect of the female makes him vulnerable to her. So the course for me to follow is obvious."

"Do tell."

"I shall. No doubt you will find the process useful yourself in the near future. Firstly, I am going to be so sweetly generous and charming and modest toward Stonehaven that he will become a calm and entirely satisfied man.

"Next, I intend to present an appearance to him that is so demure that not a single notion of *Sitting With Me* will ever enter his head."

"How—"

"How shall I accomplish that?" Grace held out her arms and made a circle. "See? Skin is the problem, dearest Melony. The display of too much skin. Take it from me, that is absolutely the most dangerous element of all in this male-female thing. If a man can see and touch *naked* skin, he is lost!"

Melony shuddered and let out a small moan.

"Disturbing indeed," Grace agreed. "So I stand before you as a solution to the dilemma. I need to see and smell and hear and eat—and use my hands. The rest, every inch of me, is covered in the most unappealing manner possible."

"I see."

"I knew you would. He will be forced to address matters of higher importance. Stonehaven will realize that it is my mind he loves, not my body, and that will cause him to become the sweetest-mannered of men!"

Chapter 20

❝You are particularly bloody this evening, Arran.❞

"I am busy." *And in no mood for brotherly advice.*

Struan moved a chair close to the piano where Arran sat and picked up a violoncello. "Choose a fiddle, Calum. We haven't done this in too long."

"You play with Arran. I'm not sure I remember how."

Arran spread his hands on his thighs. "You two don't intend to go away, do you?"

"No." Struan began to tune the violoncello, then stopped. "What . . . ? " He leaned the instrument into his lap and bent over. "What in God's name is *that?*"

"The spike on the bottom? It's my invention. Try it. You'll find playing much easier. One day all violoncellos will be played balanced on the floor with a spike."

"If you say so, then they probably will," Struan said doubtfully. He swung the instrument this way and that, played a little, and swung some more. "I do believe you're right. My brother the genius. When will you stop hiding and share yourself with the world?"

"Whatever little good I do will not be wasted. Someone will take it where it can be best utilized. Fuss bores me. I don't want public recognition. This is where I want to be, and without intrusions."

The unexpected sound of Calum stroking an almost forgotten melody from a fiddle silenced them both. That fiddle had been given to Calum by Arran's father.

Arran caught Struan's eye, and there was between them the old closeness, the ties of two brothers who had shared many interests, a love of poignant music well played being one of the best.

Calum played on. " 'The Heather Road,' " Struan said softly enough, only Arran could hear him. "He always played with his heart. He makes me see what he plays."

"Aye," Arran said, because it felt right. "Moors. High moors beneath a sky brushed free of cloud by the wind that bends the purple heather. He was always gentle inside that tough hide of his."

"He needed the tough hide to survive," Struan said. He lowered his voice even more. "Does he ever speak of—"

"No. But the day will come when he'll have to confront the past."

Struan rested his chin on the scroll and stroked the strings until they whined a little.

Calum's eyes were closed. He drew the bow, and a muscle in his cheek flickered.

"Father gave us so much when he gave us the music," Struan said. "I wish Calum had been our brother, too."

"So do I."

"Does Calum?"

Arran considered. "I think not. I think perhaps there's something stronger that's starting to call him now."

"Call him to what?"

With a smile, Arran began to play with Calum. "Some things are inside us, Struan. You know that. Inside Calum there's something as strong as the winds over the moors that he loves so much. And it's wild—perhaps with anger. That troubles me. There may come a day when he'll need us as much as he needed us as a small boy.''

''Perhaps, perhaps. He's a man who ought to marry.''

''He almost did. Or have you forgotten. That brought him close to despair, and it may have been the beginning of this anger I feel in him.''

''Marriage could make him whole,'' Struan persisted.

''You're hardly a man to have strong opinions on that subject,'' Arran said, leaning into the gentle music.

''And you are?'' When Arran's fingers grew still, Struan was already shaking his head. ''Forget my careless tongue. I didn't mean to say that.''

''Yes you did. You always were an irritating devil. And you're right, so that's an end of it.'' Raising his voice for Calum to hear over the sound of the piano, Arran said, ''It must be past your bedtime, Struan—and Calum's.''

''Oh, we're not at all tired. We've got a thing or two to discuss with you.''

Arran rested an elbow above the keyboard and regarded Struan. ''Discuss away. My life is completely turned upside down. I am no longer master in my own home. My decisions are made for me. Discuss—'' He stopped. Struan was looking past him and smiling.

Calum's violin fell silent.

''Good evening, gentlemen.''

Arran gritted his teeth. *Grace,* for God's sake. He turned slowly—in time to see her cross the gallery carrying a small tray upon which sat a delicate cup and saucer.

''My, my, all three of you,'' she said, smiling as if it were four in the afternoon and this were tea at Marlborough House with the duchess presiding, not

two in the morning in a place to which she had not
been invited. "If I'd known you were together here,
I would have been sure to bring enough. No matter.
I'll give this to Stonehaven and return with more as
soon as possible."

Arran caught Calum's eye and saw a threat there.
He, Arran Rossmara, Marquess of Stonehaven, was
to humor this strange female who had been foisted
upon him or risk his old friend's wrath.

"You should have retired hours since," Arran
said, trying not to sound as truculent as he felt.

"Not at all," Grace said lightly, and still smiling.
"It has become obvious that it is your habit to be
about in the night hours. Therefore, as your future
wife, it is my place to adapt my habits to yours. You
see, I am already learning to be awake at night.
Sleeping in the day may be a trifle more difficult,
but I shall conquer that problem."

From the corner of his eye, Arran saw Struan put
a hand over his mouth. Damn him—and Calum—
they were enjoying this.

"It will not be necessary for you to change your
habits." Hell's teeth, he could *not* abide thinking of
her tripping in and out whilst he attempted to work.

"It certainly will be. Now, enough of that. I have
brought you something I know you will enjoy." She
frowned down into the cup. "Oh, dear, I'm afraid
it may have cooled. There is quite a stretch between
my room and the gallery, you know."

"It will be fine," Arran said, reaching for the saucer. "What is it?"

"Hot chocolate."

"I—"

"He *loves* hot chocolate," Struan said. "Doesn't
he, Calum?"

"Oh, indeed. When we were boys together, he
used to drink his own hot chocolate, then try to steal
ours."

Arran narrowed his eyes. Later there would be ways to extract his revenge.

"Melony is *such* a help," Grace said, clearly delighted. "She said she was certain she had heard that you liked chocolate, and she was right, wasn't she?"

Arran was still formulating a reply when Grace simply slipped from the room without another word.

"Pincham is a bitch," he said through his teeth.

"She is sexually obsessed," Struan commented, tightening pegs on the violoncello. "Isn't she, Calum? Tell Arran how she tried to lure you into the butler's pantry."

"I hardly think the Pincham's attempts to seduce me would be near as interesting to Arran as the fact that she managed to get you to meet her in the chapel yesterday and then she asked you to hear her confession!" He slapped a thigh.

"That was not to be repeated," Struan said sternly. "I should not have confided in you."

"Why?" Calum laughed. "Because you've betrayed something sacred by telling me about it?"

"I told you she asked me to hear her. I did not do so. Therefore nothing has been betrayed."

Calum swaggered forward, pointing at Struan, *en garde*, with his bow. "No, no, Father, you protest entirely too much." He tapped the other man's shoulder. "Did she or did she not swoon?"

The rise in Struan's color made Arran chuckle. "Come, brother, don't keep me in suspense."

"She swooned into his arms," Calum said with evident relish. "Struan was forced to catch the succulent piece—"

"Calum!"

"*Struan*. You caught her, and she attempted to have you right there on the chapel floor."

"My God," Arran shouted. "That's rich. And did she?"

"Did she what?" Struan said, scowling.

"*Have* you, of course. Did she manage to tempt you out of your priest's garb and into her plump, white arms?"

"Have your fun," Struan said. "Then we shall discuss more important matters."

Calum smothered his laughter. "Indeed we shall. But first, Arran, does Grace know . . ." He indicated scattered sheets of music. "Does she?"

"That I compose? No. She does not know this music is my own. And it will remain so."

Calum inclined his head. "I merely wanted to be certain. Now to the most important issue. Arran, do not allow Mortimer and Theodora to take Grace to Edinburgh tomorrow."

"No," Struan said. "We think it would be better to cancel the trip. Safer."

"Safer how?"

"You know they do not want this marriage," Calum said. "We fear they may come up with some means to ruin everything."

"Ruin a match made in heaven, do you mean?" Arran said.

Calum set down the violin and bow. "A day will come when you'll thank me for finding Grace for you. She's a delight."

"A delight indeed," Struan said. "She'll make you a good wife and be a good mother to your children."

"I *hate* chocolate," Arran said, knowing he sounded pettish.

"We know," Calum and Struan said in unison.

In unison they turned to watch as Grace entered once more. She carried the tray again, this time with two cups and saucers. Squeezed beneath her arm was a flat parcel. "Here we are." The sparkling smile was there, too.

"Thank you, Grace," Calum said, rising to relieve

her of the tray. "We shall become accustomed to
such charming kindnesses just in time for you to
take your place as Arran's marchioness. Then you
will be too elevated to make hot chocolate."

"Nonsense." She raised her chin. "I do not believe in elevation."

Arran regarded her thoughtfully. What, he wondered, was this all about? What had brought about
this display of self-deprecating charm? He studied
the green dress she wore. Pretty enough and well
cut, but draped about the neck and shoulders with
one of those frightful, dowdy falling collars. The
damned things had obviously been invented by
some prune-faced old maid determined to deprive
men of pleasure.

"This is for you, Stonehaven," Grace said, handing him the parcel. "It is a very small thing. Of no
consequence at all, in fact. It's just something I
thought you might appreciate—since I thought of it
for you, that is . . ."

Arran watched her falter and wet her lips. "Are
you prepared for your journey tomorrow?" he
asked. He avoided looking at Calum or Struan. "No
doubt you are delighted by the prospect of so much
excitement."

She stood before him with the parcel held in both
hands. "It will be interesting, my lord; of that I have
no doubt."

"Yes, well, since you have only hours before your
departure, you'd do well to attend to your rest."
She was capable of incredible deceit. How innocent
she appeared, even now, standing before him whilst
he knew that she'd gleefully shared her plot to use
him with Mrs. Pincham.

"The chocolate is delicious," Struan said loudly.

"I'm glad you like it," Grace said. She continued
to look only at Arran.

The fact that Pincham had also duped Grace

brought Arran some satisfaction. So Melony had said she thought him fond of chocolate, had she? *Vixen*.

"That dress is unusual," he said.

"Do you like it?"

"It . . . it puzzles me somewhat. I cannot imagine why you would choose such a fashion."

The brilliant smile appeared once more. "You will, my lord. In time you will understand and appreciate the subtlety of it. Please accept this."

He had little choice but to take the package.

"Consider it a remembrance of me and look at it whilst I'm in Edinburgh."

Arran found his eyes drawn to hers, such softly golden eyes. Her face was devoid of any artifice. Lovely in her sharp-boned, delicate way. All of her was lovely.

He turned away abruptly. "There is no need to give me anything." Impatiently he unfolded the heavy paper and revealed a small canvas.

With measured steps, he walked across the room and sat on a chaise.

"Well?" She pressed her hands together.

Arran studied what she had given him.

"Do you like it?"

"When did you paint this?"

"Yesterday. In the afternoon. It didn't take long."

"No."

"Do be careful. The paint isn't quite dry."

"Mm."

Struan and Calum assembled behind him and looked down at the painting. Arran glanced up, caught first Struan's, then Calum's, eye and found no flicker of reaction in either.

"Interesting," Calum said.

"Most," Struan echoed.

Arran sighed. They were relishing his misery. "You are too kind, Grace. Will you explain this work to me? I wouldn't want to miss a single nuance."

"Oh, you *do* like it. I'm so glad." She rose to her toes and bobbed. "It's a woman. But of course, you will have gathered as much."

"Indeed." No doubt the yellow thing amid stripes of brown would be the subject of the painting. "Clothes?"

"You toy with me, Stonehaven." Grace approached with exaggerated steps. "No, naturally there are no clothes. We know I don't paint clothes."

"We do indeed."

"He jests with you," Struan said. "Anyone can see she's not wearing anything."

Arran glanced at Grace. She was so intent, she didn't meet his eyes.

"I . . . The woman in the painting fears she may be a disappointment to the object of her affections. So she does not look at him."

"Ah," Calum said.

"Yes. She is sitting with her back to you, Stonehaven. Hiding that which might present the possibility for compromise."

"Compromise?" This began to sound like a conversation carried on in code.

"She does not wish to put the one for whom she cares deeply at risk—of endangering his principles, his honor. Therefore she does not present him with temptation."

Her tone, the plea for understanding he sensed, disturbed Arran. He said, "Thoughtful of her."

"I knew you'd approve."

"What are the brown stripes?" he asked.

Grace frowned. "They are a curtain, a screen, if you will."

"Why does she need a screen if she thinks she's hidden?"

"Well, her back is naked, so I decided to hint at a screen just to make sure there is no question of implying seductive intent."

Arran shook his head. Muffled noises from behind suggested his allies were having difficulty not laughing. He turned a hard stare at Struan and Calum, and all vestiges of humor vanished.

"I knew it," Grace said when Arran failed to comment further. "It was my one mistake on this piece. Never mind. Use it as it is and I'll correct it when I return from Edinburgh."

Arran had to smile at her. "It's . . . delightful just as it is." Damn, if she didn't have the power to wind him in like a great, hungry fish. Her passion for her peculiar art drew him; it formed a bond he could not completely dismiss.

He studied the painting again. "I wouldn't have you change this, Grace."

"No, no," she said, her smile utterly open now. "You are kind, but no. On this occasion I tried to be too clever. I should have forsaken suggestive technique and followed my instincts. They were definitely correct. I should have painted her in clothes."

Arran sat back and looked at her profile, at the shimmer of white-blond hair.

Could he have been entirely wrong about Grace? God help him, but he hoped so.

Chapter 21

Humming, Arran strode across the stable yard. Warm early afternoon air carried the scent of hay and horses and leather. The ring of steel on steel came from the blacksmith's shop.

Arran nodded briskly to a lad who doffed his cap and instantly scurried away. Nearby, two men fell idle over pitchforks and gaped at the master they knew by his bearing but had not seen before.

He slapped his crop against a boot and smiled grimly. He would not spend many days doing his dear brother's bidding, but he'd promised Struan to at least let himself be seen about the castle in daylight. "Make the effort, Arran," Struan had said earnestly. "Still their foolish tongues so that Grace need not listen to the old lies about your supposed madness."

And here he was, wasting time in playing the idle nobleman when his energies would be better spent helping with the lambing in the more distant reaches of Kirkcaldy land.

"Good afternoon," he said to a tweeded young man leading a pretty chestnut mare.

"Aye . . ." Bright blue eyes slowly registered amazement before a cap was tugged off to reveal untidy red hair. "The Sava— My lord?"

Arran raised a brow and said shortly, "Quite," before approaching an open door into the stables.

Savage. Perhaps it was indeed time to stamp out stupid rumors.

He passed inside thick, cool stone walls and scuffed through straw. On either side of him stretched stalls where fine horseflesh stirred and whinnied and blew. There was the sound of soft muzzles nuzzling feed.

"*No!*" A male voice reached Arran from the tack room. "Jacob's bringin' your horse, Calum. In God's name, go alone."

Hector?

"How can I, man?" Calum spoke clearly.

"If ye tell him, I'm done for."

Calum swore and raised his voice, "There's *no* choice, Hector."

"I came t'ye because I thought it'd be a way out wi'out puttin' the noose around my own neck." This Hector MacFie sounded nothing like the controlled man Arran had always known him to be. "Surely y'see how it'll go for me if his lordship . . . Ye do see?"

Calum said, "I see that we must act quickly. And I also see that we have a dilemma."

Arran's way was to be direct, but some instinct told him to hold back. He stepped into an empty stall beside the tack room.

"Well," Hector said after a pause. "I've said my piece."

"Hell and damnation! If—"

The clop of hoofs approaching from the opposite end of the stables covered Calum's angry voice.

Arran remained hidden, waiting for the horse to be led from the building. The animal scuffled, leather creaked, and something scraped metal.

"Yes!" It was Calum's shout that carried over all the din. "Pray no harm has come to her or it'll be both of our necks."

There was a great crashing of hoofs and then the

animal left the building to clatter at high speed through the cobbled yard.

Arran stepped from the stall . . . and came face-to-face with his estate commissioner. "Pray no harm comes to whom?" Arran demanded.

Hector fell back. "Your lordship, I—"

Arran looked through the open stable door and had no difficulty identifying Calum, mounted on his gray and already dropping from sight as he descended the castle mound.

"Answer me." Arran's heart quickened. He turned on Hector. "Answer me, *now*. Where is Calum bound? *Why* should I not know?"

"I . . . He doesna want me t'tell—"

"Damn you!" Arran grabbed Hector's neckcloth and jerked him close. "Don't lie to me. I heard some of what just passed between you. *You* were the one who wanted information withheld from me, not Calum. Even now it is *you* he seeks to aid in some manner."

He saw Hector give up. The man sagged. "I learned something I wish I hadna learned." He shook his head defeatedly. "It's Miss Wren who's in danger."

Arran let out a slow breath. "Miss Wren left three days ago."

"Aye. And I was mistaken t'hold my tongue so long. But it's tonight when they plan to do her harm, and . . . I should have come t'you sooner, but I'd have had to tell about—"

"Good God," Arran said. He whirled about. "My horse!"

"It *isn't* London," Mama said, pointing her nose at a sky that continued to hold its sun inside a web of fine clouds.

Grace met Melony's eyes, and they hid giggles behind their hands.

"Edinburgh is not London," Grace said indulgently. "But do look at its castle, Mama. It is so wonderful. *Look.* In the middle of the city. Right in the middle of *everything.* Why, one feels one could reach out and touch it."

"A black-looking thing," Mama said. "Give me Windsor."

"The king will come in a few months," Grace commented. "He is said to be most pleased at the prospect. That must mean Edinburgh is considered very important."

"Wait until this evening, Mrs. Wren," Melony said. "The musicale at Sir Alistair and Lady Muir's will be splendid. Everyone who *is* anyone will be there."

"*Is* there anyone who *is* anyone in this provincial little city?"

Grace met Melony's eyes again and had to turn and stare unseeingly into the closest shop window. Thank goodness for Melony. She managed to make every moment fun and to help Grace cope with Mama's efforts to belittle everyone and everything in "this provincial little city."

"Where *is* the coach?" Mama said. "In London one never has to wait for one's coach at such times."

"We've never exactly *had* such times as these in London," Grace reminded her mother gently. "And poor Angus Creigh is doing his best, I'm sure. Princes Street seems as busy as Bond Street, and we've taken so long with our errands."

"Kennedy's gone for Angus," Melony said. "They'll be along soon enough." Dressed in a brilliant blue pelisse and a matching bonnet of crepe with a flaring brim trimmed in swansdown, she swayed and smiled and looked, Grace decided, perfectly charming. Why, every gentleman who passed looked their way to see Melony.

"There's Angus," Melony said, moving closer to the edge of the flag-way.

The handsome black town coach bearing the Stonehaven coat of arms rolled to a stop before them. Kennedy, a prim, humorless maid Lady Cuthbert had made available to Grace, alighted and promptly disappeared back into the glove-maker's establishment from which they had most recently departed.

Angus climbed down from the box. "Let's get ye settled inside, ladies," he said. Apparently Stonehaven had insisted that his own most trusted coachman should convey Grace wherever she needed to go—a thought that made her glow.

He *did* care. And regardless of Mairi's dire predictions of disaster if Grace did not cry off entirely, she was determined to pursue her course of teaching the noddycock to admit his love for her.

Of course, there was the matter of her discovery that he'd made an allotment for her trousseau and that it was strictly limited. That, Mama had informed her stridently, did not suggest a generous heart on the part of Grace's fiancé—a matter that must be remedied as soon as possible.

"There ye are," Angus said when he had his charges settled. "No doubt there's a mountain o' finery to be taken along wi' ye."

Grace hurried to reassure the old man. "Not a mountain at all. Very few things, really." There had been a rather embarrassing moment at the dressmaker's when it became evident that the budget for Grace's gowns would mean she must choose with great care and trim whatever corners could be trimmed.

Angus set off in the direction of the shop.

"Really," Mama said. "That man speaks as if he were a *relation*. Such familiarity on the part of servants should not be tolerated. Your sister agrees with me, Mrs. Pincham, I can tell you that."

"You and Theodora appear to be fast friends," Melony said.

"I admire her deeply."

"As she does you," Melony responded.

Grace allowed the chatter to flow over and around her. Before long, Angus and Kennedy returned with those items that could be immediately transported, and they set off for Charlotte Square.

"The wedding dress is a dreadful disappointment," Mama said. "Not at all what I had in mind for my only daughter. But then, one becomes accustomed to disappointment when one is alone in the world and dependent upon but one child—and a *daughter*—to provide for one's small need for happiness.

Melony said nothing, and neither did Grace. The wedding gown—the style and materials having been already picked out by Lady Cuthbert before Grace arrived—was made overly fussy by a profusion of inexpensive flounces and bows.

They swept past the elegant curves of Edinburgh's crescents where houses, three and four stories high, touched shoulders in a most agreeably complementary way. White stone steps, flanked by glossy black railings, rose to mahogany doors sporting highly polished knockers and letter boxes. Edinburgh's servants were less well dressed than those in London, but they appeared ruddy-faced and cheerful as they went about their business.

The Charlotte Square house was reached by driving around a pretty garden at the center of the square. Daffodils and narcissus nodded their cheerful heads in a warm breeze, and attentive nannies watched their small charges gambol on the grass. Beech trees, their new leaves bright green and trembling, spread lofty shadows over clumps of stubby crab apple trees. Spring's warm, fragile scent was in the air.

The thought that this was a place Stonehaven knew well made it engrossing to Grace. The house—referred to by Lady Cuthbert as overly modest—had been his Edinburgh home when he was a single young man coming and going from Scotland in the service of the king. "In the days before Stonehaven became so very strange," Lady Cuthbert had said ominously. "Forgive me, Grace. I should not speak so carelessly, but I am concerned for your happiness—and your well-being."

A small knot of apprehension formed in Grace's stomach, but she refused to allow it to shake her conviction that her marriage would be a blessed event. She had made great progress with Stonehaven—even if he didn't appear to have noticed the fact—and she would continue to make progress.

She missed him.

Grace felt startled. A week ago she'd been ready to dash back to England and try to forget she'd ever met him. Now she was actually grateful for Mama's rash behavior and . . . "Oh, dear."

"What did you say?" Melony asked as they arrived at Stonehaven's house.

"I said, *oh dear*," Grace said. "I will not pretend to you, Melony. I am surprised to find myself so committed to my marriage with Stonehaven." And she was also surprised to find herself remembering Mama's frightful gambling disaster without cringing. Really, she had changed terribly much in a few weeks.

Grace became aware that Melony was staring at her, and smiled. "I'm sorry. I'm blatherin', as Mairi would say. But I'm happy, Melony. Truly happy. I am convinced that Stonehaven and I shall have a congenial life together."

Angus handed Blanche down, but Melony hung back. "Tell me, Grace, why are you so certain of this?"

"Assisted by your insights into the opposite sex, I have had a revelation. Men in general are very susceptible to women. Given that situation, and adding Stonehaven's commitment to our match, success is inevitable because I intend to ensure that he views me kindly. I am going to be so considerate of him that he will come to bless the day I came into his life."

An unusual expression entered Melony's face. She seemed to stare through Grace as if she weren't there at all. Then she started and smiled. "I'm sure he will. Come, Grace, let us prepare for the musicale. Thank goodness it is in Charlotte Square. I don't give a fig for Theodora's opinion. I consider this among the most desirable locations in Edinburgh."

"I'm not sure I want to go. They say Sir Walter Scott may be there, and any number of other important people."

"You will enjoy yourself." Finally Melony allowed a footman to assist her from the carriage, and Grace followed. "Wear the red this evening."

"Oh, no!" Instantly Grace collected herself. "I mean, I am exceedingly grateful to you for giving me the gown, but it will need some slight alterations before I can wear it." The bodice alone needed a number of inches removed, and the waist did not fit as it should.

"I'll have Kennedy do what's necessary," Melony said. "She shall come to you at once. Mrs. Wren is looking forward to the event. So is Theodora, and so am I."

Grace saw her mother disappear into the house. "I'll think about it," she said. What she wished to do was be alone to think about Stonehaven and how she would pursue her quest to overcome his ill humor as soon as she got back to the castle.

"We shall leave promptly at eight," Melony announced, falling back to follow Grace up the front steps.

In the pale green entrance hall, Grace paused beside a brass vase overflowing with white lilac that sat upon a demilune mahogany side table. She tried to decide how she could manage to remain at home this evening.

"Don't forget it's to be the red," Melony said, passing through an archway leading to the inner hall. "Since you did not bring the marvelous jewels Stonehaven gave you, I shall lend you my pearls."

Grace arrived at the bottom of the stairs. Melony walked ahead now.

"I shall not go to the musicale." Grace jumped at the sound of her own clear voice.

Melony paused, then turned around. "Don't be a silly goose. Of course you will."

"No. No, I've decided to remain here."

Slowly Melony descended until she stood a single step above Grace. "I don't know what to say. He will be so disappointed."

Grace frowned. "Who will be disappointed?"

"Why, Stonehaven, of course."

"He will not know. And anyway, he also would not care. He did not even particularly want me to come to Edinburgh at all."

"That was all an act," Melony said. Finger by finger she removed her gloves. "And he will know because he has instructed a certain party to take note of your every move."

"What certain party?"

"All I know is that there is someone who was appointed to the position."

Grace swallowed and pressed a hand to her stomach. "But *why* does Stonehaven care if I go to this musicale?"

"Because, my dearest little friend . . ." Melony bowed her head. "It pains me to say this, but it is for your own good. Stonehaven is resigned to the match, but he is concerned at your lack of . . . shall we say, social savoir faire?"

"Oh," Grace said softly.

"Yes, well, to that end—to correct the deficiency—he regards it as most important for you to become exposed to situations in which a marchioness should be more than comfortable."

"Such as the musicale?" Grace asked, annoyed that her voice was so small.

"Such as the musicale. You are tired, Grace. Rest for a while. But if you wish to prove to your future husband that you will do anything to please him, and make him proud of you, you will attend this evening's affair."

"I see. And I'm to wear the red satin?"

"The red satin."

"Very well." Grace climbed past Melony and continued up. "I shall be ready at eight." *For Stonehaven's sake alone.*

Calum and his gray had covered some miles before Arran finally sighted his friend's flying cloak. Arran half-closed his eyes against the wind that tore at his face and closed distance until he drew within yards of the gray.

"Stop!" Arran shouted.

Calum looked over his shoulder, but urged his horse on.

Arran grimaced and leaned into Allegro's neck until he drew alongside Calum's mount.

"Stop," Arran demanded again.

Calum ignored him.

Leaning dangerously, Arran caught at the reins of Calum's horse.

"In God's name!" Calum cursed loudly. "You'll unseat me, man."

"If that's what it takes to find out what's afoot here, so be it." With a mighty yank, Arran brought the gray rearing to a halt.

"There is no time for chitchat," Calum said through his teeth. "Go back. I'll do what must be done."

Arran controlled his own skittering mount. "Enough of this gammon. Out with it, Calum. What is it that you are *not* to tell me?"

"I swore I would not reveal the source of my information."

"Your first allegiance is to me. That aside, I overheard much of what you spoke of with MacFie. Only the details remain unknown to me."

"Very well," Calum said. "Anything, as long as what must be done is done. Grace is to attend a musicale at the Muirs' this evening. There is a strong possibility that she will be lured away and . . . and seduced. Even riding as fast as we can, there's a chance we'll be too late."

Arran shifted to see Calum's face more clearly. "The devil you say." Calum wasn't given to idle invention. "Are you sure?"

"No. But I'm damned afraid I should be."

"Lured away by whom?"

"You will have to know eventually. Hector told me he'd . . . he was in the way of being in a position to overhear an exchange between Melony Pincham and your damnable cousin Mortimer. The subject of their conversation concerned you."

"So why didn't Hector come to me direct?"

"Because he was afraid you might ask for particulars."

"Explain," Arran said. "Quickly."

Calum bowed his head. "The fool has made some mistakes, not that they should matter. He had been with Lady Cuthbert in her chamber. To be precise, he was in the dressing room between that chamber and Sir Mortimer's. Lady Cuthbert was—er—*resting*. Hector overheard Melony talking to Mortimer.''

''In *his* chamber?''

Calum shrugged. ''Busy people, Sir Mortimer and Lady Cuthbert.''

''I'm damned,'' Arran muttered. ''Surely Hector misunderstood. Mortimer's a fool, but he'd hardly risk being overheard while he was plotting the seduction of *my* fiancée.''

''Mortimer and Pincham were—'' Calum cleared his throat ''—in the throes of passion, so to speak.''

Arran sat perfectly still. Then he gave a short laugh. ''Mortimer and La Pincham? In the *throes?*''

''Exactly. And quite something to behold, from what I could gather. Evidently Hector had been . . . he'd been taking a nap. Mortimer and Pincham must have come in and not had any idea that Lady Cuthbert and Hector were . . . Anyway, when Hector went into the dressing room, Mortimer's door wasn't quite shut. Pincham's into pain. Silk bonds and flagellation. She likes to be hurt.''

''And Mortimer—?'' His cousin's appetite for sex had never been in question, but Arran had always assumed him to be the passive type who would take his pleasure with leisurely command. ''Mortimer? By God, Calum, Pincham's his wife's sister!''

''If you ask me, the sister thing adds to the spice for Mortimer's type. Anyway, they were in the thick of it all when Pincham suddenly says that Mortimer should regard what they're doing as practice for what he's to do to Grace.''

Arran's gut snapped in. ''I would kill . . . The fact that Melony said that—if she did—doesn't mean they would ever really attempt such a perversion.''

''They will, I tell you.''

''I don't believe it.''

''*Believe* it.'' Calum's horse skittered sideways. ''I'm going to Edinburgh.'' He began to ride.

Arran tucked his heels into Allegro's sides. "Mortimer's a greedy fool, but he wouldn't risk this."

"I think he will. This is his last desperate chance to get what he's spent years lusting for."

They galloped side by side, spurring the horses on to greater speed.

"What exactly is it that Mortimer and Pincham plan?" Arran cried. "Finish the story."

"Gladly. Melony spoke of Mortimer hiding in the pavilion at the Muirs' place tonight. And Mortimer agreed that it would be a perfect spot for . . ." Calum's voice trailed away.

"For . . . ?" Arran prompted. His breath jammed in his throat.

"Soiling the goods. Putting any paternity in question. Initiation and ruination, my friend."

"How very grand it all is," Grace whispered to Melony behind the red painted fan that went so well with the satin gown Kennedy had contrived to fit to Grace's small figure.

They sat on little ivory-colored tapestry chairs in the last row assembled in the Muirs' elegant green drawing room. The company was richly dressed. Everywhere Grace looked, jewels flashed and the colors of the ladies' dresses made a brilliant collage amid the gentlemen's mostly dark evening dress.

"I do think Madame Constanza may have an almond caught in her throat, don't you?" Melony remarked, hunching her shoulders above the daringly low neckline of her magenta gros des Indes, and speaking behind her own delicate ivory fan.

Grace rolled in her lips and willed herself not to laugh aloud. The soprano, who had been singing for a very long time, did indeed sound as if something wobbled in her throat, rather like the little bobbling ball that produced birdlike sounds in a water whistle.

"What do you think of Sir Walter Scott?" Melony asked.

On Grace's other side, Mama, who was sitting with the Reverend Mr. Felix Bastion, leaned to frown absolutely ferociously at Grace.

Grace smiled demurely and looked straight ahead at the florid-faced, straining Madame Constanza. The Reverend Bastion had hung on Mama's every word from the moment they'd been introduced. He was, according to Lady Cuthbert, "a nonentity. A widower with a small living in some godforsaken place in Somerset. However, he is very respectable." Lady Cuthbert, openly annoyed with Sir Mortimer for refusing to escort them to the musicale, had been contentious all evening.

Respectable was the only word Grace had heard and noted. Let Mama enjoy whatever brief attentions came her way.

"He is puffy-faced and sickly-looking," Grace murmured to Melony, speaking of Sir Walter Scott. "His eyes are shrunken to little slits. He and his wife both appear to be ailing."

"I understand it is the pressure of preparing for the royal visit," Melony said, also looking straight ahead. "This room is horribly hot. We could excuse ourselves and find some lemonade."

"Would that not be considered rude?"

"Not at all. Lean on me and use your fan vigorously. If we are questioned, we shall say you were overcome by the vapors and that I am conducting you to find some fresh air."

Grace did not like deceit, but she longed for a little peace and a place to be cool. "Very well." She inclined her head to Mama. "Melony and I are going to find some lemonade. I am overheated."

Mama tutted and returned her attention to the singer.

WIth her hand through Melony's elbow, Grace allowed herself to be led past Lady Cuthbert—whose tutting sounded exactly like Mama's—and from the room.

"Whew," Melony said as soon as a footman closed the drawing room doors behind them. "I thought I should *die* in there."

"Mm. I don't care for the soprano, but I am looking forward to some of the other music later on."

"That won't be for *ages*," Melony said, starting downstairs. "There'll be an intermission. Then they will serve refreshments. That will take *forever*. Do let's go out into the gardens."

"I thought you said we should go for lemonade."

"And so we shall. Later. For now I think I may just *die* if I do not get out of this house for a while."

Grace was certain they should do no such thing, but she seemed to have no choice but to follow Melony down flight after flight until they reached the ground floor.

"Surely it is not wise for us to venture forth—alone?"

"Nonsense. Don't be such a cuckoo."

At french doors that opened from a small parlor onto a terrace, Grace stopped. "Really, Melony, I should prefer to have lemonade now."

"Oh—" Melony closed her mouth and considered. "Very well. We shall compromise. I'll go with you for lemonade. *Then* you'll come with me outside. It will be so very exciting."

"Exciting?" Grace echoed dubiously.

"Absolutely. We shall be like two jolly boys on a lark. I know of a place I can take you where no one ever goes."

That did not sound at all appealing to Grace.

"It isn't far. And you will have a most exhilarating time there, I promise you."

"I believe I am tired."

Melony caught her hand. "Lemonade will refresh

you, and then we shall go. Lovely gardens with an elegant white marble pagoda beside a small lake. At night it will be beautiful—and wonderfully tragic by moonlight. Of course, if you are afraid of adventure, then—''

"Like a temple to the moon," Grace said, imagining the picture. "How romantic."

"Very."

"Moonlight on water is so lovely."

"Ah, you have experienced moonlight on water many times," Melony said.

"Never," Grace told her. "But I have imagined it."

"Then you must see it for yourself one day, but I quite understand if you are afraid at present."

Grace peered through glass panes and said firmly, "I have changed my mind. Take me now."

Once they were outside, dew on the grass quickly soaked Grace's red satin slippers and the feet of her lace stockings.

"Hurry," Melony cried when they were beyond a wall that separated the formal part of the Muirs' garden from an area choked with trees. "Quickly. We must not take too long."

"I'm coming," Grace said unhappily. Her lust for adventure had rapidly sped away, and now she wished she had stood fast and refused to come outside.

"Ooh, this is so thrilling," Melony said in hushed tones, running ahead of Grace. The trees were so close that the two women had to dodge between trunks. Dense foliage closed out the moon.

"It's very dark," Grace said, after almost bumping into a jagged stump. "How much farther is the lake?"

"Not far at all." Melony found Grace's hand in the darkness and held on tightly. "See? The water's ahead. You can see it shimmer."

Almost as soon as Melony mentioned the water,
they were upon it.

"So black," Grace said. Her heart knocked hard.
"Like swelling ink. It looks very deep."

"They say it is," Melony responded. "Very deep
and filled with the bones of forsaken lovers."

"Oh!" Grace tried to tug away.

"Silly," Melony said, laughing. "I'm only joking.
There's the pavilion."

Grace stood still, pulling Melony to a stop beside
her. "It's *beautiful*. Absolutely glorious. So mysterious. I've never seen anything so wonderful."

"Yes, yes, yes. We must hurry. If we don't get
back before the intermission, we'll be missed. You
do still want to see it up close?"

"Of course." Shedding her fear, Grace flew
around the edge of the lake with Melony toward the
little white gem of a building. Its dome and the four
miniature minarets at its corners shone like freshly
frozen pond ice in the moon's light.

Three curving steps led to a narrow entrance.

"The door's open," Melony said, hanging back
for the first time. "Shall we go in?"

"We certainly shall." Grace relished the thought
of being able to remind Melony that in the end, she,
Grace, had been the brave member of their expedi-
tion.

"I don't believe I can go first," Melony whispered.

"Well, I believe I can," Grace said, releasing
Melony's hand and marching upward toward the
black opening into the building. "Come along. If you
were a man, I should call you jinglebrains. There is
nothing to fear."

"Of course not," Melony said from behind.

Grace entered the pavilion and drew in a hushed
breath. Inside, beams of white light as thin as
threads crisscrossed the darkness from tiny holes in

the dome. The beams caught glittering speckles in the marble walls.

"Come on, do, Melony. This is like nothing I've ever experienced before."

A crash brought a shriek to her lips. "Melony!" Grace whirled around. "Melony! Where are you?"

There was no reply.

She took a few steps and stopped. The entrance no longer showed as an oblong in white walls. Running, Grace reached the place where she thought the doorway had been—and found it.

Closed.

Closed and apparently jammed.

"Melony! The door's stuck. Help me!"

A scratching sound sent her whirling around. She pressed her back to the wall. "What is it? Who's there?"

It was probably a *rat.* "Melony!"

"Hush, Grace."

A man's voice spoke very nearby.

Fingers sought her face.

Grace screamed.

"Hush, Grace," he repeated. "It's all right. You're safe with me."

She closed her eyes and almost collapsed with relief. "Sir Mortimer. Thank goodness it's you."

Chapter 22

A man ought to make a habit of having himself a virgin from time to time.

Exhilarating, Mortimer decided, resting his hands about Grace's neck, her slender, unsuspecting neck.

"The door must have blown shut," she said. Her face was a pale blur touched by pinpoints of light from the holes in the dome. "Quickly, Sir Mortimer, we must open it."

"We will," he told her, ensuring that his voice remained warm. "We will."

She stepped away, and he made no attempt to stop her. "Poor Melony will be out of her mind with worry. Melony! Melony, it's all right."

After several seconds, she turned, and he heard her fumbling with the door. "It . . . it is really stuck," she said.

Smiling, he fingered the key in his waistcoat pocket. "Let me try." Settling a hand on her cool shoulder, he reached around and made a satisfactorily loud noise rattling the handle. "Dash me, the thing won't open. Melony! Melony, are you out there?"

"Perhaps she can't hear us."

"Unlikely." This must be handled exactly as he and Melony had planned.

"She must have gone for help."

"You don't know Melony as I do. Highly strung

creature. This will have frightened her. Mark my words, she'll go home to get me."

Grace faced him once more. "Oh." He stood so close, she automatically settled her hands on his chest and looked up into his face. "But you are not at home. You are here."

"Melony doesn't know that, does she?"

"I suppose not."

"So she will go home, discover I'm not there, and then try to decide what to do next."

"Oh, my."

"Oh, my indeed. She will not go back to the company for fear of Theodora's—and your mama's— wrath at her for bringing you out here."

Grace's fingers curled on his chest. "So what will she do?"

"I'm afraid she may take a very long time deciding what to do at all. We shall just have to find our own way out."

"Why *are* you here?"

He'd been prepared for the question. "I felt a pang of guilt for not accompanying Theodora, so I decided to come on over. Popped along the gardens from Arran's place. Used a route we knew as boys. Got this far and decided to put off the awful musicale a bit longer. I was wandering. What more can I tell you?"

"I'm very glad you were wandering."

She sounded so sincere, he almost laughed aloud. "Y'know, if I remember correctly, there's a trap thing above the door. To let more air in during the heat of summer. Opens inward on hinges from the bottom."

Grace clutched his waistcoat lapels. "Can we open it and get out?"

"Possibly. Although I can't think how to reach the thing. There's nothing to stand on in here." Marble benches lined walls on three sides of the pavilion; there were no other furnishings. "I recall getting shut in here with Arran when we were boys. If memory serves, he stood on my shoulders and made it out through that trap, but . . ."

"*I* shall do it."

Mortimer swallowed a chuckle. "Course not. Wouldn't hear of it, m'dear."

"Well, you're going to have to hear of it." She moved beside him and peered upward. "I'm not terribly heavy. If you were to sort of curl over and lean against the door, I could step upon your back."

"I absolutely forbid it," he said, and crossed his arms.

Grace caught at his sleeve and tried to shake him. *"Please.* It is so frightening . . . not being with you, but the thought of not being able to get out for goodness knows how long."

"I'm certain Melony will do something by morning."

"Morning!"

"Hm. Perhaps that is too long to wait. I could lift you to sit upon my shoulder. That should be relatively safe."

"Do it." Grace faced the door and spread her arms. "We shall do this very well together."

Oh, very well indeed.

Mortimer clasped Grace's tiny waist and felt a deep surge of heat in his loins. "Here we go. We must be very careful." He hoisted her easily to sit on his left shoulder. "Can you reach it?"

"I . . . Yes! Yes, here it is." She strained, searching for the catch. "It's . . . Oh, dear, I think it opens from the top."

"Then we shall give it up." He tightened his grip on her waist.

"No! Help me stand on your shoulder. I shall reach it easily then."

"Are you certain you—"

"Absolutely certain." With one hand on the door and the other firmly anchored in his hair, she shifted. "Steady me. I'm really very nimble."

Yes . . . This was working even better than he had dared hope.

Grace weighed so little—yet was so femininely shaped. His hands slid down over her hips, and blood began to pump, hot and hard, in his veins. Then she was hitching up her skirts and scrambling upward. Mortimer assisted until she stood upon his shoulder and reached for the top of the trap.

He held her ankles.

She stretched farther. "I think I feel a bolt."

"Good." Slipping his hands up to her calves was so natural. "Can you move it?" Holding her knees would make her so much more secure.

"It's . . . *stiff*."

The effort to shoot open the bolt caused her to wobble.

Mortimer shifted his grip rapidly up Grace's thighs. "Careful," he said, hearing the thickening of his own voice. "Be very, very careful."

"I do believe someone has closed it permanently."

Another wobble took Mortimer's hands even higher, past garters to such soft skin.

"They have! It's nailed shut and . . . Oh, Sir Mortimer!"

The tensing of her body let him know she'd finally noticed how intimately he touched her. "You're perfectly safe. I'll help you down."

A slight, deliberate shift on his part and she started to fall.

Mortimer grappled and it simply happened; her silk drawers parted to admit one of his hands.

"Sir Mortimer!"

He could not do other than save her from a terrible accident. "Trust me," he said, bundling her

skirts at her hips, cupping her delightfully rounded
bare bottom, and swinging her legs around his waist.
"Ah, yes. My poor Grace. Trust me and I shall make
certain you forget to be frightened."

At the sight of Arran, the Muirs' butler all but
staggered backward. "My . . . lord?"

Arran, with Calum at his elbow, swept off his hat
but made no attempt to remove his mud-splattered
cloak. They strode into the foyer and glanced quickly
around.

The butler, a thin, white-haired ancient who
walked like a puzzled partridge in his shiny black
slippers, tilted his head and peered up into Arran's
face. "Lord . . . Stonehaven?" His filmy eyes shifted
to Calum. "And the boy?"

"Good evening, Jarvie," Arran said. The servant
had been with the Muirs since before Arran first visited with his father in the summer of 1800. "You're
correct. I'm Stonehaven—the younger," he added
lest the old man think he was talking to Arran's father. "And this is my friend, Mr. Innes."

Jarvie hitched rheumatic shoulders. "Your father
died some years since, my lord. I was merely taken
aback to see you. I had heard you no longer—"

"Yes, yes," Arran said. "I no longer *do*. But I'm
here now and I'd appreciate your assistance. I'm
looking for my cousin, Sir Mortimer Cuthbert, and
his party. I believe they were to attend a musicale
here this evening."

"Indeed," Jarvie said. "Third floor. The green
drawing room."

"I'll check there," Calum said, starting up the
stairs, taking several steps at a time.

"Lady Cuthbert arrived," Jarvie said. "And her
sister and the quiet young lady and her mother. But
I don't believe I saw Sir Mortimer."

Calum hesitated, looking down at Arran.

"They're about to go in for refreshments, sir," Jarvie said loudly. "Supper's set in the little drawing room and Lady Muir's parlor. Second floor for the little drawing room. Third floor, Lady Muir's parlor."

"We can't afford to waste more time," Calum said.

Arran nodded. "I'll go to the gardens. Just in case."

"The gardens, my lord?" Jarvie's impressive brows jutted over a beaked nose. "The party is assembled above, not outside."

"Do not concern yourself," Arran said. "Go on up, Calum. I'll head for the pavilion. I know where it is."

She would be embarrassed for the rest of her life!

"I'm so sorry," Grace said. "I slipped."

"Think nothing of it." Sir Mortimer's voice was muffled. "But I fear we have a small problem. I must ask you to keep your legs where they are for a moment."

Her legs were still wrapped around his waist. "Why?"

"We . . . A part of your, er, *apparel* has become attached to a . . . A moment and I'm sure I can undo the problem."

"Oh!" His fingers pressed into her most private places. "Really, I insist you let me down. Move your hand at once."

He did move his hand—in a rubbing motion that sent a burning sensation into her thighs. Grace tried to clamp herself together, to shut him out.

"I shall simply have to loosen my own clothing," Sir Mortimer said. "Otherwise we shall tear your dress. Then how shall we explain where you've been when we get you back inside?"

Another stroke of his fingers caused a fresh rush of hot tension.

His face was pressed to her breasts!

"You are very soft, Grace."

"I do not care if my clothes are torn," she said, struggling.

"Of course you do."

He moved all about her, rubbing between her legs, lifting her higher whilst he hitched at she knew not what. And his very mouth grazed beneath the neckline of the bodice that was still too large.

"Sir Mortimer!"

Arran leaped up the steps to the pavilion and pounded on the door. It had been Grace's voice he heard. Calum had been right. She was in there.

"Grace! It's all right, my love. I'm here. Open this door, Mortimer."

"Stonehaven?" she called. "Oh, thank goodness."

He heard Mortimer curse.

"The door won't open," Grace said. "It's stuck."

Arran remembered another time, years ago, when he'd chased Mortimer, threatening him with the thrashing he richly deserved for tormenting a kitten. On that occasion Mortimer had also become "stuck" in the pavilion.

He drew in a calming breath. "The lock must have shot home by itself. Remember how it did that time when we were boys, Mortimer?"

Silence.

"I'm sure that's what happened. Check the wall to the left of the door. There should be a key on a ledge."

"Is it there?" Grace sounded near hysterical.

He would *kill* Mortimer if he'd . . . Later must be soon enough to deal with that.

"Dash me," Mortimer said loudly. "Here it is."

In seconds the door swung open and Grace tumbled out. "Stonehaven! Oh, thank you. Thank you. I was so—"

"Dashed grateful, old man," Mortimer thundered with spurious enthusiasm. "Quite forgot that key."

"Are you all right?" Arran asked Grace. He gathered her against him and said softly, "You aren't hurt?"

"N-No."

"She almost was," Mortimer said. "We were trying to open that trap above the door. Grace is a game little thing, Arran. You've a good woman there. Insisted upon climbing on my shoulder and—"

"The trap was nailed shut when we were children," Arran said.

"Well, no harm done," Mortimer said, and his eyes met Arran's above Grace's head.

If there was no harm done, it was only because Calum had managed to virtually drag Arran to Edinburgh. "No," he said slowly. "No harm." Keeping communication open with Mortimer would be the best course. Easier to watch him that way.

"Mama will be so concerned by now," Grace said. "I cannot imagine how long I've been out here."

"Not long, I should think, m'dear," Mortimer said heartily. "But Arran had better get you back inside before you catch your death. Flimsy gown, that."

Arran's spine ached with the longing to knock the bastard down. "Lead the way, Mortimer." In future he intended always to be where he could see his cousin's back.

"No. Think I'll pass. Thanks all the same. I'll pop on back to our place."

"*My* place, d'you mean?"

"Exactly. Who would have thought they'd have nailed that trap shut?"

Arran helped Grace down the steps. "You would, Mortimer. Muir caught you climbing through it once too often. Don't you remember? He had you do the nailing.''

He didn't wait for a response from Mortimer. Once back inside the Muirs', and with Jarvie hovering nearby, he inspected Grace. ''Best make sure you don't look as if you've been *building* a pavilion,'' he temporized. ''Are you certain you aren't at all hurt?''

She shook her head.

''Miss Wren went for a walk in the garden,'' Arran told Jarvie. ''She got herself stuck in that pavilion.''

Jarvie tutted. ''You don't say, my lord.''

Arran raised Grace's chin and looked into her eyes. ''There is absolutely nothing I should know? About your unpleasant experience?''

''Nothing.''

He didn't miss the unhappy shadow in her golden eyes. Little imagination was needed to suggest what might have caused Grace to scream Mortimer's name in the pavilion. The debauched scoundrel had been in the process of forcing himself upon her; Arran would make a wager on that.

''Well, you certainly look marvelous.'' And she did. In red satin, she was startling. Automatically Arran smoothed back a silver-blond lock that had begun to work free of the tight chignon that had become her preference in the past few days. ''You are a jewel in that dress. A fascinating scarlet jewel. You should be wearing the rubies.'' His attention dropped lower. The bodice did not fit particularly well—which was all to the good in this instance. The satin dipped loosely between her pretty breasts. How easily accessible they would be. His body's response was predictable.

Mortimer could have . . . Arran clamped his teeth together.

''Do you have a kerchief, Stonehaven?''

His gaze shot back to her eyes. "A kerchief?"

Grace tugged her bodice higher and spread a hand over her décolletage. "Yes. A kerchief."

"I'm afraid not. Are you injured?"

"No." To Jarvie she said, "Could you find me a kerchief—something in lace, perhaps?"

The man's face showed no sign of surprise. He left the hall, and Grace promptly turned her back on Arran.

"*Is* something wrong, Grace?"

"No."

"Then we really should be getting upstairs."

"You seem quite changed, Stonehaven. Quite good-tempered."

Could he be blamed for his previous ill humor toward her? "The circumstances of our meeting were not the best." Yes, he could be blamed. "You were misled. I may have behaved badly. I regret that. Perhaps it is time for us to make a better beginning." After all, he needed a wife, and quickly.

And he found he . . . liked her?

"It was wrong of me to come to Scotland as I did. In such a calculated manner."

Arran raised a hand to touch her hair, but dropped it back to his side. "You were desperate to find a way to support yourself and your mother. A marriage such as Calum offered was bound to seem like an answer to your prayers."

"It did!" She looked over her shoulder at him. "But I do not feel good about agreeing simply because I wanted security."

He wanted to . . . He *wanted* her. "I think you were very brave," he told her. The way her sun-tipped lashes made a golden shadow in her eyes fascinated him. "You feel great responsibility for your mother. That has become obvious to me. For her—more than for yourself—you took an enormous risk."

Rosy color rose in her cheeks. *Charming*.

"You are so very kind, Stonehaven," she said, and for an instant he thought her mouth quivered. "But I *knew* you were. Just as I know what it is that made you so horrid—and you were very horrid for a while."

The scuff, scuff of approaching slippers heralded the return of Jarvie. "I trust this will do, miss," he said, holding out a white lace kerchief as if it were a fish too long from the water.

"Oh, *perfect*. Thank you."

Grace's head bent forward, and Arran watched the interesting spectacle of elbows rising and falling as she did something with the "perfect" kerchief.

"There!" She came to his side and smiled gaily. "You see? You have no need to fear being compromised by me again."

He could only stare. "Compromised? By *you?*"

"Don't shilly-shally about it, Stonehaven." She sounded positively exuberant. "You are an exceedingly principled man. I caused you—although I hope you will believe that I did not know it at the time—but I caused you to be drawn away from your principles. An excessive display of female *skin* caused you to desire to Sit With Me. You could do nothing to help yourself. I expect it's all part of the mysteriousness that is the marriage—that part of a marriage that occurs strictly between a man and a woman, that is—in private—when they are alone?"

"Good God," he muttered, unable to stop himself.

"May I ask you a question?"

"Why not?" He had never encountered a female like her.

"Did we do quite *everything* that occurs between a man and a woman—in private?"

He looked past her at Jarvie. The old man's chin jutted, and his neck. His eyes revealed nothing.

"This is hardly the time or the place to discuss such . . . personal matters." His gaze settled on the lace kerchief and he frowned. "What . . . ? *Why* have you . . . ? Grace, why have you stuffed that ridiculous little kerchief into your bodice?"

"You see?" She jabbed him with a forefinger. "You looked at the very spot where the most purely female skin is located. If I had not thought very quickly, my wretched skin would have been turning you into a tyrant again. But I am beginning to understand you very well, Stonehaven. Trust me. Your principles will be safe in my hands."

"*Good God!*" The woman was amazing. He had to restrain himself from removing her foolish little modesty frill. "Since we seem to be having the most outrageous conversation, there is a small matter that has concerned me. It continues to concern me."

She settled her hand on his arm. "You may ask me anything. *Anything.*"

Really, she did have marvelous eyes . . . and marvelous skin . . . and her face was *different*, unforgettable, intelligent, ethereal . . . Damn it, he was becoming obsessed with the chit. Unbelievable.

"Stonehaven? Please don't hesitate to trust me with your problems."

Exasperated but amused, he ushered her to the stairs. "You are too kind, Grace." They started up. "The matter I wished to discuss was your . . . *friendships* with men to whom you are not related."

"I only have one."

He stopped. "Me? Yes, at the moment. But I was referring to previous, er . . ."

Grace appeared puzzled. "You know there have been no previous friends such as you."

"I know no such thing for sure. I thought . . ."

"What could you possibly have thought?" She went to remove her hand from his arm, but Arran covered her fingers and held them. "You thought I had . . . you thought I had experienced with other men what I experienced with you? You believed I was a female with no sense of propriety at all and that I was accustomed to being alone with men?''

How could he tell the girl that he knew in his heart that she had not and was not, but that his head required reassurance?

She tugged her hand free and continued upstairs. Arran caught up at the top of the flight. Grace said, "My mother will be beside herself with worry at my absence. Kindly excuse me.''

"You are my fiancée and you will not walk away when I am speaking to you.''

Her chin came up. "I am and always will be a woman with a strong mind. If you remember that, we shall do tolerably well.''

"If I . . . You are *impossible*. Are you telling me that when you spoke of pursuing a friendship with me after your marriage—before you knew I was the marquess—you meant nothing more than that? *Friendship?*''

"What else could I possibly have meant?''

Arran expanded his chest and expelled the breath slowly. "Indeed. What else could you possibly have meant?'' His damnable suspicion of all women had come close to robbing him of incredible happiness. Gratitude at his having stopped—for whatever reason—on the very brink of seducing an innocent mingled with the anticipation of doing that very thing: on his wedding night.

Grace advanced, and he fell in at her shoulder. "May I ask you to do something for me?'' he said.

She paused, and he saw emotions flit over her features. "Yes. Yes, of course.''

"Would you please forgive my bad behavior toward you in the past?''

Her sudden smile was radiant. "Consider it forgiven and forgotten. Will you forgive me for taking

so long to understand the battles you waged with
your principles until it was almost too late?"

"Consider yourself forgiven."

"Thank you. Oh, dear, the music has already begun again. That means I was missing throughout
the refreshments. What will Mama think?"

A footman opened the door to the Muirs' green
drawing room, where the expected array of brilliantly dressed guests sat in rows. Laboring before
the company, a misguided violinist struggled
through part of a Paganini concerto.

Arran heard Grace murmur, "Oh dear," and
smiled.

"Mother Wren appears . . . occupied?"

Grace placed a hand in front of her grin. "*Mother*
Wren? Mama would hate that. But she does seem
quite happy, don't you think?"

"I do think." Mrs. Wren sat with a thin, graying
man in exceedingly conservatively cut clothing who
gazed at her with open admiration. "In fact, I wonder if she even knows you were not here."

"Melony!" Grace whispered harshly. "I cannot
believe it. There she sits, when she must think me
still trapped in that beastly pavilion."

Melony Pincham sat next to Blanche Wren, with
Theodora to her right. As if she felt their presence,
Mrs. Pincham turned. Her horrified gaze met Arran's, then moved on to Grace. Even at a distance
he saw the woman whiten.

"Why," Grace said in a low voice, "I do not think
Melony is at all glad to see that I am safe."

Arran did not reply. Theodora hissed something
into Mrs. Pincham's ear, and she returned her attention to the front of the room.

There were several vacant seats on the other side
of a narrow aisle, and Arran led Grace to sit down.
He felt, as well as saw, heads begin to swivel in his
direction. He heard, very clearly, murmured com-

ments across the room, and he held his mouth in a grim line. Let them exclaim at the sight of Stonehaven. They'd thought him gone from their midst forever. He would be glad to absent himself again as soon as he'd made certain every one of them knew he'd made another trip to the altar.

The painful performance drew to a close, but instead of the expected swell of conversation, a storm of whispers passed through the assembly. One pair of eyes after another made brief contact with Arran's before swiftly moving away. And there were the eyes of young women that tried to hold his, to gain his attention—and the gracious nods of more than one or two hopeful mamas. They had enjoyed their shredding of his reputation, but they would be more than happy to secure entrance to Kirkcaldy and a right to the Stonehaven fortune.

"They are all looking at you," Grace said. "And they look so spiteful. I should like to tell them all exactly what I think of them." She slipped her hand through his arm.

"I do believe you feel protective of me," he said. "Tell me what you would tell these magpies."

"That they are nothing and you are everything, of course."

"How have I managed to earn such esteem, I wonder?"

"You have earned it despite yourself," she told him tartly. "Fortunately, I am very perceptive and I was able to see through your nasty humors. There are still things I wish to know about you, but I'm persuaded that your answers—when you choose to give them—will satisfy me. In the meantime, I am not going to speak to a single one of these *avid* people. *Look* at them. They are positively *popping* with curiosity about you."

"Let them pop," he said mildly. The feel of

Grace's hand tightly holding his arm was more than pleasant—so was the warmth of her shoulder.

Lady Muir, florid but distinguished in plum-colored velvet, rose and stood before her guests. "And now we come to the portion of the program for which we have all waited," she said. "May I present to you the most distinguished pianist to grace any Scottish drawing room at any time. Mr. Gallatin Plethero."

Arran opened his mouth but found the air in the room had been entirely removed. Darkness gathered at the edges of his mind. He must remain calm and he must show nothing of what he felt.

"Have you heard this musician?" Grace asked. She continued to catch glances cast in their direction and to deliver deathly glares in response.

Arran said, "I may have heard him."

"Good evening," Plethero said, arrogantly putting aside polite address. "And it is indeed a good evening for all of us. I am grateful to Sir Alistair and Lady Muir for inviting me to play for you. The following are several works by an anonymous composer. Some of you will have heard me play them before."

A presence arrived at Arran's side, and he looked up into Calum's face. He bent to speak into Arran's ear. "This is long overdue."

Arran didn't reply. Calum pulled up a chair and sat beside him.

Plethero played brilliantly, with absolute control and confidence—and with an empathy with the music that turned Arran's heart. Plethero played as if Arran's music had been drawn from his own soul.

The first arrangement was "The Children." Arran had composed it with visions of the tenant children at play romping across his mind. He closed his eyes and saw whirling arms and legs and bright smiles beneath a bright sun. He saw little hands clasping little hands and swinging and swinging—and he heard the sound of children laughing.

Then there was silence.

But only for a moment before applause, delighted, enthusiastic applause, broke out amid cries of "Bravo!"

Plethero turned on his piano bench and made a deep, self-contained bow.

"You are inspired," Calum said in low tones. "A genius."

"I am an interpreter," Arran responded. "I take other people's moments and write them as notes. There is your genius." He indicated Plethero.

"Thank you," the pianist said loudly. "Thank you."

Arran heard his "Seashore" and knew once more the wonder of soft surf seeking purchase on dark gold sand, and falling back again, bubbling, popping—and returning again and again, endlessly.

When the ovation finally subsided, Gallatin Plethero swept the fingers of his right hand over the keys, raised a knowing brow at his rapt listeners, and paraded Arran's "Girls at a London Ball" for all to hear.

Grace shook Arran's arm. "Listen," she whispered.

"He's very good." Arran felt half-sick, half-thrilled to his core. He'd been right to choose this man. Plethero was indeed the genius. He took a muddler's rough efforts and smoothed them into wonders.

"He doesn't play it as well as you," Grace said.

Everything within him became instantly, utterly, still. He could not breathe. He was not sure he still thought at all. Surely his heart did not beat.

"Arran, when you play this, the colors are brighter," Grace murmured, leaning against him as if they were the oldest of friends between whom there were no constraints. "I'm sure whoever wrote this was thinking of a grand ball. But there is a sadness. A whimsical sadness. Only, you make me feel it more.''

She spoke as if she'd heard him play the piece many times, rather than once and incompletely.

Again, as Plethero finished, the audience leapt to their feet, clapping madly and shouting for more. Arran found himself standing beside Grace, with Calum at his other elbow, applauding with the rest.

''More!'' a man's voice demanded.

''More! More!'' went up the echo from dozens of others.

Plethero, standing to take his leave, held up humble hands and waited for the din to subside. ''Very well. For you I will play one more piece. Other than by its composer, it has been played only by me. It has never been played in public before. I had thought to wait a little longer. To work with it a little longer. But now is the right moment. I'm not certain why, but I feel it. Short, but utterly haunting.''

Before a single note was played, Arran knew what he would hear. He sank back in his chair and spread a hand over his eyes. The man had it right. Skirts filling with the breeze, twirling about slender legs and falling again about slim ankles. Silver-blond hair spraying wide—like dandelion puffs beneath a blinding noon sun.

A rustle drew him partway out of his trance. Grace had moved to the front of her seat and strained even farther forward. A nimbus shimmered along her profile, her throat, over the smooth lines of her coiffure.

Notes cascaded beneath Plethero's fingers.

Come, dance with me, his imp—his imp of the sunshine now—called, offering him her hands.

Grace turned to stare at him, her amber eyes huge. Then, as if she had forgotten they were not the only two present, she touched his cheek, skimmed his mouth, and stared down at his hands.

Plethero made the music magical. He made it exactly what Arran had intended it to be.

The final notes slipped softly away, and in the momentary hush that followed, Plethero said, "The composer gave us an extra small gift this time. He let us know that the piece is entitled: 'Grace.'"

Arran returned her probing gaze. The music he'd written whilst thinking only of Grace had moved her more than all the rest. How odd.

There were no more encores. People stood and milled and chattered.

Grace let Arran draw her up, but she continued to look only at him. "You liked it, didn't you?" He hoped he sounded light, indifferent.

"Stonehaven!" Blanche Wren bobbed about beside them. "I had no idea you intended to be here. How perfectly wonderful. Please meet my friend, the Reverend Felix Bastion."

"How do you do," Arran said, never taking his attention from Grace.

"Yes, well . . ." Blanche drifted away, and others took her place. Theodora. La Pincham—babbling at Grace about not knowing what to do. He heard Grace say, "It doesn't matter," and then she smiled at him and they strolled, tightly arm in arm, from the room and downstairs.

The sight of Mortimer, slipping through the front door, caused Arran no more than an instant's irritation. The girl on his arm was different. She made *him* different.

"I want to talk about it," she told him.

"We shall talk about whatever pleases you."

Others began to stream down behind them into the hall. Melony Pincham was a splash of magenta silk that converged with Mortimer only feet away, and Arran heard him tell her, "It's all right. Everything's all right.'' Then, ''She's been found, thank God.''

Pretty. Very pretty. If anyone should overhear and know that Grace had been missing, they'd assume Mortimer to be suitably concerned for her safety.

The distance between the Muirs' and Arran's own house on Charlotte Square was short. With Grace warmly wrapped in a fur-lined cloak that matched her dress and with a draping hood over her hair, they walked very slowly home.

''Home,'' Arran said aloud at his front door. ''This is one of your homes. All of my homes will soon be yours.''

''Thank you,'' she said, and touched his mouth again in that way that caused his stomach to fall. ''The music is beautiful.''

''I'm glad you liked it. I have wanted to tell you that I hung the painting you gave me in my sitting room.''

''You did?'' She sounded vague. ''Thank you.''

''Thank *you*. I am glad Calum found you for me.''

''So am I.''

He kissed her then, gently, tasting her sweetness. Drawing her carefully against him, he moved his lips from hers and kissed his way fleetingly along her jaw until he could nuzzle into her neck.

''You named it after me.''

He grew still.

''You did, didn't you?'' Her voice broke. ''And you composed all that music, didn't you?''

''Grace—''

''The night when . . . After I threw the ruby girdle at you, I decided to go to the gallery and take my paints. I had thought to return to London, but you were there and . . . I heard you play 'Grace.' ''

''I—''

''Hush. The pianist said that before him, it had only been played by its composer. I heard you play it. That can only mean that you wrote it. And you named it for me.''

"Yes," he admitted, finally raising his face.

"I don't know exactly how I know, but I do. All of it. All of that music was yours. And you prefer to take none of the credit. You are the most wonderful man I've ever met."

Arran pushed down the hood and cradled her head, brushed his thumbs back and forth over her ears. "I am the most fortunate man you have ever met. What else can I be when outrageous chance chose to bless me with you?"

The front door opened behind Grace. Wiffen, the Charlotte Square butler for many years, cleared his throat, and Arran nodded shortly at him. Wiffen managed the serene countenance of the perfect servant, despite the fact that he was confronted with his master for the first time in more than five years.

"Good evening, Wiffen," Arran said, dropping his hands to Grace's shoulders and turning her carefully toward the house. "My fiancée and I will take brandy in the library."

"Good evening, my lord." Wiffen stepped aside to allow Arran and Grace to pass. "It would probably be appropriate for me to—"

"Thank you, Wiffen," Arran said, taking off Grace's cloak and his own and handing them to the butler. "Is the fire made up in the library?"

"It is, my lord, but—"

"Never mind. If it's a little low, I'll deal with it."

"My lord—"

"Brandy," Arran said, and caught Grace's hand. "Come, my love. We have plans to make, and very little time to do so."

He tugged her playfully into the library. "Sit by the fire and warm yourself."

"Yes . . . Oh! Arran . . ."

"What is it, my love?"

He followed the direction of her startled gaze, and narrowed his eyes. "What in God's name are *you* doing here?"

The tall, shabbily dressed woman who hovered near the fireplace clasped her hands before her. "Arran, don't speak to me like that after so long. I'm your Isabel. I'm the woman you married."

Chapter 23

Tall, with dark red hair and blue eyes, the beautiful woman before the fire held her hands imploringly toward Stonehaven.

Grace pressed a fist to her mouth. She would not faint. She would not cry out. She would show nothing at all of the insane turmoil she felt within.

"Mortimer," Stonehaven said, his voice deep and wrathful. "He found you, didn't he? He brought you here?"

"Please, Arran, don't be angry with me. I didn't want things to happen as they did."

"You didn't want them to happen as they did?" Stonehaven gave an ugly laugh. "Then what in God's name did you want, woman? You knew what you were about. When I sent you away, it was with the understanding that you were never to return."

"My circumstances have changed."

"What is that to me?"

"Now there is only you, Arran. I only want you."

Grace moved backwards, feeling her way to a chair, and slumped down.

"I want you out of this house. *Now.*"

The woman began to cry piteously. "I have sinned. But we have all sinned—"

"She is not dead," Grace heard herself say.

"Dead?" the woman said.

"When you . . . *disappeared*, Isabel, the notion became popular that I had killed you and hidden your body beneath Revelation.'' He smiled thinly. *''That* should be an idea to make you laugh. We both know it was not I who was ever with you beneath my very rooms, don't we?''

''Arran, please—''

''Get out, madam.''

''Stop it!'' Grace covered her ears. ''I cannot bear it. This woman is obviously in need. You wronged her in the worst imaginable way—and would have wronged me, too. In faith, you have planned our wedding when you are already *married!*''

A commotion sounded in the hall, and Mama bustled into the library, smiling, swinging her muff. ''There you are.'' If she noticed Isabel, she showed no sign. ''Everything is absolutely perfect, and I want you two to be the first to know. I am to be married! There, what do you think of that?''

Grace shook her head slowly. ''Mama, what are you saying?''

''Felix—that is, the Reverend Bastion—and I are betrothed. I know this is very sudden, but we loved each other on sight. We are to be married in Somerset. He has his living there. Just as soon as the banns are heard, the ceremony will take place.''

''Mama—''

''I'm sorry to desert you right before your own wedding, but I know you will not begrudge me some small happiness in my dwindling years.''

''Mama—''

''And I am determined to start afresh.'' Blanche caught Stonehaven's arm and urged him to his desk. ''I expect Grace has told you about my little problems in London? My gambling debts?''

Grace moaned.

Stonehaven muttered something unintelligible.

''Well, I've explained the whole thing to dear Felix, and he promises that the man who threatened me is all bluff. And Felix does not care that I had a

slight . . . the merest spell of bad judgment. With
him I shall be a new and completely honest woman.
He has assured me so."

"I'm delighted to hear it," Stonehaven said.
"When do you leave?"

"Almost at once," Mama responded. "But Felix
made me promise to clear up another matter. These
are yours." She ripped the lining from the voluminous muff and poured a flashing array of jewelry
and other small treasures onto the desk.

"Oh, Mama." Surely this could not be happening. Surely no human being could be expected to
tolerate so much shock and emotion in one night.

"I took them," Mama announced, indicating the
heap of valuables matching the descriptions of those
purportedly stolen from Kirkcaldy. She bent to extract something from inside one of her slippers. "I
happened upon this key in London. Felix says I
should give it to you also since I used it to gain entrance to locked rooms in your castle. It opens absolutely any door. Isn't that ingenious?"

"Most," Stonehaven agreed.

Mama made certain her muff appeared tidy and
slipped her hands inside. "I was wrong, I suppose,
but I was desperate to make certain that I had some
small resource to rely upon if Grace failed to provide
for me. And it wasn't as if you couldn't afford for
me to have such paltry trifles."

"What did you think you could do with them?"
Grace asked weakly.

"Pawn them, of course. I brought them to Edinburgh to do just that, but now it won't be necessary." Mama's brow puckered. "I do know I was
misguided, and I'm sorry. I shall not return to Kirkcaldy with you, Grace. I'll let you know when Felix
and I are ready to visit you."

Amid a rustle of embroidered satin, she departed,
leaving the door open in her wake.

The silence that followed was awful before Isabel launched herself at Stonehaven. She flung her arms around his neck, pressed her face into his shoulder, and wept with abandon.

Grace looked from the woman's heaving back, to Stonehaven's thunderous face, to the open door. Mama was to be married? She was leaving? Now?

"I must go," she said, getting up. "Um. Yes, I'll just go now."

"You will do no such thing, Grace." Stonehaven grasped Isabel's wrists and dragged her from him. "I thought you were in London. You agreed to remain there."

"I missed you."

His green eyes glittered. "Very affecting. You forget that I know all about you, Isabel." The woman's fingers had all but pulled his black hair from the ribbon at his nape.

Who had said he was a bad man? He appeared now as a dark, dangerously handsome creature of the night—wild and strong and, yes, perhaps *bad*. A buccaneer in an English gentleman's clothing.

"Have you a place to stay, madam?"

Isabel shook her head.

"Wiffen! Present yourself."

The butler did as he was asked immediately.

"Take this person and find her a place to sleep. She should have a meal and whatever else she needs for her comfort."

"Arran—"

He held up a hand and averted his face from Isabel. "Not another word or I shall have you cast out into the street."

Wiffen waved the woman past him, followed her, and shut the door.

"You cannot be so cruel," Grace said, appalled at her breathlessness.

"Can't I? Hah! I've decided I must learn to be

much more cruel in the future than I have ever been
before. People plotting against me. *God!*" He paced,
pulling off his coat as he went. "Relatives seeking
to take what is mine. Surrounded on all sides by
bloodsuckers and vagabonds. *That* woman appear-
ing as a last vicious attempt to ruin what is finally
going to be good in my life."

Grace shrank away.

"How dare they conspire against me in such a
villainous manner?" He sent her a fierce stare.
"They shall not get away with it, I tell you. And my
future mother-in-law. My future *mother-in-law*, in the
name of all that's sane and reasonable! Stealing from
me! And a gambler of some kind, to boot."

"Do not criticize my mother."

"I *will* criticize her!"

Grace backed all the way to the wall.

Stonehaven followed. "Someone should have
criticized her a long time ago for the weak, unreasonable female she is. She has clearly never understood that she has an extraordinary daughter."

"I have to think of a place to go," Grace said in
barely more than a whisper. "It may be difficult so
late at night."

He smiled then, and the effect was as terrifying as
it was—*thrilling?* She swallowed and would not let
herself look away from his mocking eyes.

"We shall leave for Kirkcaldy at first light," he
said. "When we arrive I shall arrange for us to be
married at once."

"How dare you suggest such a thing, Stonehaven."

He settled his hands on the wall above her head
and assumed an insolent, commanding slouch. "I
dare that and a great deal more. My name is Arran.
I shall expect you to use it in future."

She poked his chest, met tense, solid muscle
through his perfectly tailored waistcoat and white

linen shirt, and looked at her finger. "You told me to call you Stonehaven because the use of that name did not suggest an intimacy of the spirit."

"I've changed my mind. We certainly do share an intimacy of the spirit."

Grace poked him again. "Kindly step away."

Instead, he kissed her temple, softly, lingeringly. "I never, ever intend to step away from you, Grace."

"You are a *married* man!" But, fie, her eyes closed and her mouth became dry.

"Will you listen to me? Listen well and then we shall hear no more of this." He spoke against her hair. "I went to the altar with that woman. It was on the same day my father died. That should have been the bad omen I needed."

With the backs of his fingers, he smoothed her jaw. "Isabel became with child. We'd been married only months. I was the happiest man alive."

"Yes." She should leave this place, run away without knowing where to go if necessary.

"You already know the stories about that *infamous* night."

"When Isabel disappeared from the castle?"

"Ah, yes. And the story began that I had murdered her and our child."

Tears welled in Grace's eyes. "I heard the story."

"It was all lies. That night my *wife* informed me that she intended to leave me for another man. She had gained what she wanted from me. Jewels, money, things she had already taken to safety outside Kirkcaldy."

"Oh."

"Indeed. *Oh.* And she did leave me. Before she went, I told her that if she promised never to appear before me again, I would let her go and say no more."

"How terrible. But she is still your wife."

He tipped up his face and squeezed his eyes shut. "No, she was never my wife. Isabel Dean, the *actress* my father begged me not to marry, already had a husband. It was to him that she returned. She always said she hated Revelation and would not come to me there. Yet that night she laughed and told me how she and her husband had enjoyed one another in the chambers beneath that very tower—whilst I slept above them."

Grace gasped.

"We were never married."

"But the child? Your child?"

"Yes, the child was mine. But when Isabel admitted her guilt, she also told me she'd visited a woman skilled in *eliminating* unwanted babies. A daughter, she told me. *Born* dead. She murdered my daughter."

"Oh, Arran." Grace slipped her arms beneath his and held him tightly. "I do not understand how such things can be, but I ache for you."

Pain passed over his features. "I mourn the child, but not Isabel. For me she is more dead than my poor child."

Grace buried her face against him. "If it will bring you pleasure, we shall be married tomorrow."

His breath escaped slowly against her face. "Tomorrow," he said. "I need you, Grace."

Chapter 24

"**O**ur parents were married here," Arran said to Struan.

Struan kept pace with Arran's rapid stalking around Kirkcaldy's small chapel. "And this is the happiest occasion it's seen since."

Arran made fists at his sides. "It will be if we ever get the thing done." He could not dismiss a shadowy fear that something would yet intervene to stop him from marrying Grace.

They sidestepped three footmen carrying vases filled with spring flowers.

Shanks and Mrs. Moggach, looking officiously determined, inspected the efforts of the army of servants who had cleaned the chapel.

"I wish Calum would hurry with the damned license," Arran said through his teeth.

"He's also bringing the minister," Struan reminded him. "And everything and everyone will be here in time, so calm yourself, brother. You make even me nervous."

"Hah." Arran wrinkled his nose. "You have no nerves. A cold fish—and you always were. Now you're a *pious* cold fish. And *Catholic*. Not even able to perform a small professional service for me."

"I am useful to stop you from losing your mind while you wait for this marriage of yours." Struan cleared his throat. "Calum asked me to mention something to you."

"I can't think about estate matters at the moment. Tell him to speak with Hector."

"This is a personal matter—to Calum."

"Not now." Arran reversed direction and plodded off in another circle around the six narrow rows of pews. "I'm going to have to deal with Mortimer, damn it. I don't want them here—or anywhere near Grace, ever again. If I hadn't reached Edinburgh in time . . ."

"But you *did*."

"Theodora took it upon herself to limit expenditure on Grace's trousseau. Saving Roger's inheritance, no doubt."

"No doubt. I feel for young Roger."

"Decent boy," Arran said. "Can't imagine why."

"I promised Calum I'd speak to you on his behalf before he arrives."

"Not now." All he wanted was for Calum and the minister to arrive.

"He thinks of you like a brother."

"As I do him." A tension about Struan penetrated Arran's roiling brain. "What is it? What's wrong with Calum? He's not ill?"

"No. The time's come, that's all."

For an instant Arran couldn't think what Struan meant. "The time? Calum . . . You mean he's decided he wants to find out?"

Struan nodded once. "He knows his life did not begin when he was, as a sick child, abandoned on our doorstep. He has vague memories from before. You know that all through the years he's insisted he didn't want to find out who he really is, but now he's changed his mind. That's what he wanted me to tell you."

"Good enough. I'll help him all I—"

"No." Struan settled a hand on Arran's shoulder. "He's going alone, and he doesn't know how long it'll take or if he'll ever find anything at all."

"Going?" Arran cast about to make sense of what Struan was saying. "You mean *leave* Kirkcaldy?"

"His life began somewhere else. He intends to find out exactly where he was born, and to whom—and why strangers eventually left him to die in our stable yard."

"As if it mattered!" Arran threw up his arms. "He has *everything* here."

"Everything but what matters to him most, as it would to you, dear brother. Everything but his own history. That already cost him a woman he loved enough to want to marry."

"Alice Avery wasn't worthy of him."

"He loved her. She married someone else because he's no one."

"No one?" Arran exploded. "There's none better than—"

"In God's name, keep your voice down," Struan said urgently. "Here he comes."

"He can't leave me," Arran hissed. "He's needed here."

"Later."

Calum entered the chapel with the elderly vicar from Kirkcaldy village, a white-haired man who smiled around as if he were accustomed to being called to the castle chapel to marry the lords of Stonehaven.

Arran glared at Calum, who met his eyes directly. Between them passed the knowledge that more than one new era was about to begin. "We appear to be ready," Calum said, offering Arran his hand.

After a brief hesitation, Arran grasped his old friend's hand in both of his. "Struan told me." He bowed his head and said, "Do it if you have to, Calum. But come back to us when you can." He looked up and smiled. "Did someone go for Grace?"

"McWallop gave the nod to her maid. They'll be along soon enough."

"Shall we prepare ourselves?" the vicar said, positioning himself before the shining brass altar rail. A gold cross shone upon the lace-draped altar, and rays of the setting sun glowed crimson, purple, and emerald through brilliant stained-glass windows.

Arran looked at Calum and Struan. "I haven't done any of this as I should. I'm supposed to ask—"

"Calum will stand for you," Struan said, smiling and backing away. "I'm the lucky man who will give away your bride. Be good to her."

"Isn't it late for that lecture?"

"I think not," Struan said. "She is gentle and kind."

"And heartbreakingly untouched," Calum added. "A generous soul like Grace's is easily crushed."

Arran's lips twitched. "She should be perfectly safe with champions such as you."

"I doubt we shall be welcome to accompany her to your wedding night."

"Good God!" Fists on hips, Arran looked upward into the chapel's lushly painted domed ceiling. "I am not an animal bent on tearing her apart. Go, Stuan. I'm impatient."

Struan left. Calum fidgeted at Arran's side.

"You have the ring?" Arran asked.

"Yes."

"The license is in order?"

"Yes."

"Our wedding supper is prepared and ready in my rooms?"

"Yes. Damned strange, too."

"Strange?"

"Not sharing the moment with friends and relations. Locking yourself away."

Arran smiled broadly. "Locking myself away with my bride? Strange? I believe, Calum, that you and I have entirely different interpretations of what is most desirable at such times."

"They're coming."

Arran's stomach swooped and didn't seem inclined to return to its correct position. "Good God."

"What is it?" Calum whispered.

"Nothing . . . Everything. I'm . . . Dammit, this is most unsettling."

"Terrifying, d'you mean?"

"I'll thank you—" He stopped, absolutely unable to continue. Grace entered the chapel on Struan's arm.

Arran noted his brother as if for the first time. Tall, broad-shouldered—too handsome and youthful to have committed himself to so limited a life.

But it was Grace who smote a near fatal blow to Arran's heart. A garland of deep blue forget-me-nots wound through the crown of silver braids atop her proudly held head. She was soon close enough for him to see her trembling smile, the light in her eyes, the bloom on her smooth skin.

Despite her protests, he'd insisted upon seeing the wedding gown the wretched Cuthbert woman had chosen, and had pronounced it impossible. Grace had promptly told him she would choose a suitable dress from among those she owned.

"Look at her," Calum murmured.

"What man could do otherwise?" Arran replied.

Grace's gown was ice white satin with its own almost blue sheen and overlayed with patent net. As she moved toward him, he recognized the gown as the one Theodora had selected, but that tasteless woman could never have envisioned it like this.

Gone was every frill and bow, every loop of satin ribbon. By stripping away fussy ornamentation, a gown of startling simplicity had been created. Sleeves tightly fitted to the wrist, the bodice hugging small breasts, the skirt a slim fall that spread to a modest train behind; more could only have made the gown less.

She arrived before him and stood, looking up into his face.

Arran drew his bottom lip between his teeth. Trust, the trust of a tender creature, was an awesome burden.

By the device of adding a piece of pleated muslin, her neckline had been made demurely high. Arran almost smiled. She would do well to hide her *most female skin* from him, not that she would be successful once they were married and alone.

He picked up the enameled bluebird on its simple chain around her neck. "The lady has rubies, yet she chooses her little bluebird." Not waiting for her response, he added. "Of course she does. The lady is not concerned with *things*, is she?"

"I am concerned only with you, my lord."

His skin prickled.

"Are we ready?" the vicar asked.

They were ready. Arran had not thought his jaded heart could beat so, or that it could swell with the wanting of his soul for the woman who took him as her husband. Her clear voice accepted him and her golden eyes did not flinch away from his when he gave her his name, his protection, and his body for as long as they both might live.

"Take her and feed her," Calum said, but Arran continued to kiss his wife's soft lips.

Whispering, a few feminine giggles, and the rustle of skirts finally made him raise his head. The servants of Kirkcaldy were assembled at the back of the chapel. Arran bowed to them, and Grace turned to dip a little curtsy. The girls giggled afresh and the men smiled. Even Mrs. Moggach and Shanks appeared enormously pleased.

Arran offered Grace his arm. "Shall we, Lady Stonehaven?"

Her cheeks turned a delightful shade of pink, but she placed her hand on his.

"A moment, my friend." Calum slanted glinting dark eyes at Arran. "A kiss for the bride, I think." He touched her cheek and brushed his mouth lightly over her brow. "If this fiend is ever anything but your champion, you have only to tell me, Grace. It will be my pleasure to steal you from him."

She laughed gaily, accepted Struan's formal kiss on her hand, and made a royal procession at Arran's side past the Kirkcaldy staff.

The chapel was in the west wing. By the time Arran had ushered Grace through many long corridors toward those leading past the Eve and Adam Towers and on to Revelation, Calum and Struan had absented themselves, as had the staff. The only sound to break the silence was the click of Arran's boots on stone, the soft shush of Grace's skirts—and his own breathing, which he was almost certain she must hear.

Soon they would be together.

"I am sorry your mother . . . You should have had some family in the chapel."

Her step checked, but only for an instant. "I hope Mama will be happy with her Felix. The only one I needed was in the chapel."

He did not deserve this joy. Even now he knew the lingering shreds of dark fear that this perfect creature would somehow be torn from him.

"I have something for you," Grace said as they emerged into the entrance hall. "May I give you a present now? You have given me so much."

"I have not begun to give to you."

From a tiny pocket in a seam of her gown, she withdrew a little leather pouch. This she placed in his palm. "It has no worth, but you may like it."

The pouch yielded a perfectly smooth shell, its surface delicately striped pink and brown. Arran looked expectantly at Grace.

"Once, when I was very small, my father took

Mama and me to the beach, and I found that shell.
It has been a great treasure. Hold it to your ear."

He did so and heard the lightest whispering, as of
surf upon sand. "I never heard anything like it," he
told her.

"Oh, yes." Her face was serious and she sounded
most matter-of-fact. "It is quite like one of your
pieces of music, the second one Mr. Plethero played
at the Muirs' last night. Can that have been only last
night?"

"Only last night," he agreed, drawing her into
his arms and kissing her deeply. When he paused
for breath he said, "How well you understand me.
I wrote that piece after a visit to the seashore."

A gust of cool air whipped about them, and Arran
straightened. No member of the staff was in sight,
but the door had been flung open.

"Dash me," Mortimer said, waving Theodora and
Melony before him into the castle. "It's cold out
there."

"Oh!" Theodora stopped before Arran and Grace.
"Are we just in time for the ceremony? What are
you doing together here—alone?"

Arran felt the blackest rage he had felt since learning of the loss of the daughter he would never know.
But satisfaction tempered that rage, and he managed
a parody of a smile. "You are just in time to con-
gratulate us on our marriage, Theodora. The ceremony is over."

"Oh, I do not believe this. Your own family, Arran.
How could you exclude us? You said you intended
to be married as quickly as possible, but this?" Theodora clapped her hands to her cheeks and rocked
as if in pain.

"I say, old chap," Mortimer said. "Bit high-
handed, what? Not that I blame you for being in a
hurry to—well—in a *hurry*?" He aimed a lascivious
grimace at Arran.

"I do not recall inviting you to return to Kirkcaldy."

Grace drew in a sharp breath.

This wife of his was far too gentle a soul. "In fact, I'm sure I did not."

"Well!" Theodora's response was to snap her bonnet strings undone. "The slight of being excluded from your wedding is bad enough. But did you honestly think I would not return to ensure that my diamonds are found and returned to me?"

He'd forgotten the diamonds. A glance at Grace confirmed that she had also forgotten them. They had not been among the items Blanche produced.

"Mortie's convinced I misplaced them somewhere here. I can't begin to imagine how that could have happened, but we must certainly search. And if they are not found, then further steps must be taken."

"By all means," Arran said. "Search away. I'm sure you'll understand if my wife and I excuse ourselves."

Mortimer guffawed. "Excuse away. We men understand these things, what?" He frowned and raised a forefinger. "But before you go, there was a message I was supposed to give you—from a Mrs. *Foster?*"

Arran locked his knees. "This is my wedding night, Mortimer. I am hearing messages from no one." How the hell did Mortimer know Mrs. Foster?

"Oh, won't take but a moment. She came to Charlotte Square to let you know she wouldn't be, er, *available* to you in future." Mortimer leered. "Too bad from what I could see. Fetching piece."

Arran felt Grace shift. "Thank you for the message," he said shortly, and made to walk on.

"The lady seemed particularly keen that you should know she's also about to be married. 'Tell him we'll each be finding solace elsewhere,' is what she said. But she'll miss your times together. Yes, that was all of it."

Melony Pincham had remained quietly near the

door. She wore unusually subdued colors, and her hair was drawn severely back. Now she came forward, her eyes downcast. "Come, Mortimer. Theodora. We should leave these people to make the best they can of this arrangement of theirs."

The movement Arran saw was Grace's hand winding in the folds of her skirts. He knew she was watching his face but avoided looking at her. Getting her away from these people was essential, but it must be done with the minimum of fuss.

"I'm sure your rooms are still in readiness," he said, controlling his voice with the greatest difficulty. "We bid you a good night."

"Oh, you poor, poor things," Melony wailed suddenly. "Caught by such sad circumstances."

The woman was insane. "Good night, Mrs. Pincham," Arran said.

"Yes, indeed," Melony said with evident deep dejection. "Good night—although I know you will not sleep with the bliss that should be yours on the night of your marriage." Abruptly she grasped Grace in a tight embrace. "You poor, dear thing. You have my sympathies."

"Did someone die?" Arran asked, almost inaudibly.

"Fate can be so evil," La Pincham droned on. "But for one as gentle and dear as you, it is truly not to be borne. You of all women should not have been forced by circumstance to enter into a loveless marriage."

Arran saw Grace grow stiff in the other's arms. Her face had lost every trace of color. "Why would you presume to call our marriage loveless?" she asked in a small, clear voice.

"What else would you call an alliance made with a man who only wants one thing?"

"Come, Grace," Arran said, but she continued to stare at Melony.

"It will be all right, Grace," Melony continued.

"Arran is not as hard a man as he makes most people believe. He will not be unduly unkind to you . . . as long as he gets what he must have from you . . . very soon."

"What is that?" Grace's gaze moved to Arran.

He offered her his hand.

"He hasn't . . . Oh, of course he's told you why he's in such a hurry to marry, dearest one. And who can blame him with all this to lose." Melony's gesture took in her surroundings. "Any man of three and thirty who stood to lose control of his estate if he failed to produce an heir within two years—or rather less than two now, I suppose—would rush to marry the first potentially fertile female he could procure."

Grace's features were like carved ice. She pushed Melony from her. "Arran, when . . . On the night when you first sent for me, you said you wanted heirs. But you were angry and I did not think—that is, I had come to believe you wanted *me*. You will lose your castle if you have no heir by the time you are five and thirty?"

"He will be answerable to others for *everything* that is now his," Melony said promptly.

"Is this true, Arran?"

"No! Well, yes, in part. But I no longer feel—"

Grace gave him no chance to finish. "I must take my leave of you all. I need to go to my chamber." She hurried toward a nearby passage.

He followed her from the hall. "Grace—"

"Don't worry, Arran, I shall do my best to be whatever you need me to be. But may I first spend another night alone? I shall come to you tomorrow, if that's agreeable."

"Of course." He made a formal bow. "I'll await you until then."

Black fury entered his brain, but when he turned

back to the hall, it was to find that the Cuthberts
and their venomous relation had fled.

He opened his curled hand and saw how the shell
Grace had given him had made deep creases in his
palm. They would fade. His need for Grace's love
would not.

"God help me," he said to the emptiness. He
should have kept the solitary promise he'd made
five years ago and never allowed himself to love another woman.

"Sickenin'," Mortimer said. "Most sickenin' thing
I ever saw."

"Hush. We don't want to be heard." Melony giggled and hurried him from the stable yard and into
the castle by way of a door no one seemed to use
and which she'd previously ensured was unlocked.
"Hurry. There is a great deal to be done tonight."

Mortimer grumbled and muttered all the way to
her chamber. Once inside, she quickly lighted several candles and poked the fire to brighter life. "Sit
down and listen to me."

"Disgustin'. Woman of her years carryin' on like
that."

Melony hugged her cape about her. It was all too
perfect. "I did not want you to witness such a sight,
but you would not have believed me if I had not
insisted you go with me."

Mortimer threw off his own cloak and loosened
his neckcloth. "Did you see her . . . ? She all but
swallowed . . ." He sprawled in a chair and spread
his legs. "MacFie, in God's name. My wife having
at it with a servant."

"Hector is the best estate commissioner in the
land, Mortimer."

"She told him he was the best at . . . at a whole
lot more than managin' land." He tore the neckcloth
off and let it fall. "Depraved. What they did doesn't

bear thinkin' about—not between an animal like MacFie and my lovie—my wife."

Melony kept her smile in place. She would teach Mortimer that his *lovie* was a pale shadow of her younger sister when it came to driving a man to sexual madness.

"We don't have time for this," she told him sharply. "Things have gone well tonight."

"Well?"

"Forget Theodora for now. We did what I wanted done. We made certain that Arran and Grace did not go together into a night of wedded bliss. It was essential that we kept them apart until I can put my plan into action."

"See here—"

"*You* see here," she said, standing before him. "Do you know how to ensure that we get what we want? That we get all that is Stonehaven's?"

"Well . . . not exactly."

"No. But I do. Speed is everything."

"That's all very well, but I need a little comfort. *If* you know what I mean, lovie."

Lovie. Again he called her by the endearment he used for Theodora. She would make him pay and pay and pay for that—and for so much more. "And you shall have that comfort." With a single tug, she undid the cord closing the neck of her cloak and let the garment fall.

Mortimer fell back. "Naked! You're incredible. Come here. *Now.*" His eyes ran over her, and his tongue darted in and out of his mouth.

Melony smiled and passed her hands up her thighs, over her belly to her breasts. She pushed them up and laughed aloud.

When Mortimer made a grab for her, she dodged away. "How do they look?"

"Wonderful. Let me taste them."

"I was referring to Theodora's diamonds," she

said, fingering the flashing collar she'd stolen and which she never intended to return. "Now, go to your rooms until I send for you."

"But, lovie, I—"

"Go." It would take a very long time for Mortimer to pay all he owed her. "Before this night is out, I will have ensured that Kirkcaldy is a jewel in the crown that is to become ours."

Intelligent people recognized when a cause was lost and looked for alternatives.

Theodora hummed as she strolled toward her chambers. Such a perfect evening after all. It just showed how—with a little determination—one could turn a bad thing into something quite wonderful.

Hector was wonderful. What she wanted more than anything was to be close to him . . . available to him . . . *all* the time. Arran had married that plain little chit. That was fact. Mortimer and Melony could hope to do no more than put off the day when Arran would produce an heir. Chances were that the event would occur in time to steal Roger's inheritance— Theodora's inheritance.

But . . . fa la la, she would make the best of the situation. Ingratiate herself with Arran's colorless wife; persuade Mortimer to make the best of things also, and ensure that they could all remain at Kirkcaldy indefinitely. Yes, that could become a most pleasant arrangement after all.

Undoing her cape, she walked into her sitting room.

"There you are, Theodora." Melony whirled toward her in that irritatingly busy way she had when she was overset. "*Where* have you been?"

Wouldn't she like to know? "Out," Theodora said vaguely.

"Out? Whilst I've been worrying myself to death about you?"

"I hardly need to keep you informed of my comings and goings."

"Oh, you are . . . Theodora, I'm beside myself." Melony produced a kerchief and pressed it to her nose. "Of course I do not wish to know your comings and goings. But, Theodora, something . . . something so awful has happened . . . or it will happen if we don't *do* something."

Theodora pushed the door shut behind her. "What *are* you wailing about, Melony?"

"He called her lovie!"

"Who called whom lovie?"

"Why, Mortimer, of course. Who else calls the one he loves most dearly *lovie?*"

Theodora tugged her bonnet ribbons undone. "Are you unwell?"

"Oh, *listen* to me before it is too late. Mortimer called that insipid creature, Grace, *lovie.* He called her that and they said a great deal more."

"But—" No, Mortie would never use . . . *No.*

Melony sought Theodora's hands and held them so tightly, the bones hurt. "I will say it all in a rush. Then we shall have to act—or be destroyed by wickedness. Did you know that Mortimer and Grace became . . . good *friends* the very first evening they met?"

Theodora began to feel frightened. "They did not."

"They most certainly did. Theodora, I believe they have *Been Together.*"

"Oh!" She tugged her hands away. "How could you say such wicked things? Mortie only intended to find a way to make the foolish chit appear compromised. He would never . . . No. You are wrong."

"I wish I were. Earlier this evening Mortimer came to me. He told me you had a lover. Such foolishness. He tried to make me believe he'd actually seen you with that Hector MacFie. A *servant,* for good-

ness' sake. Anyway, Mortimer thought that would
make me understand why he'd decided to accept an
offer from Grace.''

Theodora sat down suddenly.

Melony's hands fluttered. ''Grace cannot abide
Stonehaven. Who can blame her? But be that as it
may, she invited Mortimer to help her dispose of
Stonehaven and then to become her husband in his
stead. She told him that together they would help
administer the estate—for Roger if she has no issue
at that point, or for Stonehaven's heir, should one
be produced.''

''But—'' Theodora pressed her temples. ''But why
would Mortie ask *you* to be a part of this? And anyway, he cannot marry someone else when he is already married to me.'' Perspiration broke out on her
upper lip and between her breasts.

''Evidently the new Marchioness of Stonehaven is
a creature of delicate sensibilities who must be pro-
tected from the more sinister elements of her own
designs. Mortimer wants me to help him do away
with Stonehaven.''

''That cannot be so.''

''It *will* not be so because you and I shall work
together in quite a different manner.''

She felt in danger of swooning. ''I must go to
Mortie at once. He will reassure me that this is all
foolishness.''

Melony fell to her knees before Theodora. ''You
will not go to Mortimer. You will listen to me and
do what I tell you to do.''

''Please stop this . . . Why? Why shouldn't I go
to Mortie?''

''Because once Stonehaven is dead, Mortimer
wants me to help him to do away with you.''

Chapter 25

If only she didn't love him.

Grace tore another sheet of paper into small pieces and dropped them on the pile beside her chair. Sketching usually had the power to divert her, but she couldn't concentrate tonight.

Mairi had not returned to her mistress. Why should she? No doubt she'd been told that Grace would be with her husband.

She dashed lines onto a fresh sheet and tried to concentrate. Very quickly the bold shapes of tree limbs emerged.

She'd taken off the wedding gown and pushed it to the back of the wardrobe, where she need not set eyes upon it. Now she wore the simple dark blue velvet in which she'd first arrived at Kirkcaldy. A gown that made her appear dull and serious was exactly right for the occasion. Married solely for the purpose of safeguarding a man's estate . . . a man who received intimate messages from another female person—a person who was probably a *courtesan—on his wedding day.*

The door, flying open to admit Mairi, caused Grace to jump.

"Och, miss . . . I mean, m'lady. I'd didna expect ye t'be here."

Grace did not feel like discussing her very personal disaster with anyone. "It's all right. I don't need anything."

Bundled in her gray wool cloak and wearing a simple bonnet, Mairi shifted from foot to foot. She carried a willow basket.

"What is it, Mairi?"

"Well . . . Deary me."

"Mairi? Are you all right?"

"*I'm* fine. Och, I'll just out wi' it and take the consequences. I'd come for that." She pointed to a tray on a table beside the bed.

In the middle of the day, when Grace had arrived from Edinburgh, an array of delicious-looking food had been delivered. She'd been too excited to touch it. "The food? You came to take the food away?"

"I'm not given to falsehoods," Mairi said stoutly. "I came to put the food in this basket and take it to someone who could use it. I'd have gone to the kitchens for something, only Grumpy would have found out and dismissed me. There. Now y'know I'm a thief."

"Oh, don't be silly. If you need—"

"*I* don't need anythin'. And I wasna only about to steal your food. I was goin' t'take the blanket ye're not usin'. And maybe even one o' the nightrails ye'll probably not be needin' now ye're a marchioness— on account o' ye'll have too many fine things to—"

"*Mairi.*" Grace got up and pressed her fingers to the girl's mouth. "Stop blatherin' and tell me what this is all about."

Huge tears sprang into the girl's eyes.

"Oh, Mairi." Grace pulled her into a fierce hug. "What's the matter? Has something happened to your family?"

"N-No. It's Gael Mercer. She's the sweetest thing ye'd ever be likely t'meet, and it's likely she's dyin'."

"Hush," Grace said, rocking Mairi. "Tell me about her. Let me help you."

"Well, she's Robert Mercer's wife. And they've a

dear wee lassie named Kirsty. They're tenants here
at Kirkcaldy. Gael's havin' another babbie and she's
not strong enough. One o' my sisters told me. She
said Gael's time has come and she's . . . The baby
doesna want t'be born.''

"Surely there's someone who knows about such
things who can help."

"Aye. The midwife, only she's been called away
to help wi' another difficult birth and she canna leave
t'be wi' Gael. I dinna know what t'do except take
somethin' to tempt Gael to eat. She's but a weak
thing hersel'. And I thought a soft blanket and a
pretty, delicate nightrail . . . Och, I know I was
wrong.''

Grace released Mairi and retied her trailing bonnet
strings. "Enough of that. Put all of the food in the
basket while I get the blanket. I think there may even
be two. And I'll get a nightrail. I've a little woolen
spencer, too, in a pretty rose color. We'll take that.''

Mairi hurried to do as she was told. "Thank ye,''
she said, sweeping small sandwiches and little cakes
from beneath a silver cover. "But I canna let ye come
out into the night. It wouldna be right or proper.
And what would his lordship say?''

"That's the blankets,'' Grace said, ignoring the
reference to Arran. "And I think the nightrail with
the embroidered poppies would be just the thing.
Wait whilst I put on my boots. Kindly remember
that I'm the mistress of Kirkcaldy now, and its people are *my* responsibility, too.''

Grace had never before been out beneath the stars
in wild country where she did not know the way.
She sat beside Mairi in an ancient cart pulled by an
equally ancient-looking shaggy pony. Ignoring
Mairi's pleas to the contrary, Grace had slipped in
through the kitchen gardens and entered the castle
dairy to grab up a wheel of yellow cheese and a crock
of fresh cream.

"There it is," Mairi said, when they broke from a stand of trees and started down a hill. "Ye can see the cottages from here. Och, poor Gael and Robert. Their love is somethin' to make ye cry wi' longin' for the same yoursel'."

When they rolled to a stop before one of a cluster of cottages at the foot of the hill, Grace realized for the first time that she was afraid.

Mairi jumped down and began gathering the supplies they'd brought. She paused and glanced at Grace. "Och, look at ye. Fair pinched, ye look. I shouldna have let ye come wi' me. Stay where ye are and I'll be as quick as I can."

"I'll do no such thing," Grace said firmly, and climbed down from the cart. "They'll need whatever help they can get."

A murmuring group of people clustered about the cottage door, but they parted to allow Mairi and Grace to enter. Once inside, Grace wrinkled her nose in pleasure at the pungent scent of peat burning in the fireplace.

"Hello, Mistress Tabby," Mairi said to a rotund woman placing a kettle over the fire. "We've come t'do what we can to help."

Wiping her hands on her apron, the woman turned around, saw Grace, and appeared to lose the gift of speech.

"This is . . . this is the new Marchioness of Stonehaven," Mairi said, and to Grace, "Ye dinna look like one o' us in your fine clothes, y'see. She'd notice that."

Mistress Tabby bobbed a curtsy, and her florid face glowed even redder. "Your visit'll be royally received, I'm sure," she said, and bobbed again.

"I'm not here to be royally received," Grace said, but she smiled. A lot of this curtsying could become most trying.

The cottage appeared to have two rooms. The one

they were in served all of the family's needs but
sleep. Mairi approached a low door. "Is it all right
for me t'go in?" she asked Mistress Tabby.

The woman was too much occupied with a curious assessment of Grace to respond.

A sudden shrill moan from the other room
stopped Mairi where she stood.

Mistress Tabby's lips set in a firm line. She poured
boiling water into a basin, gathered a pile of clean
cloths, and bustled past Grace.

As the woman opened the door, there was another sound, a wail that went on and on; then, as
abruptly as it started, it faded away.

"Mairi?" Grace whispered. "What is that?"

"It's—" Mairi made a silent "ooh," and shook a
hand for silence, and they listened to a grating cry
that was part hiccup, part outrage. "The babbie! It's
the babbie."

Grace had heard whispers about women who
were increasing—and had noted voluminous, heavy
gowns associated with the condition. "Why is it
crying?"

"It's just the way o' it," Mairi said. "My mother
used t'say a wee babbie cried because it was born
wi' sense."

To her surprise, Grace felt a bubbling excitement.
The baby's wail grew louder and she heard another
noise, the sound of men's laughter and a woman
crying—crying happy tears between calling a name
Grace could not make out.

"It sounds like Gael," Mairi said, smiling while
tears slid down her cheeks. "God's good. He'd no
take one so needed."

"Tell me about the sense a baby's born with,"
Grace said, deeply fascinated.

"Och, it's just women's talk. She meant a babbie
knows that when it's born, it's left the best place

it'll ever be and that all the hardest times are yet t'come.''

"Oh," Grace said, although she did not understand at all. "Mairi, the baby's inside the mother till it's born, isn't it?" She'd never before had the courage to ask such a question.

Mairi stared at her. "It must be hard to be a gentlewoman," she said. "I'm probably not supposed t'say, but yes, the babbie's inside its mother." She put a hand on her own stomach. "And they say it's the most wonderful feeling, the feeling o' your own babbie movin' within ye."

"And then the baby is born." Grace puzzled over what that might mean.

"Your mother didna tell ye anythin', did she?"

Grace shook her head.

"It's a pity and a shame. But ye'll learn soon enough when ye have babbies o' your own. Hush, now." She put her head inside the bedroom, then went all the way in.

Grace's heart beat hard and fast. What could it all mean? She put her hands on her own stomach. A baby inside? How?

"Miss . . . I mean, my lady." Mairi's head stuck out of the bedroom door. "They're all busy here, but I reckon ye could see the wee bairn."

At first Grace shook her head. She filled her fingers with her skirt.

"He's beautiful," Mairi said, smiling. "Do come and see."

Grace went slowly, hesitantly, until she stood just inside a room where the only furnishing was a roughly fashioned bed and a single chair. In a distant corner stood a small cot upon which sat a little girl with blond hair that rose around her head like spun white gold.

"Come on." Mairi beckoned, but Grace only ventured a few steps closer to the bed. A red-haired young woman lay against the pillows, her face very white, her big eyes very blue. And she smiled up at a slender, blond man who leaned over her and whispered words Grace could not hear.

Another man, this one exceedingly tall and with wild dark hair, stood with his back to Grace and Mairi. He rocked and made clucking sounds.

"The worst came and went," Mairi said in low tones. "She dinna lose the blood this time the way she did wi' Kirsty." She indicated the little girl.

Grace heard, but still had little idea what was meant except that the bringing forth of a baby from a woman's stomach was a complicated thing. She watched the mother's face and decided it was also a wonderfully happy thing.

Something brushed her leg and she jumped. Looking down, she saw that the child had left her bed and come to stand beside her. She stroked the velvet of Grace's dress and gazed up at her.

"She's not seen anythin' so fine as your gown," Mairi said.

A fresh wail snatched their attention. The big man laughed and rocked harder.

"He's a bonny wee laddie," the fair young man said. "A bonny son."

"Aye," his wife said softly. "But not as bonny as his father."

"Oh," Mairi said softly. "Y'see how they love?"

A tug returned Grace's attention to the little one at her side. She smiled down.

"Kirsty's babbie," the child said. Tight beneath one arm she held a small, jointed teddy bear.

"Kirsty's baby," Grace agreed.

"He needs feedin'," the woman in the bed said, and a fretfulness entered her voice. "I should nurse him."

"You don't have the strength," the big man said.

Grace clasped her hands tightly together. It could not be. It *could not*.

"Dinna worry your head," Mistress Tabby said, spreading cloths on the bottom of the bed. "There's a good woman who'll take care o' that for ye."

"I want to nurse my own—"

"It's for the best." The man who must be Robert Mercer smoothed his wife's glorious hair and kissed her brow. "The sooner ye've your strength back, the sooner ye'll be takin' care o' all o' us again."

The big man turned and bent over the bed, carefully lowering the tiny, spindly-limbed creature he'd held against his chest. "There, my fine boy. You'll do very well now." Deftly he folded the soft cloths around the baby, then lifted his fragile bundle so that Mistress Tabby could swathe a white wool blanket about it. "You did well, Gael. You and Robert did well. It's time you showed Kirsty her brother."

He put the baby into his father's arms and looked around for the girl. "Kirsty—" His eyes met Grace's, and the smile on his face became fixed.

Surely . . . Grace pressed her hand over her heart. The man wore rough clothes and heavy, worn boots. His tousled black hair fell to his shoulders, and although the tone of his voice had alerted her, he spoke with a softly Scottish brogue that was never heard in the clipped speech of the Marquess of Stonehaven. Yet it was into Arran's clear green eyes that she looked.

"What will ye call the babbie?" Mairi said. "Will it be Robert, like his father?"

"No," Robert Mercer said at once. "It'll be Niall, after the man who helped birth him."

Grace found she could not move, could not breathe.

"Gael and Robert," Mairi said, moving forward. "This is Lady Stonehaven, the Savage's—I mean, the marquess's new lady. She became his bride today. She heard about your trouble and came t'see if she could do anythin'."

There was complete silence before Robert Mercer came around the bed to bow. "I . . . We thank you." He bowed even deeper. "We'd heard the marquess was t'take a wife."

"Thank you," Gael Mercer said. Her smile made her eyes luminous. "I'm sure ye'll make the marquess a happier man. Will ye look at our babbie?"

It was "Niall" who placed the baby in Grace's inexperienced arms. The soft bundle wiggled and stretched. "Oh, look," Grace said. The wrinkled little face jerked back and forth until a tiny fist found a place against the baby's mouth. "Look!"

"Aye. Nature's wonderful."

She looked up into Arran's face, her dark angel's face, and saw such deep gentleness there that she felt its impact like a glowing blow deep inside.

"Niall's as good as his name to all o' us, m'lady," Robert Mercer said. "Champion. There's never a hardship at Kirkcaldy that Niall doesn't find a way to help us. Not that I'd expected him to be a practiced hand at birthin' babbies." He laughed.

"With a good mother's help and common sense, it's not such a problem," Arran said, never looking away from Grace. "You can thank my horses for giving me the practice." Making certain no one else saw what he did, he put a single finger to his lips.

Grace nodded faintly and their pact was sealed. He could not know the joy she felt. Regardless of how she'd come to him. Regardless of why he'd wanted her as his wife—this man was so much more to her than any other.

Very carefully she raised the light bundle to her face and touched her cheek to the baby's downy head. He squirmed, and she felt his little fingers jerk against her chin.

"I don't want to give him up," she said, going to

Gael Mercer's side. "But you'll want to hold him. Mairi and I brought a few things. Some food. Blankets. And there's a pretty nightrail for you, Mrs. Mercer."

"I'm Gael."

"Gael. May I come again to see . . . Niall?"

"We'd be proud. And we do thank ye. Ye'd best away back to your bed. We wouldna want his lordship t'be angry."

"The marquess isn't a man to be angry over such things," Grace said, careful not to look at Arran again. She started for the door.

"Be careful how you go, my lady," Arran said. "Did you ride?"

"We came by cart," she told him.

"You were dutiful to come on your wedding day, but your husband will expect you to await his pleasure. Do not delay in returning to the castle."

A thrill of pleasure went through her at his words. "We won't delay," Grace said.

Kirsty stood, sucking a thumb and swaying, near the door. Her cotton nightshirt showed signs of many washings, and her feet were bare.

"You're going to catch a cold," Grace said, gathering her up and depositing her back on her bed. "You've had a busy night. Now it's time for you to sleep. Here . . ." She slipped the gold chain holding the little enameled bluebird over her head and put it on the child. "This is for you because you managed to have such a lovely baby brother."

Kirsty picked up the bird, and pure wonder filled her pale face. "Look." She showed the necklace to her bear. "Pretty."

"Ye're too good, m'lady," Robert Mercer said. "And ye're a spoiled one, Kirsty Mercer. A bear from Niall and a beautiful necklace from the lady, and all in a matter o' weeks."

With Mairi, Grace took her leave of the company

and felt Arran's eyes on her back until the bedroom door closed behind her.

They went out into the night and found the tenants about the door chuckling quietly and raising glasses whilst they toasted new life and the deliverance of a woman who was clearly very dear to them all.

"I've heard o' the man, Niall," Mairi said when they were safely in the cart and making their slow way back to the castle. "The tenants talk about all his good works. He saved a man from drownin' once. Another time, when there was a big snow, he carried two children out o' the hills when everybody'd given them up for dead. And . . Well, there's many a story about the good he's done."

"A special man," Grace said, hugging her knees against the chill. "How lucky we are to have him at Kirkcaldy."

"Indeed," Mairi agreed. "But y'know, I'd never seen him for mysel' before tonight. I don't know, but . . . but I could have sworn I'd seen him somewhere else. Ah, well, it's probably because I'm so tired."

Chapter 26

"**A**rran!"

He whirled around. "Theodora?" Dressed in a voluminous white night robe and with her hair tangled about her face, she rushed toward him from the direction of his chambers.

"Oh, Arran, we've been waiting for you. You've got to help us with Grace."

"Grace?" He dropped the bundle that was "Niall's" garb and grasped her shoulders. "What about Grace?"

"She went out somewhere."

He relaxed instantly. "Did she?"

"Yes. Then she came back and . . . Oh, please do hurry!"

"Speak plainly," Arran said, watching her narrowly. "She came back, and . . . ?"

"And she was distraught. We think she was upset by the unfortunate mention of . . . of, well, things from your past."

He caught her shoulders again. "Stop chattering, you fool." They'd done something to Grace. "Where is she?"

"Melony had one of her feelings. She has them, you know. She senses things and—"

Arran shook her. "*Where* is Grace?"

"Melony went to her room and found her gone. She waited until she returned, and then Grace insisted upon going into the vaults beneath Revelation. We tried to stop her.''

The vaults? ''There's nothing down there.''

''We know that. Nothing, but who knows how many miles of passageways? Grace said she had to find out if it was true that Isabel Dean could have gone down there to be with . . . to be with Mr. Dean.''

''Why would she do such a thing?''

''I have no idea—unless her mind is unhinged because of your betrayal of her feelings for you.''

He dropped his hands lest he shake the female again, and harder. ''I will not discuss these matters with you, madam.''

''Mortimer went out to search for you.''

''Calum? Struan? You did not think to ask for their help?''

Her hands went to her face. ''No. Oh, we have not managed this well enough. Do go down and try to find her.''

His stomach turned. ''Try to find her? She can go no farther than the old wine cellar—if the key is in the trap. The door to the catacombs has always been locked.''

''The key was in the trap.'' Theodora shook her head. ''I thought the catacombs were locked, too, but they were not. She climbed the rungs from the wine cellar and ran into the darkness. We dared not follow since we might not find a way back.''

Slowly he understood what she was telling him. ''Get out of my way, madam,'' he said, pushing past. ''I must go to her.''

''I hope you can. But I fear she's gone, Arran, gone into all those black places beneath Kirkcaldy.''

Grace twisted and turned before the dressing table glass and smiled at the sparkle of firelight caught in silver lilies scattered over her white robe.

When Arran got back from the Mercers', he would come to her.

Would he like the robe?

Certainly very little skin showed, yet the effect was pleasing.

Returning to find Melony waiting in her room had disturbed Grace. The other woman's commiseration had annoyed her, and she'd been glad to be left alone. Melony's doleful sympathy at Arran's "betrayal" of Grace had not seemed sincere. There had been no question of mentioning what had happened at the Mercers' cottage. No doubt all would be well once the marriage . . . once whatever was supposed to happen in a marriage had happened.

What could be taking Arran so long? Perhaps she should have waited longer to ensure Gael was indeed doing well enough.

Shapes blurred in the glass . . . until a square of white just barely shifted into sight. A note pushed beneath her door.

Smiling, walking on tiptoe, Grace went to retrieve and unfold the paper. She saw at once that Arran's name was boldly written at the bottom. How romantic. She had never received any written communication from him before.

"Grace," the note said. "We must put aside the past. Come to me at once and we shall forget all differences. I want to show you where Isabel betrayed me. The entrance to the vaults is beneath the wheel-stair. Remember? When you visited me at Revelation, you came that way. Arran."

What had changed after she left the Mercers?

Careful to protect the flame of his candle, Arran strode past the bottom of the stairs to his rooms, crossed the lofty hall, ducked beneath a low archway, and took a downward flight several steps at a time. Almost no light penetrated the gloom, and the deeper he went, the less he could see outside the yellow arc the candle cast.

He reached the bottom and paused for the instant it took to note that the door to the vaults was indeed open.

Grace, why, in God's name?

Pressing on, he passed through the door and down a narrow passage to the storeroom. No one had been in here since . . . since Isabel.

"Grace?" He held the candle aloft, and shadows leapt over rough stone walls. Crates and trunks stood jumbled together, and buckets and implements and a heap of cushions.

Grace wasn't in the storeroom. He scarcely spared a glance for the cushions that had no doubt been useful to his former "wife."

More steps, these even narrower than the passageway into the storeroom, led deeper through the earth to a circular chamber few knew existed.

"Grace! Grace, answer me!"

He halted. A long-ago Stonehaven with a fear of being cut off by siege had designed the vaults and catacombs beneath Kirkcaldy. He had wanted assurance of a water supply from underground springs in the hills and, as a last resort, escape through an impossible warren of passageways no one, to Arran's knowledge, had ever used.

"Grace." He scrubbed at his eyes. She was a brave little thing, but surely she wouldn't venture here. And surely, if she got this far, she'd go no farther.

There was not time to see if she'd returned to her rooms. Arran ran his eyes over the complicated system of chains and pulleys that operated the ancient water supply. A crank turned the pulleys to raise a metal plate that opened pipes beyond the chamber. Then, in theory, water would fill a shallow well in the next subterranean cavern—which lay beneath this one—and be readily available to the castle.

He *had* to be certain she wasn't hiding somewhere in this forsaken place.

An open trapdoor and yet another short flight of steps took him down into his eccentric ancestor's final circular cavern, where a hole in the floor covered by a grille was the only evidence of the well. Here the walls were lined with wine racks . . . all empty. Arran's father had insisted the stock be moved years ago.

Then he saw what he'd most dreaded. A rack on the farthest side of the chamber had been swung away from its neighbors. Arran knew that hinges made it operate as a convenient screen for metal rungs that rose to the last door he would encounter: the door to the catacombs.

Open.

Theodora had not lied when she'd said they followed Grace this far only to watch her pull open the rack, scramble up the embedded rungs, and rush into the darkness.

Arran quickly climbed the rungs. He'd thought to pack his pockets with candles, but they would not last forever. Bending, he moved into the low-roofed tunnel. Damn Theodora and Mortimer. They hoped Grace would die here.

From somewhere in the distance came a tap-tapping. Arran stood still. "Grace?" His voice echoed back, "Grace, Grace, Grace," and faded into silence.

Then came the tapping, only not tapping. *Running feet.* Running feet in light shoes and pounding . . . *downward.* Someone ran downward from above him. Someone was following the route he'd just taken.

He turned around, keeping his head down, and climbed back to the cellar floor.

The scuffling steps grew closer.

Arran held his breath and drew behind the hinged rack.

"I will not be afraid," a very familiar voice said, and promptly cracked into a squeak. "I will not turn back. I am brave."

Glaring, he stepped from behind the rack.

"I am *very* brave. Oh!" Grace barreled into his chest and dropped the guttering candle she carried. It rolled away and went out.

Grace shrieked.

"You are indeed brave, my lady," Arran said, crushing her to him. "The bravest. Only an extremely brave . . . and an extremely foolish woman would risk enraging a *savage* husband."

She giggled wildly.

Arran gave her a single shake . . . before he kissed her. He kissed her and his tension only swelled. She tasted so sweet, so druggingly, achingly sweet. "How did I pass you?" He breathed in the scent of spring flowers that hovered in her hair. "What possessed you to come down here?"

"Don't make fun," she told him, burying her face in his chest. Beneath his fingers, fine, soft lawn slid over her skin.

"My God, Grace. There's no humor here. Theodora said you'd gone into the catacombs."

"Theodora?" She raised her face. "*You* sent for *me*. You told me to meet you here."

Arran framed her face. "You came down here because you were upset and wanted . . . Theodora said you insisted upon coming here."

"But I *didn't*. After I left you at the Mercers', I returned to Kirkcaldy to wait for you." She lifted a crumpled piece of paper into the candlelight. "You had this note put under my door. I thought it odd, but I came at once."

Arran took the note and read the words someone

else had written in his name. "Oh, my God," he
said slowly. "Quickly, we've got to get out of here."

Grabbing Grace's hand, he ran for the steps to the
trap.

It slammed and the key clicked in the lock . . . on
the other side.

"You are certain this will work, Melony?"

"Absolutely. Turn the crank."

Theodora's hands shook so, that when she clasped
the ancient, rusting crank handle, she could barely
close her fingers. "Oh, Melony, listen. They're
banging on the trap."

"Let them bang. Here, I'll help you."

Melony's strong hands clamped Theodora's to
cold metal, and the sound of long-unused pulleys
creaked, gathering speed. Chain began to rotate, link
by link, clacking loudly.

The banging on the trap to the lower chamber became a ceaseless thunder, and she could hear the
muffled sounds of Arran shouting.

"Hurry," Melony said. "We have more work to
do tonight."

"Persuading Mortimer to return to Edinburgh?"

"It's the best way. We'll insist it is wise to lull
Arran into thinking we've retreated peaceably. We'll
tell him that we'll return later to make the best of
things."

Theodora looked toward the steps leading down
to the other chamber. "And by the time we come
back, they'll . . ."

"You are such a peagoose, Theodora. Push!"

With a long, grating squeal, a handle attached to
the pulleys rose from a slot in the floor, drawing a
thick metal plate with it. Instantly the sound of
rushing water followed.

"There," Melony said triumphantly. "It does still

work. First the well will fill. Then the chamber will begin to flood.''

"Oh, Melony!"

"Don't forget, Grace intended to have you killed,'' Melony said. "Eventually there will be so much water that they'll only be able to crouch beneath the trap. Then they'll grow too tired and . . . Yes. In time the water will rise to the level of the catacombs. When Arran and Grace slip away, they'll be carried into those passageways, and that will be that.''

"And you're sure Mortimer won't be angry?''

Melony looked at her sister and wondered, as she had so often wondered, how it could be possible that they were related at all. "Mortimer won't know, Theodora. Only you and I know. Arran and Grace will never be found. The story we make up will convince the world that they rode into the night and never came back.'' What a stupid woman Theodora was.

"How long will it take?''

"Stop turning now,'' Melony said, and when Theodora withdrew her hands and stood staring toward the lower cellar, she eased off the crank handle—just as she'd practiced doing earlier—and held it behind her back. "It won't take too long, Theodora. Hear how fast the water pours in. Bend over a little and you'll be able to tell where the pipe runs.''

Theodora bent and put her ear close to the wall.

Melony raised the heavy handle over her shoulder and brought it down on the back of Theodora's head.

Her sister flopped to the stone floor. Blood spread from her upturned ear onto ridiculously girlish white garments.

Lady Theodora Cuthbert died without a sound.

Chapter 27

❦❦❦

"No," Arran told Grace. "No, it's out of the question." They stood on the steps to the upper chamber. Water pumped upward through the well grille with incredible power and grew closer with every second.

"But the catacombs go somewhere, don't they? Surely they must have been dug so that people could come and go from the castle that way if they had to."

She was calm, and he loved her for that. One of the many things he loved her for. "My sweet, as far as we know, there was never any occasion for someone to find out if they went anywhere at all."

"In time the water will run away into the passages." Grace held his coat with one hand. "But surely it could never flood them."

"Believe me when I say the catacombs are not the answer." In darkness, with no idea which turn to take, they would grovel along until they died.

"This chamber may fill entirely," Grace said, voicing his own thoughts."

"I want to try the door again . . . Just hold on to me!"

With a mighty surge, the well grille was thrown upward, and Arran watched the level rise with nightmarish rapidity. He all but dragged Grace to the top of the steps.

"Perhaps a sort of air bubble will form at the top,"

375

she said, looking at the ceiling that sloped up a little from the trap. "We could hold our faces into that."

Lucid thoughts, but one as small and slender as Grace would not have enough strength to withstand the dragging pressure from below, or sufficient flesh to ward off the cold for long.

He wanted to shout his rage, to punish . . . He wanted his hands around his cousin's throat.

"Why do Mortimer and Theodora want us dead?"

Fury took another grinding hold upon him. "They have everything to gain by ensuring that you and I never produce an heir."

"But—" Although they stood halfway up the steps, water had already risen over their feet. "Please, Arran, let's go into the catacombs."

Go, and they would die. Stay, and they would die. But to die without audacity was out of the question.

"You're right, my lady. We'll go together now." He must not let himself picture her drifting, lifeless, into eternity.

Keeping an arm around her, gripping the fresh candle he'd lighted in a curled finger, he worked his way along the racks, towing Grace beside him.

Then the unthinkable happened. When they were only feet from the passageway, a rumble rolled toward them, and with it, a mass of earth and rock that burst from the catacombs and plunged into the water.

"What's happening?" Grace said, panting. The spewing debris sent a swell over her, and she sputtered as she bobbed up.

"I'm not sure," Arran admitted. There was *no* way out. "Probably a cave-in somewhere in the passageway. It's blocked."

"The water may stop rising," she said, and his gut clenched. Her voice was growing weaker.

"I'm sure it will," he told her. "We'll be all right.

Sooner or later one of the servants will think to come down here, and we'll be found." Found dead after water was finally seen escaping from the vaults.

"Yes," she said.

Her grip started to slide.

"Hold on," Arran ordered. "I'm going to get to the door again. The wood is old. Perhaps it'll give— or the lock." Or any other damfool impossible thing.

His heart hammered, thundered in his ears. Dragging Grace, he made his way through the chilling water. At least the sound of the thrusting current had dulled. He looked at Grace and saw her eyes drifting shut.

"Grace! Stay awake!" He could not shake her, could not try to kiss or console her. "Grace! Wake up!" Please let him live to *kill* Mortimer Cuthbert and his evil wife.

Grace opened her eyes very wide. "I'm sleepy."

"I know. It's the cold and the shock. You must not sleep. I need you, Grace. I need your help."

She smiled, and Arran reached the steps.

Hopeless. With his head touching the trap, the water already washed above his waist.

The candle went out.

Arran closed his eyes. The air was growing thinner.

Thanking God he'd been born with extraordinary strength, Arran hauled Grace over his shoulder. All he could do was keep them both alive for as long as possible.

Absently he felt in his pocket for another candle, then grimaced, realizing that even if they were not wet, he had no means of lighting one.

His fingers closed on something long and round, thin and smooth. For an instant his heart almost ceased beating.

Blanche Wren's "ingenious" key. *The key that opened any lock.*

Very carefully, terrified he would drop it, he eased the precious device out. Anchoring Grace with an arm, he fumbled until he found the keyhole in the darkness and slipped the strange key in.

It met resistance. The key that had been used to lock them in was still in place. Cursing aloud, he poked and shoved . . . and their last hope for life jolted all the way into the lock as it pushed the other key out.

Arran turned and turned the thin key. Nothing happened. He turned the other way. And he felt the sluggish opening of the latch.

A roar sounded from somewhere in the earth below. The water bubbled toward his shoulders—and Grace's head.

Arran prayed that he could summon one last burst of strength from his sorely tested body, and with a great shove, threw the heavy trap upward with one hand.

Cradling Grace in his arms like a child, he barely staggered past the final step to the middle chamber. A mighty blast of water followed, sweeping almost instantly to his knees. Struggling, he waded through the darkness with the oozing mass tearing and sucking around him.

A sodden heap of something that gleamed palely blocked his path. He pushed it with one leg until it rolled heavily away, then he leaned to jerk at the pulleys that controlled the water trap.

With a mighty clang, the great plate slid down into place again.

"Thank you, God," Arran said loudly.

He made his way from the hell his ancestor's folly had become until he once more set his feet on the dry stone flags at the base of the great wheel-stair.

"I told you we'd find a way out," Grace heard herself say. Disoriented, she looked up at Arran's jaw—a sharp jaw, dark with the beginnings of a beard. She wriggled and shoved. "Put me down, please. I can walk perfectly well."

"Hold your tongue, madam," he roared.

Grace turned her mouth down. "We have both had a great trial, Stonehaven. But that does not mean you should shout at me." He was striding up the stairs to his chambers, jarring her against his chest.

Arran did not so much as favor her with a glance. Just as well since she could *feel* anger in him.

She felt jumpy, excited—afraid not to be afraid anymore. The cavern had been so dark and the water had risen so fast.

Arran's black hair, wet and curly, hung loose in a manner that reminded her of a pirate. Some women would be afraid of being carried by a man who looked like a pirate. "I am not afraid."

"You no longer have to be afraid. But you have been more afraid than any woman—or man—should ever be."

She had an outrageous urge to giggle. "It was horrible." Stifled laughter erupted as a hiccup. "So horrible. We were meant to drown. Very soon the room would have filled . . . We would try . . . How could being captured by a pirate seem like *anything* after that?"

He kicked open the door to his sitting room and marched to the fireplace. "You are hysterical, madam. I suggest you hold your tongue."

"I most certainly shall not hold my tongue." She tried to push away, but he held her tightly while he stooped to throw coals onto a fire that had burned very low. "I very nearly did not have the use of my tongue at all. I shall certainly not—"

His hand, clapped over her mouth, reduced Grace to mumbling.

"They tried to kill us," he said. His eyes glittered

menacingly. "But they failed. And now, finally, we are alone."

He was behaving strangely. "I want you to put me down." Suddenly she was aware of how small she was, and how pathetic in her wet finery. Arran was exceedingly large and strong. He was also wet, but there was nothing pathetic about the figure he made. Grace swallowed. "I said—"

"*I* said you are to say nothing." His shirt clung, transparent, to his chest. Dark hair showed clearly, and the defined lines of his muscles.

A fine quiver passing through him struck trepidation into Grace. He quivered with energy, with tension. His eyes seemed not quite focused, yet she knew his concentration was centered on her.

"Are you angry?" she said in a small voice, and felt foolish. "Naturally you are. Forget I—"

"I almost lost you—just as I almost had you—completely."

There was something in his unflinching gaze that suggested she was right to be nervous. "We have to think carefully," she told him, doing just that herself. "Yes, we had better sit quietly and decide what to do next."

"I *know* what I'm doing next, and I have no intention of sitting quietly, I assure you."

Oh, dear, there did seem to be some threat in his words. "The Cuthberts will come," Grace said, and shuddered. "And Melony. I do not believe she is at all what she appeared."

"She is exactly what she appeared to be. You are too trusting, but you will learn better. I shall teach you."

"Oh."

Quite abruptly, but carefully, he lowered her feet to the floor. "In future you will make no friend without consulting me. You will *need* no friends for a very long time." He settled his hands loosely around her neck, and his thumbs brushed back and forth along her jaw.

"One always needs friends. I know, because I never had any before you."

"Now you *do* have me," he told her. "Any other friend will be superfluous. And you will have no time to spare away from my needs."

"Oh." Really, she wished she didn't say that so often. "Well, back to the issue at hand."

"I am referring to the issue at hand."

"They will come, Stonehaven. We must be prepared for them. Lock the door."

"My name is Arran. They will not come. And the door is locked . . . for quite different reasons."

"Oh."

"My cousin and his female accomplices will come nowhere near this room. They plan to wait until morning. Then, when McWallop announces we are nowhere to be found, they will appear surprised and concerned. There will be a great search, and eventually our disappearance will be pronounced a great unsolved mystery. At that point Mortimer will be appointed administrator of my estates. We will speak more of all this later."

"You *do* appear angry."

"I *am* angry." His narrowed gaze rested on her mouth. "I want to be with you, to lie with you."

Her stomach made a quick little jump. "Is that . . . is that a euphemism, Arran? For *Sit with Me?*"

He tipped up his chin and looked down at her. "Give me patience," he said. "I have waited longer than any man should wait—endured more in the time I've known you than any man should endure. Come with me."

As he caught her wrist, she held up her other hand. "Arran! Arran, I am beginning to think you have not been honest."

''Come with me. I'm about to be absolutely honest.'' His eyes moved over her.

Hot. He looked at her body, and his gaze was heated. Her sodden gown and robe stuck to her in places she wished she could hide.

''You failed to tell me the truth,'' she said weakly, backing rapidly away from him.

He followed with measured steps. ''Your clothes are wet. Take them off.''

Her heart pounded. ''No.''

''Take them off.''

Grace sidestepped behind a chair. ''That will make you angrier.''

''I think not.''

''I'm certain I'm right.'' Grace vacated her spot behind the chair and dodged for the writing table—with Arran closing the space between them as slowly or as rapidly as he chose. ''If I am undressed before you, your principles will be compromised.''

''Hold your tongue, madam.''

''You have already said that.'' She made a run for it but didn't cover a yard before he caught her waist and hauled her to sit upon the writing table. ''You are overbearing,'' she told him. Straightening her back, she crossed her arms over her breasts, glanced down, and lowered one hand to rest in her lap—her very revealed lap.

''You fascinate me, imp,'' Arran said. He lifted her heavy, damp hair away from her shoulders and studied her carefully. ''So delicate, but so strong. Yes. Yes, I think we shall do very well together.''

''I shall not continue to be subtle,'' Grace announced. ''We have *not* already done absolutely *everything* that is done by a man and a woman. In private. Have we?''

''God, in heaven . . .''

''There is no need to speak the Lord's name in vain.''

"I assure you I spoke from the heart."

"We haven't, have we? Not *everything*? That's done in private? Between a man and a woman? When they are completely alone? There, I have asked you."

"You have asked me."

"What else is there?"

Arran parted her knees and stood close to her against the table. Grace had to raise her chin to see his face. Shrugging, he worked off his coat, dropped it to the floor, and took off his waistcoat. "I don't think I shall ever wear those again," he said, undoing his shirt. "It is quite possible that I am about to embark on a long period when I do not wear anything at all."

Her stomach fluttered. "Kindly be direct with me."

"I am direct. And I intend to be more so." His shirt went the way of his coat and waistcoat.

He was big, overwhelmingly big. The hair on his chest made an intriguing pattern, wide over the broadest part, narrow over the narrowest part—that part where it disappeared into his trousers.

"They're wet, aren't they?"

She jumped. "What?"

"My trousers. You are noting that they are wet and should be removed."

"Well, no—at least, perhaps not."

With one hand he cupped her bottom on the table and steadied himself whilst tugging off his boots.

Grace grew hot.

He smiled at her, a smile that reminded her of a tiger . . . a tiger who had yet to eat the meal he'd waited too long to eat. Now his trousers received his attention.

"Oh, I don't think—"

"*Don't* think," he ordered, and continued until the trousers lay atop the rest.

Grace raised her face sharply, to be confronted by

the altogether unsettling spectacle of Arran's mockingly intense stare.

Ignoring her flapping hands, he untied her robe and pulled it off. He lifted her against his very bare chest and slid the robe away.

"Grace." He anchored her face between his hands. "We have not done everything that happens between a man and a woman—his wife—in private. We are going to do it now. At first you may not enjoy every moment of the experience, but I promise that you will soon become addicted."

She frowned. "How do you know?"

"Because I already know how passionate you are. You are ready for what we are about to do."

"But if I'm not going to enjoy—"

His mouth, sealed to hers, shut off the words. He kissed her deeply as if applying his brand, making his mark.

"I am chilled, Grace," he said when he finally raised his head. "Dry me. Rub me, Grace."

Deep places, nameless places, pulsed again as he had made them pulse before. "I have nothing to rub you with."

He laughed and pulled a stool from beneath the table. "This is how you shall start." The scanty nightrail was jerked up about her hips. Arran braced a foot on the stool and lifted Grace astride his thigh. "Yes. Oh, yes, I think I like the way that feels. Do you, Grace?"

She drew in a sharp little breath and scrabbled for his arms. Her eyes widened. "It feels . . . Oh, it *feels!*"

"I quite agree." He covered her breasts and squeezed gently.

Grace made a grab for his wrists, almost fell, and clutched his naked shoulders instead.

Arran laughed deep in his throat. "You had best

hang on, imp. This stuff is so thin, it is quite dry now.'' He fingered her nightrail. ''I don't think I like it anymore.''

Instantly he bowed his head and licked the fabric over a nipple, opened his mouth wide and sucked until the fine lawn was soaked. ''Mm. Wet again. Much better.'' He nibbled and nipped at first one, then the other breast. ''Lovely. But you aren't rubbing me.''

A blaze of white heat shot from her breasts into her belly. ''I . . . I can't.''

''You will.''

He rocked her back and forth on his thigh until she cried out. ''It's . . . Oh, it's . . .''

''I quite agree.'' His voice sounded so strange now. ''That's what I want for you, my sweet one. You are going to learn the power you have—to take and to give.''

Rocking, rocking, rocking. A sharp ache started between her legs. Grace panted and felt perspiration pop out on her brow and her back.

''Touch me,'' Arran said huskily. ''Hold me.''

The tensing in those mysterious places drew tight. Shaking steadily, Grace stroked his shoulders.

''Not there,'' Arran said. ''The part of me that so fascinated you before. Hold me there, sweet Grace.''

She was afraid.

Arran looked into her eyes—and ripped the nightrail from neckline to hem.

Grace gasped aloud.

''Very soon you will hold me—and do a great deal more.''

The nightrail went the way of the rest of their clothes, and without another word, Arran shifted Grace farther onto the table, tipped her to her back, and pulled her knees over his shoulders.

''Arran!''

She was open to him. He could see all that should

be kept hidden. And he leaned over her, swaying a little. The part of him he wanted her to hold jabbed insistently against the place between her legs that was embarrassingly moist and achy.

"I do not think this is appropriate," she said, listening to the wobble in her voice.

"Anything we do is appropriate," he told her. "Tonight we almost died together. Now we will celebrate living together. And we will celebrate it again and again. Let me give to you first, Grace."

He spoke so strangely sometimes.

Arran went to his knees between her thighs.

"What—"

"Hush." He reached to cover her breasts, to pinch and roll her nipples until she writhed.

"*Arran!*"

He did not reply. He could not. His mouth was *there*. His tongue was *there*. Flicking, nuzzling.

"No! *Arran!*" The burning darts became searing fire. "Arran!" She found his hair and tugged. "Ooh! Ooh. Oh, Arran."

Wave after wave of rippling pleasure burst, spread outward, upward. Her legs felt boneless, and her arms, her whole body.

Then he was on his feet again, still holding her helpless by the legs, and leaning to kiss her with violent possessiveness.

And whilst he kissed her, she became aware that even as the throbbing at her center faded, he parted slippery folds and eased a finger inside.

"Why are you doing that?" She clamped down with muscles of which she'd never before been aware. "Why?"

"To help ease the way, sweet one." With gentle persistence, he used more fingers, and Grace bit her bottom lip hard. His fingertips stroked higher and she twisted, found his hand and held it to her.

"You are right for me, Grace. And ready."

Arran withdrew his fingers and jutted his hips closer. He pressed that heavy, hard part of him to her body.

"I want you now, Grace."

"Yes." Without knowing what he wanted, she knew she wanted it, too.

The pressure increased and he began to push into her body. Velvety smooth, but so large, so hard. "There will be a little pain, but not too much, I hope." His breath hissed between his teeth. "You are very small."

She squeezed her eyes shut. "I think I know about everything now. Perhaps there is no need to continue."

"*Grace,*" he cried, and the impossible occurred, he slid all of that great hardness inside her.

"It burns." She pushed on his chest and felt something break inside her. "Arran!"

"Hold on, sweet one," he said against her ear when she flailed, trying to stop him from hurting her. "It will soon pass."

She panted, attempted to fill her lungs, and the pain subsided.

Arran held still. "Is there still pain?"

"No." Grace shook her head. "What are we to do now?"

He smiled, a smile that warmed his green, green eyes. "You will do nothing. I will do everything. Just trust me and very soon you will want me to do it again."

She eyed him dubiously.

Arran began to move, very slowly at first, in and out of her clenching body. In and out whilst she held his arms and watched his face. He smiled again, and she smiled back.

"Pain?"

"No. Please don't stop."

He didn't.

Grace forgot to hold on, forgot to be frightened. When she closed her eyes, it was with the vision of Arran's tensed face, the straining of veins at his temples and in his neck.

Faster and faster he drove into her, and amazingly, the darts of searing heat burst to life again.

This time, when she cried out she heard, just faintly, Arran's triumphant shout.

"Beautiful," he said in a voice that broke. "You are absolutely beautiful. Perfect. Perfect with me. I can't believe it."

He was still inside her.

Grace could scarcely breathe at all. She felt hot tears course into her hair. "Good."

"And all by chance. You came to me by chance."

"I was brought to you deliberately."

"Yes." He laughed, and Grace's eyes popped wide open at the feeling it caused inside her. "Yes, you were brought to me, but there were no guarantees. I never could have hoped for this."

"It was all right, then."

"All right?" He pulled her legs down and around his waist and hauled her up into his arms. His hands supported her bottom. "It was fantastic."

The hair on his chest teased her sensitive nipples. She brushed back and forth a little, experimenting. So good.

Arran made a slight adjustment and finally slid out of her.

"Do you have to do that?" she asked.

"What?" He strode toward the bedchamber.

She buried her face in his shoulder. "Take it away."

He laughed, and the sound in his throat vibrated. "Not for long. Now I shall do what I should have done before. I'm going to lie with you in my bed."

"Oh, good." Grace twined her arms around his

neck and kissed him with all her might. "How exciting. Now you will show me the next thing."

"The *next* thing?" He threw back his counterpane and placed her on the bed.

"Whatever else husbands and wives do in private. When they are alone? With nobody else—"

He gave a barking laugh. "You're amazing. Whatever else? Oh, Grace—Lady Stonehaven—*my* lady—I do love you."

She stopped smiling. Her throat grew tight and her foolish eyes filled with tears once more.

"I love you, Grace," he repeated, lifting her against the pillows, lying beside her, stroking her hair.

"I like what husbands and wives do together," she finally managed to say.

Arran frowned. "Is that all you like about being with me?"

The tears overflowed and she caught her quivering lower lip in her teeth.

"My sweet," he said, brushing drops from her cheeks. "What is it? What's wrong?"

"If we'd died in the vaults, we would never have discovered exactly what it is that a man and woman—"

He groaned and his mouth on hers cut off the rest of what she would have said. "I am truly fascinated by you," he whispered against her lips.

"Not as fascinated as I am by you, my lord." Grace eased away until she could see his face. "You look like a barbarian in a gentleman's clothing . . . or you do when you're dressed. I'm in love with a barbarian. Totally, absolutely, completely in love with a barbarian with the face of a dark angel."

He chuckled.

She found that part of him he so enjoyed having held, and noticed that he stopped chuckling.

* * *

Distant noises fingered a path through heavy sleep.

Pounding.

Arran opened his eyes in the darkness. The soft nakedness curled into his body was Grace, the softness filling his hand, her breast.

"Open . . . !"

Someone was pummeling the sitting room door—with both fists by the sound of it.

Arran became wide-awake. If that was Mortimer, he had badly miscalculated. Easing himself away from Grace, he went swiftly into the sitting room and closed the door to the bedchamber.

"Arran? Arran, are you in there? In God's name, answer me."

Calum. Relief swamped Arran. Not bothering to cover himself, he went to fling the door open.

"Thank the Lord," Calum said, and looked from Arran's face to points much lower. "I take it congratulations are in order?"

"Remind me to give you a medal one day," Arran said. "For your incredibly good taste. Now, enough said on that topic. What's happened?"

"You'd better come with me now. Struan's standing guard over Mortimer."

Arran turned away and snatched up trousers. In seconds he was more or less dressed and following Calum through the castle. He asked no more questions, and Calum offered no comments.

At the entrance to the corridor leading to Mortimer's rooms, Arran stopped. "Hell's teeth," he said under his breath.

"Arran!" Mortimer's voice came to him from a doorway where Struan stood with a pistol in his hand. "Arran, speak to them. Make them let me go to her."

"He hasn't made a damned bit of sense yet," Calum said.

Arran looked not at Calum, or Struan—or Mortimer. The ghastly sight that squeezed his gut was what had once been Melony Pincham.

In death, her face drained of all natural color, she was an overly rouged woman with garish red hair. She lay on her side in an impossibly bowed arch, her stomach thrust forward, her feet and head thrown back.

"She took a shot in the back," Calum said tonelessly.

Struan held up the pistol. With his free arm he restrained Mortimer's feeble efforts to rush at Arran. "Evidently she tried to shoot him with this."

"She tried to shoot me," Mortimer wailed. "She's mad."

"*Was* mad," Calum corrected dispassionately.

"In the struggle, Melony was shot instead," Struan said.

Arran looked at the corpse. "Accidentally? In the back?"

"In the head first," Struan said. "Evidently she fell on him, and that's when the second shot hit her back."

"She wouldn't let me go to her," Mortimer said. His eyes wandered vaguely from Melony's body to Arran's face. "Said she'd drowned you and Grace. Said she did it all for me. Can you credit that? I just wanted Kirkcaldy. Never wanted you dead. Wouldn't have gone *that* far."

"I'm touched."

A sudden, wild cry erupted from Mortimer. He rushed forward, arms flailing. Struan moved to stop him, but Arran waved his brother aside.

"I've got to go to her," Mortimer screamed. "I've got to go to Theodora."

Arran looked to Struan and Calum, but they both shook their heads.

"Melony killed Theodora in the vaults." Mortimer, feet bare, shirttail flapping, ran past. "She killed my lovie."

Epilogue

October 1822. Kirkcaldy Castle, Scotland

"A mighty, monstrous excess of a place," Arran said, standing beside Allegro. "That's what my father called it. And his father before him."

Grace, sitting sidesaddle on her amiable chestnut, eased her position and reached her gloved hand toward her husband. "Didn't they like the castle?"

He wound their fingers together. "They loved it. We all have, for as long as there have been Stonehavens here. I imagine it was their way of pretending nonchalance."

"How foolish." From their spot at the edge of a stand of massive beeches, they looked across the valley at Kirkcaldy's imposing bulk.

"Men can be foolish," Arran said, and quickly added, "on very rare occasions."

Grace laughed lightly, reveling in her surroundings. The beech leaves were turning the glorious shade of orange that heralded winter's first quickening. She studied her husband with loving concentration. Today there was some news to share, news that would make him happy, she knew. But he was preoccupied, and she must be certain he did not fail to tell her why before she completely distracted him.

"Calum sent word."

Ah. Grace bent to kiss Arran's fingers, to press them against her cheek.

393

He raised troubled eyes to hers and turned up the corners of his marvelous mouth. "Sometimes I think you feel my very heart—how it beats—how it hurts."

"Is Calum well?"

"Well enough, but angry, I think. He's in Cornwall."

"Cornwall?" Grace echoed in surprise. "So far? I thought he remained in Edinburgh."

"Evidently he has made a discovery."

"Oh, Arran!" Excitement bubbled in Grace. "He knows who he really is?"

"Perhaps. He did not exactly tell me the details of his findings. But he is not happy, my love, and when Calum isn't happy, it's hard for me not to feel the anguish with him."

"Should you like to go to him?"

"No. He would not want that." He smiled, pulled her head down until he could kiss her soundly, then turned to swing into his saddle. "Let us return to Kirkcaldy. Already the afternoons seem more chill."

They rode awhile in silence. The breeze whipped at Arran's hair, and his proud profile was sharp against a brittle blue sky. The scent of coming winter was in the air.

"I think we should warm ourselves, my lady."

Grace ducked her head and smiled. "Warm ourselves?"

"Yes, yes. I fear I have developed a terrible weakness. More an addiction, really, for becoming warm with you. Being close to you—simply seeing you—or even *thinking* about you, causes an overwhelming desire to strip away your clothes and do all the wonderful things you make so very pleasurable."

"Arran!" She glanced around. "Hush. You should not speak so when someone might overhear."

"Who might overhear?" He also looked around at moorland and wood, at soft hill and gentle valley and the clusters of buildings where his tenants lived and worked—and laughed and cried and loved. "I think I may speak safely, madam wife. I lust after your body."

"Arran!"

"You *don't* lust after mine?"

Grace trotted the chestnut a few yards before smiling back at Arran. "Yes, I do. Race you home!"

The chestnut was game, but within seconds Allegro galloped alongside and Arran had to hold him back from running ahead of the smaller animal.

"How do you think Roger does?" Arran called.

"Well," Grace said. "He's a dear boy. I'm so glad you insisted upon keeping him with us."

"He has an aptitude for figures. It'll make him useful to me one day—since everyone else I trusted deserted me."

Calum and Struan. How Arran missed his brother and his best friend. "Have you heard news of Mortimer's progress in the Indies?"

"Very little, except that he's apparently consoling his loss of Theodora with the charming daughter of another planter."

"I hope he is happier."

"As usual, you are too generous. I'd have called him out if you hadn't intervened."

"He'd suffered enough," Grace shouted. "And he didn't have anything to do with the things Melony . . . She acted alone." Her jaws tightened as they always did when she remembered the horrors of that awful night.

A hard gallop brought them to the fortifying wall at the base of Kirkcaldy's mound. Arran raced through first, drew up, and wheeled around to await Grace.

As she joined him, a figure in a flapping gray cloak hurried from the nearby gatekeeper's lodgings.

"Arran," Grace cried. "Look. It's Struan."

In an instant Arran was off his horse and striding

to embrace his brother. The two laughed and thumped backs and then simply clung to each other.

"Damn, but it's good to see you," Arran said at last. "You took off with barely a word, and there's been barely a word from you since."

"I had matters to attend," Struan said, walking toward Grace. He placed his hands at her waist and lifted her to the ground. "Let me look at you, little sister. Yes, you are even more beautiful than before. This marriage is agreeing with you, and well it should if I am not to rattle your husband's teeth."

"Hah!" Arran clapped Struan's shoulders—and frowned. "You look different."

"I've been in Dorset," Struan said, as if answering a question. "I came by a small holding there some years ago, and I've been putting it into proper order. Now I'd like to help at Kirkcaldy awhile, if that would suit you."

Arran's lips had parted and remained so.

"When I returned early in the year, I intended to speak to you of these matters, but there were certain other . . . well, you were otherwise occupied, and I wanted to do nothing to interfere with that."

Arran's mouth snapped shut.

"We are so happy you've come back," Grace said. She scowled at Arran. "Aren't we, Stonehaven?"

"She always calls me Stonehaven when she's out of sorts with me," Arran said plaintively. "She can be a very hard woman."

"No doubt."

"You want to come back to Kirkcaldy?"

"Yes."

Arran ran his fingers through his hair. "What of your calling? How does the church view lengthy absences on the part of her priests?"

"When I came before, I intended to speak of this."

"So you said."

"I am not a priest."

Grace paused in the act of stroking the chestnut's neck.

Arran appeared bemused. "What in God's name are you talking about?"

"I left the priesthood three years ago."

"And you never said a word until today?" Arran thundered.

"Don't shout at me, you arrogant bastard," Struan roared in response. "The reason I let you keep on thinking I was wedded to the church was because if I hadn't, you might never have married again after Isabel. You were so filled with rage and self-pity that you wanted to shut yourself away with your precious music and foresake the world."

"You *lied* to me." Arran's jaw jutted.

Struan's chin matched his brother's. "I didn't lie. I merely failed to give you certain information. I decided that if I did not hide the fact that I was no longer a priest, you would step back and wait for me to marry and produce a Stonehaven heir for you. I wanted you to find your own happiness, you cabbagehead! I wanted you to learn to *love*."

Arran raised his fists, and let them drop to his sides. He looked at Grace, held an arm toward her.

She hurried to him and flinched at the power of his embrace.

"Seeing the two of you together makes me very happy," Struan told them quietly. He stroked a blond curl away from Grace's face. "I'm not too sorry I deceived the two of you. It was worth it to see how you are together. Can I be of service to you, Arran?"

"By heaven, *can* you be of service?" Arran grinned and his eyes glittered with satisfaction. "As of this moment you are my right hand and my left."

"I'm so happy you've returned," Grace said, making up her mind to say what she was bursting to say. "And I have something to tell, too. Arran is to have an heir—in early spring of next year. There. What do you think of that?''

"Wonderful," Struan said. He kissed Grace's cheek and shot a hand in Arran's direction. "Congratulations, brother. Many congratulations."

Arran didn't seem to notice Struan's hand. "I'm going to have an heir," he said as if trying out the words for texture and sound. "I'm going to have an heir. *I'm going to have an heir!*" With a whoop, he swept Grace from the ground and whirled her around.

She laughed down into his face and then shrieked with excitement.

Arran frowned, caught her up into his arms, and studied her closely. "Do you feel well? Did you call in the physician? We must ensure an appropriate nanny is engaged forthwith. And a tutor. Yes, a tutor must be chosen with great care."

Grace caught Struan's eye and they chuckled. "Perhaps we should attend to the birth before the tutor," she suggested.

"You did not *tell* me," Arran said suddenly, and glared. "You did not tell me, and when you did, it was in front of my treacherous brother."

"I'm sorry," she said, not sorry at all. "It seemed the appropriate moment."

"A man who *posed* as a priest."

"I did not pose," Struan said mildly. "I merely failed to deny that I was a priest."

"You wore clerical garb."

Struan crossed his arms and rolled onto his toes. "I wore conservative garb."

Gently Grace threaded one arm through Arran's and one through Struan's and let their deep voices rumble over her head.

Her hair shone silver in the candlelight. With difficulty, Arran stopped himself from leaving the piano and going to take her into his arms. They'd left his bed barely an hour since, and she was still flushed from their lovemaking.

"What shall I play for you?" he asked.

"Surprise me." She leaned over one of her delightfully awful paintings, her brow puckered in concentration.

The melody of "Grace" flowed automatically from his fingers, and their eyes met. She set down her palette and brush and came to stand beside him.

"This has been a perfect day," she said. "I'm so glad Struan has come back to us—even if only for a while. He ought to marry and have children of his own."

"Yes." He stopped playing and raised her hands to his lips. "Our child will be lovely. As lovely as you are."

"Stop flattering me and play."

Arran kissed her fingers slowly, one by one, and turned on the bench. He pulled her between his knees and studied her face. "I can never flatter you enough."

"Stop." Her smile slipped away. "I love you, Arran."

"I love you."

She took a breath, and so did he. There was no need for more words.

It was as if the air between them changed shape, shifted and settled, aglitter now and faintly singing.

"I've just remembered something," he said when he could finally speak again. "Would you please marry me?"

She blinked. "I already have, you buffoon."

"How very good of you. I'm almost certain I forgot to ask."

Now that you've enjoyed
Stella Cameron's
FASCINATION,
Sample her next romance
Coming soon from Avon Books—
BREATHLESS

"Stella Cameron leaves you *breathless* . . ."
Elizabeth Lowell

"Stella Cameron is pure magic . . ."
Jayne Ann Krentz

"Love, greed, romance, revenge! Stella Cameron casts another seductive spell."
Katherine Stone

An island called Hell. A man called Sin. A woman called Angel. Revenge, desire, and danger . . . and nowhere to hide.

*The moon was his enemy.** Slipping from the cover of a dense clump of hibiscus, Sinjun hugged a fringe of shadow at the edge of the grassy slope that swept down to the lagoon cottage. A group of ancient hala trees, balanced crookedly on their tepees of air roots, offered a fresh blind. He threw himself across a swath of light and landed against a ridged trunk.

Standing there, he felt stupid. He'd undoubtedly knock on the door and be confronted by a myopic female in a flannel nightie who wouldn't know one end of a gun from the other.

On the other hand . . .

"What the—" Something cold and wet touched his wrist. Fists curling, he swung around.

Instantly a shaggy shape reared out of the gloom. Sinjun braced and whispered urgently, "Down, Swifty." *Too late.* Eighty pounds of ungrateful hound planted his front paws on Sinjun's chest and flattened him against the tree.

---

*Copyright © 1993 by Stella Cameron

"Down, dammit." With both hands, he shoved the dog off. "And stay down. And *stay* put. Mangy, useless pest. Never around if you could be useful. *Down.* Go *home!"*

Swifty whined. Slowly he lowered his belly and slunk away.

Sinjun turned back and peered out from the trees. The cottage had been built on a low but sheer bluff above the small lagoon. From where Sinjun stood, the building stood between him and the ocean. Glass backed by wooden jalousies formed most of the wall facing him.

The jalousies were open . . . all of them. And bright lights showed every detail of the living room that ran the length of the cottage.

Every detail included rattan furnishings, tapa wall hangings, a white shale fireplace, logs on the hearth, books on a glass-topped table, wood carvings of mythical gods—everything.

There was no sign of a woman, myopic or otherwise.

Sinjun waited, and watched . . . and fingered the Beretta tucked into the waistband of his jeans.

This was ridiculous.

But nothing moved.

Nothing.

Muscles in his belly clenched. He withdrew. She'd only been there half an hour—forty-five minutes at the most. Hardly enough time to cozy up in bed. And if she had, would she leave the living room lighted up like a Christmas tree?

She could be expecting him to come after her.

She could be here somewhere, expecting to see him while he would be unable to see her.

Logic suggested he should ring the doorbell

and introduce himself. Caution squelched the idea.

Ribbons of pewter cloud eased across the moon, and the light over Hell went out.

Leaving the protection of the trees, Sinjun edged forward, keeping his head down.

The cloud passed. Silver stroked every surface once more.

Managing to stick to what shadow the shrubs threw, Sinjun made speedy progress to the corner of the cottage. There he rested and waited for his breathing to calm down.

Coming on his own might have been the dumbest move he'd ever made. Regardless of how confident he felt, he should have stationed good buddy Chuck as backup. Better yet, Sinjun's cool-headed, resourceful sidekick-cum-personal-servant, Walter Lloyd-Worthy, an Englishman who scorned Chuck's ''vulgar tantrums,'' would have made the perfect shotgun for this occasion.

Then there was Willis—always Willis—the deceptively taciturn Samoan who tended the compound grounds with loving care. Willis's gratitude to Sinjun ran deep; it was Sinjun to whom he owed his life. Anyone who threatened Willis's benefactor would wish he'd thought longer, much longer, before drawing the attention of the strongest, most physically impressive man Sinjun had ever personally encountered.

Unfortunately, chances for careful contingency planning had been passed up. And, according to Chuck, there was only one small, smart-mouthed woman to be dealt with. Sinjun pushed up far enough to peer through the jalousies at sill level.

This would all prove unnecessary anyway.

If Chuck hadn't said he'd dropped the woman here, Sinjun would have thought some staff member left on the lights.

He frowned, and searched the room again . . . and finally located what he'd been looking for: something that didn't belong. Just inside the front door stood a dark gray suitcase.

Just inside the front door.

Still closed.

Placed where it could be grabbed by someone in a hurry to leave.

Crouching beneath the windows, Sinjun ran rapidly past the front door and on until he could turn a corner and reach a door that led to the kitchen.

Catching his bottom lip between his teeth, he pressed his ear to a panel. No sound came from inside. He eased the doorknob to the left. The door swung silently open and he stepped into the unlighted room.

Moonlight sliced through skylights and back windows to print squares of white brilliance over pale tile and stainless steel appliances. Smiling grimly, Sinjun softly closed the door behind him and pulled the gun into his palm. On tiptoe, he crossed to the short passage that led to the living room. Regardless of her reason, that small, mouthy blonde was lurking somewhere, anticipating catching him flatfooted.

Swiftly and silently, he moved into the cottage's one bedroom and found it empty. The same proved true of a small laundry room, a guest bathroom, a sauna and a mudroom and shower at the back of the building.

Standing to one side, Sinjun peered through the mudroom window and into an area between the cottage and the edge of the bluff.

The cottage—built by the man who had willed the island to Sinjun—stood a short distance from a shallow drop into the odd, deep little lagoon.

He began to feel the woman wasn't there. Cautiously he let himself outside and stood listening. A nearby chorus of bullfrogs, the rustling click of palm fronds overhead, and a soft shush of surf into the lagoon were all he heard. The night wind brought a heavy scent of salt from the sea, mixed with fragrant frangipani.

Letting out the breath he'd held, Sinjun walked toward the spot where the land fell away. Tension ebbed a little, but his muscles remained tensed. Damn Chuck. He'd left Angelica Dean here, and she'd already sneaked out to go hunting. If he was lucky, all she hoped to find were some titillating snippets of information about his private life. If he wasn't so lucky, she hoped to find him—and really ruin his already lousy day by turning out to be an agent for whoever wanted him dead.

Who did want him dead?

The question was the same one that had roamed his brain daily in the six weeks since his first "accident" when he'd come close to being the victim in a drive-by shooting. And, as always, he began an inventory of business dealings, of people involved in those dealings who might have reason to think less than kindly of him. Unfortunately, there were more than a few. Investment magnates didn't always make a lot of friends; even if they were as scrupulously ethical as Sinjun Breaker.

He stepped back and froze. A movement at the edge of the cliff had caught his eye. Fingers searched this way and that and then dug in to find a hold in the bank.

The lord of the clouds had an evil sense of humor. Grayness blanketed everything again.

With his eyes narrowed on the place where the fingers had appeared, Sinjun waited.

A small grunt preceded the appearance of a head. Next came hunched shoulders draped with long, dripping hair, and finally, the rest of a body that appeared to be clad in a transparently thin, white swimsuit. Evidently Angelica Dean, rather than lying in wait for Sinjun, had chosen to leap headlong into the sea and swim—alone—at night.

She managed to haul herself up until she crouched, knees jackknifed, like an oversized, pale and dripping, frog.

"Ms. Dean, I presume?"

The form at his feet didn't move; in fact, it was his feet that appeared to hold her attention.

"Are you having difficulty getting up?"

"No." Her voice was muffled.

"Good. Hasn't anyone ever mentioned to you that it's dangerous to swim alone—particularly at night?"

"Yes."

"Then you're a fool."

She muttered something unintelligible.

Sinjun began to lose patience. "I'm sure you want to get off Hell as much as I want you off. I hadn't anticipated your being brought here at this time of day—or should I say, night? But we might as well discuss this project you've been hounding me with now. Then you can be on your way first thing in the morning."

Her next words were perfectly audible. *"Arrogant bastard"* wasn't something he enjoyed being called, particularly by someone who'd been pushing him for a favor for weeks.

Still the woman hunched on the ground.

Sinjun stooped and touched her shoulder with his left hand.

She jumped.

"This is ridiculous. Give me your hand."

Without looking up, she did as he asked, and he hauled her up. Standing straight, the top of her head didn't reach his chin.

Something broke in Sinjun. "Lady," he said, not caring how harsh he sounded, "I've had a hell of a day and I'm very, very jumpy. For your own good, I'd advise you to quit playing games."

"I'm not." The wobble in her voice suggested chattering teeth.

He couldn't afford to sympathize with his potential enemy, or an agent of a potential enemy.

"You're out of time," he informed her. "We'll do this my way . . . openly. I expect you to put your cards on the table . . . now. No holding back, Ms. Dean. Let me see what you're holding in your hand. We'll decide where to go from here."

He didn't imagine it; she cried out softly, as if anguished.

Slowly, very slowly, she raised her face, and Sinjun swallowed once, hard, and with difficulty. Chuck hadn't quite painted an accurate picture. Small, yes. Blond, yes. Mouthy? The lady had a beautiful, full, soft mouth—that much Sinjun could see in the moon-tinged darkness. And he could see that her face was oval, the chin pointed, the nose pert and slightly tip-tilted, the hairline heart-shaped above finely arched brows, and she had the biggest pair of eyes he'd ever seen. Blue? Gray? Green? That was one thing he'd have to look at in the light, because the coy moon didn't tell him.

Muscles in his jaw flexed. "I told you what I want."

"Hands," she mumbled, and gradually she lifted her arms until her hands were above her head. White teeth dug into her bottom lip before she whispered, "Are you going to shoot me?"

Sinjun frowned and glanced down . . . and his thighs locked. The muzzle of the gun he'd forgotten he still held was pressed into a full, white breast.

He started violently. Tension could make a man damned unobservant. His first impression had been almost accurate.

Ms. Angelica Dean was naked.